YET MOTHER HAD HER WAY, AS SLYBOOTS MOTHER WAS always to have her way . . . one March morning soliciting the help of several of us, who were sworn to secrecy, and delighted to be her handmaidens, in a simple scheme: Lona being asleep in the attic, Mother led the baby out of the house by holding a piece of bread soaked in chicken blood in front of its nostrils, led it crawling across the hard-packed wintry earth, to the old hay barn, and, inside, led it to a dark corner where we helped her lift it and lower it carefully into an aged rain barrel empty except for a wriggling mass of half-grown rats, that squealed in great excitement at being disturbed, and at the smell of the blood-soaked bread which Mother dropped with the baby. We then nailed a cover in place; and, as Mother said, her skin warmly flushed and her breath coming fast, ''There, girls—it is entirely out of our hands.''

Tor books edited by Dennis Etchison

MASTERS OF DARKNESS I
MASTERS OF DARKNESS II
MASTERS OF DARKNESS III

MASTERS OF DARKNESS III

EDITED BY

DENNIS ETCHISON

TOR

A TOM DOHERTY ASSOCIATES BOOK
NEW YORK

MASTERS OF DARKNESS III

Copyright © 1991 by Dennis Etchison

A Tor Book
Published by Tom Doherty Associates, Inc.
49 West 24th Street
New York, N.Y. 10010

ISBN: 0-812-51766-0

Printed in the United States of America

First edition: May 1991

0 9 8 7 6 5 4 3 2 1

To my wife,
KRISTINA ROBIN ANDERSON

ACKNOWLEDGMENTS

P.32,42

CONTENTS

PREFACE

Welcome to *Masters of Darkness III*.

This is the third in a series of authors' choice anthologies, presenting outstanding short fiction selected by the finest writers of horror/dark fantasy, with new commentaries composed by them especially for this book.

The format is deceptively simple. I have asked fifteen distinguished authors to choose a favorite story, to correct or restore it if necessary, and to provide comments for this edition. As you will see, the result is a revelation, not only for what is discussed in the Authors' Notes or variances in texts (for example, Joyce Carol Oates thoroughly revised her story "Family" for this edition, and James Herbert provided a longer version of "Hallowe'en's Child" to be published here for the first time) but in the choices of material. The particular work that holds special meaning for a writer may have received little notice at the time of original publication; it may not even be widely known or acknowledged today. In some cases the representative piece is a classic well worth rereading in a new light. But just as often it is a relatively obscure entry worthy of greater attention, one that for subjective reasons is close to the author's heart and at odds with what is popularly perceived as the author's strong suit. Hence you may find quietly realistic autobiography from an acclaimed writer of escapist thrillers, a study of psychological disintegration from one famous for his neatly-plotted ghost stories, a bitter political warning from a light satirist, or an emotional meditation on love from a bestselling chronicler of supernatural terrors. I hope you find these unexpected turns as fascinating as I do, that they will serve to deepen your respect for those who are capable of more than their streamlined commercial backlist might suggest, and that they will introduce you to others whose works you may want to know better.

As in previous volumes, you will note certain names more commonly associated with other fields: science fiction, fantasy, mystery and the literary mainstream. I have said before that no writer worth his or her salt is long content to work within the confines of a single circumscribed area. The stereotype of image may be a straitjacket that permits a writer to publish only what fulfills reader expectations. These anthologies aim to dispel some unfortunate preconceptions, pointing up the truth that a writer can no more be judged by reputation than a book can be known by its cover. Genres exist to satisfy the marketing needs of professional publishing, not because of any inherent artistic limitations on the part of the writers who are packaged for a particular target audience.

In that regard this volume may seem to be something of a contradiction in terms, since it is nominally a book of horror stories. Closer examination reveals it to be nothing less. But I trust that it is also something more—a demonstration of versatility that may broaden the understanding of "horror" and lead to a fuller appreciation of that word's relevance in today's world and the literature that reflects and reinforces it. Reality is known by the language used to describe experience, the future built from the template of ideas that directs its construction. If the shape of our dreaming creates the form of our lives, then I would suggest that it may be time to break with the constraints of habit in order to reshape what is to come. Fiction is the wellspring of our imaginings, and our legacy. What better place to begin than by reconsidering the true constituents of darkness and light, and to take responsibility for the larger implications of these expanded definitions?

I would like to offer my thanks to all the writers who have participated in *Masters of Darkness* since its inception. Included in these three volumes are many of the most brilliant dark dreamers of our time. Originally I conceived of only one volume under this title, but the number of important contributors squeezed out of the first by limitations of space made the sequels a necessity. We have seen works by Ray Bradbury, Robert Bloch, Richard Matheson, Manly Wade Wellman, Richard McKenna, Fritz Leiber, Nigel Kneale and Jack Williamson alongside stories by newer masters like Karl Edward Wagner, Ramsay Campbell, Richard Christian Matheson, Whitley Strieber, Charles L. Grant, Clive Barker, James Herbert and Stephen King—some 45 in all. Were this series not finite we would see many more, for with each new compilation I am reminded of the multiplicity of first-rate talent that deserves representation in any anthology aspiring to be definitive. A few renowned authors declined the invitation for personal reasons, and others proved frustratingly elusive in my efforts to locate them. Nonetheless the degree of enthusiastic cooperation has been deeply gratifying, enabling me to deliver a series that is finally worthy of its title.

My part in shaping the character of these books has been minimal, the role of the contributors all and everything. To them, and to Melissa Singer and Tom Doherty, the editors who originally recognized the potential of this project, I extend my lasting gratitude. And to readers, who are the real beneficiaries of this effort, I wish to say that I sincerely hope your reading in this field has been provoked and enriched. Literature as a whole can only gain from your curiosity and continuing appetite for the best that short fiction has to offer, a form I believe to be the richest and most potent yet devised for readers and writers everywhere.

—Dennis Etchison
September 1989

THE SECRET
Jack Vance

SUNBEAMS SLANTED THROUGH CHINKS IN THE WALL OF the hut; from the lagoon came shouts and splashing of the village children. Rona ta Inga at last opened his eyes. He had slept far past his usual hour of arising, far into the morning. He stretched his legs, cupped hands behind his head, stared absently up at the ceiling of thatch. In actuality he had awakened at the usual hour, to drift off again into a dreaming doze—a habit to which lately he had become prone. Only lately. Inga frowned and sat up with a jerk. What did this mean? Was it a sign? Perhaps he should inquire from Takti-Tai. . . . But it was all so ridiculous. He had slept late for the most ordinary of reasons: he enjoyed lazing and drowsing and dreaming.

On the mat beside him were crumpled flowers, where Mai-Mio had lain. Inga gathered the blossoms and laid them on the shelf which held his scant possessions. An enchanting creature, this Mai-Mio. She laughed no more and no less than other girls; her eyes were like other eyes, her mouth like all mouths; but her quaint and charming mannerisms made her absolutely unique: the single Mai-

1

Mio in all the universe. Inga had loved many maidens. All
in some way were singular, but Mai-Mio only recently had
become a woman—even now from a distance she might
be mistaken for a boy—while Inga was older by at least
five or six seasons. He was not quite sure. It mattered
little, in any event. It mattered very little, he told himself
again, quite emphatically. This was his village, his island;
he had no desire to leave. Ever!

The children came up the beach from the lagoon. Two
or three darted under his hut, swinging on one of the poles,
chanting nonsense words. The hut trembled; the outcry
jarred upon Inga's nerves. He shouted in irritation. The
children became instantly silent, in awe and astonishment,
and trotted away looking over their shoulders.

Inga frowned; for the second time this morning he felt
dissatisfied with himself. He would gain an unenviable
reputation if he kept on in such a fashion. What had come
over him? He was the same Inga that he was yesterday
. . . except for the fact that a day had elapsed and he was
a day older.

He went out on the porch before his hut, stretched in
the sunlight. To right and left were forty or fifty other such
huts as his own, with intervening trees; ahead lay the lagoon blue and sparkling in the sunlight. Inga jumped to
the ground, walked to the lagoon, swam, dived far down
among the glittering pebbles and ocean growths which
covered the lagoon floor. Emerging he felt relaxed and at
peace—once more himself: Rona ta Inga, as he had always
been, and always would be!

Squatting on his porch he breakfasted on fruit and cold
baked fish from last night's feast and considered the day
ahead. There was no urgency, no duty to fulfill, no need
to satisfy. He could join the party of young bucks now on
their way into the forest hoping to snare fowl. He could
fashion a brooch of carved shell and goana-nut for Mai-
Mio. He could lounge and gossip; he could fish. Or he
could visit his best friend Takti-Tai—who was building a
boat. Inga rose to his feet. He would fish. He walked

along the beach to his canoe, checked equipment, pushed off, paddled across the lagoon to the opening in the reef. The winds blew to the west as always. Leaving the lagoon Inga turned a swift glance downwind—an almost furtive glance—then bent his neck into the wind and paddled east.

Within the hour he had caught six fine fish, and drifted back along the reef to the lagoon entrance. Everyone was swimming when he returned. Maidens, young men, children. Mai-Mio paddled to the canoe, hooked her arms over the gunwales, grinned up at him, water glistening on her cheeks. "Rona ta Inga! Did you catch fish? Or am I bad luck?"

"See for yourself."

She looked. "Five—no, six! All fat silver-fins! I am good luck! May I sleep often in your hut?"

"So long as I catch fish the following day."

She dropped back into the water, splashed him, sank out of sight. Through the undulating surface Inga could see her slender brown form skimming off across the bottom. He beached the canoe, wrapped the fish in big sipi-leaves and stored them in a cool cistern, then ran down to the lagoon to join the swimming.

Later he and Mai-Mio sat in the shade; she plaiting a decorative cord of colored bark which later she would weave into a basket, he leaning back, looking across the water. Artlessly Mai-Mio chattered—of the new song Ama ta Lalau had composed, of the odd fish she had seen while swimming underwater, of the change which had come over Takti-Tai since he had started building his boat.

Inga made an absentminded sound, but said nothing.

"We have formed a band," Mai-Mio confided. "There are six of us: Ipa, Tuiti, Hali-Sai-Iano, Zoma, Oiu-Ngo and myself. We have pledged never to leave the island. Never, never, never. There is too much joy here. Never will we sail west—never. Whatever the secret we do not wish to know."

Inga smiled, a rather wistful smile. "There is much wisdom in the pledge you have made."

She stroked his arm. "Why do you not join us in our pledge? True, we are six girls—but a pledge is a pledge."

"True."

"Do you want to sail west?"

"No."

Mai-Mio excitedly rose to her knees. "I will call together the band, and all of us, all together: we will recite the pledge again, never will we leave our island! And to think, you are the oldest of all at the village!"

"Takti-Tai is older," said Inga.

"But Takti-Tai is building his boat! He hardly counts any more!"

"Vai-Ona is as old as I. Almost as old."

"Do you know something? Whenever Vai Ona goes out to fish, he always looks to the west. He wonders."

"Everyone wonders."

"Not I!" Mai-Mio jumped to her feet. "Not I—not any of the band. Never, never, never—never will we leave the island! We have pledged ourselves!" She reached down, patted Inga's cheek, ran off to where a group of her friends were sharing a basket of fruit.

Inga sat quietly for five minutes. Then he made an impatient gesture, rose and walked along the shore to the platform where Takti-Tai worked on his boat. This was a catamaran with a broad deck, a shelter of woven withe thatched with sipi-leaf, a stout mast. In silence Inga helped Takti-Tai shape the mast, scraping a tall well-seasoned pa-siao-tui sapling with sharp shells. Inga presently paused, laid aside the shell. He said, "Long ago there were four of us. You, me, Akara and Zan. Remember?"

Takti-Tai nodded.

"We pledged never to leave the island. We swore never to weaken, we spilled blood to seal the pact. Never would we sail west."

"I remember."

"Now you sail," said Inga. "I will be the last of the group."

Takti-Tai paused in his scraping, looked at Inga, as if

he would speak, then bent once more over the mast. Inga presently returned up the beach to his hut, where squatting on the porch he carved at the brooch for Mai-Mio.

A youth presently came to sit beside him. Inga, who had no particular wish for companionship, continued with his carving. But the youth, absorbed in his own problems, failed to notice. "Advise me, Rona ta Inga. You are the oldest of the village and very sage." Inga raised his eyebrows, then scowled, but said nothing.

"I love Hali Sai Iano, I long for her desperately, but she laughs at me and runs off to throw her arms about the neck of Hopu. What should I do?"

"The situation is quite simple," said Inga. "She prefers Hopu. You need merely select another girl. What of Talau Io? She is pretty and affectionate, and seems to like you."

The youth vented a sigh. "Very well. I will do as you suggest. After all one girl is much like another." He departed, unaware of the sardonic look Inga directed at his back. He asked himself, why do they come to me for advice? I am only two or three, or at most four or five, seasons their senior. It is as if they think me the fount and source of all sagacity!

During the evening a baby was born. The mother was Omei Ni Io, who for almost a season had slept in Inga's hut. Since it was a boy child she named it Inga ta Omei. There was a naming ceremony at which Inga presided. The singing and dancing lasted until late, and if it were not for the fact that the child was his own, with his name, Inga would have crept off early to his hut. He had attended many naming ceremonies.

A week later Takti-Tai sailed west, and there was a ceremony of a different sort. Everyone came to the beach to touch the hull of the boat and bless it with water. Tears ran freely down all cheeks, including Takti-Tai's. For the last time he looked around the lagoon, into the faces of those he would be leaving. Then he turned, signalled; the young men pushed the boat away from the beach, then jumping into the water, towed it across the lagoon, guided it out into the ocean. Takti-Tai cut brails, tightened halyards; the big square sail billowed in the wind. The boat surged west. Takti-Tai stood on the platform, gave a final flourish of the hand, and those on the beach waved farewell. The boat moved out into the afternoon, and when the sun sank, it could be seen no more.

During the evening meal the talk was quiet; everyone stared into the fire. Mai-Mio finally jumped to her feet. "Not I," she chanted. "Not I—ever, ever, ever!"

"Nor I," shouted Ama ta Lalau, who of all the youths was the most proficient musician. He reached for the guitar which he had carved from a black soa-gum trunk, struck chords, began to sing.

Inga watched quietly. He was now the oldest on the island, and it seemed as if the others were treating him with a new respect. Ridiculous! What nonsense! So little older was he that it made no difference whatever! But he noticed that Mai-Mio was laughingly attentive to Ama ta Lalau, who responded to the flirtation with great gallantry. Inga watched with a heavy feeling around the heart, and presently went off to his hut. That night, for the first time in weeks, Mai-Mio did not sleep beside him. No matter, Inga told himself: one girl is much like another.

The following day he wandered up the beach to the platform where Takti-Tai had built his boat. The area was clean and tidy, and tools were hung carefully in a nearby shed. In the forest beyond grew fine makara trees, from which the staunchest hulls were fashioned.

Inga turned away. He took his canoe out to catch fish, and leaving the lagoon looked to the west. There was nothing to see but empty horizon, precisely like the horizon to east, to north and to south—except that the western horizon concealed the secret. And the rest of the day he felt uneasy. During the evening meal he looked from face to face. None were the faces of his dear friends; they all had built their boats and had sailed. His friends had departed; his friends knew the secret.

The next morning, without making a conscious decision, Inga sharpened the tools and felled two fine makara trees. He was not precisely building a boat—so he assured himself—but it did no harm for wood to season.

Nevertheless the following day he trimmed the trees, cut the trunk to length, and the next day assembled all the young men to help carry the trunks to the platform. No one seemed surprised; everyone knew that Rona ta Inga was building his boat. Mai-Mio had now frankly taken up with Ama ta Lalau and as Inga worked on his boat he watched them play in the water, not without a lump of bitterness in his throat. Yes, he told himself, it would be pleasure indeed to join his true friends—the youths and maidens he had known since he dropped his milk-name, whom he had sported with, who now were departed, and for whom he felt an aching loneliness. Diligently he hollowed the hulls, burning, scraping, chiselling. Then the platform was secured, the little shelter woven and thatched to protect him from rain. He scraped a mast from a flawless pa-siao-tui sapling, stepped and stayed it. He gathered bast, wove a coarse but sturdy sail, hung it to stretch and season. Then he began to provision the boat. He gathered nut-meats, dried fruits, smoked fish wrapped in sipi-leaf. He filled blowfish bladders with water. How long was the trip to the west? No one knew. Best not to go hungry, best to stock the boat well: once down the wind there was no turning back.

One day he was ready. It was a day much like all the other days of his life. The sun shone warm and bright, the lagoon glittered and rippled up and down the beach in little gushes of play-surf. Rona ta Inga's throat felt tense and stiff; he could hardly trust his voice. The young folk came to line the beach; all blessed the boat with water. Inga gazed into each face, then along the line of huts, the trees, the beaches, the scenes he loved with such intensity. . . . Already they seemed remote. Tears were coursing his cheeks. He held up his hand, turned away. He felt the boat leave the beach, float free on the water. Swimmers thrust him out into the ocean. For the last time he turned to look back at the village, fighting a sudden maddening urge to jump from the boat, to swim back to the village. He hoisted the sail, the wind thrust deep into the hollow. Water surged under the hulls and he was coasting west, with the island astern.

Up the blue swells, down into the long troughs, the wake gurgling, the bow rising and falling. The long afternoon waned and became golden; sunset burned and ebbed and became a halcyon dusk. The stars appeared, and Inga, sitting silently by his rudder, held the sail full to the wind. At midnight he lowered the sail and slept, the boat drifting quietly.

In the morning he was completely alone, the horizons blank. He raised the sail and scudded west, and so passed the day, and the next, and others. And Inga became thankful that he had provisioned the boat with generosity. On the sixth day he seemed to notice that a chill had come into the wind; on the eighth day he sailed under a high overcast, the like of which he had never seen before. The ocean changed from blue to a gray which presently took on a green tinge, and now the water was cold. The wind blew with great force, bellying his bast sail, and Inga huddled in the shelter to avoid the harsh spray. On the morning of the ninth day he thought to see a dim dark shape loom ahead, which at noon became a line of tall cliffs with surf beating against jagged rocks, roaring back and forth across coarse shingle. In mid-afternoon he ran his boat up on one of the shingle beaches, jumped gingerly ashore. Shivering in the whooping gusts, he took stock of the situation. There was no living thing to be seen along the foreshore but three or four gray gulls. A hundred yards to his right lay a battered hulk of another boat, and beyond was a tangle of wood and fiber which might have been still another.

Inga carried ashore what provisions remained, bundled them together, and by a faint trail climbed the cliffs. He came out on an expanse of rolling gray green downs. Two or three miles inland rose a line of low hills, toward which the trail seemed to lead.

Inga looked right and left; again there was no living creature in sight other than gulls. Shouldering his bundle he set forth along the trail.

Nearing the hills he came upon a hut of turf and stone, beside a patch of cultivated soil. A man and a woman worked in the field. Inga peered closer. What manner of creatures were these? They resembled human beings; they had arms and legs and faces—but how seamed and seared and gray they were! How shrunken were their hands, how bent and hobbled as they worked! He walked quickly by, and they did not appear to notice him.

Now Inga hastened, as the end of the day was drawing on and the hills loomed before him. The trail led along a valley grown with gnarled oak and low purple-green shrubs, then slanted up the hillside through a stony gap, where the wind generated whistling musical sounds. From the gap Inga looked out over a flat valley. He saw copses of low trees, plots of tilled land, a group of huts. Slowly he walked down the trail. In a nearby field a man raised his head. Inga paused thinking to recognize him. Was this not Akara ta Oma who had sailed west ten or twelve seasons back? It seemed impossible. This man was fat, the hair had almost departed his head, his cheeks hung loose at the jawline. No, this could not be lithe Akara ta Oma! Hurriedly Inga turned away, and presently entered the village. Before a nearby hut stood one whom he recognized with joy. "Takti-Tai!"

Takti-Tai nodded. "Rona ta Inga. I know you'd be coming soon."

"I'm delighted to see you! But let us leave this terrible place; let us return to the island!"

Takti-Tai smiled a little, shook his head.

Inga protested heatedly, "Don't tell me you prefer this dismal land? Come! My boat is still seaworthy. If somehow we can back it off the beach, gain the open sea . . ."

The wind sang down over the mountains, strummed

through the trees. Inga's words died in his throat. It was clearly impossible to work the boat off the foreshore.

"Not only the wind," said Takti-Tai. "We could not go back now. We know the secret."

Inga stared in wonderment. "The secret? Not I."

"Come. Now you will learn."

Takti-Tai took him through the village to a structure of stone with a high-gabled roof shingled with slate. "Enter, and you will know the secret."

Hesitantly Rona ta Inga entered the stone structure. On a stone table lay a still figure surrounded by six tall candles. Inga stared at the shrunken white face, at the white sheet which lay motionless over the narrow chest. "Who is this? A man? How thin he is. Does he sleep? Why do you show me such a thing?"

"This is the secret," said Takti-Tai. "It is called 'death.'"

AUTHOR'S NOTE

LONG AGO—I FORGET THE EXACT DATE—I WROTE A STORY which I called "The Secret." It was rather a strange story; I recognized this at once, but science fiction is a strange field, and I am a strange writer, and most of my friends are somewhat strange. In any event, I sent the story back to my agent in the ordinary way, using ordinary stamps and an ordinary post office, and confidently awaited the usual sale, check and publication.

However, "strangeness" superseded the usual. Nothing happened. No sale, no check, no publication. I shrugged and put the story and its lack of success to the back of my mind.

Some months later, during a telephone conversation with my agent, I thought to inquire about "The Secret." The response was strange: puzzlement and the news that no such story had ever been received at the agency, hence never marketed nor sold.

Odd, I said, but still no problem. I would make a copy from the carbon and send it back in short order, and all would be well. But—when I went to look for the carbon, I found that this had likewise disappeared. In short, all trace of "The Secret" was gone.

The incident gave me pause. I wondered if in "The Secret" I had blundered upon concepts for which humanity was not ready, and which the Upper Entities had discreetly expunged from existence. It was an unsettling idea. I wondered if I should not accept the events as a portent and a warning, and erase "The Secret" and its dangerous content from my mind. I could find no persuasive reason to challenge the Quintessentials and annoy them a second time, so I turned my attention toward other matters.

Several years went by, and living the life of a science-fiction writer hardened me and made me bold. To make a long story short, I dared Destiny and wrote a new version of "The Secret." The aftermath was somewhat anticlimactic, and as I recalled my bravado I felt a bit foolish. No difficulties whatever presented themselves. The manuscript reached New York unmolested and was safely delivered into the hands of my agent. The story was sold and published and no one seemed to care one way or the other.

As I reflect upon the two stories, it seems to me that they are much alike. Still, the doubt persists. Is it possible that in the second version, subconsciously or inadvertently I skirted the tendentious areas which had caused the previous trouble? I have no clear conviction in either direction; perhaps I will never know.

—Jack Vance

THE PATTER OF TINY FEET
Nigel Kneale

"HOLD ON A MOMENT. DON'T KNOCK," JOE BANNER SAID. "Let me get a shot of the outside before the light goes."

So I waited while he backed into the road with his Leica. No traffic, nobody about but an old man walking a dog in the distance. Joe stuck his cigarette behind one ear and prowled quickly to find the best angle on Number 47. It was what the address had suggested: a narrow suburban villa in a forgotten road, an old maid of a house with a skirt of garden drawn round it, keeping itself to itself among all its sad neighbours. The flower beds were full of dead stems and grass.

Joe's camera clicked twice. "House of Usher's in the bag," he said, and resumed the cigarette. "Think the garden has any possibilities?"

"Come on! We can waste time later."

Weather had bleached the green front door. There was a big iron knocker and I used it.

"It echoed hollowly through the empty house!" said Banner. He enjoys talking like that, though it bores everybody. In addition he acts character—aping the sort of

small-town photographer who wears his hat on the back
of his head and stinks out the local Rotarians with damp
flash powder—but he's one of the finest in the profession.

We heard rapid footsteps inside, the lock clicked, and
the door swung open, all in a hurry. And there appeared—
yes, remembering those comic letters to the office, it could
only be—our man.

"Mr. Hutchinson?"

"At your service, gentlemen!" He shot a look over Joe's
camera and the suitcase full of equipment, and seemed
pleased. A pale pudding-face and a long nose that didn't
match it, trimmed with a narrow line of moustache. He
had the style of a shop-walker, I thought. "Come inside,
please. Can I lend you a hand with that? No? That's it—
right along inside!" It sounded as if the word "sir" was
trembling to join each phrase.

We went into the front room, where a fire was burning.
The furniture was a familiar mixture: flimsy modern ve-
neer jostling old pieces built like Noah's Ark and handed
down from in-laws. Gilt plaster dancers posed on the sideboard and the rug was worn through.

"My name is Staines," I said, "and this is Joe Banner,
who's going to handle the pictures. I believe you've had a
letter?"

"Yes, indeed," said Hutchinson, shaking hands.
"Please take a seat, both of you—I know what a tiring
journey it can be, all the way from London! Yes. I must
say how extremely gratified I am that your paper has shown
this interest!" His voice sounded distorted by years of
ingratiating; it bubbled out of the front of his mouth like
a comic radio character's. "Have you . . . that is, I understand you have special experience in this field, Mr.
Staines?" He seemed almost worried about it.

"Not exactly a trained investigator," I admitted, "but
I've knocked out a few articles on the subject."

"Oh . . . yes, indeed. I've read them with great interest." He hadn't, of course, but he made it sound very
respectful. He asked if we had eaten, and when we reas-

sured him he produced drinks from grandmother's sideboard. Banner settled down to his performance of the "Hick-in-the-Sticks Journal" photographer out on a blind.

"You—you seem to have brought a lot of equipment," Hutchinson said quickly. "I hope I made it clear there's no guarantee of anything . . . visible."

"Guarantee? Why, then you *have* seen something?"

He sat forward on his chair, but immediately seemed to restrain himself and an artfully stiff smile appeared. "Mr. Staines, let's understand each other: I am most anxious not to give you preconceived ideas. This is your investigation, not mine." He administered this like a police caution, invitingly.

Joe put down his empty glass. "We're not easily corrupted, Mr. Hutchinson."

To scotch the mock-modesty I said: "We've read your letters and the local press-clipping. So what about the whole story, in your own way?" I took out my notebook, to encourage him.

Hutchinson blinked nervously and rose. He snapped the two standard lamps on, went to the window with hands clasped behind him. The sky was darkening. He drew the curtains and came back as if he had taken deep thought. His sigh was full of responsibility.

"I'm trying to take an impersonal view. This case is so unusual that I feel it must be examined . . . *pro bono publico*, as it were. . . ." He gave a tight little laugh, all part of the act. "I don't want you to get the idea I'm a seeker after publicity."

This was too much. "No, no," I said, "you don't have to explain yourself: we're interested. Facts, Mr. Hutchinson, please. Just facts."

"For instance, what time do the noises start?" said Joe.

Hutchinson relaxed, too obviously gratified for the purity of his motives. He glanced at his watch brightly.

"Oh, it varies, Mr. Banner. After dark—any time at all after dark." He frowned like an honest witness. "I'm trying to think of any instance during daylight, but no. Sometimes it comes early, oftener near midnight, occasionally towards dawn: no rule about it, absolutely none. It can continue all night through.''

I caught him watching my pencil as I stopped writing; his eyes came up on me and Joe, alert as a confident examination-candidate's.

''Footsteps?''

Again the arch smile. ''Mr. Staines, that's for you to judge. To me it sounds like footsteps.''

''The witness knows the rules of evidence, boy!'' Joe said, and winked at us both. Hutchinson took his glass.

''Fill it up for you, Mr. Banner? I'm far from an ideal observer, I fear; bar Sundays, I'm out every evening.''

''Business?''

''Yes, I'm assistant headwaiter in a restaurant. Tonight I was able to be excused.'' He handed us refilled glasses. ''A strange feeling, you know, to come into the house late at night, and hear those sounds going on inside, in the dark.''

''Scare you?'' Joe asked.

''Not now. Surprising, isn't it? But it seems one can get used to anything.''

I asked: ''Just what do you hear?''

Hutchinson considered, watching my pencil. He's got the answer all ready, I thought. ''A curious pattering, very erratic and light. A sort of . . . playing, if that conveys anything. Upstairs there's a small passage between the bedrooms, covered with linoleum: I'll show you presently. Well, it mostly occurs there, but it can travel down the stairs into the hallway below.''

''Ever hear—'' Joe began.

Hutchinson went on: ''It lasts between thirty and forty seconds. I've timed it. And in a single night I've known the whole thing to be repeated up to a dozen times.''

''—a rat in the ceiling, Mr. Hutchinson?'' Joe finished. ''They can make a hell of a row.''

''Yes, I've heard rats. This is not one.''

I frowned at Joe: this was routine stuff. ''Mr. Hutchinson, we'll agree on that. Look, in your last letter you said you had a theory—of profound significance."

"Yes."

"Why don't we get on to that, then?"

He whipped round instantly, full of it. "My idea is—well, it's a terribly unusual form of—the case—the case of a projection—how can I put it? It's more than a theory, Mr. Staines!" He had all the stops out at once. His hands trembled.

"Hold it!" Joe called, and reached for his Leica. "I'll be making an odd shot now and then, Mr. Hutchinson. Show you telling the story, see?"

Hutchinson's fingers went to his tie.

"You were saying—?" I turned over a leaf of the notebook.

"Well, I can vouch for this house, you know. I've lived here for many years, and it came to me from my mother. There's absolutely no . . . history attached to it."

I could believe that.

"Until about six years ago I lived alone—a woman came in to clean twice a week. And then . . . I married." He said this impressively, watching to see that I noted it.

"A strange person, my wife. She was only nineteen when we married, and very . . . unworldly." He drew a self-conscious breath. "Distant cousin of mine actually, very religious people. That's her photograph on the mantelpiece."

I took it down.

I had noticed it when first we entered the room; vignetted in its chromium-plated frame, too striking to be his daughter. It was a face of character, expressive beyond mere beauty; an attractive full-lipped mouth, eyes of exceptional vividness. Surprisingly, her hair was shapeless and her dress dull. I passed the portrait to Joe, who whistled.

"Mr. Hutchinson! Where are you hiding the lady? Come on, let's get a picture of—"

Then he also guessed. This was not a house with a woman in it.

"She passed away seven months ago," said Hutchinson, and held out his hand for the frame.

"I'm sorry," I said. Banner nodded and muttered something.

Hutchinson was expressionless. "Yes," he said, "I'm sorry too." Which was an odd thing to say, as there was evidently no sarcasm in it. I wondered why she could have married him. There must have been twenty-five years between them, and a world of temperament.

"She was extremely . . . passionate," Hutchinson said. He spoke as if he were revealing something indecent. His voice was hushed, and his little moustache bristled over pursed lips. When his eyes dropped to the photograph in his hand, his face was quite blank.

Suddenly he said in an odd, curt way: "She was surprisingly faithful to me. I mean, she was never anything else. Very religious, strictest ideas of her duty." The flicker of a smile. "Unworldly, as I said."

I tried to be discreet. "Then you were happy together?"

His fingers were unconsciously worrying at the picture frame, fidgeting with the strut.

"To be honest, we weren't. She wanted children."

Neither Banner nor I moved.

"I told her I couldn't agree. I had to tell her often, because she worked herself up, and it all became ugly. She used to lose control and say things she didn't mean, and afterwards she was sorry, but you can't play fast and loose with people's finer feelings! I did my best. I'd forgive her and say: 'I only want you, my dear. You're all I need in the world,' to comfort her, you see. And she'd sob loudly and . . . she was unnecessarily emotional."

His voice was thin, and tight. He rose and replaced the photograph on the mantelpiece. There was a long silence.

Joe fiddled with his camera. "No children, then?" Cruel, that.

Hutchinson turned, and we saw that somehow he had managed to relax. The accommodating smirk was back.

"No, none. I had definite views on the subject. All quite rational. Wide disparity in the prospective parents' ages, for instance—psychologically dangerous for all parties: I don't know if you've studied the subject? There were other considerations, too—financial, medical; do you wish me to go into those? I have nothing to hide."

It was blatant exhibitionism now: as if he were proffering a bill on a plate, with himself itemized in it.

"There's a limit even to journalists' curiosity," I said.

Hutchinson was ahead of me, solemnly explaining. "Now! This is my theory! You've heard of poltergeist phenomena, of course? Unexplainable knockings, scratchings, minor damage, and so on. I've studied them in books—and they're always connected with development, violent emotional development, in young people. A sort of uncontrolled offshoot of the . . . personality. D'you follow?"

"Wait a minute," Joe said. "That's taking a lot for granted if you like!"

But I remembered reading such cases. One, investigated by psychical researchers, had involved a fifteen-year-old boy: ornaments had been thrown about by no visible agency. I took a glance at the unchipped gilt dancers on the sideboard before Hutchinson spoke again.

"No, my wife may not have been adolescent, but in some ways . . . she was . . . so to speak, retarded."

He looked as pleased as if he had just been heavily tipped. If that was pure intellectual triumph, it was not good to see.

"Then . . . the sounds began," Joe said, "while she was still alive?"

Hutchinson shook his head emphatically.

"Not till three weeks after the funeral! That's the intriguing part, don't you see? They were faint and unidentifiable at first—naturally I just put down traps for rats or mice. But by another month, they were taking on their present form.''

Joe gave a back-street sniff and rubbed a hand over his chin. ''Hell, you ask us to believe your poltergeist lies low until nearly a month after the—the—''

''After the medium, shall we say, is dead!'' His cold-bloodedness was fascinating.

Joe looked across at me and raised his eyebrows.

''Gentlemen, perhaps I'm asking you to accept too much? Well, we shall see. Please remember that I am only too happy that you should form your own—your own—'' Hutchinson's voice dropped to a whisper. He raised his hand. His eyes caught ours as he listened.

My spine chilled.

Somewhere above us in the house were faint sounds. A scuffling.

''That's it!''

I tiptoed to the door and got it open in time to hear a last scamper overhead. Yes, it could have been a kitten, I thought; but it had come so promptly on cue. I was on the stairs when Hutchinson called out, as if he were the thing's manager: ''No more for the present! You'll probably get another manifestation in forty minutes or so.''

Cue for the next performance, I thought.

I searched the staircase with my torch. At the top ran the little passage Hutchinson had described; open on one side, with banisters, and on the other, a dark papered wall. The linoleum was bare. There was nothing to be seen, nor any open doors. The very dinginess of this narrow place was eerie.

Downstairs I found Joe feverishly unpacking his apparatus. Hutchinson was watching, delighted.

''Anything I can possibly do, Mr. Banner? Threads across the passage—oh, yes? How very ingenious? You've your own drawing-pins?—excellent! Can I carry that lamp for you?''

And he led the way upstairs.

We searched the shabby bedrooms first. Only one was in use, and we locked all of them and sealed the doors.

In half an hour preparations were complete. Hair-thick threads were stretched across the passage at different levels; adhesive squares lay in patterns on the linoleum. Joe had four high-powered lamps ready to flood the place at the pressure of a silent contact. I took the Leica; he himself now carried an automatic miniature camera.

"Four shots a second with this toy," he was telling Hutchinson, while I went to check a window outside the bathroom. I still favoured the idea of a cat: they so often make a habitual playground of other people's houses.

The window was secure. I was just sticking an additional seal across the join when I sniffed scent; for a moment I took it to be from soap in the bathroom. Sickly, warm, strangely familiar. Then it came almost overpoweringly.

I returned as quickly and quietly as I could to the stairhead.

"Smell it?" Joe breathed in the darkness.

"Yes, what d'you suppose—?"

"Ssh!"

There was a sound not four yards away, as I judged it: a tap on the linoleum. Huddled together, we all tensed. It came again, and then a scamper of feet—small and light, but unmistakable—feet in flat shoes. As if something had run across the far end of the passage. A pause—a slithering towards us—then that same shuffle we had heard earlier in the evening, clear now: it was the jigging, uneven stamp of an infant's attempt to dance! In that heavy, sweet darkness, the recognition of it came horribly.

Something brushed against me: Banner's elbow.

At the very next sound he switched on all his lamps. The narrow place was flung into dazzling brightness—it was completely empty! My head went suddenly numb inside. Joe's camera clicked and buzzed, cutting across the baby footsteps that came hesitating towards us over the floor. We kept our positions, eyes straining down at nothing but the brown faded pattern of the linoleum. Within inches of us, the footsteps changed their direction in a quick swerve and clattered away to the far corner. We waited. Every vein in my head was banging.

The silence continued. It was over.

Banner drew a thick raucous breath. He lowered the camera, but his sweaty face remained screwed up as if he were still looking through the viewfinder. "Not a sausage!" he whispered, panting. "Not a bloody sausage!"

The threads glistened there unbroken; none of the sticky patches was out of place.

"It *was* a kiddie," Joe said. He has two of his own. "Hutchinson!"

"Yes?" The flabby face was white, but he seemed less shaken than we others.

"How the hell did you—?" Banner sagged against the wall and his camera dangled, swinging slowly on its safety strap. "No—it was moving along the floor. I could have reached out and touched— My God, I need a drink!"

We went downstairs.

Hutchinson poured out. Joe drank three whiskies straight off but he still trembled. Desperate to reassure himself, he began to play the skeptic again immediately. As if with a personal grievance, he went for Hutchinson.

"Overdid that sickly smell, you know! Good trick—oh yes, clever—particularly when we weren't expecting it!"

The waiter was quick with his denials: it had always accompanied the sounds, but he had wanted us to find out for ourselves; this time it had been stronger than usual.

"Take it easy, Joe—no violence!" I said. He pushed my hand off his arm.

"Oh, clever! That kind of talc, gripe-watery, general baby smell! But listen to this, Mr. Bloody Hutchinson: it should be much more delicate, and you only get it quite that way with very tiny babies! Now this one was able to walk, seemingly. And the dancing—that comes at a different stage again. No, you lack experience, Mr. H! This is no baby that ever was!"

I looked at Hutchinson.

He was nodding, evidently pleased. "My theory exactly," he said. "Could we call it . . . a poltergeisted maternal impulse?"

Joe stared. The full enormity of the idea struck him.

"Christ . . . Almighty!" he said, and what grip he still had on himself went. He grabbed at his handkerchief just in time, before he was sick.

When he felt better, I set about collecting the gear.

Hutchinson fussed and pleaded the whole time, persuasive as any door-to-door salesman in trying to make us stay for the next incident. He even produced a chart he had made, showing the frequency of the manifestations over the past three months, and began to quote books on the subject.

"Agreed, it's all most extraordinary," I said. "A unique case. You'll be hearing from us." All I wanted was to be out of that house. "Ready, Joe?"

"Yes, I'm all right now."

Hutchinson was everywhere, like a dog wanting to be taken for a walk. "I do hope I've been of some service! Is there anything more I can possibly—? I suppose you can't tell me when the publication date is likely to be?"

Nauseating. "Not my department," I said. "You'll hear."

Over his shoulder I could see the girl's face in her chromium frame. She must have had a very great deal of life in her to look like that on a square of paper.

"Mr. Hutchinson," I said. "Just one last question."

He grinned. "Certainly, certainly. As the prosecution wishes."

"What did your wife die of?"

For the first time he seemed genuinely put out. His voice, when it came, had for the moment lost its careful placing.

"As a matter of fact," he said, "she threw herself under a train." He recovered himself. "Oh, shocking business, showed how unbalanced the poor girl must have been all along. If you like, I can show you a full press report of the inquest—I've nothing to hide—absolutely nothing—''

I reported the assignment as a washout. In any case Banner's photographs showed nothing—except one which happened to include me, in such an attitude of horror as to be recognizable only by my clothing. I burnt that.

''Our Mr. Hutchinson's going to be disappointed.''

Joe's teeth set. ''What a mind that type must have! Publicity mania and the chance of a nice touch too, he thinks. So he rigs a spook out of the dirty linen!''

''Sure he rigged it?''

Joe hesitated. ''Positive.''

''For argument's sake, suppose he didn't; suppose it's all genuine. He manages to go on living with the thing, so he can't be afraid of it . . . and gradually . . . 'new emotional depths' . . .'' The idea suddenly struck me as having a ghastly humour. ''Of course, publicity's the only way he could do it!''

''What?''

''Banner, you ought to be sympathetic! Doesn't every father want to show off his child?''

AUTHOR'S NOTE

I WROTE THIS 40 YEARS AGO, SPECIALLY FOR THE AMERican edition of a bunch of my stories called Tomato Cain. *It replaced one that I wasn't so keen on in the original English version.*

That 40-year gap shows itself in one or two ways. People who read about the scurrility of British tabloid newspapers of the present day, and the crooked ruthlessness of their reporters and paparazzi, may be surprised at Joe Banner and Staines in this story, by their (relative) sensitivity. But these two are men of their time. They would take some pride in not falling for a cheap, obvious hoax. It would be shaming.

Something else I notice on rereading. The very concept of a poltergeist needed a touch of explanation in those pre-Spielberg days. You couldn't take the general reader, for whom it was intended, for granted. Because Tomato Cain *wasn't a cult collection of creepies. There were all sorts in it, from comic to pathetic to ironic. And if there was any kind of horror, I tried to keep it to unease that would linger in the mind.*

What else? The photographic methods? Quite hi-tech for 1949. Even a Leica discarded in favour of an automatic miniature with electric wind, and by a professional at that. Ahead of his time, even by 1989.

Sex? Writing the story today, I might be more explicit. But it belongs to its time, like the characters. I shan't change it.

—Nigel Kneale
April 1989

THE TENANT
Avram Davidson

BALTO, THE SLUMLORD, A LITTLE GREY SUIT OF A MAN
with a long, hairy nose, hired Edgel. That is, not just this
one time or any one particular time, or steadily, but every
now and then, Balto hired Edgel. Edgel was sort of large,
and sort of lopsided, and for this last he drew a disability
pension on which he drank more than was good for him.
Often, when his full and sallow face was flushed with some
bargain in bottled goods, he'd look down and there was
Balto.

Persuasively, he'd tell Edgel that this was no life for
him, that there was no future in it, that he ought to be
looking around for something to do. But Edgel never
needed to be persuaded, as he fully agreed. And so he'd
go to work for Balto as agent/collector in some one or
other of the heaps of vertical ratholes from which Balto
drew great sums of money. And he pictured himself growing respectable. Often, of course, it turned out that in the
house Edgel was charged with was a tenant who had—for
one reason or another, generally a good one—promised to
cut Balto open and draw his tripes if he dared present his

face again. And as soon as this particular menace ceased, Balto dismissed Edgel with a sigh. Or it might be that the housing and health people were anxious to close in on Balto, in which case they were baffled by seeing only Edgel, who was not summonsable. And when the heat was off, Balto, with a sigh— And so on.

Edgel never learned. But, anyway (as Balto pointed out), he was no worse off than before, he'd made some money, and it wasn't like he had nothing to fall back on: He had his pension.

One night, teetering on a dirty curbstone, wondering if he should venture over to a new bar reputed to give an ounce and a quarter of whiskey for the price of an ounce, or perhaps to scout around for a certain taxi driver who had made an agreement with a new woman, Edgel looked down and there was Balto.

"I will not deceive you, Edgel," he said, "I have a job to be done and there is no one I trust to do it except you." For this was a fact: Edgel was honest. His accounts often didn't balance and were short, but he made up the difference himself. Scrupulously. "Furthermore," said Balto, with great earnestness, "I'll tell you immediately that the job isn't permanent. In fact, the better you do your work, the sooner the job is over. But there is money in it." And he named impressive sums.

"Do you think I like this rotten business?" Balto asked. "I would much rather own clean property. All I've ever asked was a decent chance. And now I have it. And I want to share it with you."

In short, no less than six of Balto's rat-eaten tenants were included in a section which was to be torn down and new housing put up. The authorities had condemned the properties on behalf of the builders. The builders were offering the contractor a bonus for speedy completion, the contractor was passing on part of the bonus to owners (including Balto) for speedy vacating, and Balto (Great-Heart) was dividing part of it between Edgel and the tenants.

"And," he wound up, "as a matter of fact—I tell you in confidence, Edgel—I am very familiar with the men in this new syndicate. We, I mean they, will need a staff of dependable people, experienced and honest. A word to the wise. I really mustn't say any more." The long, hairy nose looked up at Edgel, significantly.

The next day, Edgel met by appointment a man named Hallam, who had a wen and who worked for a real estate firm that was engaged in relocating tenants who didn't relocate themselves. "They don't appreciate it," he told Edgel. "You might think they'd be glad to leave these rat-holes, but they aren't. Of course," he pointed out, walking rapidly down the littered street, "the places we're moving them into are also ratholes, but what the Hell, it's a change of scenery."

They passed a tiny store that sold textile remnants, ready-made rejects in factory clothes, and all sorts of things; and a dark little man crouching in the doorway like an upright bat uncurled himself and fluttered at them. "Remember, you find me a good new place, now? Remember."

"Yes, yes," Hallam assured him. "We certainly will. You start getting packed." To Edgel, he said, "He'll take what we give him, or find his own self a place."

Then they started climbing scabby stairs. By noon they were in the last house on Edgel's list. "With this building," said Hallam, "we've got both good luck and bad. Good luck—the middle floor tenants took the bonus and moved right into the place I offered them. Bad luck—this lady on the top floor. She's the main problem. Some of the people, now, they say they won't move and then you got to evict them and that could lead to all kinds of trouble. This one, she doesn't exactly say she *won't* move, but she don't make no *move* to move, if you folla me. I feel sorry for them when they get that sick look on their face."

The downstairs hall, where they paused, was dark and damp and fetid. "It can make you feel like a criminal, some of these people that are afraid to move because they've forgotten they ever lived anywhere else. Because, really, she's a nice, quiet person." *Some* of the tenants were neither nice nor quiet, and it had become easier for Edgel to understand why Balto was parting with money for a surrogate. Hallam said, now, "Don't pay no attention if that old bum downstairs says anything. He's just a dirty old bum. Not sorry for *him*, you can betcher life."

The dirty old bum downstairs looked, sounded, and smelled like a dirty old bum. He began to curse as soon as they knocked; he cursed in English, a tongue singularly poor in obscene invention, and he repeated his scant store over and over. Then he stopped. He leered at them, tiny filmed eyes squinting and winking from his ruined face. "Going upstairs, boys?" he asked. Softly, slyly. "She'll let you—if she's in the mood. If she's in the mood, she'll let anybody. And when Old Larry says, 'Anybody,' that's just what he means. *Anybody*."

The stairs creaked and shifted. There was more light on the top floor because of a dirty hall window. An odd noise came from somewhere. Hallam knocked. The woman who answered did not come out to the hall but stood behind the half-closed door and peered out. Edgel couldn't see her clearly, but she was just an ordinary-looking woman.

"Mrs. Waldeck, this is Mr. Edgel, the landlord's agent." Silence. "Have you been getting ready to move? If you move before the end of next month, we find you another place—"

"I don't want another place," she said, in a quick, weak, fearful voice.

"—and we give you a bonus. How much of a bonus, Edgel?"

"Maybe even a hundred dollars," Edgel said.

"I don't want a bonus. I can't move. I lived here thirty-two years. I'm a sick woman. You can't make me move out."

Edgel said, brusquely, "That's a lot of nonsense, Mrs. Waldeck. We can come here with a cop and a marshal tomorrow and throw you out on the sidewalk. But we don't want to do that," he said, wheedlingly. "We'll get you a place on the ground floor, you won't have to climb all these stairs, and we'll give you a bonus. They're going to tear this house down, you know."

The woman had begun to shake her head while he was talking. Then she said, "Maybe they won't tear this one down. I could pay more rent. Two dollars more?—three? You tell them I'll pay more rent, because I'm a sick woman and I can't move, and so they won't tear this house down. Because I can't *move*!" Her voice rose to a shriek and she slammed the door. After a minute they started down the steps.

"What we could do, maybe," Edgel suggested, "is we could get a guy with a badge and a paper, like they both look real, and she wouldn't know the difference. A dumb broad who thinks they'll leave the house stay up for her extra three dollars! And we move her and her things into one of those places you got. That way, we can still collect the bonus."

Hallam said, yeah, maybe they could do that, if they were real careful about it. "You hear that funny noise?" he asked.

"Sounded like a parrot?"

"Sounded more to me like a frog."

"Maybe she keeps frogs to feed the parrot?" And they both laughed, and they went somewheres to get a bite to eat and a glass of beer.

It was late one night, some weeks after, when Edgel walked with careful feet along the dark sidewalk. He told himself that he was not—was *not*—drunk. Only a little wine. The air would clear his head. But the air, instead of affecting his head, affected his kidneys. Edgel stepped into the blackness of an alley. The tap-tap of a woman's heels on the cracked sidewalk made him draw deeper into the darkness. At the same time the sound put an idea or two into his fuddled mind. Hot, urgent, ugly ideas. What sort of woman, what kind of woman, would be out on the prowl on the streets at night . . . ?

Then she stopped just at the lip of the alley, and in the thin shaft of lamplight. She turned her face to and fro as if she sensed someone's presence. A feathered hat was on her head, and her dress, low-cut, was of a rich fabric. Her mouth shone red. She smiled, her brows arched. He took a silent half step forward. Then his bleared vision cleared.

Edgel saw that the hat was an old ruin of a hat and that the dress was spotted and gappy. The flesh that had seemed rounded and ivory just a second ago, was sagging and raddled with hollows, in which the skin was yellow wrinkles or knotted folds of fat. The eyes were painted; the lips revealed a thin, loose line beneath smears of greasy rouge inexpertly applied to paint a floppy paraphrase of a mouth. And the eyes rolled and winked, and the painted lips made mouthings that hinted of hard-lost memories of smiles.

And he saw that it was Mrs. Waldeck. And he shrank into his clothes.

She saw someone. Her hands smoothed her dress. Her face simpered. She walked off with a roll of her hips and the tip-tap of her heels. Suddenly, the street went quiet. When he emerged from the alley, there was no one in sight. There was nothing in sight. He scuttled away, and he thought of Old Larry's words. *When she's in the mood, she'll let anybody . . . Anybody . . .*

One by one, the tenants moved on. Edgel paused to speak to the batlike little dark man in the shop, whose plaint that they find him a good new place had begun to assume a querulous tone. "Listen," Edgel asked him, "who is this Mrs. Waldeck? What kind of a—"

He stopped. The little man was making gestures, his face gone yellow the while. He touched his hand to his fly. He made a V of two fingers and peered through it, then he pushed the thumb up and closed the same fingers around it, and he spat three times with desperate vigor. And from within his greasy shirt he pulled out a cord from which hung a cross, a medallion, a tiny coral hand with open palm, and a black obsidian longhorn— These he kissed with fervor and with noises of heavy breathing. Then he looked up at Edgel, thin waxy lids drawn back from shining, frightened eyes.

"I don't talk to her," he said. "I don't talk about her. She bring me those quilts she make—I sell them to Gypsy peoples—that's all. I don't know no more. *Please*. No more!" And he scurried into his pack-rat's nest of a store.

And so Edgel set his vigil. Into an empty flat on the other side of the street he moved a big chair and some food and a few bottles. She'd have to go out for food herself, sooner or later. And finally, at the start of the blue dusk the afternoon of the second day of his vigil, she did go out. She stood at the steps for a long while. She moved away slowly. But she moved away! She had several quilts and a shopping bag with her; so she would be gone for some time. How long? Long enough. Edgel crossed the street, entered her house, and sped up the stairs on his toes. Silent, though no one was left in the house to hear him (Old Larry having succumbed to the lure of the bonus and quitted the place, foul mouth and handcart of fetid plunder off to some unknown hole). Edgel told himself, as he fumbled with the keys, that he had a right to do what he was doing—he was the landlord's agent (and damn Balto for making him do his dirty work!); she, tenant—ex-tenant, really—was living there by sufferance and not by right, her rent refused. And the day of reckoning near. But his heart beat in sickly beats, and it told him that what he was doing was vile and cheap. And the key rasped in the old lock, and then the door opened.

The room he entered was dim and crowded with old furniture. He saw something to one side, flashed his pocket light. The quilting frame and a bag of dirty-looking cotton padding. It was very warm, and there was a bad smell. Something moved, something sounded. It was in the opposite corner—a mound, like a vast tea cozy, and on top of it a pair of heavy leather gloves.

Edgel stood there another minute. Then he pulled off the cover, and again he heard movement, sounds, but the light was dim and he could see nothing. So he turned on the electric light and turned to face what seemed to be a huge birdcage.

At first glance he thought he saw a child inside of it—a child like one of those in the hideous photographs of famines: all bloated huge belly and sticklike arms and legs—but in just an instant he saw it was no child. Nor was it starving, not that way it moved so quickly again and again, throwing itself against the heavy wires, beating with its tiny fists and gibbering and yammering in that hateful voice, half shrill scream and half thick croak—and both sounds together.

The fists uncurled and made wrinkled palms and twiggy fingers with yellow, twisted talons—cracked-skin fingers with bitten-looking warts and dirty flaps of skin between them, which at once stretched out to become webs up to the first joint. (How many joints there might be, he could not afterwards remember, but more than on his own fingers; and he had been put in mind, by those fingers, of the bandy, loathsome legs of some huge bird-eating spider.) On the lips and chin and paps were scatterings of long hairs, and there were clotted tufts in the armpits. Its coloring was dead and litchlike, and the skin glistened with a dewy sheen. Edgel felt that if he himself had no mind at all, even, and no sense or reckoning, that if he should feel the creature touch against him ever so briefly or slightly, that his body of its own would recoil and quake and fling itself, babbling, away.

And the head thrust against the wire of the cage, worried at it with tiny sharp teeth, and licked at it with a blue-black tongue.

Edgel flung himself around. Mrs. Waldeck was there. She came at him. There was a flatiron in her hand. Her face was white and blank. He seized her wrist, struggled, and she spat at him. Then he twisted, and the iron fell. Her eyes looked into his and her lips moved.

"Sometimes he is very sweet," she said. "Sometimes he'll take food from my fingers."

"What—?" Edgel babbled. "What—?" And he thrust her away from between him and the door. The bag she had in her other hand broke and scattered, and he saw the grey, coffin-shaped tablets, with the skull and bones embossed on them.

After the second double shot he felt able to unclench his fists, and it was safe to relax a bit without fear of the quick, spasmodic grunting noises he had heard himself making (five hundred years ago) as he fled down the rotting stairs. Swallowing, swallowing the quick flow of spittle which the drinks produced, taking the chaser at a gulp to wash away the taste of his own bile, he stared at a mass of color before his eyes. It came into focus just as the dull roaring in his ears did. A calendar of a naked woman with great gourds of breasts, and the pounding brass of a jukebox, and on his right the hoarse and knowing voice of some barroom brave:

"Whuddiya mean, 'd he make out? Whuddiya mean? He never did 'n he never will, not unless he pays fr it, *an'* no wonder. *You* seen whuttee looks like? Christ! that, only a mother could love!"

AUTHOR'S NOTE

IN THE LATE FIFTIES AND EARLY SIXTIES I LIVED IN A NEW *York City neighborhood which had come down in the world (it has since come up in the world but that's another story), and was still going down. I was searching for a lost cat and in the course of the quest I encountered an empty lot. The tenants in the tenements on its sides, as an easy method of garbage disposal, had been throwing their garbage out of the windows into it, and the lot was piled high with it and had become a vast rat ranch. This provoked me to think of other tenement neighborhoods I had known, and as I thought of them I peopled them with inhabitants real and fictitious, and the problems which many of them faced in their daily lives and in facing removal when the old slums were torn down. Some of them had never known that they were living in slums and lived in the same apartments for ages. One old man had lived in the same flat for seventy-five years and had never learned English. An old woman neighbor of the artist Hannes Bok was still using a coal stove and gas lamps when she died. And one morning I observed three little girls, evidently sisters, going to or from church; I was admiring their pretty, neat, clean and pious appearance when the eldest said to the youngest, "Mary Agnes Theresa, get the hell away from the gutter, or I'll kick the shit outta yiz!" This story owes something to one by Judith Merril, "That Only a Mother," which appeared in* Astounding Stories; *but Miss Merril, after murmuring something about imitation being the sincerest form of flattery, said she didn't mind. And now you may go on to the next story. I am sure that it is very good.*

—Avram Davidson

HALLOWE'EN'S CHILD
James Herbert

IF I HADN'T BEEN IN SUCH A RUSH IT PROBABLY WOULDN'T have happened.

And if I hadn't been so tired.

Maybe if I hadn't been so scared.

Yes, that above all. So scared for Anne. Our first baby meant seven months (once we knew for sure) of scariness for both of us. Eleven years of hoping—the last few of those we spent in despair—then those torturous/ecstatic months after we were informed that, yes, something was there and all we now had to do was be patient. Twenty weeks into Anne's pregnancy and the amniocentesis results told us to expect a girl. Everything appeared to be fine, but we took no chances, none at all. Anne had already given up her secretarial job the moment we knew the egg really had embraced the seed, but now she went into underdrive—that is, she cut out all unnecessary effort. Totally. She invalidized herself. You see, Anne was thirty-eight, an uneasy time for some women, and even worse for those who've never given birth before. "Barren" is an appropriate word—"desolate" might be even better. I'm

35

not sure that men, even the most sensitive, truly appreciate the condition. Those of us who have been as desperate for offspring as our wives or lovers might catch a glimmer, but there's no way we can experience the real trauma. Anne explained that to me.

The labour pains started around eight o'clock on a Sunday evening. We were prepared; we'd been prepared the whole of that month of October. Anne was perfectly calm and I did my best to appear that way too (she offered no criticism of my two abortive attempts at ringing the doctor—my index finger was wayward). When I got through, Dr. Golding asked me the usual questions (usual for *him*, that is; it was all new to me) about time lapses between pains, where the actual pain was coming from, Anne's general condition, etc. He was kind, as if he cared as much about me as he did my wife. But then, I was the one paying for his services for, selfishly, although perhaps understandably given the circumstances, I'd decided our baby would be born privately rather than nationally, if you get my meaning. Besides, the National Health Service had enough to cope with, so if I could ease their burden in some small way by taking my custom elsewhere, well that was fine by me and I'm sure by them also.

The doctor informed me he would alert the hospital but that it was too early for panic stations just yet. I was to ring him again when the contraction pains regularized.

That happened around midnight, maybe just a little after. This time Dr. Golding told me to get moving.

It was about twelve miles to the hospital, a long drive through country lanes and villages, but Anne, unlike me, was serene throughout the journey. Uncomfortable true, but every time I glanced her way, she was smiling (I tried *not* to look at her during the spasms). The hospital itself was small and cosy, a country establishment that had a few private rooms for those who were willing and able to pay. The night sister herself took charge, leaving me alone while they got Anne settled in. When I next saw my wife she was sitting up in bed looking plump and content, although her smile was a little strained by now.

I stayed for an hour before they told me to go home and get some sleep. Nothing was going to happen for a while and when they were sure things were about to break—literally—they would phone Dr. Golding first and then me.

Fine, I said. But it wasn't. I was scared. It was our first time and I for one had all the pessimism that comes with maturity. I agreed to leave though; Sister gave me the impression that choice was not really involved.

Nothing at all happened that day. I rang the office and let them know my week's leave had just begun. My business partner informed me of his favourite brand of cigar. I moped around the house for most of the morning, watching the telephone, hoovering, watching the telephone, loading the washing machine, watching the telephone, dusting and . . . you know what.

I went back to the hospital twice, once in the afternoon and then again in the early evening. Anne was still the blissful Buddha, the swelling she cradled in her arms showing no imminent signs of collapse. Dr. Golding looked in on my second visit and uttered reassuring words. However, just before he ducked out the door he mentioned something about "inducement" if nothing had happened by tomorrow. It was Anne who patted *my* hand and told me not to worry.

I returned home and cooked a meal, leaving most of it uneaten on the plate. I was overanxious, to be sure, but after waiting eleven years for this event, who could blame me? The phone call came at quarter to ten that night.

Things were beginning to move, Dr. Golding informed me. My daughter had suddenly became curious about the outside world. If I got to the hospital soon enough, I'd be there to greet her when she arrived.

The night was chilly, but I didn't bother with an overcoat. I grabbed my jacket, scooped up the car keys, and was inside the car without taking a breath.

It wouldn't start. The bugger wouldn't bloody start.

I smacked the wheel, but that had no effect. I stomped the accelerator, and the engine rasped drily.

Then I swore at my own stupidity. The night *was* chilly. The car needed some choke.

It roared fruitily enough when I corrected my mistake. I had to brake hard as another vehicle rushed past my drive.

Take it easy, I scolded. Getting myself killed wouldn't have pleased anybody, least of all me. I eased the car out gently and gathered speed once I was on the highway. A truck coming towards me flashed its beams and I quickly switched on my own headlights.

As I left the quiet streets of the town and headed across country, I saw there was a low-lying mist rolling over the fields. The moon was bright though, its cold glow bringing a spookiness to the landscape.

I passed through a village and my mouth dropped open. Soon, despite my anxiety over Anne and the baby, I was grinning.

They were cute, these little kids togged up in their witch and monster outfits, several bearing homemade lanterns and broomsticks. I could hear their giggling and excited chatter as they trick-or-treated their way along the high street and tried to scare the hell out of each other.

October 31st. My daughter was going to be born on Hallows' Eve. Hallowe'en. I was neither pleased nor dismayed at the idea. I just wanted her there, safe and sound.

A kid jumped to the curbside and leered crazily at me as I passed, his green face lit by a flashlight beneath his chin. My mind was too preoccupied to retaliate with a leer of my own.

My foot stamped on the brake pedal as the headlights picked out more of the stunted ghouls on the crossing ahead. The car rocked and the kids laughed. They crowded around the side window and tapped on the glass. "Trick or treat, trick or treat," they demanded.

Tempted to drive on, I nevertheless dug into a pocket for loose change; maybe the fact that two of the masqueraders had remained on the crossing and were leaning on my car bonnet, luminous plastic fangs caught by the moonlight, had something to do with my decision. Better to pay up rather than waste time arguing my case. Winding down the window I dropped coins into the greedy hands that thrust in. One of them smacked the bodywork as I drove on.

Out into the cold night again, the mist enveloping the car as though it had been waiting for me to leave the village refuge. I shivered, reached forward, turned up the heater. Still a ways to go yet. Hold on, Anne, don't start without me.

Now I saw the lights of a hamlet ahead, just a street with a few houses on either side and nothing else. I didn't slow the car; in fact, I increased speed, for the mist had little substance beneath the sodium lights. Just beyond the last houses masked faces turned to watch my approach. A witch in cape and pointed hat waved a broomstick at me. I sped on, waving in response to their banshee wails.

Darkness dropped heavily once again, the car's headlights bouncing back at me from the rolling grey blanket (which seemed even thicker now). I slowed down, dipped the beams. Again I slapped the steering wheel in frustration.

Dear God, let it lift. Please let me get to Anne.

And you know, the mist actually seemed to lift; or at least, a hole in the whiteness opened up before me. Taking full advantage, I accelerated; unfortunately, the relief was only temporary. The swirling clouds came back at me with a vengeance.

I braked, tightening my grip on the wheel, keeping the vehicle in a straight line. I heard the thump—*felt* it—and shouted something, Lord knows what.

Rubber scraped tarmac as the car screeched to a halt. I sat frozen, the engine stalled; a sickness swelled inside me.

I'd hit something. No, the thump had a softness to it. I'd hit *someone*. For the second time that night, this time with a cold dread dragging at me, I beseeched God. Let it be an animal, I said. Please, an animal. But I'd seen a small black bundle hurl over the side of the bonnet an instant after the impact. Its apparent size suggested I'd hit a child.

I think I was mumbling a prayer as I lurched from the car.

There wasn't too much to see out there, although the mist didn't seem quite as dense in the open. Only in the light beams was there real substance; beyond them the low fog was more tenuous, less compact. I searched around the car, stumbling over the grass verge on the left, moving in a crouched position, fearful of what I might find.

I called out, but there was no reply. And there was nothing lying close to the vehicle. For one wild—almost feverish—moment, I considered jumping back into the car and driving on. There was nobody there, I told myself. I hadn't run into anything; the haste, the anxiety, had got the better of me. Maybe a bird, a large crow perhaps, had flown up in front of me. I returned to the car.

But a sudden rush of guilt (and reality) prevented me from climbing in.

And a faint scratchy moan caused me to look back along the road.

I moaned myself. The mist had drifted enough for me to glimpse a dark shape crawling along the roadside.

My steps were slow at first, as though apprehensive of what they would lead me to; compassion however soon hurried me forward. As I approached the moving figure, my worst fears were realized: I *had* hit a child.

He or she appeared to be clothed in a long black cloak or gown—not the first such costume I'd seen that night. Except that whereas most of those other children had elected for pointed hats, this one had favoured a cowl, one that covered his or her head completely. Why was the kid out here alone? What the hell were the parents thinking of to allow their child to be unaccompanied at this late hour? These were minor considerations on my part, probably no more than a feeble attempt to shift the blame for the accident from myself.

I reached the crawling figure and bent low to touch its shoulder, the tenderness and pity I felt all but consuming. I became weak; my outstretched hand trembled.

The shoulder beneath the black cape felt fragile, somehow brittle, as if the bones were like those of a small bird.

"You'll be all right," I said softly and with no confidence in my heart. "I'll get you to a hospital, you'll be fine."

I knelt, reaching round to turn the child over, my face close to the hood.

Something sharp raked across my eyes. The figure had twisted suddenly, lashing out in panic (I thought then) or in pain. Blinded for the moment, I sensed the child scrambling away; its cries were sharp little sounds, that were not unlike the yelps of a wounded animal.

"Stop!" I called. "I want to help you."

All I heard was a scurrying.

The sting left my eyes, although a wetness still blurred my vision. I managed to discern a dark shape shuffling away from me though, heading back towards the car.

"Stop! I'm not going to hurt you." I shouted and took off after the cloaked figure. He or she leaned against the bodywork for support, staggering onwards, one leg dragging behind. With surprising speed, considering the injuries the child must have sustained, it was beyond the car and moving into the beams of the headlights. I gave chase, afraid for the poor little wretch, afraid that it might come to more harm because of its hysteria.

I quickly caught up and yelled, "Wait!" A tiny scream that was curious in its fierceness was the reply.

I snatched at the cloak, grasped cloth and held firm. But fear or confusion had lent the child unreasonable strength, for it was I who was tumbled onto my knees in the roadway. As I fell, my other hand clutched the figure so that it was forced down with me. The child squirmed in my grip as we rolled over the hard surface and I had to hold fast to prevent damage to either of us. I could scarcely credit the energy of the tiny brute (I admit it—I was getting somewhat exasperated by now).

"Be still," I ordered, feeling inadequate, frustrated, and impatient—all those things.

And then I turned the child over to face me.

It was a few seconds before I staggered away to fall heavily onto my elbow. A few seconds of staring into the most grotesque, the most evil, face I'd ever seen in my life.

The cowl had dropped away as she—yes, it was a woman, at least I *think* it was a woman—raised her head from the road to stare with filmy yellow eyes into mine, her ravaged and rotting countenance caught in the full glare of my car's headlights. But it wasn't just the shock of seeing the sharp, hawked nose, swollen near its tip with a huge hardened wart from which a single white hair sprouted, the cheeks with hollows so deep they seemed like holes, the thick grey eyebrows that joined across her wrinkled forehead, the cruel, lipless mouth from which a black tongue protruded, that made me throw myself away.

Oh no, it was when that pointed black tongue slicked from sight and she spat a missile of green slime into my face, screeching as she did so, that did that.

Shocked, bubbly liquid dripping from my chin, I stared across the tarred surface at her. She sat up, thin grey strands of hair stiff against her shoulders. Her dwarfish legs were splayed, the long gown she wore beneath the cloak risen above bony knees, high boots laced around her ankles.

Something moving beneath the hem of her skirt captured my attention. It slid from cover as if uncurling. A grey-pink tip appeared. It slithered further into view, growing thicker. It was ringed with horny and hairy scales.

She watched my astonished face and then she laughed, a high squawky sound, a witch's—yes, a *witch's*—cackle (at least, how I'd always *imagined* a witch's laughter to be—and this was Hallowe'en, after all).

Probably, if I hadn't already been in such an extreme state of tension, I might have behaved more calmly. As it was, that scaly tail weaving between her legs tipped the balance between rational reaction and blind panic. Her gnarled and ravaged features, the scratchy, high-pitched laughter, the sheer aura of *malevolence* around her, didn't help; but no, it was definitely that horny swaying thing that sent me tearing back to the car.

I'd left the door open and I bundled in, the cackling chasing through the mist after me. I flicked the ignition and moaned at the engine's grinding. It fired on the third attempt.

The road ahead, or what I could see of it, was now deserted. I pushed down on the accelerator and tires spun on the damp road before gripping. The car shot forward.

And suddenly she, it, the *thing*, was on the bonnet, peering through the windscreen at me. The grotesque creature mouthed something, something that I didn't hear but which *looked* foul. She grinned toothlessly, that black tongue flicking out to lick the glass. My brain told me this was all impossible; my emotions were not prepared to listen.

Then she began to scratch the windscreen with clawed fingers, her long, curling nails screeching against the glass. The scratchmarks she left were clearly visible.

Those wicked, filmy eyes glared into mine, and they mocked me, they challenged me, they dared me to *dis*-believe this was happening. Her laughter penetrated the screen; and so, too, did those taloned fingernails that she swept down again and again into the grooves already made.

I think I screamed. Certainly the car's brakes did as I jammed my foot on the pedal.

The midget monster disappeared from view, propelled by the abrupt halt. Immediately, in a reflex action, I stepped on the accelerator again. The brief bump I felt was sickening: I was *sure* I heard the crunching of crushed bones.

My inclination was to drive on, to leave the nightmare behind. But basically, and as far as any of us are, I'm a normal human being: I have a conscience. I also possess— at least I did then—some soundness of mind. I'd hurt someone, someone unlike you or me, but a person, dwarf-ish and deformed though she was (my mind was already refusing to acknowledge what I'd seen with my own eyes— the tail, the black tongue, the fingernails tearing through glass). I stopped the car.

Once outside I shivered, the night air having grown even more chilled. Or perhaps something else was chill-ing my bones; maybe it was the prospect of what I would now find lying in the road. My footsteps dragged but I knew I could not just leave her there, no matter how fearful I was.

The low mist had thinned considerably, possibly due to the rush of air the speeding car had created. The body was easy to find. It lay in the road, unmoving, one part—the chest—strangely deflated. A further coldness ran through me when I realized that it was my car's tyres that had flattened her little body like that.

There was no need to look closer to conclude she was dead; yet closer I did look. Her eyes were half-open, just a crescent of watery yellowness showing on either side of her hooked nose. This time I really had killed her.

But as I watched, her eyelids slid fully open, an al-most languid movement, and her pupils seemed to float to the surface from deep within the eyeballs themselves.

Her voice was no more than a peculiar croaking:

> *Hallow's Eve, Hallow's Eve*
> *Beware hobgoblins on Hallow's Eve.*

Those taloned claws grabbed my clothing and pulled me down onto her. We rolled and rolled in the road, this way and that, with me yelling and her screeching, and when I felt those fingernails digging into my chest, reaching for my heart, I knew I was in mortal danger (and knew, had I had any doubts, that this was no dream).

Despite the terrible injury, the thing was strong; but I was bigger and more afraid. I managed to rise over her, my hands clasped tight around her scrawny neck. I could feel bones breaking beneath my fingers.

She smiled blackly up at me.

"Can't kill me, can't kill me," she chanted.

Her pointed tongue shot from her toothless mouth like a long, striking snake. She scratched (the tongue was *rough*) the tip of my nose.

"Beware hobgoblins," she warned when the tongue had slithered back.

My only excuse is that total, mind-shocking hysteria took over. I cracked her head against the shiny surface of the road. And then again. Then again. More, until a thick gooey liquid spread from the back of her skull onto the tarred surface. Her eyes blinked.

"Can't kill me," she taunted.

The last crack had a mushy softness to it, like delicate porcelain filled with sugar shattering inwards.

With a rasping sigh, she finally lay still. Then she said: *"We don't die."*

Enraged, and mindless, I screamed.

I scooped up the limp form, my intention, I think, to lay it on the grass verge, or perhaps even in the back seat of the car; but I became overwhelmingly repulsed by what I held in my arms when I heard her say: *"You'll be sorry. You and the baby."*

I threw the little monster over the hedge beyond the verge and was startled to hear a splash. There must have been a water-filled ditch or a pond on the other side. I listened to the gurgling that came through the leafy hedge, not letting my breath go until the bubbly sound had ceased. Dread upon dread. She, it—the *thing*—had said *"the baby."* What the hell had she meant? I actually clutched my hands to my chest, so powerfully portentous was the sensation that struck me.

I fled the scene (of the crime, I suppose it's not unreasonable to add) and scrambled back into my car. What had she meant? Dear God, what had she meant? Surely . . . I blanked the terrifying thoughts from my mind. I had to get to the hospital, that was the important thing. I could bring the police back here later, tell them the whole story, how it wasn't my fault. Tell them the *whole* story? I gazed at the long scars in the glass before me. Tell them about that? About the creature's black tongue. About how she'd fought even though her chest had been completely crushed? About the horned tail hanging between her legs? Tell them about that? They'd think I was insane, even when they examined the body. *If* they ever found the body. Why did I need to show them where it was? Nobody had witnessed the accident. In all likelihood, it would take ages for the corpse to be discovered, so who could connect it with me? The holes etched in the glass—*should* anyone enquire—might possibly have been caused by a tree branch. That was more feasible than clawed fingers, at any rate.

The car was already in motion as all these thoughts tumbled through my head. I drove crazily, and it was only because I soon approached the town that I didn't have another accident. The lights shone ahead and I increased speed, desperate to get to Anne and my unborn/born (?) child.

By the time I reached the hospital, the long cracks in the windscreen had healed over; by the time I drew the car to a halt near the maternity unit, the marks had disappeared altogether. I spared myself no time to wonder.

Anne's private room was empty. I hurried through the main ward, searching for a nurse, a doctor, anyone who could give me a hint as to my wife's whereabouts. Those women still awake in the ward, some of them suckling newborn infants, looked up, startled at my unkempt appearance (I'd been rolling around in the road remember; I suppose I was looking pretty wild-eyed too). A nurse came striding towards me.

Fortunately she recognized me. "Your wife went up to the delivery room twenty minutes ago," she said, her voice low. "Now calm yourself, everything's fine."

I brushed by her, heading for the stairs beyond the far doors. I climbed them two at a time, my chest hurting from the exertion, my hand clammy damp as it slid along the stair rail. The waiting room was empty, the door to the delivery room closed. Resisting the urge to rush through, I rapped on the wood.

Someone on the other side murmured something, then I heard approaching footsteps.

"Just in time," the midwife said as she peered out at me. "Come inside and hold your wife's hand. My goodness, I think she might need to comfort you."

Dr. Golding smiled at me, then frowned. "Sit yourself down," he said, indicating a chair beside the high bed. He returned his attention to my recumbent wife.

Anne looked drained, but she managed a smile. She clasped my hand and I winced when she squeezed hard as a spasm hit her. Her eyes had a dreamy look that even the pain could not cut through.

"Wonderful," I heard the doctor say. "That's wonderful. Your daughter's well on her way. One last push, I'm sure that'll do the trick. You'll doing marvellously."

"You'll be sorry. You and the baby."

The voice was in my mind, not in the room.

Anne gasped, but it was not from childbirth pains; she swung her face towards me questioningly and I realized it was *I* who had clutched *her* hand too tightly.

". . . You and the baby . . ."

A voice as shrivelled as the creature who had uttered the words.

"Excellent," said the doctor.

It couldn't have happened, I told myself. Stress, exhaustion, the culmination of months of anxiety, praying that finally a child would be ours, that nothing would go wrong, nothing would spoil our ultimate dream. . . .

I'd imagined everything that had happened during the rushed journey to hospital. My mental state had induced an hallucination. That had to be the answer. Hadn't the car's windscreen been unmarked by the time I'd arrived at the maternity unit? Reason encouraged the explanation.

And the ugly, guttural voice in my head at last withered away.

"Welcome," said Dr. Golding.

For my daughter had slid smoothly and effortlessly, it seemed, after so many hours of labour, from her mother's body into the ready hands of the doctor.

The room dipped and banked around me; my head felt feather-light.

"Good God, catch him," I heard someone say as if from a great distance.

Firm hands gripped my waist and I blinked my eyes to find the midwife's face staring down at me.

"It's not the first time the proud father has fainted on us," Dr. Golding said cheerily. "You take yourself outside for a moment or two while we tidy things up in here. Stick your head between your knees; you'll soon feel better."

Anne nodded at me and I could see just how depleted was her strength in the wanness of her smile.

"The baby . . . ?" I said.

"A perfect little girl," the midwife said as she whisked the pink, glistening bundle away to the scales.

I rose, just a bit unsteady, and bent to kiss Anne's lips. "You're both perfect," I whispered to her.

I went to the door and turned to catch sight of my child swaddled in white in the arms of the midwife before I stepped outside. With relief I sank into a stiff-backed chair in the waiting room. Thank God, I said silently to myself. Thank God . . .

But I heard a muffled shout from back there in the delivery room. I was frozen, body and senses, as I listened:

"It's impossible." It was the doctor's voice. "There can't be another—"

The woman's shriek drove me to my feet. The delivery room door opened before I could reach it. The midwife's face appeared whiter than the uniform she wore. A hand shot to her mouth as her chest seemed to heave. Bending forward, she pushed past me.

I prevented the door from swinging closed with a raised arm. I entered the room.

Anne, our baby held tight to her breasts, was staring from the bed to the doctor, a look of abject horror frozen on her face.

Dr. Golding had his back to me. He, too, was strangely immobile. And he, too, held something in his arms.

I knew it was another baby, my daughter's twin.

I heard a tiny, scratchy cry.

And as I watched, a small, scaly tail curled up around the doctor's elbow.

AUTHOR'S NOTE

MY YOUNGEST DAUGHTER, CASEY, REALLY WAS BORN ON Hallowe'en, and I did get the call that she was on the way around nine o'clock at night, and there was a low-lying mist and a clear moon as I drove through the English countryside to get to the little hospital where the event was taking place, and I did speed through tiny villages where kids were appearing from doorways dressed as witches and ghouls and carrying lanterns, and my wife's bed was empty when I arrived at the hospital, and I did race up to the maternity room with a terrible sense of foreboding.

The rest, however, is make-believe.

I was in time for the delivery, the baby was fine (although let's be honest here—slick, fresh babies are pretty gruesome in their own right), and my wife, Eileen, was happy, if exhausted. Casey is now five years old and, while I'll admit she sometimes gets the devil in her, there are, as yet, no signs of claws and scaly tails.

—James Herbert

AFTER THE FUNERAL
Hugh B. Cave

AFTER THE FUNERAL HARRY DROVE OLD CLAYTON LAN-
dry back to the house. It was nearly five o'clock. "I suppose I'd better plan on staying the night," Harry said.
"I'm not keen about starting home at this hour."

Home was in Providence, Rhode Island, a long way
from this northern Vermont village. The day had dragged
and he was weary.

Old Clayton, who had looked after Father for the past
two years, prepared a meal of cabbage and pork, and they
ate it together in the farmhouse kitchen. As a boy Harry
had eaten breakfast at the same table every day of his life
from the time he left his high chair until he was fifteen
years old. On his fifteenth birthday he had run away.

"Tell me again how you found him, Clay," he said to
push back the silence.

Clayton frowned at him as though bewildered by the
question. He was a white-haired seventy-seven and had
looked a little ridiculous in his black funeral suit. Having
changed now to his usual overalls, he blended a bit better

into the surroundings. "I found him in the attic, Mr. Harry."

"I know *that*, Clay."

"On the bed up there."

"You told me that, too."

"Then what else can I tell you, Mr. Harry?"

"He'd been going up there every night, you say?"

"Almost every night, since the letter came from the asylum."

"And you would hear him pacing back and forth up there, reading his Bible?"

"That's right. But, like I said, it wasn't at all the way he used to read the Bible in the parlor, downstairs here. Down here he used to read about sex and sin. Up there it was forgiveness."

"You could hear what he was saying?"

"My Lord, yes, Mr. Harry. Both down here and up there he yelled out the words like he wanted the whole county to hear him. But you must know that. He carried on the same way when you was here, I'm told."

"Not in the attic, Clay."

"He did down here, though. Every housekeeper he ever had talked about it."

Yes, Harry thought, Father had certainly carried on down here, even before Mother went away. He would never forget how the man marched around the parlor every evening with the Book in his out-thrust hands, bellowing the words so that the very windows rattled. There were passages in the Old Testament about the sinfulness of sex that Harry remembered to this day, though they had made his head ache something awful when Father roared them out.

He could shut his eyes right now and see the man marching—six-foot six-inches tall, straight as the flagpole that stood in the front yard at that time, his voice a deep, booming bass and his hair a mass of white topping a handsome face that always seemed about to burst into flames.

The Reverend Jason W. Callinder had been preaching at the local village church before Harry was born. At fifty-four he married for the first time, taking twenty-five-year-old Yvonne Marcotte for his bride. Harry was born a year later. Six years after that, Yvonne Marcotte Callinder was declared insane and put away in an asylum, where she had died just seven months ago.

Harry had come from Providence to attend that funeral, too. But Father hadn't gone to it.

Seated now at the old kitchen table with the last of his father's many housekeepers, Harry recalled his unhappy childhood in this house and wondered how he had endured it so long. He remembered his mother as two entirely different persons. One was a pretty, flashing-eyed woman (she was French-Canadian) who sang and laughed a lot and played bright melodies on the old upright piano in the parlor. The other, later, was a pathetically subdued creature who performed her household duties in almost total silence.

Night after night, while Father rattled the parlor windows with his Bible readings, she sat with her head bowed over her mending, never once attempting to make conversation—not even with the little boy who sat beside her, frightened half out of his wits by his father's shouting.

Then she was sent away, and there were only Father and himself and the first of the many housekeepers.

He remembered the first housekeeper rather more clearly than some of the others, perhaps because she *was* the first to take his mother's place. A busy, bustling woman, Mrs. Osborne had treated the six-year-old boy with kindness, even criticizing Father for being too strict with him. "Now he's just a child, Reverend, and you're not to expect all that much from him," he remembered her saying more than once.

But she did not last. "When I came here I expected my evenings to be peaceful," she told Father with her hands on her hips the day she quit. "I did not expect to be subjected to a noisy sermon on sin and sex every night. Good day to you, sir. It is my considered opinion that the wrong member of this family was sent away to the asylum!"

But the Bible reading did not stop, even when other housekeepers walked out because of it. Father was always able to find someone else to cook his meals and do the housework.

Harry recalled most of the later ones only vaguely. At age eleven he had faced a larger problem. Father decided he was old enough to be of interest to the Devil.

"Harold"—plucking the gold watch from his waistcoat pocket and scowling at it—"you should have been home from school thirty-five minutes ago! Where have you been?"

Even a truthful answer was certain to elicit a suspicious stare from under those lowered white brows. An answer not quite the truth . . . well, Father always seemed to know, somehow. Punishment varied, from being deprived of supper to being sent to the attic.

Ah, the attic! How many hours had he spent up there? In summer it was stifling hot there under the shingled roof; in winter it was freezing cold. Always it was dark, because the two windows were too small to let in more than slivers of light.

There was a bed, an old iron thing with a torn and musty mattress on it, but he was forbidden to use it. Even the old rocking chair was denied him. If he wished to sit, he must use either the floor or the straight-backed chair with the broken cane seat.

There was a big wooden box of old books and magazines up there, too, but he was not allowed to touch it. Once he dared to peek anyway, and discovered the magazines were Sunday School publications for children—at least, the ones on the top were, and he was not brave enough to probe more deeply. As it was, he was terrified that Father would discover what he had done and find some way to punish him. Being sent to the attic was awful enough.

Frowning across the kitchen table now at old Clayton Landry, Harry said, "When did you say Father moved to the attic for his Bible readings?"

"Right after the letter came from the institution."

"Did he tell you what was in the letter?"

Clayton shrugged his bony shoulders. "From the day I come here to work, sir, he never confided in me. As a matter of fact, he never even mentioned the letter. I wouldn't've known he got it except he was out of the house that day when the postman came." His shoulders twitched again. "All I know is, he asked me could I run an extension cord from his bedroom so's he could have a light in the attic. I done it, and the next thing I knew, I was hearing him up there every evening instead of in the parlor. But, like I told you, the words were different."

"No more sex and sin."

"Nope."

"Now he wanted forgiveness."

"I didn't say that. What I said was he read a lot of Bible words having to *do* with forgiveness. I can't imagine him ever thinking *he* needed forgiving for anything."

He did, though, Harry thought bitterly. *Oh, but he did!*

Vividly to mind came the terrible Sunday evening when Father, home from church ahead of him, had thundered at him to come into the parlor the moment the front door clicked shut behind him. Sitting there like a god of judgment in his chair, the white-haired man roared, "Where have you been? I have been home for nearly an hour!"

"I walked Amy Leslie home, Father."

"For what? To have sex with her?"

"Father, please. We are just friends. We're in the same home room in school."

Father stabbed a finger at him, and it was like being menaced by a bolt of lightning with the man's face an awesome thundercloud behind it. "I saw you talking to her. I saw you *touching* her!"

"People touch each other all the time, Father. It only means they are friends and like each other. It doesn't—"

"Be quiet! I have seen this coming on in you. You are your mother's son! Go to the attic and remain there until I come for you!"

He went to the attic. Even there, with the trapdoor at the top of the ladder closed, he heard his father thundering in the parlor about the sinfulness of sex and about temptation—all passages he had heard many times before but delivered now with a fervor that terrified him. That evening in the attic he felt hatred for his father for the first time. But when the white-haired man climbed the ladder and pushed up the trapdoor and came to him with a leather belt dangling from one huge hand, the hatred turned again to terror.

"Take down your trousers!"

All the next day his bottom bled, staining his clothes. The housekeeper then was Miss Emily Adlam, younger than most, and she washed him and put salve on him. More important, she sympathized when he announced he was going to run away.

"I'll help you," she said.

They planned it together. Both would leave the following Sunday while Father was in church, preaching against sin and sex and the Devil. He would pretend to be too ill to go to church; she would insist on staying at home in case he needed her.

"My brother will drive you to Waterbury in his car," she said, "and you can take a bus there for Boston, where I have a married sister. I'll give you a letter, and they will help you."

The last time he saw his father alive was that Sunday morning, when from the window of his room he looked down and watched the Reverend Jason W. Callinder, then seventy, stride bareheaded down the road with a Bible in one hand and the sun all aglitter in his mane of white hair.

A week later, in Boston, he obtained a job as a messenger boy with Western Union and moved into an inexpensive rooming house to begin a life on his own.

"I wonder," said Harry to the man at the kitchen table with him, "what made him change from sin and sex to forgiveness. Was it the letter, Clay?"

"I wouldn't know, sir. But that's *when* he changed—right after it came."

"He shouted about the sinfulness of sex all the time I can remember. You were a neighbor of ours then. Did he do it when I was very young?"

"Even before you were born, Mr. Harry."

"And he changed to forgiveness after the letter came. M'm . . . Very interesting, don't you think?"

"To say the least, sir."

"Do you suppose that letter might still be around here somewhere, Clay? In his room, perhaps?"

"We could look."

"Finish your food first. We have all evening to solve the mystery of my dear father. I doubt we'll be able to, anyway."

They finished eating. Clayton carried the dishes to the sink and filled the sink with water to make the washing up easier when he returned to it. Climbing the wide, uncarpeted stairs to the floor above, they went together along the hall to the big front bedroom that had been used by Harry's father—and also, at one time, by his French-Canadian mother.

A search of the old maple chest of drawers there turned up nothing of interest. Peering back into the hall, Harry said, "Do you suppose the attic . . . ?"

"It's possible. He spent every evening up there toward the end."

"We'll need flashlights."

"Uh-uh. You're forgetting I installed a light up there, Mr. Harry. It works from here." Kneeling, Clayton took up a wire with a plug on the end of it, and inserted the plug into a baseboard outlet. "She's on now 'less the bulb burned out. You still remember how to get up there, sir?"

"I will till I die."

"Well, that shouldn't be soon, you being a young man yet."

"Let's hope not."

"*He* died up there, though," Clayton said. "And they

don't know yet what of.'' With a sidelong glance at Harry
he added, ''*Do* they, sir?''

''If they do, I haven't been told, Clay.''

''But you want to go up there, even so?''

''I think I want to read that letter.''

Night was falling now. It came early at this time of year,
and they had spent a long time in the kitchen, eating and
talking. Clayton switched on the hall light as they went
along to the attic ladder.

The ladder was just as Harry remembered it: a pair of
nearly vertical two-by-fours rising to the trapdoor in the
hall ceiling, with shorter lengths of the same wood nailed
on for rungs. As a boy he had always found the rungs too
far apart and supposed Father had made them that way on
purpose, to add to his punishment. Now as he climbed up
after old Clayton they seemed less taxing.

Clayton pushed open the trapdoor and, indeed, the
opening was yellow with light as he had predicted. Not a
bright light, but better than nothing. Boosting himself onto
the attic's rough board flooring, Harry straightened and
looked about, remembering.

How many times before running away had he been sent
up here as punishment for the sins of his childhood, such
as daring to be alone with a girl? How often, even before
the last terrible flogging, had he been whipped up here?
Bitterness burned in him like swallowed acid as he thought
about it.

And the room had not changed, even in the smallest
detail. Over there was the forbidden bed, over there the
rocker he had never been permitted to use. And almost
directly under the dangling light bulb was the box of magazines he had once almost dared to delve into.

He knelt beside the box now, saying to Clayton, ''If the
letter's up here at all, this is probably where we'll find it.
He told me time and time again if I ever disturbed this
box he would hand me over to the Devil.''

''Did you believe him, sir? I mean, when you was that
young did you belive in the Devil?''

"I did, Clay. Indeed I did."

"And do you now, sir, if I might ask? You're not a preacher like he was, are you?"

"No, I'm not a preacher."

"What *do* you do down there in Providence, sir, if I might ask?"

Harry did not answer. While talking he had been tossing magazines out of the box—the same Sunday school papers he had found when he dared to look before. Now in his hands he held something different. Oh, but *different*. What he held in his hands now, with the overhead light shining directly down on it, was a handsome, smooth-paper magazine with a nude woman on its cover.

"So," Harry said in a barely audible whisper. "So!"

He opened the magazine. It consisted almost solely of photographs in color of nude women and nude men engaged in sex in a variety of ways. On one such picture was written in what he recognized as Father's handwriting, 'This is sinful. Never would I do this!' On another was written, 'Oh, God, why must I be so everlastingly tempted? Why can I not have peace?'

Harry handed the magazine to the man watching him and dug deeper into the box. There were many such magazines. There were thirty, at least. All of them bore comments in Father's unmistakable script:

'No man should permit this to be done to him. It can only lead straight to Damnation.'

'This woman should be condemned to Hell.'

'How loathsome! Yet I know that if it were offered to me, God forgive me, I could not refuse it.'

Harry looked at his companion. "Did you expect anything like this, Clay?"

"Lord, no, Mr. Harry! Never!"

"Notice the dates. Not all of these are recent. Some must have been here when I was here. Even before I was born."

"And all the time he thundered about the sinfulness of sex, he was tormenting himself with these." Clayton shook his head in wonder. "The poor man. With two such powerful urges pulling at him, he must have felt he was being torn apart all the time." He leaned forward to see what Harry has just lifted from the box. "Mr. Harry, that's the letter! That's it in your hand. The letter from the asylum!"

Harry rose from his knees and walked to the rocking chair he had so often wanted to sit in. He sat. He took the letter out of its envelope and saw that it was typewritten. Before starting to read it, he looked to see who had written it.

The signature was a scrawl, but under it was typed, 'Adrian McFarlane, M.D., Chief of Staff.'

'Dear Mr. Callinder,' the letter began. 'Just before her death here your wife asked me to take a message for you, and I did so because she was at that time unusually lucid even though physically very weak. She asked to make a statement that could be delivered to you after her death. I might add that I tape-recorded our conversation. If you wish, I will send you a copy of the tape so that you may check the accuracy of what I am about to tell you.

'Your wife said that you savagely turned against her when you learned that she was pregnant, because you knew the child could not be yours. You believed sex was sinful and never had intercourse with her—in fact, never even allowed yourself to touch her. You assumed that her pregnancy was the result of her having been unfaithful to you with some other man.

'This, your wife told me, is not true. She was never touched by another man. What happened is that on a night when you were away from home, preaching in another part of the state, she had a dream. It was an unusually vivid dream. I will not go into details here, but nearly ten minutes of the tape are taken up by her account of this strange dream. In it, she says, she was assaulted by what she called a minion of the Devil whose objectives was to humiliate _you_. This demon overpowered her and raped her, she told me. When she awoke he was gone. But, she insists, it could not have been merely a dream, for she was made pregnant in fact.

'You may ask why she did not tell you this at the time. *I* asked her this and her answer was that you were so violently opposed to anything pertaining to sex that she kept silent out of pure terror.

'It is for you to evaluate all this, Mr. Callinder. I myself am an atheist, believing in neither God nor Devil. I can only say that at the time of our conversation your wife was not insane. Perhaps if she had found the courage to tell you this when it happened, she would never have become a patient of ours.'

Harry had read the letter to himself, in silence. Now before handing it to his companion he said, "Tell me something, Clay. You found my father on the bed, here, I believe you said."

"Yes, sir."

"Are you telling me everything?"

"Well, sir . . . he was naked."

"I see. Go on."

"On his back, sir. With his hands on his—you know."

"And?"

"He was a mess, sir, all wet and well—messy. The bed, too. And you know something? *I* think that's what killed him. The shame of doing it, I mean. To him it must have been like surrendering to the Devil after all the years of fighting him."

"I wouldn't be surprised," Harry said. "Here." He held out the letter. "Read this."

Clayton was a slow reader. It took him a long time to reach the end of the letter. Even then he did not grasp its major implication right away.

"My goodness, Mr. Harry," he said. "If this is true, what she says, she was drove crazy for a thing she never did."

"Of course."

"No wonder your father switched over from sin and sex to forgiveness. He needed all the forgiving he could get!"

"He must have believed her, too, you know," Harry said gently.

"Huh?"

"That she was raped by a demon."

"Well," Clayton said, still clutching the letter and scowling at it, "don't *you* believe her? Your own mother?"

"Of course I do."

That was when Clayton got it. He looked up from the letter. He looked at Harry. His eyes grew large, and a little twitch drew the corners of his mouth down. "But," he said, "but . . . if it was a demon got your mother pregnant . . . then you . . . you must be . . ." Swaying on his feet, he dropped the letter and sucked in a breath. "What *do* you do there in Providence, Mr. Harry? You never did answer me when I asked you!"

Harry sardonically grinned at him. "Well, of course, Clay, one thing I *had* to do there was grow up, and I guess I've done that. At least, I'm pretty sure I wouldn't let Father have his way with me now." Still grinning, he glanced up at the dangling light bulb.

The light went out. When it came on again of its own accord a few seconds later, old Clayton Landry saw that he was alone in the attic.

On groping his way downstairs he found he was alone there, too. Harry's car was still in the yard, but Clayton had an idea cars were not very necessary to a person like Harry. It had been a rented car anyway, he remembered.

One thing he knew for certain: he sure to God wasn't going to stay in that house overnight, even with Harry gone.

Shaking all over and moaning with terror, he fled into the night.

AUTHOR'S NOTE

Why this particular story and not some other of the few I've written? Well, now, it appeared first in Fantasy Tales, *that marvelous magazine edited by Stephen Jones and David Sutton. Published in England,* Fantasy Tales *is a World Fantasy Award winner and has won the British Fantasy Award so many times that most of us have lost count.*

Moreover, this story was voted by the readers of that magazine to be the best story in the issue in which it appeared, and those readers are a pretty sophisticated bunch when it comes to tales of this sort. And the issue contained so many well-known names that the editor felt compelled to put five of them on the cover.

I chose this story, too, because it was written and published fairly recently—the winter of 1986—and therefore hasn't already been anthologized. And finally, I fingered it because when I was asked by Dennis Etchison to pick out something of mine for this volume, I couldn't decide among four that appeared to be likely prospects. So I read the four aloud to a certain lady named Peggie, whom some of you may know, and this is the one she liked best. Which is enough for me, any day.

—*Hugh B. Cave*

SHE PHONED AGAIN LAST NIGHT. AT 3 A.M. THE WAY SHE always does. I'm scared to death. I can't keep running. On the hotel's register downstairs, I lied about my name, address, and occupation, hoping to hide from her. My real name's Charles Ingram. Though I'm here in Johnstown, Pennsylvania, I'm from Iowa City, Iowa. I teach—or used to teach until three days ago—creative writing at the University. I can't risk going back there. But I don't think I can hide much longer. Each night, she comes closer.

From the start, she scared me. I came to school at eight to prepare my classes. Through the side door of the English building I went up a stairwell to my third-floor office, which was isolated by a fire door from all the other offices. My colleagues used to joke that I'd been banished, but I didn't care, for in my far-off corner I could concentrate. Few students interrupted me. Regardless of the busy noises past the fire door, I sometimes felt there was no one else inside the building. And indeed at 8 A.M. I often *was* the only person in the building.

That day I was wrong, however. Clutching my heavy

64

briefcase, I trudged up the stairwell. My scraping foot-steps echoed off the walls of the pale red cinder block, the stairs of pale green imitation marble. First floor. Second floor. The neon lights glowed coldly. Then the stairwell angled toward the third floor, and I saw her waiting on a chair outside my office. Pausing, I frowned up at her. I felt uneasy.

Eight A.M., for you, is probably not early. You've been up for quite a while so you can get to work on time or get your children off to school. But 8 A.M., for college stu-dents, is the middle of the night. They don't like morning classes. When their schedules force them to attend one, they don't crawl from bed until they absolutely have to, and they don't come stumbling into class until I'm just about to start my lecture.

I felt startled, then, to find her waiting ninety minutes early. She sat tensely: lifeless dull brown hair, a shapeless dingy sweater, baggy faded jeans with patches on the knees and frays around the cuffs. Her eyes seemed haunted, wild, and deep and dark.

I climbed the last few steps and, puzzled, stopped be-fore her. "Do you want an early conference?"

Instead of answering, she nodded bleakly.

"You're concerned about a grade I gave you?"

This time, though, in pain she shook her head from side to side.

Confused, I fumbled with my key and opened the office, stepping in. The room was small and narrow: a desk, two chairs, a wall of bookshelves, and a window. As I sat behind the desk, I watched her slowly come inside. She glanced around uncertainly. Distraught, she shut the door.

That made me nervous. When a female student shuts the door, I start to worry that a colleague or a student might walk up the stairs and hear a female voice and won-der what's so private I want to keep the door closed. Though I should have told her to reopen it, her frantic eyes aroused such pity in me that I sacrificed my principle, deciding her torment was so personal she could talk about it only in strict secrecy.

"Sit down." I smiled and tried to make her feel at ease, though I myself was not at ease. "What seems to be the difficulty, Miss . . . ? I'm sorry, but I don't recall your name."

"Samantha Perry. I don't like 'Samantha,' though." She fidgeted. "I've shortened it to—"

"Yes? To what?"

"To 'Sam.' I'm in your Tuesday-Thursday class." She bit her lip. "You spoke to me."

I frowned, not understanding. "You mean what I taught seemed vivid to you. I inspired you to write a better story?"

"Mr. Ingram, no. I mean you *spoke* to me. You stared at me while you were teaching. You ignored the other students. You directed what you said to *me*. When you talked about Hemingway, how Frederic Henry wants to go to bed with Catherine—" She swallowed. "—you were asking me to go to bed with you."

I gaped. To disguise my shock, I quickly lit a cigarette. "You're mistaken."

"But I *heard* you. You kept staring straight at *me*. I felt all the other students knew what you were doing."

"I was only lecturing. I often look at students' faces to make sure they pay attention. You received the wrong impression."

"You weren't asking me to go to bed with you?" Her voice sounded anguished.

"No. I don't trade sex for grades."

"But I don't care about a grade!"

"I'm married. Happily. I've got two children. Anyway, suppose I did intend to proposition you. Would I do it in the middle of a class? I'd be foolish."

"Then you never meant to—" She kept biting her lip. "I'm sorry."

"But you speak to me! Outside class I hear your voice! When I'm in my room or walking down the street! You talk to me when I'm asleep! You say you want to go to bed with me!''

My skin prickled. I felt frozen. ''You're mistaken. Your imagination's playing tricks.''

''But I hear your voice so clearly! When I'm studying or—''

''How? If I'm not there.''

''You send your thoughts! You concentrate and put your voice inside my mind!''

Adrenaline scalded my stomach. I frantically sought an argument to disillusion her. ''Telepathy? I don't believe in it. I've never tried to send my thoughts to you.''

''Unconsciously?''

I shook my head from side to side. I couldn't bring myself to tell her; of all the female students in her class, she looked so plain, even if I wasn't married I'd never have wanted sex with her.

''You're studying too hard. You want to do so well you're preoccupied with me. That's why you think you hear my voice when I'm not there. I try to make my lectures vivid. As a consequence, you think I'm speaking totally to you.''

''Then you shouldn't teach that way!'' she shouted. ''It's not fair! It's cruel! It's teasing!'' Tears streamed down her face. ''You made a fool of me!''

''I didn't mean to.''

''But you did! You tricked me! You misled me!''

''No.''

She stood so quickly I flinched, afraid she'd lunge at me or scream for help and claim I'd tried to rape her. That damned door. I cursed myself for not insisting she leave it open.

She rushed sobbing toward it. She pawed the knob and stumbled out, hysterically retreating down the stairwell.

Shaken, I stubbed out my cigarette, grabbing another. My chest tightened as I heard the dwindling echo of her wracking sobs, the awkward scuffle of her dimming footsteps, then the low deep rumble of the outside door.

The silence settled over me.

An hour later I found her waiting in class. She'd wiped her tears. The only signs of what had happened were her red and puffy eyes. She sat alertly, pen to paper. I carefully didn't face her as I spoke. She seldom glanced up from her notes.

After class I asked my graduate assistant if he knew her.

"You mean Sam? Sure, I know her. She's been getting Ds. She had a conference with me. Instead of asking how to get a better grade, though, all she did was talk about you, pumping me for information. She's got quite a thing for you. Too bad about her."

"Why?"

"Well, she's so plain, she doesn't have many friends. I doubt she goes out much. There's a problem with her father. She was vague about it, but I had the sense her three sisters are so beautiful that Daddy treats her as the ugly duckling. She wants very much to please him. He ignores her, though. He's practically disowned her. You remind her of him."

"Who? Of her father?"

"She admits you're ten years younger than him, but she says you look exactly like him."

I felt heartsick.

Two days later I found her waiting for me—again at 8 A.M.—outside my office.

Tense, I unlocked the door. As if she heard my thought, she didn't shut it this time. Sitting before my desk, she didn't fidget. She just stared at me.

"It happened again," she said.

"In class I didn't even look at you."

"No, afterward, when I went to the library." She drew an anguished breath. "And later—I ate supper in the dorm. I heard your voice so clearly, I was sure you were in the room."

"What time was that?"

"Five-thirty."

"I was having cocktails with the Dean. Believe me, Sam, I wasn't sending messages to you. I didn't even *think* of you."

"I couldn't have imagined it! You wanted me to go to bed with you!"

"I wanted research money from the Dean. I thought of nothing else. My mind was totally involved in trying to convince him. When I didn't get the money, I was too annoyed to concentrate on anything but getting drunk."

"Your voice—"

"It isn't real. If I sent thoughts to you, wouldn't I admit what I was doing? When you asked me, wouldn't I confirm the message? Why would I deny it?"

"I'm afraid."

"You're troubled by your father."

"What?"

"My graduate assistant says you identify me with your father."

She went ashen. "That's supposed to be a secret!"

"Sam, I asked him. He won't lie to me."

"If you remind me of my father, if I want to go to bed with you, then I must want to go to bed with—"

"Sam—"

"—my father! You must think I'm disgusting!"

"No, I think you're confused. You ought to find some help. You ought to see a—"

But she never let me finish. Weeping again, ashamed, hysterical, she bolted from the room.

And that's the last I ever saw of her. An hour later, when I started lecturing, she wasn't in class. A few days later I received a drop-slip from the registrar, informing me she'd canceled all her classes.

I forgot her.

Summer came. The fall arrived. November. On a rainy Tuesday night, my wife and I stayed up to watch the close results of the election, worried for our presidential candidate.

At 3 A.M. the phone rang. No one calls that late unless . . .

The jangle of the phone made me bang my head as I
searched for a beer in the fridge. I rubbed my throbbing
skull and swung alarmed as Jean, my wife, came from the
living room and squinted toward the kitchen phone.

"It might be just a friend," I said. "Election gossip."

But I worried about our parents. Maybe one of them
was sick or . . .

I watched uneasily as Jean picked up the phone.

"Hello?" She listened apprehensively. Frowning, she
put her hand across the mouthpiece. "It's for you. A
woman."

"What?"

"She's young. She asked for Mr. Ingram."

"Damn, a student."

"At 3 A.M.?"

I almost didn't think to shut the fridge. Annoyed, I
yanked the pop-tab off the can of beer. My marriage is
successful. I'll admit we've had our troubles. So has every
couple. But we've faced those troubles, and we're happy.
Jean is thirty-five, attractive, smart, and patient. But her
trust in me was clearly tested at that moment. A woman
had to know me awfully well to call at 3 A.M.

"Let's find out." I grabbed the phone. To prove my
innocence to Jean, I roughly said, "Yeah, what?"

"I heard you." The female voice was frail and plain-
tive, trembling.

"Who *is* this?" I said angrily.

"It's me."

I heard a low-pitched crackle on the line.

"Who the hell is *me*? Just tell me what your name is."

"Sam."

My knees went weak. I slumped against the wall.

Jean stared. "What's wrong?" Her eyes narrowed with
suspicion.

"Sam, it's 3 A.M. What's so damn important you can't
wait to call me during office hours?"

"Three? It can't be. No, it's one."

"It's three. For God sake, Sam, I know what time it is."

"Please, don't get angry. On my radio the news announcer said it was one o'clock."

"Where *are* you, Sam?"

"At Berkeley."

"California? Sam, the time-zone difference. In the Midwest it's two hours later. Here it's three o'clock."

". . . I guess I just forgot."

"But that's absurd. Have you been drinking? Are you drunk?"

"No, not exactly."

"What the hell does *that* mean?"

"Well, I took some pills. I'm not sure what they were."

"Oh, Jesus."

"Then I heard you. You were speaking to me."

"No. I told you your mind's playing tricks. The voice isn't real. You're imagining—"

"You called me. You said you wanted me to go to bed with you. You wanted me to come to you."

"To Iowa? No. You've got to understand. Don't do it. I'm not sending thoughts to you."

"You're lying! Tell me why you're lying!"

"I don't want to go to bed with you. I'm glad you're in Berkeley. Stay there. Get some help. Lord, don't you realize? Those pills. They make you hear my voice. They make you hallucinate."

"I . . ."

"Trust me, Sam. Believe me. I'm not sending thoughts to you. I didn't even know you'd gone to Berkeley. You're two thousand miles away from me. What you're suggesting is impossible."

She didn't answer. All I heard was low-pitched static.

"Sam—"

The dial tone abruptly droned. My stomach sank. Appalled, I kept the phone against my ear. I swallowed dryly, shaking as I set the phone back on its cradle.

Jean glared. "Who was that? She wasn't any 'Sam.' She wants to go to bed with you? At 3 A.M.? What games have you been playing?"

"None." I gulped my beer, but my throat stayed dry. "You'd better sit. I'll get a beer for you."

Jean clutched her stomach.

"It's not what you think. I promise I'm not screwing anybody. But it's bad. I'm scared."

I handed Jean a beer.

"I don't know why it happened. But last spring, at 8 A.M., I went to school and . . ."

Jean listened, troubled. Afterward she asked for Sam's description, somewhat mollified to learn she was plain and pitiful.

"The truth?" Jean asked.

"I promise you."

Jean studied me. "You did nothing to encourage her?"

"I guarantee it. I wasn't aware of her until I found her waiting for me."

"But unconsciously?"

"Sam asked me that as well. I was only lecturing the best way I know how."

Jean kept her eyes on me. She nodded, glancing toward her beer. "Then she's disturbed. There's nothing you can do for her. I'm glad she moved to Berkeley. In your place, I'd have been afraid."

"I *am* afraid. She spooks me."

At a dinner party the next Saturday, I told our host and hostess what had happened, motivated more than just by need to share my fear with someone else, for while the host was both a friend and colleague, he was married to a clinical psychologist. I needed professional advice.

Diane, the hostess, listened with slim interest until halfway through my story, when she suddenly sat straight and peered at me.

I faltered. "What's the matter?"

"Don't stop. What else?"

I frowned and finished, waiting for Diane's reaction. Instead she poured more wine. She offered more lasagna.

"Something bothered you."

She tucked her long black hair behind her ears. "It could be nothing."

"I need to know."

She nodded grimly. "I can't make a diagnosis merely on the basis of your story. I'd be irresponsible."

"But hypothetically . . ."

"And *only* hypothetically. She hears your voice. That's symptomatic of a severe disturbance. Paranoia, for example. Schizophrenia. The man who shot John Lennon heard a voice. And so did Manson. So did Son of Sam."

"My God," Jean said. "Her name." She set her fork down loudly.

"The parallel occurred to me," Diane said. "Chuck, if she identifies you with her father, she might be dangerous to Jean and to the children."

"Why?"

"Jealousy. To hurt the equivalent of her mother and her rival sisters."

I felt sick; the wine turned sour in my stomach.

"There's another possibility. No more encouraging. If you continue to reject her, she could be dangerous to you. Instead of dealing with her father, she might redirect her rage and jealousy toward you. By killing you, she'd be venting her frustration toward her father."

I felt panicked. "For the *good* news."

"Understand, I'm speaking hypothetically. Possibly she's lying to you, and she doesn't hear your voice. Or, as you guessed, the drugs she takes might make her hallucinate. There could be many explanations. Without seeing her, without the proper tests, I wouldn't dare to judge her symptoms. You're a friend, so I'm compromising. Possibly she's homicidal."

"Tell me what to do."

"For openers, I'd stay away from her."

"I'm *trying*. She called me from California. She's threatening to come back here to see me."

"Talk her out of it."

"I'm no psychologist. I don't know what to say to her."

"Suggest she get professional advice."

"I tried that."

"Try again. But if you find her at your office, don't go in the room with her. Find other people. Crowds protect you."

"But at 8 A.M. there's no one in the building."

"Think of some excuse to leave her. Jean, if she comes to the house, don't let her in."

Jean paled. "I've never seen her. How could I identify her?"

"Chuck described her. Don't take chances. Don't trust anyone who might resemble her, and keep a close watch on the children."

"*How*? Rebecca's twelve. Sue's nine. I can't insist they stay around the house."

Diane turned her wineglass, saying nothing.

". . . Oh, dear lord," Jean said.

The next few weeks were hellish. Every time the phone rang, Jean and I jerked, startled, staring at it. But the calls were from our friends or from our children's friends or from some insulation/magazine/home-siding salesman. Every day I mustered courage as I climbed the stairwell to my office. Silent prayers were answered. Sam was never there. My tension dissipated. I began to feel she no longer was obsessed with me.

Thanksgiving came—the last day of peace I've known. We went to church. Our parents live too far away for us to share the feast with them. But we invited friends to dinner. We watched football. I helped Jean make the dressing for the turkey. I made both the pumpkin pies. The friends we'd invited were my colleague and his wife, the clinical psychologist. She asked if my student had continued to harass me. Shaking my head from side to side, I grinned and raised my glass in special thanks.

The guests stayed late to watch a movie with us. Jean and I felt pleasantly exhausted, mellowed by good food, good drink, good friends, when after midnight we washed all the dishes, went to bed, made love, and drifted wearily to sleep.

The phone rang, shocking me awake. I fumbled toward the bedside lamp. Jean's eyes went wide with fright. She clutched my arm and pointed toward the clock. It was 3 A.M.

The phone kept ringing.

"Don't," Jean said.

"Suppose it's someone else."

"You know it isn't."

"If it's Sam and I don't answer, she might come to the house instead of phoning."

"For God's sake, make her stop."

I grabbed the phone, but my throat wouldn't work.

"I'm coming to you," the voice wailed.

"Sam?"

"I heard you. I won't disappoint you. I'll be there soon."

"No. Wait. Listen."

"I've been listening. I hear you all the time. The anguish in your voice. You're begging me to come to you, to hold you, to make love to you."

"That isn't true."

"You say your wife's jealous of me. I'll convince her she isn't being fair. I'll make her let you go. Then we'll be happy."

"Sam, where are you? Still in Berkeley?"

"Yes. I spent Thanksgiving by myself. My father didn't want me to come home."

"You have to stay there, Sam. I didn't send my voice. You need advice. You need to see a doctor. Will you do that for me? As a favor?"

"I already did. But Dr. Campbell doesn't understand. He thinks I'm imagining what I hear. He humors me. He doesn't realize how much you love me."

"Sam, you have to talk to him again. You have to tell him what you plan to do."

"I can't wait any longer. I'll be there soon. I'll be with you."

My heart pounded frantically. I heard a roar in my head. I flinched as the phone was yanked away from me.

Jean shouted into the mouthpiece, "Stay away from us. Don't call again. Stop terrorizing—"

Jean stared wildly at me. "No one's there. The line went dead. I just heard the dial tone."

I'm writing this as quickly as I can. I don't have much more time. It's almost three o'clock.

That night, we didn't try to go back to sleep. We couldn't. We got dressed and went downstairs where, drinking coffee, we decided what to do. At eight, as soon as we'd sent the kids to school, we drove to the police.

They listened sympathetically, but there was no way they could help us. After all, Sam hadn't broken any law. Her calls weren't obscene; it was difficult to prove harassment; she'd made no overt threats. Unless she harmed us, there was nothing the police could do.

"Protect us," I insisted.

"How?" the sergeant said.

"Assign an officer to guard the house."

"How long? A day, a week, a month? That woman might not even bother you again. We're overworked and understaffed. I'm sorry—I can't spare an officer whose only duty is to watch you. I can send a car to check the house from time to time. No more than that. But if this woman does show up and bother you, then call us. We'll take care of her."

"But that might be too late."

* * *

We took the children home from school. Sam couldn't have arrived from California yet, but what else could we do? I don't own any guns. If all of us stayed together, we had some chance for protection.

That was Friday. I slept lightly. Three A.M., the phone rang. It was Sam, of course.

"I'm coming."

"Sam, where are you?"

"Reno."

"You're not flying."

"No, I can't."

"Turn back, Sam. Go to Berkeley. See that doctor."

"I can't wait to see you."

"Please—"

The dial tone was droning.

I phoned Berkeley information. Sam had mentioned Dr. Campbell. But the operator couldn't find him in the yellow pages.

"Try the University," I blurted. "Student Counseling."

I was right. A Dr. Campbell was a university psychiatrist. On Saturday I couldn't reach him at his office, but a woman answered at his home. He wouldn't be available until the afternoon. At four o'clock I finally got through to him.

"You've got a patient named Samantha Perry," I began.

"I did. Not anymore."

"I know. She's left for Iowa. She wants to see me. I'm afraid. I think she might be dangerous."

"Well, you don't have to worry."

"She's not dangerous?"

"Potentially she was."

"But tell me what to do when she arrives. You're treating her. You'll know what I should do."

"No, Mr. Ingram, she won't come to see you. On Thanksgiving night, at 1 A.M., she killed herself. An overdose of drugs."

My vision failed. I clutched the kitchen table to prevent myself from falling. "That's impossible."

"I saw the body. I identified it."

"But she called that night."

"What time?"

"At 3 A.M. Midwestern time."

"Or one o'clock in California. No doubt after or before she took the drugs. She didn't leave a note, but she called you."

"She gave no indication—"

"She mentioned you quite often. She was morbidly attracted to you. She had an extreme, unhealthy certainty that she was telepathic, that you put your voice inside her mind."

"I know that! Was she paranoid or homicidal?"

"Mr. Ingram, I've already said too much. Although she's dead, I can't violate her confidence."

"But I don't think she's dead."

"I beg your pardon?"

"If she died on Thursday night, then tell me how she called again on *Friday* night."

The line hummed. I sensed the doctor's hesitation. "Mr. Ingram, you're upset. You don't know what you're saying. You've confused the nights."

"I'm telling you she called again on Friday!"

"And I'm telling you she died on *Thursday*. Either someone's tricking you, or else . . ." The doctor swallowed with discomfort.

"Or?" I trembled. "*I'm* the one who's hearing voices?"

"Mr. Ingram, don't upset yourself. You're honestly confused."

I slowly put the phone down, terrified. "I'm sure I heard her voice."

That night, Sam called again. At 3 A.M. From Salt Lake City. When I handed Jean the phone, she heard just the dial tone.

"But you know the goddamn phone rang!" I insisted.

"Maybe a short circuit. Chuck, I'm telling you there was no one on the line."

Then Sunday. Three A.M. Cheyenne, Wyoming. Coming closer.

But she couldn't be if she was dead.

The student paper at the University subscribes to all the other major student papers. Monday, Jean and I left the children with friends and drove to its office. Friday's copy of the Berkeley campus paper had arrived. In desperation I searched its pages. "There!" A two-inch item. Sudden student death. Samantha Perry. Tactfully, no cause was given.

Outside in the parking lot, Jean said, "Now do you believe she's dead?"

"Then tell me why I hear her voice! I've got to be crazy if I think I hear a corpse!"

"You're feeling guilty that she killed herself because of you. You shouldn't. There was nothing you could do to stop her. You've been losing too much sleep. Your imagination's taking over."

"You admit you heard the phone ring!"

"Yes, it's true. I can't explain that. If the phone's broken, we'll have it fixed. To put your mind at rest, we'll get a new, unlisted number."

I felt better. After several drinks, I even got some sleep.

But Monday night, again the phone rang. Three A.M. I jerked awake. Cringing, I insisted Jean answer it. But she heard just the dial tone. I grabbed the phone. Of course, I heard Sam's voice.

"I'm almost there. I'll hurry. I'm in Omaha."

"This number isn't listed!"

"But you told me the new one. Your wife's the one who changed it. She's trying to keep us apart. I'll make her sorry. Darling, I can't wait to be with you."

I screamed. Jean jerked away from me.

"Sam, you've got to stop! I spoke to Dr. Campbell!"

"No. He wouldn't dare. He wouldn't violate my trust."

"He said you were dead!"

"I couldn't live without you. Soon we'll be together."

Shrieking, I woke the children, so hysterical Jean had to call an ambulance. Two interns struggled to sedate me.

Omaha was only one day's drive from where we live. Jean came to visit me in the hospital on Tuesday.

"Are you feeling better?" Jean frowned, troubled.

"Please, you have to humor me," I said. "All right? Suspect I've gone crazy, but for God sake, humor me. I can't prove what I'm thinking, but I know you're in danger. I am too. You have to get the children and leave town. You have to hide somewhere. Tonight at 3 A.M. she'll reach the house."

Jean stared with pity.

"Promise me!" I said.

She saw the anguish on my face and nodded.

"Maybe she won't try the house," I said. "She might come here. I have to get away. I'm not sure how, but later, when you're gone, I'll find a way to leave."

Jean peered at me, distressed; her voice sounded totally discouraged. "Chuck."

"I'll check the house when I get out of here. If you're still there, you know you'll make me more upset."

"I promise. I'll take Susan and Rebecca, and we'll drive somewhere."

"I love you."

Jean began to cry. "I won't know where you are."

"If I survive this, I'll get word to you."

"But how?"

"The English department. I'll leave a message with the secretary."

Jean leaned down to kiss me, crying, certain I'd lost my mind.

* * *

I reached the house that night. As she'd promised, Jean had left with the children. I got in my sports car and raced to the interstate.

A Chicago hotel where at 3 A.M. Sam called from Iowa. She'd heard my voice. She said I'd told her where I was, but she was hurt and angry. "Tell me why you're running."

I fled from Chicago in the middle of the night, driving until I absolutely had to rest. I checked in here at 1 A.M. In Johnstown, Pennsylvania. I can't sleep. I've got an awful feeling. Last night Sam repeated, "Soon you'll join me." In the desk I found this stationery.

God, it's 3 A.M. I pray I'll see the sun come up.

It's almost four. She didn't phone. I can't believe I escaped, but I keep staring at the phone.

It's four. Dear Christ, I hear the ringing.

Finally I've realized. Sam killed herself at one. In Iowa the time-zone difference made it three. But I'm in Pennsylvania. In the East. A different time zone. One o'clock in California would be *four* o'clock, not three, in Pennsylvania.

Now.

The ringing persists. But I've realized something else. This hotel's unusual, designed to seem like home.

The ringing?

God help me, it's the doorbell.

AUTHOR'S NOTE

HOW DOES A WRITER CHOOSE A STORY, AMONG MANY, THAT typifies what he or she has been trying to accomplish? Prior to selecting "But at My Back I Always Hear," I reread several others and finally settled on this one, not because it's my most horrific (although I did find my skin go cold but not to the frigid degree that was caused by "For These and All My Sins" or the middle section of my novel, Testament*) and not because its style was experimental (as was "The Hidden Laughter"), but precisely because this story was typical, an example of a technique and various themes I've returned to again and again.*

Let's deal with the technique first. Like many novelists, I find the discipline, the compression, of a story enormously difficult. There's an irony here. My initial effort at fiction was First Blood, *but after I sent it to my agent, I had a nightmare that so compelled me I wrote it verbatim, a story called "The Dripping," which was purchased by Ellery Queen's Mystery Magazine and became—two weeks before my agent phoned to tell me a publisher had accepted* First Blood—*my first . . . my God, a check! . . . my first sale. Other writers will understand. "The Dripping," to me, will always be special. A validation of my dreams.*

But as I labored on my next book (the dreaded second-novel syndrome: Can I possibly do it again?*), short-story nightmares failed to visit me. And as that second novel,* Testament, *continued to give me problems, to aggravate my insecurity, I craved the satisfaction of writing another short, macrocosmic, "I can do it with luck in a couple of days" validation of my ambition to be a hypnotist, a magician, a teller of tales.*

I was then a professor of literature at the University of Iowa, and by chance, preparing for a class, I picked up Robert Browning's "My Last Duchess" and felt a prickle of revelation. You see, "The Dripping" had been a first-person narrative, but I've always been suspicious of first-person narratives because of my admiration for Henry James.

"The master," commenting on his consummate horror novel, The Turn of the Screw, *had called his tale a "trap for the unwary"—because its first-person technique made*

it impossible to decide if the narrator was telling the truth about the ghosts she encountered or if she was hopelessly insane. James in fact disdained the first-person technique, calling the device a trick in which the only interest for the reader was to decide if the "I" of the story was self-deluded, a liar, or crazy. So how could I, devoted to "the master," feel justified in following my instincts to repeat, to build on, what I'd done in "The Dripping" if the viewpoint I felt compelled to use had been dismissed by one of my literary heroes?

Robert Browning's "My Last Duchess" supplied the answer. It's called a "dramatic monologue," a technique he's given credit for creating, not in a play (where a soliloquy's an accepted convention) but on a page, in a poem! "That's my last Duchess painted on the wall," Browning begins, or rather his narrator does. And I thought, Who is the speaker addressing? And how did the reader happen to receive these words? The technique is unbelievable, artificial, yet wonderfully effective. Around the same time, I fell in love with the novels of James M. Cain. "They threw me off the hay truck about noon." That's how The Postman Always Rings Twice begins, one of the all-time great first sentences, in one of the greatest thrillers ever written. But Cain's narrator wasn't addressing an imagined audience viewing a stage. No, that damned fate-controlled aggressor/victim was writing his story as a form of confession while he waited, tough and controlled, to be executed for murder.

So I asked myself, Why not pretend you never read James? Why not concentrate on Browning and Cain? And that decision broke my short-story writer's block. I embraced the first-person technique. It's direct. It's intimate. It's vivid. And it allows a writer to compress. The tormented narrator blurts out his tale of horror. Until the end of "But at My Back . . ." the story is due to Browning. But when the hero-victim picks up the pen and paper in his hotel room and reveals that all along he's been writing his tale of terror, as a document, so the people who find

*his body will understand his predestined doom, that's
Cain, and God bless him. He showed me the way.*

Now about theme. For reasons too complex to elaborate
in this brief space, I'm obsessed about security. That topic
is manifest in all of my work. The worst horror I could
ever imagine was to lose my family, to lose a member of
my family, to be separated from those I love. In real life,
that horror became all too factual. On June 27, 1987, my
wonderful fifteen-year-old son, Matthew, died (after six
months of unbelievable agony) from bone cancer. I described that ordeal in a book called Fireflies. But in "The
Dripping" and in many stories since then, before Matthew's death, I've been terrified by that ultimate horror.
The narrator in "But at My Back . . ." loses everything
he holds dear. Not because it's his fault. But because of
fate. *Because sometimes things don't work out. Lord help
me, yes. In case you don't already know it, life isn't fair.*

Then too (and I'm struggling to suppress emotion now),
I was a professor of literature, and I did have a student
who claimed I was sending sexual telepathic messages to
her. She did keep calling, threatening, haunting—not only
me (I can deal with that) but my family. Most of "But at
My Back . . ." is true. Except that the student is still alive
and, for all I know, lurking.

Finally, after I moved from Canada to Pennsylvania and
then to Iowa, I fell in love with the boundless sky and
incredibly fertile beauty of my adopted state. I call it exotic. Watch the movie Field of Dreams to understand what
I mean. It occurred to me that horror didn't have to fester
in the traditional Hawthorne-invented gloom of New England, or in the oppressive ghettos of decaying major cities, but in bright sunlight, in the midst of splendor.
Remember Cary Grant racing desperately to escape the
machine-gun bullets from the "innocent" cropduster in
Hitchcock's North by Northwest? I began to envision a
series of stories that would take advantage of the broad
Midwest and Highway 80 and the space, the sublime,
hence terrifying space *from one isolated community to an-*

other. I explored that notion in several stories: "The Storm," "For These and All My Sins." Others. Even the time-zone *changes are fraught with danger.*

So if you desperately need security (as the hero of "But at My Back . . ." does, as its author *does), you choose this story as representative of your work. My alter-ego professor sacrifices his life and his soul for his family. Good man. I understand him all too well. Because given the chance (which, damn it, I never had), I'd gladly have sacrificed* my *life and soul to save my son.*

—*David Morrell*

THE WHISPERER
Brian Lumley

THE FIRST TIME MILES BENTON SAW THE LITTLE FELLOW
was on the train. Benton was commuting to his office job
in the city and he sat alone in a second-class compartment.
The "little fellow"—a very *ugly* little man, from what
Benton could see of him out of the corner of his eye, with
a lopsided hump and dark or dirty features, like a gnomish
gypsy—entered the compartment and took a seat in the far
corner. He was dressed in a floppy black wide-brimmed
hat that fell half over his face and a black overcoat longer
than himself that trailed to the floor.

Benton was immediately aware of the smell, a rank
stench which quite literally would have done credit to the
lowliest farmyard, and correctly deduced its source. Despite the dry, acrid smell of stale tobacco from the ashtrays
and the lingering odour of grimy stations, the compartment had seemed positively perfumed prior to the advent
of the hunchback. The day was quite chill outside, but
Benton nevertheless stood up and opened the window,
pulling it down until the draft forced back the fumes from
his fellow passenger. He was then obliged to put away his

flapping newspaper and sit back, his collar upturned against the sudden cold blast, mentally cursing the smelly little chap for fouling "his" compartment.

A further five minutes saw Benton's mind made up to change compartments. That way he would be removed from the source of the odorous irritation, and he would no longer need to suffer this intolerable blast of icy air. But no sooner was his course of action determined than the ticket collector arrived, sliding open the door and sticking his well-known and friendly face inside the compartment.

"Mornin', sir," he said briskly to Benton, merely glancing at the other traveller. "Tickets, please."

Benton got out his ticket and passed it to be examined. He noticed with satisfaction as he did so that the ticket collector wrinkled his nose and sniffed suspiciously at the air, eyeing the hunchback curiously. Benton retrieved his ticket and the collector turned to the little man in the far corner. "Yer ticket . . . *sir* . . . if yer don't mind." He looked the little chap up and down disapprovingly.

The hunchback looked up from under his floppy black hat and grinned. His eyes were jet and bright as a bird's. He winked and indicated that the ticket collector should bend down, expressing an obvious desire to say something in confidence. He made no effort to produce a ticket.

The ticket collector frowned in annoyance, but nevertheless, bent his ear to the little man's face. He listened for a moment or two to a chuckling, throaty whisper. It actually appeared to Benton that the hunchback was *chortling* as he whispered his obscene secret into the other's ear, and the traveller could almost hear him saying: "Feelthy postcards! Vairy dairty pictures!"

The look on the face of the ticket collector changed immediately, his expression went stony hard.

"Aye, aye!" Benton said to himself. "The little blighter's got no ticket! He's for it now.".

But no, the ticket collector said nothing to the obnoxious midget, but straightened and turned to Benton.

"Sorry, sir," he said, "but this compartment's private. I'll 'ave ter arsk yer ter leave."

"But," Benton gasped incredulously, "I've been travelling in this compartment for years. It's never been a, well, a 'private' compartment before!"

"No, sir, p'raps not," said the ticket collector undismayed. "But it is now. There's a compartment next door; jus' a couple of gents in there; I'm sure it'll do jus' as well." He held the door open for Benton, daring him to argue the point further. "Sir?"

Ah, well, Benton thought, resignedly, I was wanting to move. Nevertheless, he looked down aggressively as he passed the hunchback, staring hard at the top of the floppy hat. The little man seemed to know. He looked up and grinned, cocking his head on one side and grinning.

Benton stepped quickly out into the corridor and took a deep breath. "Damn!" he swore out loud.

"Yer pardon, sir?" inquired the ticket collector, already swaying off down the corridor.

"Nothing!" Benton snapped in reply, letting himself into the smoky, crowded compartment to which he had been directed.

The very next morning Benton plucked up his courage (he had never been a *very* brave man), stopped the ticket collector, and asked him what it had all been about. Who had the little chap been? What privileges did he have that an entire compartment had been reserved especially for him, the grimy little gargoyle?

To which the ticket collector replied: "Eh? An 'unchback? Are yer sure it was *this* train, sir? Why, we haint 'ad no private or reserved compartments on this 'ere train since it became a commuter special! And as fer a 'unchback—well!"

"But surely you remember asking me to leave my compartment—*this* compartment?" Benton insisted.

" 'Ere, yer pullin' me leg, haint yer, sir?" laughed the ticket collector good-naturedly. He slammed shut the compartment door behind him and smilingly strode away without waiting for an answer, leaving Benton alone with his jumbled and whirling thoughts.

"Well, I never!" the commuter muttered worriedly to himself. He scratched his head and then, philosophically, began to quote a mental line or two from a ditty his mother had used to say to him when he was a child:

> *The other day upon the stair*
> *I saw a man who wasn't there . . .*

Benton had almost forgotten about the little man with the hump and sewer-like smell by the time their paths crossed again. It happened one day some three months later, with spring just coming on, when, in acknowledgement of the bright sunshine, Benton decided to forego his usual sandwich lunch at the office for a noonday pint at the Bull & Bush.

The entire pub, except for one corner of the bar, appeared to be quite crowded, but it was not until Benton had elbowed his way to the corner in question that he saw why it was unoccupied; or rather, why it had only one occupant. The *smell* hit him at precisely the same time as he saw, sitting on a bar stool with his oddly humped back to the regular patrons, the little man in black with his floppy broad-brimmed hat.

That the other customers were aware of the cesspool stench was obvious—Benton watched in fascination the wrinkling all about him of at least a dozen pairs of nostrils—and yet not a man complained. And more amazing yet, no one even attempted to encroach upon the little fellow's territory in the bar corner. No one, that is, except Benton . . .

Holding his breath, Benton stepped forward and rapped sharply with his knuckles on the bar just to the left of where the hunchback sat. "Beer, barman. A pint of best, please."

The barman smiled chubbily and stepped forward,

reaching out for a beer pump and slipping a glass beneath the tap. But even as he did so the hunchback made a small gesture with his head, indicating that he wanted to say something . . .

Benton had seen all this before, and all the many sounds of the pub—the chattering of people, the clink of coins, and the clatter of glasses—seemed to fade to silence about him as he focussed his full concentration upon the barman and the little man in the floppy hat. In slow motion, it seemed, the barman bent his head down toward the hunchback, and again Benton heard strangely chuckled whispers as the odious dwarf passed his secret instructions.

Curiously, fearfully, in something very akin to dread, Benton watched the portly barman's face undergo its change, heard the *hisses* of the beer pump, saw the full glass come out from beneath the bar . . . to plump down in front of the hunchback! Hard-eyed, the barman stuck his hand out in front of Benton's nose. "That's half a dollar to you, sir."

"But . . ." Benton gasped, incredulously opening and closing his mouth. He already had a coin in his hand, with which he had intend to pay for his drink, but now he pulled his hand back.

"Half a dollar, sir," the barman repeated ominously, snatching the coin from Benton's retreating fingers, "and would you mind moving down the bar, please? It's a bit crowded this end."

In utter disbelief Benton jerked his eyes from the barman's face to his now empty hand, and from his hand to the seated hunchback; and as he did so the little man turned his head toward him and grinned. Benton was aware only of the bright, bird-like eyes beneath the wide brim of the hat—not of the darkness surrounding them. One of those eyes closed suddenly in a wink, and then the little man turned back to his beer.

"But," Benton again croaked his protest at the publican, "that's *my* beer he's got!" He reached out and caught the barman's rolled-up sleeve, following him down the bar until forced by the press of patrons to let go. The barman finally turned.

"Beer, sir?" The smile was back on his chubby face. "Certainly—half a dollar to you, sir."

Abruptly the bar sounds crashed in again upon Benton's awareness as he turned to elbow his way frantically, almost hysterically, through the crowded room to the door. Out of the corner of his eye he noticed that the little man, too, had left. A crush of thirsty people had already moved into the space he had occupied in the bar corner.

Outside in the fresh air Benton glared wild-eyed up and down the busy street; and yet he was half afraid of seeing the figure his eyes sought. The little man, however, had apparently disappeared into thin air.

"God damn him!" Benton cried in sudden rage, and a passing policeman looked at him very curiously indeed.

He was annoyed to notice that the policeman followed him all the way back to the office.

At noon the next day Benton was out of the office as if at the crack of a starting pistol. He almost ran the four blocks to the Bull & Bush, pausing only to straighten his tie and tilt his bowler a trifle more aggressively in the mirror of a shop window. The place was quite crowded, as before, but he made his way determinedly to the bar, having first checked that the air was quite clean—ergo, that the little man with the hump was quite definitely *not* there.

He immediately caught the barman's eye. "Bartender, a beer, please. And—" he lowered his voice, "—a word, if you don't mind."

The publican leaned over the bar confidentially, and Benton lowered his tone still further to whisper. "Er, who *is* he—the, er, the little chap? Is he perhaps, the boss of the place? Quite a little, er, *eccentric*, isn't he?"

"Eh?" said the barman, looking puzzledly about. "Who d'you mean, sir?"

The genuinely puzzled expression on the portly man's

face ought to have told Benton all he needed to know, but Benton simply could not accept that, not a second time. "I mean the hunchback," he raised his voice in desperation. "The little chap in the floppy black hat who sat in the corner of the bar only yesterday—who stank to high heaven and drank *my* beer! Surely you remember him?"

The barman slowly shook his head and frowned, then called out to a group of standing men: "Joe, here a minute." A stocky chap in a cloth cap and tweed jacket detached himself from the general hubbub and moved to the bar. "Joe," said the barman, "you were in here yesterday lunch; did you see a—well, a—how was it, sir?" He turned back to Benton.

"A little chap with a floppy black hat and a hump," Benton patiently, worriedly repeated himself. "He was sitting in the bar corner. Had a pong like a dead rat."

Joe thought about it for a second, then said: "Yer sure yer got the right pub, guv'? I mean, we gets no tramps or weirdos in 'ere. 'Arry won't 'ave 'em, will yer, 'Arry?" He directed his question at the barman.

"No, he's right, sir. I get upset with weirdos. Won't have them."

"But . . . this *is* the Bull and Bush, isn't it?" Benton almost stammered, gazing wildly about, finding unaccustomed difficulty in speaking.

"That's right, sir," answered Harry the barman, frowning heavily now and watching Benton sideways.

"But—"

"Sorry, chief," the stocky Joe said with an air of finality. "Yer've got the wrong place. Must 'ave been some other pub." Both the speaker and the barman turned away, a trifle awkwardly, Benton thought, and he could feel their eyes upon him as he moved dazedly away from the bar towards the door. Again lines remembered of old repeated themselves in his head:

> *He wasn't there again today—*
> *Oh, how I wish he'd go away!*

"Here, sir!" cried the barman, suddenly remembering. "Do you want a beer or not, then?"

"*No!*" Benton snarled. Then, on impulse: "Give it to—to *him*!—when next he comes in . . ."

Over the next month or so certain changes took place in Benton, changes which would have seemed quite startling to anyone knowing him of old. To begin with he had apparently broken two habits of very long standing. One: instead of remaining in his compartment aboard the morning train and reading his newspaper—as had been his wont for close on nine years—he was now given to spending the first half hour of his journey peering into the many compartments while wandering up and down the long corridor, all the while wearing an odd, part puzzled, part apologetic expression. Two: he rarely took his lunch at the office any more, but went out walking in the city instead, stopping for a drink and a sandwich at any handy local pub. (But never the Bull & Bush, though he always ensured that his strolling took him close by the latter house; and had anyone been particularly interested, then Benton might have been noticed to keep a very wary eye on the pub, almost as if he had it under observation.)

But then, as summer came on and no new manifestations of Benton's—*problem*—came to light, he began to forget all about it, to relegate it to that category of mental phenomena known as "daydreams," even though he had known no such phenomena before. And as the summer waxed, so the nagging worry at the back of his mind waned, until finally he convinced himself that his daydreams were gone for good.

But he was wrong . . .

And if those two previous visitations had been dreams, then the third could only be classified as—nightmare!

July saw the approach of the holiday period, and Benton had long had places booked for himself and his wife at a sumptuously expensive and rather exclusive coastal resort, far from the small Midlands town he called home. They went there every year. This annual ''spree'' allowed Benton to indulge his normally repressed escapism, when for a whole fortnight he could pretend that he was other than a mere clerk among people who usually accepted his fantasies as fact, thereby reinforcing them for Benton.

He could hardly wait for it to come round, that last Friday evening before the holidays, and when it did he rode home in the commuter special in a state of high excitement. Tomorrow would see him off to the sea and the sun; the cases were packed, the tickets arranged. A good night's rest now—and then, in the morning . . .

He was whistling as he let himself in through his front door, but the tone of his whistle soon went off key as he stepped into the hall. Dismayed, he paused and sniffed, his nose wrinkling. Out loud, he said: ''Huh! The drains must be off again.'' But there was something rather special about that poisonous smell, something ominously familiar; and of a sudden, without fully realising why, Benton felt the short hairs at the back of his neck begin to rise. An icy chill struck at him from nowhere.

He passed quickly from the hall to the living room, where the air seemed even more offensive, and there he paused again as it came to him in a flash of fearful memory just *what* the awful stench of ordure was, and *where* and *when* he had known it before.

The room seemed suddenly to whirl about him as he saw, thrown carelessly across the back of his own easy chair, a monstrously familiar hat—a floppy hat, black and wide-brimmed!

The hat grew beneath his hypnotized gaze, expanding until it threatened to fill the whole house, his whole mind, but then he tore his eyes away and broke the spell. From the upstairs bedroom came a low, muted sound: a moan of pain—or pleasure! And as an incredibly obscene and now well-remembered chuckling whisper finally invaded Benton's horrified ears, he threw off shock's invisible shackles to fling himself breakneck up the stairs.

"Ellen!" he cried, throwing open the bedroom door just as a second moan sounded—*and then he staggered, clutching at the wall for support, as the scene beyond the door struck him an almost physical blow!*

The hunchback lay sprawled naked upon Benton's bed, his malformed back blue-veined and grimy. The matted hair of his head fell forward onto Ellen's white breasts and his filthy hands moved like crabs over her arched body. Her eyes were closed, her mouth open and panting; her whole attitude was one of complete abandon. Her slender hands clawed spastically at the hunchback's writhing, scurvy thighs. . . .

Benton screamed hoarsely, clutching wildly at his hair, his eyes threatening to pop from his head, and for an instant time stood still. Then he lunged forward and grabbed at the man, a great power bursting inside him, the strength of both God and the devil in his crooked fingers—but in that same instant the hunchback slipped from the far side of the bed and out of reach. At an almost impossible speed the little man dressed and, as Benton lurched drunkenly about the room, he flitted like a grey bat back across the bed. As he went his face passed close to Ellen's, and Benton was aware once again of that filthy whispered chuckle as the hunchback sprang to the floor and fled the room.

Mad with steadily mounting rage, Benton hardly noticed the sudden slitting of his wife's eyes, the film that came down over them like a silky shutter. But as he lunged after the hunchback Ellen reached out a naked leg, deliberately tripping him and sending him flying out onto the landing.

By the time he regained his feet, to lean panting against the landing rail, the little man was at the hall door, his hat once more drooping about grotesque shoulders. He looked up with eyes like malignant jewels in the shadow of that hat, and the last thing that the tormented householder saw as the hunchback closed the door softly behind him was that abhorrent, omniscient wink!

When he reached the garden gate some twoscore seconds later, Benton was not surprised to note the little man's complete disappearance. . . .

Often, during the space of the next fortnight, Benton tried to think back on the scene which followed immediately upon the hunchback's departure from his house, but he was never able to resolve it to his satisfaction. He remembered the blind accusations he had thrown, the venomous bile of his words, his wife's patent amazement which had only served to enrage him all the more, the shock on Ellen's reddening face as he had slapped her mercilessly from room to room. He remembered her denial and the words she had screamed after locking herself in the bathroom: "Madman, madman!" she had screamed, and then she had left, taking her already packed suitcase with her.

He had waited until Monday—mainly in a vacant state of shock—before going out to a local ironmonger's shop to buy himself a sharp, long-bladed Italian knife. . . .

It was now the fourteenth day, and still Benton walked the streets. He was grimy, unshaven, hungry, but his resolution was firm. Somewhere, *somewhere*, he would find the little man in the outsize overcoat and floppy black hat, and when he did he would stick his knife to its hilt in the hunchback's slimy belly and he would cut out the vile little swine's brains through his loathsomely winking eyes! In his mind's eye, even as he walked the night streets, Benton could *see* those eyes gleaming like jewels, quick and bright and liquid, and faintly in his nostrils there seemed to linger the morbid stench of the hybrid creature that wore those eyes in its face.

And always his mother's ditty rang in his head:

> *The other day upon the stair*
> *I saw a man who wasn't there!*
> *He wasn't there again today—*
> *Oh, how I wish . . .*

* * *

But no, Benton did *not* wish the little man away; on the contrary, he desperately wanted to find him!

Fourteen days, fourteen days of madness and delirium; but through all the madness a burning purpose had shone out like a beacon. Who, what, why? Benton knew not, and he no longer wanted to know. But somewhere, *somewhere* . . .

Starting the first Tuesday after that evening of waking nightmare, each morning he had caught the commuter special as of old, to prowl its snakelike corridor and peer in poisonously through the compartment windows, every lunchtime he had waited in a shop doorway across the street from the Bull & Bush until closing time, and in between times he had walked the streets in all the villages between home and the city. Because somewhere, *somewhere!*

"Home." He tasted the word bitterly. "Home"—hah! That was a laugh! And all this after eleven years of reasonably harmonious married life. He thought again, suddenly, of Ellen, then of the hunchback, then of the two of them together . . . and in the next instant his mind was lit by a bright flash of inspiration.

Fourteen days—*fourteen days including today*—and this was Saturday night! Where would he be now if this whole nightmare had never happened? Why, he would be on the train with his wife, going home from their holiday!

Could it possibly be that—

Benton checked his watch, his hands shaking uncontrollably. Ten to nine; the nine o'clock train would be pulling into the station in only ten more minutes!

He looked wildly about him, reality crashing down again as he found himself in the back alleys of his home town. Slowly the wild light went out of his eyes, to be replaced by a strangely warped smile as he realised that he stood in an alley only a few blocks away from the railway station. . . .

* * *

They didn't see him as they left the station, Ellen in high heels and a chic outfit, the hunchback as usual in his ridiculous overcoat and floppy black hat. But Benton saw them. They were (it still seemed completely unbelievable) arm in arm, Ellen radiant as a young bride, the little man reeking and filthy; and as Benton heard again that obscene chuckle he choked and reeled with rage in the darkness of his shop doorway.

Instantly the little man paused and peered into the shadows where Benton crouched. Benton cursed himself and shrank back; although the street was almost deserted, he had not wanted his presence known just yet.

But his presence *was* known!

The hunchback lifted up Ellen's hand to his lips in grotesque chivalry and kissed it. He whispered something loathsomely, and then, as Ellen made off without a word down the street, he turned again to peer with firefly eyes into Benton's doorway. The hiding man waited no longer. He leapt out into view, his knife bright and upraised, and the hunchback turned without ceremony to scurry down the cobbled street, his coat fluttering behind him like the wings of a great crippled moth.

Benton ran too, and quickly the gap between them closed as he drove his legs in a vengeful fury. Faster and faster his breath rasped as he drew closer to the fugitive hunchback, his hand lifting the knife for the fatal stroke.

Then the little man darted round a corner into an alleyway. No more than a second later Benton, too, rushed wildly into the darkness of the same alley. He skidded to a halt, his shoes sliding on the cobbles. He stilled his panting forcibly.

Silence . . .

The little devil had vanished again! He—

No, *there* he was—cringing like a cornered rat in the shadow of the wall.

Benton lunged, his knife making a crescent of light as it sped toward the hunchback's breast, but like quicksilver the target shifted as the little man ducked under his pursuer's arm to race out again into the street, leaving the echo of his hideous chuckle behind him.

That whispered chuckle drove Benton to new heights of raging bloodlust and, heedless now of all but the chase, he raced hot on the hunchback's trail. He failed to see the taxi's lights as he ran into the street, failed to hear its blaring horn—indeed, he was only dimly aware of the scream of brakes and tortured tyres—so that the darkness of oblivion as it rushed in upon him came as a complete surprise. . . .

The darkness did not last. Quickly Benton swam up out of unconsciousness to find himself crumpled in the gutter. There was blood on his face, a roaring in his ears. The street swam round and round.

"Oh, God!" he groaned, but the words came out broken, like his body, and faint. Then the street found its level and steadied. An awful dull ache spread upwards from Benton's waist until it reached his neck. He tried to move, but couldn't. He heard running footsteps and managed to turn his head, lifting it out of the gutter in an agony of effort. Blood dripped from a torn ear. He moved an arm just a fraction, fingers twitching.

"God mister what were you doing what were you *doing*?" the taxi driver gabbled. "Oh Jesus Jesus you're hurt you're hurt. It wasn't my fault it wasn't me!"

"Never, uh . . . mind," Benton gasped, pain threatening to pull him under again as the ache in his lower body exploded into fresh agony. "Just . . . get me, uh, into . . . your car and . . . hospital or . . . doctor."

"Sure, yes!" the man cried, quickly kneeling.

If Benton's nose had not been clogged with mucus and drying blood he would have known of the hunchback's presence even before he heard the terrible chuckling from the pavement. As it was, the sound made him jerk his damaged head round into a fresh wave of incredible pain. He turned his eyes upward. Twin points of light stared down at him from the darkness beneath the floppy hat.

"Uh . . . I suppose, uh, you're satisfied . . . now?" he painfully inquired, his hand groping uselessly, longingly for the knife which now lay halfway across the street.

And then he froze. Tortured and racked though his body was—desperate as his pain and injuries were—Benton's entire being *froze* as, in answer to his choked question, *the hunchback slowly, negatively shook his shadowed head!*

Dumbfounded, amazed, and horrified, Benton could only gape, even his agony forgotten as he helplessly watched from the gutter a repeat performance of those well-known gestures, those scenes remembered of old and now indelibly imprinted upon his mind: the filthy whispering in the taxi driver's ear; the winking of bright, bird eyes; the mazed look spreading like pale mud on the frightened man's face. Again the street began to resolve about Benton as the taxi driver walked as if in a dream back to his taxi.

Benton tried to scream but managed only a shuddering cough. Spastically his hand found the hunchback's grimy ankle and he gripped it tight. The little man stood like stone, like an anchor, and once more the street steadied about them as Benton fought his mangled body in a futile attempt to push it to its feet. He could not. There was something wrong with his back, something broken. He coughed, then groaned and relaxed his grip, turning his eyes upward again to meet the steady gaze of the hunchback.

"Please . . ." he said. But his words were drowned out by the sudden sound of a revving engine, by the shriek of skidding tyres savagely reversing; and the last thing Benton saw, other than the black bulk of the taxi looming and the red rear lights, was the shuttering of one of those evil eyes in a grim farewell wink. . . .

Some few minutes later the police arrived at the scene of the most inexplicable killing it had ever been their lot to have to attend. They had been attracted by the crazed shrieking of a white-haired, utterly lunatic taxi driver.

AUTHOR'S NOTE

"THE WHISPERER" WAS MY ATTEMPT TO WRITE A WEIRD tale without reference to the standard props of the game. None of your typical monsters here but something inexplicable. How do you deal with someone like the Whisperer? With a crucifix? A silver bullet? With an outraged, torch-wielding gang of peasant villagers? This guy does his thing in broad daylight, and afterwards people won't even admit that he was there! Except his victims . . .

The "sex" scene was important. One of a man's worst nightmares has to be the rape of his wife or woman. Or that she is stolen away from him by some Other. Bad enough when the Other is another guy—another ordinary guy—but when it's the Whisperer?

Kirby McCauley said I had "created a character for the supernatural gallery who bids well to be long remembered." His words pleased me, and I hope "The Whisperer" gives you as much pleasure. . . .

—Brian Lumley

DOPPELGÄNGER
R. Chetwynd-Hayes

MRS. FORTESCUE'S PARTY WAS IN FULL SWING WHEN THE
Bayswaters arrived, which enabled her to greet Matthew
in a loud voice and thus warn her guests that the time had
come to stop whatever they were doing and pay homage
to the long awaited lion. She used Jennie as a sounding
board.

"How nice of you to come, my dear." She raised her
eyebrows and assumed an expression of arch surprise.
"And you managed to bring your handsome and so brilliant husband! I was so afraid he just wouldn't find time
to honour my little gathering."

Jennie gave her a dazzling smile and nudged Matthew
who was examining the running buffet with a critical eye.

"So sorry we are so late, but the car broke down and
Matthew is hopeless with engines. He just raises the bonnet and swears."

Mrs. Fortescue's bosom quivered ominously and a fat,
rumbling laugh gradually dissolved into words.

"Genius is rarely practical. We've been discussing *Man
on a Roof*. So original. Where does he get those wonderful

102

ideas from?'' She ventured to address Matthew, possibly a little disconcerted by his air of barely polite boredom. ''Where *do* you get your ideas from, Mr. Bayswater?''

''My head.''

Jennie slid a hand round his arm and nodded gently.

''He does. Get them from his head. He frightens himself sometimes. Particularly when he shaves. Says the sight of that head in the mirror is very unnerving first thing in the morning. Understandable in a way, isn't it?''

Mrs. Fortescue could be likened to a lady adrift in an open boat who is quite unable to read a compass.

''Yes . . . I mean no. Do help yourself to a drink or something.''

''First sensible words I've heard yet,'' Matthew remarked. ''What are those things on sticks?''

''Stuffed olives.'' Jennie edged him away from the temporarily speechless Mrs. Fortescue. ''And that stuff on tiny biscuits is slivers of fried chicken.''

''Good grief!''

A butler who had doubtlessly learnt his trade from P.G. Wodehouse, stood behind a long table and inclined his head when Matthew pointed to the whisky decanter, then poured a generous measure into a thick-based glass.

''Soda water or ginger ale, sir?'' he asked.

''Ginger ale for the lady, more whisky for me.''

A slight tightening of the man's lips might have been interpreted as an expression of disapproval, but he added the extra whisky, then removed a cap from a bottle of ginger ale with a quick flick of his wrist.

''Rudeness and booze act tonight?'' Jennie enquired.

Matthew shrugged and took a tiny sip from his glass.

''Might as well. Give 'em something to talk about.''

''So long as you don't drink all that whisky. You know alcohol upsets your stomach.''

He raised a finger to his lips. ''Hush, child. Do you want to spoil my image as the hard-drinking author? If anyone asks you, say my stomach is lined with asbestos.''

Jennie giggled and smiled kindly at a tall, long-nosed

young man who was gazing at her with gaping mouth and wide-open eyes.

"Well, you'd better take a good swig now, because here comes the real McCoy. Old Jeffrey Makepiece and I'd say he's as pickled as a soused herring."

The short fat man with the bright-red face, eased his way through the crowd, then laid a mottled hand on Jennie's bare arm. His watery eyes gleamed with tired lust.

"Jennie, me dear, I'd swear you're more beautiful than ever. Damn me eyes if you're not."

Jennie gently removed his hand, then performed a little curtsey. "Thank you, kind sir. And you're no less handsome that when I saw you last."

Makepiece pulled his stomach in, raised the discarded hand to this thinning hair, then stared unhappily at his empty glass.

"Why not apply for a refill?" Matthew suggested. "After all it's free."

"Damn me, I believe I will. The doctor's warned me off whisky, you know. Said it would kill me. So, I've gone over to gin. No point in paying a doctor if you don't follow his advice."

Instantly Jennie was the epitome of solicitous concern; gripping Matthew's arm, trying to arouse his sympathy for someone held between the claws of an irresistible vice.

"But you mustn't drink at all. That's what the doctor meant. Matthew, please—you tell him that. Surely he'll listen to you."

Makepiece watched his glass being replenished with gin, then chuckled with the satisfaction of a man who mistakes despair for bravery.

"Sweet child, how sweet of you to be so concerned. But if I cease to drink, what on earth will I do?"

"Face reality," Matthew said softly.

"Good heavens, you're the last man to recommend that course of action. Matthew Bayswater, the weaver of fantasies! Daring to speak of reality! Maybe you have no need of that sadly neglected glass in your hand, but you have nevertheless built a bridge that spans the terrible gulf of what-is to what-might-be. Allow lesser men to seek a more mundane avenue of escape.''

Matthew nodded slowly and took a rather longer sip from his glass. "You're so right. Drink what you will and God guide you through the mists.''

"And now," Jeffrey Makepiece looked round the room, "I will perform at least one good deed. Unless I'm greatly mistaken our hostess has that young actor pinned against the wall and is about to introduce him to Maudie Perkins. Such an experience could well dry up the well of youth. Bless you, my children.''

He ambled back into a forest of bodies and, so it seemed to Matthew, ceased to exist. Jennie sighed and slipped her hand into his.

"How sad, he used to be a fine actor—didn't he?''

Matthew grimaced. "He made a few ripples in a small pool. Frankly he terrifies me. There but for the grace of God . . . It only takes a few cosmic seconds to roll back down the hill.''

"Matthew, you're being morbid.''

"I know. These gatherings depress me. Why the hell did we come?''

"Because I made you. But we needn't stay long. Oh, Lord! Here comes Mr. What-can-you-do-for-me.''

Leslie Mortimer still retained some vestige of the conventional good looks that had pulled in the bobby-soxers a generation ago, but now he wore the faintly desperate expression of a man who has retained his youth long past its grave time. The suspiciously dark hair flopped down over a grotesquely unlined brow, the full lips were parted in a perpetual charming smile, thus revealing prettily capped teeth. But the fine eyes were hungry and raked Matthew's face.

"Matthew, my dear fellow! The veritable island of success in a vast sea of failure. A little bird informs me that *Grey Dawn* is about to be made into a film. And you've written the script.''

"Such has been my fate," Matthew admitted.

"And," the actor went on, still maintaining his carefully adjusted faintly interested expression, "I am also given to understand, you have formed a company to handle production."

"That little bird appears to have a long beak."

Leslie Mortimer released a peculiar rumbling laugh that had been waiting for some kind of humorous encouragement and now seemed reluctant to go back into retirement. A slim, white-faced girl who clung to the actor's arm, as though it were the only available straw in a sea of uncertainty, giggled and jerked her head forward, looking rather like a pretty lizard that has spotted a particularly succulent fly.

"This is Lottie," Mortimer made a belated introduction. "I've promised her a part in my next film. She's got talent."

Matthew gave the girl a quick glance. "So I see. I understand the studios are rather quiet at the moment."

The laugh came again, only now it contained a rather strained quality. "There's always work for talent, dear boy. Of course if you have a part that would suit me, I might be able to spare a month or so."

Matthew looked thoughtfully at his half empty glass and seemed to find its contents of enthralling interest.

"As a matter of fact I had thought of recommending you for the Harold Larkin role. Not the lead of course, but meaty for the right man. Has a few scene stealers."

The mask slipped. Matthew experienced an upsurge of pure happiness when he saw the gaping mouth, the expression of dawning delight, and wondered how he would have reacted, were he the suppliant and not the donor of cinematic crumbs. He waited for the gratitude explosion, the ego-boosting joy.

"You're not joking?"

"I never joke about the ridiculous."

"What can I say? I'm most tremendously grateful. I promise—faithfully promise—you won't regret this."

Matthew sighed deeply and appeared to be rather bored with a matter of little concern.

"That's settled then. Pop along to Pinewood on Tuesday and I'll arrange for a few preliminary tests. Always supposing," he permitted himself a pale smile, "your busy programme allows you the time."

"I can manage it. Yes, indeed. It might mean cancelling one or two things, but I'll be there."

Lottie did a little dance and in consequence was in danger of revealing more than is considered acceptable in polite society.

"And what about me, Mr. Bayswater? I don't suppose you've anything at all that would fit me?"

Matthew was aware of the warning pressure of Jennie's hand and resisted the urge to make an obvious answer. Instead he raised an enquiring eyebrow and considered the distinct possibility of the casting office giving him hell on Tuesday morning.

"I don't know. Maybe a bit part with a few lines tacked on. Bring her along, Mortimer."

There was a moment of panic; a feeling that his generous hand had already given more than his credit allowed and at any moment he would be shown up as a worthless bankrupt. He heard Jennie's soft, lilting voice sending out an even flow of small talk, as always defending him from the slings and arrows of mediocrity. Possibly he had drunk more of the whisky than he had intended, because suddenly the room seemed to move slightly out of perspective, creating the impression he was standing on a slightly elevated position, looking down on a sea of white faces that elongated and pulsated, rather like a television picture when the outside aerial has fallen down. Then a man with a completely bald head suddenly flashed into being and shouted:

"For God's sake, wake up, man."

He vanished and all the faces took on their normal appearance, the room slid back into focus and all was as it had been, only he was left with an irrational fear, a strange notion that he had fallen into a deep pit and there was no guarantee that the experience would not occur again. There were more people round him now, all talking at once, their eyes devouring him and Jennie; and he suddenly wanted to be faraway, walking across a desolate moor, knowing that eternity slept under a benign sky.

The voice of James Fisher—agent, profit-seeking friend—rose up above the jungle of sound and told him what he always wanted to hear.

"Matthew, you're a damned lucky bastard. You sit on a throne and accept the homage of your worshippers and curse me liver if you've done all that much to deserve it. There's no democracy in life. Most of us are born with ugly bodies, no gifts worth talking about, and have to spend our days crawling in the mud. Others like you have it made from cradle to grave. It's not fair."

Jennie of course gave a pretty demonstration of outraged indignation.

"He works very hard. And you've got a lot of room to talk. Ten percent of his earnings, just to retype a contract and the cost of a postage stamp. It's the jackals who grow fat on the lion's . . . the lion's . . ."

"Kill," Matthew suggested.

She pushed back a lock of hair with her left hand.

"Well—the lion's something. And the jackals raise their young and keep wives and mistresses—all because Matthew sometimes sits up all night and uses his clever brain."

James winked at Matthew. "Oh come off it! He's only a high-paid liar."

"He's not a liar."

"Yes he is. He hasn't written a word of truth in his entire life. What is a novel but one long lie? An author creates a world of make-believe and expects everyone to share his illusion. When you come right down to it, the entire writing fraternity are nothing more than a crowd of psychopaths."

A roar of laughter greeted this definition and even Jennie was forced to smile.

"Anyway," she placed her two hands round Matthew's left arm, "he's a very nice psychopath."

"Let's settle for a thirsty psychopath and get me another drink. The one I had seems to have disappeared in one way or another."

"You drank it."

"I never did."

"Darling, I really do think it's about time we went home. You have to be up early tomorrow."

"Suppose I don't want to go home?" Matthew enquired.

"Then we stay here."

He smiled complacently. "That being the case we'll go."

James Fisher grinned and slowly shook his head.

"Oh, happy man who can spell the word freedom as he shakes his velvet chains. Are you permitted to come to my office tomorrow?"

"So long as I wear my woollen vest."

Mrs. Fortescue expressed deep regret when she found her star guest was leaving early, although she had been heard to remark that his heavy drinking might prove an embarrassment.

"So soon, Mr. Bayswater! How sad. And there were so many interesting people I wanted you to meet."

Jennie put up a smoke screen and made a retreat sound like a victory. "We simply hate to go, but Matthew has a very early appointment tomorrow morning and he's not all that well."

"Indeed! Nothing serious, I hope."

"No. Just been overdoing it. You understand?"

The lady nodded with due solemnity. "Indeed I do. He must take care of himself."

When they were in the car Jennie looked at him and smiled gently. "She's rather a duck and clearly thinks you're something that dropped from the sky."

Matthew swung the car round into the main road, then changed gear. "At this moment she's telling everyone who will listen that drink's my problem and how marvelously you cope."

"But isn't that what you want people to think?"

He shrugged. "It's a game I like to play. Does no one any harm."

"Yes, but why?"

"Because I'm terrified of ending up like Mortimer. Sucking up to someone like me and really hitting the bottle. Playing a game, having people think I'm already on the skids, is like pretending you're broke when there's a lot of money in the bank. Understand?"

Jennie's eyes glittered softly in the light cast by a passing car. "No. You have a lot of money in the bank and even if you never published another book, you'd never have to—well—act like Leslie Mortimer. These fits of depression worry me."

"Worry you! They murder my sleep."

He pulled up at the traffic lights and glanced out of the side window. People were passing along the pavement; each one a self-contained unit, but sharing a common fund of hopes and fears, looking forward to or dreading the birth of the next hour, day or month. Then he became aware of a particular face; thin, drawn, the eyes clouded by melancholy that was framed by a glass shop door. A hauntingly familiar face surmounted by untidy blond hair. A tall, bald-headed man came from behind a counter and apparently called out, for the face jerked round and looked back over one shoulder.

"Matthew," Jennie's voice came from beside him, "wake up, darling. The lights have changed."

Matthew was able to catch a glimpse of the shop facia board before he drove off. He read: L.W. SMITH. LTD. KITCHENWARE EQUIPMENT.

"What's bothering you now?" Jennie asked after a while.

"I don't know. Only . . . there's a man in that hardware shop by the traffic lights and I've a feeling I've seen him before, but for the life of me I can't think where."

"You'll remember," Jennie said consolingly. "When you least expect it, the memory will come back. But I know the feeling. It's damned irritating."

"Somehow I feel sorry for him. He looked damned miserable and I suppose that's no wonder. It must be a hell of a life selling pots and pans to bitchy old women."

"Perhaps he owns the store and is making a bomb."

Matthew shook his head and turned into the drive.

"I don't think so. It looked as if the owner was choking him off for something. Come to think of it that old basket looked familiar as well."

But it was later that night when they were both in the king-size bed and Matthew was allowing his brain to dim down its awareness that the spark of memory flared up into a revealing flame.

"I remember where I saw that man before."

Jennie turned on her bedside lamp and blinked at her husband with sleep-glazed eyes.

"What man? What on earth are you talking about?"

"The man in the shop. I see that face every morning in the shaving mirror. Take off a few pounds, add a generally unkempt appearance—and we might be twin brothers."

Jennie displayed mild interest. "That means you have a double! How extraordinary! You must invite him to tea."

"Good God! What a thought."

Presently Jennie turned out the light and Matthew lay back trying to come to terms with a situation that should have been both amusing and intriguing. Having a double that worked in a hardware shop was surely unique. But it was for some reason disturbing.

James Fisher emptied his glass, then replenished it from an adjacent bottle. He watched Matthew push his plate to one side and looked idly round the restaurant, then expressed his concern.

"You haven't eaten enough to keep a fly alive. You need a holiday."

Matthew shrugged and sipped from a glass of water.

"I'm all right. Jennie makes certain I eat a good break-fast and the old hag who rules our kitchen crams roast beef and Yorkshire pud down my throat come sunset. But lunch is a bad time for me. No appetite—no any-thing."

Fisher ran a forefinger round the rim of his glass.

"I often wonder—who shouldn't—why you don't pack it in for a bit. The stuff you've got in the pipeline will keep you in the super-tax bracket for quite some time."

Matthew shook his head and spoke without really think-ing.

"That would mean letting go and God knows where I would fall."

"You've lost me. Explain."

"I can't. Look, something happened last night which still bothers me. It's damned ridiculous really, but I'd be obliged if you would accompany me to a certain shop and supply moral support."

James Fisher lit a cigarette and blew out a nigh perfect smoke ring.

"What kind of shop?"

"One that sells hardware—kitchen stuff. Last night I saw my double looking out of the doorway and damned if I can get the memory out of my mind."

Fisher assumed an expression of mock horror.

"For Chrissake! Don't tell me there's another face like yours floating around! This I must see."

Matthew beckoned to a waiter. "That's what I intend. The chances are on closer inspection the fellow will prove to have only a superficial resemblance. The place isn't far. By the traffic lights on the corner of Denby Street."

"Everything all right, sir?" the waiter enquired, as he accepted Matthew's luncheon card.

"Well, the steak tasted like burnt leather and the roast potatoes like underdone tennis balls. Otherwise I've no complaints."

"Thank you, sir. There's a ten percent cover charge."

* * *

The long shop-lined street looked so different in daylight; all the shops open and despite the bright sunshine, transformed into brilliantly lit grottos by overhead neon strips. Matthew looked at the large, double-fronted shop on the corner and realised it presented a much fresher, glossy appearance than he remembered; was in fact a creation of chrome and glass with an illuminated sign on the facia board that caused his heart to thud alarmingly. He braked the car to a halt and stared up at the blue, neon letters and tried to understand.

KITCHEN KIT KAMP

This was far different from the W.L. SMITH KITCHEN-WARE EQUIPMENT painted in large black letters on an off-white background that he distinctly remembered seeing the night before. Neither did the interior of this ultramodern establishment offer much comfort. In place of a long counter and rows of laden shelves, were several model kitchens, each one resplendent with stainless-steel and brightly plastic doors and drawer fronts. He felt like someone who has come to view a cottage and is confronted by a palace.

"Well," James Fisher enquired, "are we going to meet your double or not?"

"It's all wrong," Matthew said in a low voice. "All terribly wrong."

"You don't have to tell me. The best part of seven hundred quid for a lot of plastic covered chipboard. But that long-haired twit who appears to be flogging his rubbish to an old lady, certainly doesn't look much like you."

Matthew looked up and down the street, took note of the chemist shop, the traffic lights and knew there was no possible doubt that he had driven to the correct location. Everything was as it should be—except the kitchen equipment shop.

"Let's go in," he said quietly, "but I've a feeling I'm just going to make a fool of myself."

He opened the door and stepped onto a gleaming, orange-coloured tiled floor, then walked boldly towards a large, imitation leather-covered desk where the young man with long hair, who, having bowed politely to the old lady, was now sorting through some papers. He looked up and bared his teeth in an engaging smile.

"How can I help you, gentlemen?"

Matthew found he was quite unable to speak, for it now seemed to be the height of absurdity to ask this callow youth if there was anyone employed on the premises who resembled him. But James suffered from no such reticence.

"We would like to settle a little argument. A friend of ours swears to God he's seen someone who is the spitting image of this gentleman in this shop . . ."

"Showrooms," the young man corrected.

"Pardon me. Well—have you anyone that looks like this guy?"

The young man shot Matthew one quick glance then shook his head.

"No. Anyway the only people employed here are my wife and myself."

"Perhaps a customer who was here late last night," James suggested.

"I was out last night. But Eileen was here. Hold on a sec and I'll fetch her."

He disappeared into an alcove that was hidden behind an eye-catching mauve curtain and presently returned accompanied by a very pretty girl with short auburn hair and the mien of a mature child. Matthew thought they might have been both manufactured in the same factory. She nodded vigorously.

"Oh, yes. I've seen him before."

James exclaimed: "Well, well, the mystery is about to be solved. Tell us, sweet one, where did you see this gentleman before?"

"On telly. When he was being interviewed about his last book. He's Matthew Bayswater."

James Fisher slapped him on the back. "May that teach

you to keep your ugly mug off the box. Once seen it's never forgotten. However, it would appear that no one that looks like you works here.''

''No such luck,'' the girl breathed.

''Daresay we can fit you in,'' her husband said quietly, possibly not all that pleased by her unrestrained enthusiasm. ''If you get a bit hard up, there's worse jobs than selling kitchen furniture.''

''Harold, really! What will Mr. Bayswater think?''

Matthew began to edge towards the door, anxious to terminate this ridiculous charade. ''Thank you. . . . Sorry to have taken up your time.''

''Pleasure,'' the young man intoned, then added: ''Pop in any time you're passing.''

''I can't wait to tell my sister.'' His wife stared. ''She'll never believe I've actually talked to Matthew Bayswater.''

James Fisher nodded. ''I know what you mean. Well, be good. Don't sell any wooden kitchens.''

''There's a willing number there,'' he murmured, once they were back in Matthew's car. ''Ready for a quick 'ow's yer father over the kitchen sink. Very nice too.''

Matthew did not answer, but slid the gear lever into third, then drove the car over the traffic lights. He took careful note of the houses they passed, the TO BE SOLD sign that stood in front of one empty shop and knew he had not mistaken the route taken the night before. There was no point in toying with such words as imagination, illusion, dined-well-but-not-wisely, or any other well-worn clichés that were apt to be used when the unusual raised its head. His eyes had relayed an accurate picture of an old fashioned hardware shop, with a duplicate of himself standing behind a glass door to his fully alert brain and no amount of self-deception could negate that fact. He swung the steering wheel round and began to head back to the office.

''Tell me, James,'' he said after a while, ''who am I?''

The agent gave him a long, speculative look.

''You want me to treat that question seriously?''

"Of course. Otherwise I wouldn't have asked it."

"You're Matthew Bayswater, thirty-three years old, pretty as a picture and twice as smart. After leaving a secondary school at the age of fifteen you did all manner of dead-end jobs, which appear to have covered a wide variety of trades. At one time I believe you were an errand boy in a butcher's shop. But being a bright lad, you attended night school, wrote short stories, and made a name for yourself when you won the Hickey Prize. Some rising young film producer made a film based on four of your stories, which by more luck than judgement turned out to be a blockbuster. You've never looked back since. Butcher's apron to riches. Oh, yes—you married the lovely girl who is supposed to live next door, but never does. I think that sums up your distinguished career."

"But I never worked in a kitchenware shop," Matthew said in a low voice.

Fisher nodded slowly as though he had spotted a glimmer of light in a dark room.

"This business of seeing your double in a shop doorway is getting you down, isn't it? Well, I'm no psychiatrist, but look at it this way. The chances are, if you had not had a lucky break, you might well have finished up in some such establishment. And you know it. The trouble is, success came to you too soon and too easily; and there just hasn't been time to dispel the feeling of insecurity that dominated your childhood. Last night the old subconscious flashed a picture of what-might-have-been. Now that theory might have as many holes as my grannie's drawers, but it's the best I can come up with at a moment's notice."

Matthew hooted the car horn when a thoughtless pedestrian suddenly stepped off the pavement.

"Sounds possible in an impossible sort of way. Very cut and dried. But there is much more to it. Much . . . much more."

Next day Matthew drove down to Camelot, where Henry Handel occasionally rested and pretended that his knighthood was something more than a romantic handle to put in front of his name. Originally the old house had been called Bottom Farm, but Sir Henry, after adding a few turrets and two flag poles, had boldly renamed it Camelot, possibly inspired by the role of Sir Lancelot, which he had once played in a joint Anglo-Italian film. He was a florid, well-padded man, still retaining the remnants of his former dashing good looks, who was now resigned to playing someone's father or benign uncle. Nevertheless, he had some claim to being regarded as a great actor.

This was something he could never forget and was apt to turn the most mundane conversation into well-delivered dialogue and a casual acquaintance into a captive audience. He greeted Matthew with a grave handshake, then exclaimed in a sonorous voice: "Young Bayswater, as I live and die!" then led him into a hall, that was enhanced by suits of armour, swords and some lethal-looking spears. From there they passed into what it pleased the worthy knight to call his "withdrawing room" which was equipped with pseudo-Tudor furniture and an equally fraudulent Renaissance picture of Richard I trying to cut a cushion in half with a broadsword. Matthew seated himself in an extremely uncomfortable armchair and watched the actor pour sherry into two copper flagons.

"I don't think," he began.

"Nonsense, dear boy. 'Tis but a goblet of dry sack which made our forebears the men they were. Besides it's whispered in the market place you are wont to gaze upon the grape when it is red. Take a little wine for thy stomach's sake, but for God's sake spare a thought for your liver." Sir Henry presented a full flagon to his guest, who estimated it must contain not less than half a pint of the rich brown wine. "Drink, drink and let us wash away dull care."

And he proceeded to follow his own advice with praiseworthy gusto and evident satisfaction. Then he wiped his lips on a towel-size handkerchief and waited until Matthew had taken an experimental sip.

"Well now! I learn you require me to saw the air before the camera. Tread the boards for the delectation of those who lurk in loathsome fleapits."

"You've received a copy of the script?" Matthew asked.

"Aye, that I have. I could wish the dialogue was more meaty—and more of it—but one must be thankful for what one gets these days. I am loath to sully your ears with mention of sordid monetary matters, but am I to understand that the remuneration will be . . ."

"Ten thousand for five days," Matthew stated with sordid briefness.

" 'Tis a goodly round sum that will be welcomed by my depleted coffers. I could wish it were paid out in some discreet place, so that those who issue forth from the tax collector's lair, know not of the transaction. I suppose thou wouldst not consider . . . ?"

Matthew shook his head. "I fear not. We have to make our returns."

Sir Henry sighed deeply and emptied his flagon.

" 'Tis passing sad. Not only do they consume that which is to come, but demand that which hath passed away. Can you conceive?"

"I never have. According to our time table we will require your services during the first week in September."

"I will—God willing—be there. But now you must partake with us. Take nourishment with myself and that I am wont to call my good lady. We feast at one."

"The sole reason for my visit," Matthew confessed. "One of your lunches sets me up for the next month. What is it today? Baron of beef or roast peacock?"

"Only God and the woman knows. Wait—I will summon her." And Sir Henry raised his voice and bellowed: "Matilda—come forth, woman."

Matthew heard the patter of hurrying footsteps and rose when Matilda Handel entered the room. She was a slight, middle-aged woman; a fragile creature with a kindly fresh face and neat grey hair that was cut short in the current fashionable style. She said: "Matthew! What a nice surprise,'' and presented one cheek to be kissed. "If I'd known you were here I'd have rescued you sooner. I do hope Henry hasn't been too tiresome."

"The lad is to partake with us," Sir Henry announced.

Lady Handel waved an impatient hand. "Why you can't say he's staying for lunch like a normal person is beyond me. I'm delighted, Matthew, but it's rather pot luck today, I'm afraid."

"What, no baron of beef?"

"Good heavens no! His digestion won't take that sort of thing these days. I've got some nice lamb chops with boiled potatoes and salad." She became suddenly aware of the two flagons and her hands flew to her mouth like two startled moths. "Henry, you haven't been making this poor young man drink all that awful sherry?"

" 'Tis but a modicum of sack," the knight protested.

"Nonsense. And you well know the doctor said you were to confine yourself to a small glass of burgundy at dinner time. Do you feel all right, Matthew?"

"I only drank a small amount. Besides I have a reputation of being an accomplished drinker."

"That's as may be. But a nice young actor who called the other day was incapable of speech or movement for several hours. No wonder we receive so few visitors." She turned to her husband and addressed him with maternal severity. "Henry, you will stop this period nonsense and show Matthew your knife collection."

"My armoury," Sir Henry bellowed.

"Well, show him whatever it is you've got up there, while I give cook a hand. The poor dear has back trouble and is quite unable to open the oven door."

She fluttered to the door and was soon heard pattering across the hall on her way to the afflicted cook. Sir Henry, after a few exasperated grunts, pulled in his not inconsiderable stomach and said: "Might as well see me collection. Unless you've seen it before."

"I have," Matthew admitted, "but I'm quite willing to see it again."

They crossed the hall, mounted a quite ordinary stair-case, and eventually came up into what, in a normal house would have been the attic. But dormer windows now gave a commanding view of the surrounding countryside from both side walls, while on long benches that ran the entire length of the room, were a miscellaneous collection of swords, daggers, spears, battle-axes and other instruments of mayhem. Matthew picked up an ornamental dagger.

"What period is this?"

"*Hamlet*—Oldfield Theatre 1928."

"And this sword?"

"*The Curse of the Seven Virgins*, Rome 1963."

After a few such answers Matthew remembered that Sir Henry's concept of history was strictly confined to either a theatre or a film set. He wandered round the room, ig-noring the knight's rambling monologue, until he came to a small table set in front of one window. On it lay a pair of powerful binoculars.

"*The Harsh Sea*, 1951," Sir Henry volunteered.

Matthew clamped the binoculars to his eyes and moved his head from left to right so as to obtain a wide view of the panorama laid out before him. By adjusting the view-finder he was able to make a distant house spring into close-up; every window, roof-tile, appeared but a few yards away. When the glasses were lowered he saw a child playing with a kitten in a hedge-rimmed garden; a young woman standing in an open doorway; a green car lurking on a gravelled drive. Then a clump of trees glided into view, every leaf a silent tongue as they swayed gently in response to the prevailing wind. Further to the right was a cornfield, which gave way to an expanse of open meadow land, where brown and white cows wandered with mind-less contentment. By lowering the binoculars even further Matthew found he was looking at a man leaning against a gate.

The man was staring directly at the house—even pos-sibly at the very window . . .

"Sir Henry," Matthew spoke calmly. "I would like you

to train these binoculars on that gate. The one immediately below the large oak tree."

Handel took the glasses and after squinting in the required direction, raised them to his eyes. Matthew waited.

"Got it," the knight announced. "Leads to old Jarvis's meadow. Fine example of an old gate. What wouldest thou I do now?"

"What do you think of the man leaning against the gate?"

"What man, dear boy? Apart from a few cows in the background, there's not a living body in sight."

Matthew took a deep breath and managed to subdue a pang of pure terror. "But I can still see him, even without the glasses. He hasn't moved."

Sir Henry gave him a quick glance, then again stared intently through the binoculars. "I suppose I'm looking at the right gate? For damn me soul if I can see anyone."

"There's only one gate," Matthew said quietly, "and you're looking at it. And if you can't see a man leaning against it and staring at this house, one of us is in a bad way."

The actor was now quite a different person to the rather ridiculous poser of a short time before; he handed the binoculars back to Matthew and said gently:

"Describe the fellow."

"Very well. But will you believe what I tell you?"

Sir Henry nodded very slowly. "I will—and I've no intention of questioning your sanity. All writers—and actors for that matter—are a bit cracked, but not enough to see a nonexistent man."

Matthew again trained the glasses on the gate. His double's face came into focus, the eyes unblinking, the forehead creased by a troubled frown.

"I see a man who is a nigh perfect duplicate of myself. If I start from the top and work my way down, this is a detailed description. Blond hair—like mine—but it needs cutting. My eyes, only they have a cowed expression. My height, but the shoulders seem to have acquired a stoop.

My body, but I'd say a little thinner. For the rest—he's dressed in a wrinkled, serge·suit, a dirty creased shirt, a lopsided spotted red tie. The trousers are a bit too short for him and I can see a pair of sagging socks and brown cracked shoes. That's about it. Unless I add he hasn't moved, blinked, or given the slightest sign of life.'' Matthew lowered the binoculars and looked sideways at the actor. ''And this is the second time I've seen him. The other night he was standing in a nonexistent shop doorway.''

Sir Henry drew him gently away from the window, then motioned him to a chair. When they were both seated he said: ''I've read and heard about this kind of thing, but damn me if I ever believed there was anything to it. You must have guessed what . . . that thing out there is?''

''Someone who looks too like me for comfort,'' Matthew replied, ''and apparently can't be seen by anyone else. Must be an illusion. That means I'm mad.''

The knight looked uncomfortable. ''If you're mad I'm a dutchman. Look, as a writer you must have heard of this kind of thing. Remember the oldest curse in history? 'May you meet yourself coming downstairs.' My dear fellow, you've just described your Doppelgänger.''

''What the hell is that?''

''The ghost of yourself. Damn me, I played one once. Back in the thirties. A film called *The Curse of the Double-Man*. To get into the atmosphere I must have read every word printed on the subject. A lot of quite famous people have seen the damned things. Sir Walter Scott for one.''

''With what result?''

If Sir Henry had appeared to be uncomfortable before, he now gave the impression he was sitting on a bed of hot nails.

''Well—pure coincidence of course—all getting on in years—but generally speaking they all died within a year. After seeing the Doppelgänger, that is.''

Matthew digested this information, accepted the implication, and was surprised to find that it did not cause him all that disquiet. There were worse fates than dying.

"As you appear to be an expert on this kind of thing," he said calmly, "perhaps you can tell me if these famous persons—did they always see an exact duplicate of themselves? Down to the smallest detail?"

The knight nodded. "Absolutely. Erasmus Aldridge, the seventeenth-century philosopher, records he saw a mirror reflection. The Doppelgänger was wearing his clothes, but buttoned on the opposite side. A hole that was in his right stocking was in the apparition's left."

"But this fellow isn't wearing my clothes," Matthew pointed out. "And there are other differences. Hair style, weight, expression. That doesn't fit into your theory."

Sir Henry blew out his cheeks. "Beats me. Tell you what. I've got a book in the library. What's it called now? Hang on—it's coming back . . . *Unnatural Enmities* by Conrad Von Holstein. Hell of a family, you know. All of 'em dabbled in the black arts for centuries. Old Conrad wrote this book around 1820, then disappeared shortly afterwards. And I'm damned sure there's a chapter on the Doppelgänger. Look it out after lunch. Which reminds me, the woman will be screaming to high heaven if we don't get downstairs and play with her blasted lamb chops. Mind you there's a damned good rice pudding to follow."

Matthew got up and walked back to the window. After a while he said: "He's gone now."

Sir Henry's voice came from behind him.

"Yes, well, maybe he was never there in the first place. Shouldn't take this too much to heart. Perhaps that sherry was a mite too strong and large. Fellow sees all sorts of things when he's had more than enough. Be best if we don't mention any of this to Matilda. Women never understand anything that's not connected with either the kitchen or bedroom. Let's go down."

They left the "armoury" and descended the stairs and were just in time to stop Lady Handel belabouring a large gong that was slung between two posts. She gave Matthew a sympathetic smile.

"You poor dear boy! I do hope that Henry hasn't bored you too dreadfully with the history of all those knives. I fear he has a weakness for the macabre."

Matthew allowed himself the luxury of a trite remark.

"It's all been most interesting. I've been admiring the view from the east window. It has some interesting features."

"Hasn't it?" Lady Handel agreed. "A visitor will always find something new."

Jennie had dusted everything that was available to be dusted, reluctantly refrained from doing something about Matthew's littered desk, then shot him an enquiring glance.

"Are you going to work all morning?"

"Read," he said.

"Oh! Anything nice?"

He looked down at the bulky, ancient book that Sir Henry had lent him and turned back the front cover. "Not very. *Unnatural Enmities*, by Baron Conrad Von Holstein."

"Ugh! Are you going to write about—what you said?"

"Maybe."

"I'll be across the hall if you need me. Coffee around eleven OK?"

He nodded and watched her perform that loin-warming walk that had to be seen from the rear to be really appreciated. It had something to do with the way her buttocks moved and the curve of her shoulders. Suddenly Matthew realised what a perfect partner she made; loving, but not clinging, always considering his welfare, the ideal bed companion, prepared to take part in any variation. In fact, had he created her as a character in one of his books, an editor might well be justified by saying: "Too perfect—lacks credibility."

She left the door open and presently he heard her humming a haunting tune while she cleared the dining room table. Matthew turned his full attention to the book which now lay open before him.

UNNATURAL ENMITIES
by
Baron Conrad Von Holstein: Count of Plön
Translated by
Sir James Sinclair, Bart
1933

Matthew wondered who Sir James Sinclair was—or had been—and why he should have taken the trouble to translate such a book into English. Possibly Sir Henry could enlighten him on this point. The introduction was short, but gave him some information regarding the original author.

INTRODUCTION

Very little is known about the life of Baron Conrad Von Holstein, apart from his obsession with the occult and a profound knowledge of the various folk tales and legends that the unlettered peasantry of central Europe have relayed from one generation to the next, since the dawn of history.

Certainly the von Holstein family had a most sinister reputation since Baron Heinrich was burnt at the stake in 1556; having, according to contemporary records, not only mated his only daughter to the Primate Horrific (see page 272) but did call up the dreaded Holstein Horror as well. (See page 295.)

It is interesting to learn that the baron—so far as I am aware—was the first man to coin the phrase Parallel-Universe; believing apparently that there are innumerable planes of consciousness, the lowest being the habitat of the terrible life-forms that are recorded in this book.

Conrad was born on the 30th May 1786 and disappeared under mysterious circumstances on July 7th 1820, leaving behind this work which was long banned by the Catholic Church, although copies were circulating in certain countries as late as 1893.

Matthew turned the pages over until he arrived at number 95. He sat back and read.

THE DOPPELGÄNGER

The Doppelgänger or mirror-ghost is of great antiquity, it being recorded as the earliest known apparition that did bring fear and much despondency to primitive man. A drawing, both well executed and of exceedingly well preserved colours, can be seen to this day in the Walbeck Cave, situated in the Neude-Mine district; depicting two men of same likeness, one of whom hath his hair standing on end.

The ancient Egyptians were also troubled with this affliction and it is recorded in the book of death that Rameses the third of that name, did see his other self come up from the river, thus causing the king to fall down into a great faint. In more recent times when the great Elizabeth lay dying in her palace of Richmond, one lady in waiting whose duty it was to sit by the queen's side, having strayed into the long gallery, did see the queen's mirror-self approach towards her. She, fearing that Her Majesty had arisen and would rebuke her for leaving the place of vigil, cried out and said: "I did but answer a call of nature," but when the apparition was scarce two feet away, it vanished. When the lady returned to the bed chamber, the queen was still sleeping.

The ignorant do say that the Doppelgänger is a harbinger of death, but I, being a grand master of the seventh circle, am of the opinion, nay of proven conviction, that the reason for its appearance is most complex and may well be the cause of our departure from this *place*. I speak not of the death of the material body.

On the dawn of St. Wilfred's day, I being but newly awakened, saw my Doppelgänger seated in a chair and displaying signs of deep distress. It wept and tore its hair and gazed upon me with great reproach, so that even I (who hath seen much that would cause a normal man to break his sanity) was much afraid and would have fled, had not the apparition been betwixt me and the door.

Presently it rose and walked (with resounding footsteps) to the left side of my bed and exclaimed in a loud voice:

"Why make you this hell for me?"

Then it departed, went I know not where and I—being now somewhat recovered—rose and searched my chamber with great diligence, but found no evidence of an intruder. The thought came to me that we may well form a duplicate self, who has to suffer in another place, for the sins committed here by its progenitor. Or conversely we have to endure the ills and misery of this life, because of *that* which does evil under an alien sun.

Indeed cursed is he who thirsts after knowledge, for no man, no matter how great his attainments, can entirely drain the cup of truth. Little knowledge confuses the brain, leads us into dark avenues of conjecture and awakens the gibbering ghosts of superstition. Three times more have I seen my Doppelgänger, but I pray to Almighty God that it come not again *within clutching distance*, lest that which I fear (but dare not commit to paper) come about.

Matthew slammed the book closed and looked anxiously around the room, aware of a suspicion that something—or someone—had distracted his attention. Jennie had closed the door at some time while he had been reading, but he could still hear her humming; a muted sound that seemed to come from a long way off.

Then suddenly all sound was cut off. Was succeeded by an absolute silence which made Matthew believe for one dreadful moment that he had been struck deaf. The mantelpiece clock no longer sent out its dignified loud tick, the gentle summer breeze continued to stir the leaves of the old elm tree, but there was no muted, air-borne sigh. Matthew pressed a typewriter key, it struck the white paper, formed a small *e* and fell back when he released it—but made no sound of any kind.

Then this awful, unnatural silence was shattered by a loud ranting voice that came from just behind the closed door. The voice of a woman whose spoonful of love had long since curdled and poisoned her soul. It grew louder still as the speaker approached the door.

". . . you sit there with your moon face and not a word to say for yourself and I so hate your guts I'd like to take a coal hammer and bash your head in until it bursts and stop you writing that muck that no one wants to publish . . ."

She was by the door now, the handle was turning and Matthew was whimpering, hands clasped over his ears, but the mad, bitter stream of recrimination continued to sweep across his brain.

". . . you think you're a bloody genius but you're nothing more than a gutless failure . . . bloody great fail . . . u . . . r . . . e . . . e."

The door opened and Jennie entered the room. She smiled sweetly and said: "Coffee on the boil, darling."

Instantly normal sound returned. The clock resumed its dignified tick, the wind again wooed the restless leaves and far, far away a dog barked. Matthew Bayswater pointed a quivering forefinger at his wife.

"What the hell are you playing at? Are you trying to drive me mad?"

The smile froze on Jennie's face, then gradually dissolved into an expression of horrified astonishment. She moved forward like a woman who has come face to face with a long awaited and much dreaded spectre and is determined not to appear afraid. She spoke softly.

"What's wrong, Matthew? You're so white and your hands are shaking. Are you ill? Shall I ring for Dr. Waterman?"

His throat was choked with words and there was a need to abuse, to force her to provide a rational explanation.

"A damned silly joke—if that's what you meant it to be. Shouting and roaring away like that . . . telling me I'm a failure . . . I write rubbish . . . muck . . . that will never be published . . . and wanting to kill me . . ." He looked up at her. "Do you really hate and despise me?"

Jennie instantly put an arm around his shoulders, placed her face next to his, while her soft lilting voice spoke words of comfort, loving concern.

"Of course I don't despise or hate you. I love and respect you and always will. And as for being a failure . . . You're a terrific, booming success. The great Matthew Bayswater. And don't you dare ever think otherwise."

He repeated her words in a grotesquely loud whisper.

"I'm a terrific, booming success and I must never think otherwise. Ever."

He began to feel better almost at once and decided to forget the entire episode. He was aware of a slow journey up the stairs, guided by a slender arm that encircled his waist; after a lapse of time that could have lasted from anything from ten minutes to an hour, he was between cool sheets that caressed his limbs like pleasure-seeking hands; and if the damnable logic-loving brain insisted that the problem would still be unsolved when he awoke, that, at the present moment in time, was of little importance.

Dr. Waterman put away his stethoscope and succeeded in looking very wise.

"Nothing wrong with you physically, but you certainly appear to be mixed-up mentally. Sounds like a job for one of those head-shrinkers. Probably got an anxiety complex, whatever that might mean."

"No psychiatrist for me," Matthew protested. "If I'm going nuts, I'll do it in privacy. No one is rummaging around in my brain."

The doctor shrugged. "That's up to you. But at least take a break and get away for a bit. No need to keep turning out that junk as you do. You must be worth a bomb. Now, if you were an overworked, underpaid GP, you'd have a good excuse for a nervous breakdown."

"Balls. A professional examiner of—"

"That's as may be. But yours are nothing to get excited about." Waterman turned to Jennie. "As this exchange of scintillating wit will have informed you, he's down to his usual low form. Keep him off booze, work, and how's-yer-father and he'll be all right."

"If necessary I'll tie him down to the bed," Jennie promised.

The doctor assumed an expression of shocked horror.

"Good God! Don't tell me you have to do that! No wonder he hears voices. I'll pop along tomorrow."

Scarcely had the door closed behind Jennie and the doctor than Matthew was out of bed and scrambling into his clothes. The bedroom was suddenly an evil place; the wardrobe might well conceal some as yet unthought of horror that was only waiting for the unguarded moment to emerge into grotesque life. He also experienced a reluctance to look into the dressing-table mirror, being tormented by the ridiculous notion that his reflection might rebel and not faithfully reproduce either his appearance or his actions.

He was halfway down the stairs before Jennie realised that her patient was making a bid for freedom. She remonstrated, all but laid violent hands on him, but to no avail.

"I'll really go mad in that room and I'm not really ill. Nothing wrong that work won't cure."

"But you *are* ill. I know . . . know . . ."

He paused for a moment, then looked down into her eyes and thought for a moment he detected a gleam of— what? Derision? Contempt? Or loving concern? He pushed by her and made for the front door, smothering a feeling that blended fear with irritation. Her voice came to him just before he slammed the front door.

"Be careful. Don't do anything stupid."

Of course due to the excitement, the need to get out of the house, he had forgotten the car keys and lacking the courage to face Jennie again, there was no alternative but to travel on the underground.

Grimy windows framed a view of undulating, dust-coated pipes: faces—mostly tired and drawn—stared either at the advertising cards or cast furtive glances at the graffiti that had been inscribed on the white enamel ceiling with Chinagraph. Bodies swayed when the train roared round a curve, then went over to one side when it screeched to a halt at each station. Doors sighed, then slid opened. A guard shouted something that sounded like: "Minde-daws," which was a signal for another drawn out sigh, followed by a strange vibrating rattling noise.

The train was again swallowed by the pipe-infested tunnel and Matthew began to take a real interest in his fellow passengers, as indeed had been his practice for many years, having long ago come to the conclusion that a cross-section of the entire population of London must be packed into a medium-filled tube train compartment.

He counted sixty-nine bodies and estimated that at least forty were the rightful property of office workers. A man in blue overalls with a bulging leather bag was most certainly a plumber and a plump middle-aged woman with swollen ankles most likely worked in a store. One man who was strap-hanging by the door had a dead white face and an almost completely bald head and defied definition. He stared at Matthew with unblinking eyes, then bared discoloured teeth with a mirthless grin. Matthew switched his gaze to the ceiling, but when he looked down again the man had gone. There was not the slightest sign of anyone even remotely like him anywhere.

This incident was a lesson well worth remembering. Never take anyone for granted—the dead—the misplaced— could well be moving from *here* to *there*, even as passengers are continually boarding and leaving a train.

Then he was out on the platform at Green Park Station, part of a shuffling crowd that made its way to the already packed escalators. The majority took up positions on the right, but an energetic few—Matthew was among them— began to mount the steps on the left, thus ensuring they were borne up to the light of day in the shortest possible time.

Matthew looked up and felt his heart give one sickening thud. The Doppelgänger was at the very top looking down.

There could be no doubt. His body—minus a few pounds—dressed in a cheap, shabby suit, was staring down at him with something akin to terror expressed in every line of its face. Once the initial shock had been absorbed, Matthew experienced a feeling of intense relief. Now he would be able to dispel his nightmare in the harsh light of reality. A close encounter; face to face, hear its voice, know why, explain how—pinpoint the exact location of where. He began to run up the moving stairs.

The Doppelgänger turned and disappeared into the crowd which was pouring off the escalator. Gasping like a stranded fish Matthew reached the upper region just in time to see his quarry making for the steps leading to Piccadilly. There were a lot of moving bodies between him and the steps, each one seemingly determined to retard his progress and a full three minutes had passed before he came up to street level.

He looked anxiously from left to right, then—with what relief—he saw the by now familiar figure flanked by a tall man on one side and a short dumpy woman on the other, entering the colonnaded length of pavement which ran along the entire frontage of the Ritz Hotel. Matthew ran. To make better progress he left the pavement and sprinted along the gutter, thus earning a colourful rebuke from a taxi driver who was forced to swerve out into the main stream of traffic. Heads were turned; someone called out: "Where's the fire?" as the young man raced towards what he hoped would be release from fear and doubt.

When he reached St. James's Street the tall man and the dumpy woman were standing on the kerb edge, waiting for the lights to change, before crossing the road. The short lady glared when he peered over her shoulder, then enquired in a breathless voice:

"The young man—who was walking between you and this gentleman—did you see where he went?"

The tall man provided an answer. "There never has been anyone between my wife and myself. I've been holding her arm since we came up from the station."

"But I saw him," Matthew insisted. "I saw him."

The traffic lights changed to green and the ill-assorted couple promptly crossed the road with heads held high and eyes staring resolutely to their front. Matthew allowed the crowd to flow round and past him, knowing there was little point in searching further, for if the creature had been anything more than a reflection cast out by his brain, it could have either entered a hotel or boarded one of the slow moving buses. If he were not to go completely mad, he must try to accept the unusual and give it the appearance of normality.

He hailed a taxi and was driven to his London office.

When Matthew arrived home that night he was greeted by a very anxious Jennie, who clung to him as though he had just returned from a journey of a thousand miles.

"Have you been all right?" she asked.

"Fine," he said, then kissed her hard upon the lips. "I've been just fine. I said I would be. Don't worry."

It seemed as if she couldn't bear to lose contact with him and walked with an arm around his waist. "Sorry, darling, but we've got a visitor. I mean, she just turned up."

"Who?"

"Mrs. Fortescue. Just say hallo to her, then look at your watch."

"Oh Lord!"

"But it will be good for you to talk nicely to her. Strengthen your soul."

Mrs. Fortescue was seated in Matthew's favourite chair and extended a plump moist hand when he approached. He took it, bowed over it, then restored it to its owner. In a way he was not all that sorry to find the woman there. She would act as a source of minor annoyance and stop him thinking of more pressing concerns. Jennie poured tea from a silver pot into a blue cup, added milk and two lumps of sugar, before bringing the end result over to her husband.

"Mrs. Fortescue—"

"Lydia—please."

"Oh! I forgot. Lydia was saying just before you came in, that she thinks you should write an historical novel. One with a heroine that is captured by pirates and sold to a black magician and falls in love with a wandering minstrel. That's right, isn't it—eh—Lydia?"

Mrs. Fortescue nodded so violently, her hair—about which Matthew entertained grave suspicions—jerked back and forth like a woollen cosy on an agitated teapot. "That's so right, dear, it's all in my head, but I just haven't the ability to put it down on paper."

"I'm sure you've never tried," Matthew suggested with a tired smile.

"That's so true, but I have written some extraordinary fine letters. Everyone says so. But I do so love the past. Those days when men were men and women were—"

"Glad of it," Matthew prompted and was only saved from a poke in the ribs by the distance that separated him and his self-invited guest.

"You naughty man! But don't you just hunger for those days when castles were besieged and the defenders poured boiling oil on the attackers?"

"There are times when I think that such a practice had much to commend it."

"And Protestants or Catholics of the Spanish Inquisition or someone, used to rack priests and flatten thumbs with screw things and burn people at stakes and—oh yes—there was that lovely Sir Walter Raleigh making a long speech before having his head chopped off. I mean to say, life is so tame these days."

"We've certainly gone to the dogs," Matthew agreed.

"And don't you think that lovely Henry VIII was simply wonderful? All those wives! And they all went to the block with such dignity."

"Only two. Anne Boleyn and Catherine Howard."

Mrs. Fortescue widened her eyes with surprise and gave the impression that she had not only been misinformed, but cheated out of four heads into the bargain.

"Really! I could have sworn that Mary Queen of Scots lost her head as well."

"She did. But some fifty years later."

Conversation was hard to come by after that, until Jennie, who was trying with some success to subdue a giggling fit, said:

"You have a daughter, I understand, eh—Lydia. It must be such a comfort to have children."

The lady frowned and sat upright before delivering a considered reply. "Daughters can be so sweet in the cradle, but so disappointing at the table. Such has been my experience. Susan was so cuddly when she was five—now at twenty-five—is a positive monster. I can think of no better word. A card at Christmas, a peck on my cheek at my birthday party—and three two-minute telephone calls since June." The slightly bovine eyes looked at Matthew sternly. "Do you realise I haven't seen or spoken to my daughter for six months?"

"Alas, I only read *The Times*."

Mrs. Fortescue's face had now assumed a deep red colour, as though she were either in constant and intimate contact with a whisky bottle or afflicted by high-blood pressure. Her voice was suddenly deeper and occasionally dispensed with the need for aspirates.

"It's no laughing matter. She's me daughter all said and done and it's not like 'er to disappear into the blue without so as 'ow's yer father. She must have said where she was going."

Matthew looked helplessly round for Jennie, deciding it was about time she rescued him from this mad woman, but she had disappeared, so he was obliged to fend for himself. He scowled at the lady and wondered why she suddenly looked so shabby. For some reason he shivered.

"You forget, madam, I haven't the pleasure of your daughter's acquaintance. But I'm sure you'll hear from her soon. Daughters like income-tax always return."

Mrs. Fortescue pointed a fat forefinger at him and raised her voice until it had much in common with that of a bad-tempered cat.

"Don't come the old acid with me. You were never my idea of a 'usband for my Jennie and if she's given you the elbow, well and good, but I want to know where she's gone. Now, what 'ave you done with 'er?"

"Matthew," Jennie was back, seated a little to his left, her face expressing anxiety. "What's wrong, darling? You look so strange."

Matthew blinked and stared at Mrs. Fortescue with wide-eyed horror. The lady was again fashionably, if rather over dressed; her large face pale, but expertly made-up, her bovine eyes lit by a gleam of gentle enquiry. When she spoke her voice had little in common with the ranting deep tones of a few minutes before.

"I was explaining that I hadn't seen my daughter since Easter, when you—well—looked strange. Dear me, I do hope you're not unwell."

Matthew ran a moist hand over his forehead and tried to dismiss a feeling that he was on his way down a steep hill and his descent was getting out of control.

"I'm sorry, I thought . . . You really must excuse me, but I do rather feel off colour."

Instantly Jennie was by his side, but he avoided her outstretched hand. He needed solitude where there would be no unanswerable questions posed by a lilting voice and a deep sleep that would blot out memory of all events that might have taken place in the past or the yet to be born future.

"Please," he conjured up a smile, "I'll be all right. You stay here with Mrs. Fortescue and try to atone for my rudeness." He turned to the lady who favoured him with a sympathetic smile. "It was so nice to see you again—forgive me."

Her smile became a simper. "I do understand. You talented people are so highly strung."

In fact solitude brought no relief and two pills little hope of sleep. Lying fully dressed on the bed Matthew had no power to stop his brain from raising the wraiths of memory; the Doppelgänger's terror-stricken face looking down at him from the top of the escalator and the recent transformation of Mrs. Fortescue.

If only these were the ingredients of a plot for a novel, what fun he would have finding a solution.

He closed his eyes and actually smiled. How would he set about it? To start the Doppelgänger would be cast as a miserable failure with a nagging wife and a real battle-axe of a mother-in-law. Good. Now rough in the background. Simple. Poor devil with literary aspirations, employed in a dead-end job (much like himself in the early years), who never gets the breaks, anxiety rides on his shoulders, perpetually tired, possibly impotent which would explain the wife's frustrated bitterness.

How about the wife? Imagine Jennie after being married for seven years to such a man. Not a cosseted, well-loved happy woman, but a poor miserable, deprived, ill-dressed creature, who is probably forced to go out to work to maintain a reasonable standard of living. What would she be like now? A nagging harridan? A shrieking, fault-finding, unkempt, scraggy termagant? Good God, she'd probably hit the bottle!

Mother-in-law? Have to be careful here or you'll finish up with a Dickensian monster. But most certainly an unhappy, overweight my-daughter-could-have-done-much-better-for-herself old bitch. A suitable parent for a perpetually dissatisfied wife to go home to—only of course she would always come back. A fairly basic situation that might well develop into something very nasty. Such as— and Matthew nodded gently—the possibility of the worm turning.

One day coming home and losing all control . . . Dear God why have I been gifted with such an imagination? . . . striking that yapping mouth, fastening fingers round that scrawny throat until she can't nag anymore . . . no more insults . . . then take her down the stairs . . . dig up the cellar . . . and hide . . . hide . . . and keep that old cow out . . . but above all escape . . . escape . . . into the world where one is rich and fabulously famous, with a beautiful loving wife who exists only to further one's happiness, and live there happily for evermore.

Luke began to cry softly as the luxuriously appointed bedroom shimmered and gradually changed into a place with filthy distempered walls, battered chest of drawers, scratched walnut wardrobe, faded linoleum, and unsavoury bed. The room was saturated with the stench of dead hope.

Luke got up, slid his feet into a pair of slippers and shuffled towards the door. Out on the landing he paused and looked down over the banisters. The house was cold and empty; a mausoleum where loneliness and despair kept watch over illegal dead. He slowly descended the stairs and came down into the hall where a naked floor led into an evil smelling kitchen on one side and an almost empty lounge on the other. A little further on was a flight of steps that gave access to the cellar.

Luke sank to his knees, covered his eyes with shaking hands and screamed out the eternal prayer.

"Let me not face reality . . . I don't want reality. Freeze

time here so that I can spend forever there. Please . . .
please remove from me the curse of *now*."

Gradually the house became warmer, the floor beneath
his knees softer and presently a soft lilting voice said:

"Matthew, what *are* you doing down there? Honestly
you are the limit! I thought you were upstairs resting.
Thank goodness Mrs. Fortescue has gone. What she would
have said had she seen you kneeling on the floor I cannot
imagine."

Matthew got up and slid his arm round Jennie's slim
waist. The house was warm and comfortably furnished,
outside was a world that revered Matthew Bayswater and
all his works; by his side was a lovely adoring wife. He
was a happy successful man.

"Come, darling," he said, "come and help me do that
which I cannot do by myself."

Together they mounted the stairs.

AUTHOR'S NOTE

"DOPPELGÄNGER" MUST BE ONE OF MY BETTER IDEAS,
*particularly as it was originally intended to be in the for-
mat of a novel. But wisely I came to the conclusion that
the story line just would not run to a seventy-plus-thousand
word tale and cut it down to its present length. This meant
erasing a child—the young daughter of Jennie and Matthew, a horrible cliché-mouthing little monster, a grotesque caricature of Shirley Temple. I still regret her
untimely demise.*

*Working as is my wont—sitting behind a typewriter (no
word processor for me)—a tiny spark of an idea came into
being. A young man called Matthew has an alter ego called
Luke. One is rich and famous, the other poor and miserable. Somewhere along the line they change over. Yes.
Well, many were the side roads I wandered into before
finding the main high road which led to the final story.*

But that tiny spark did flare up into a respectable flame and I can only wish it had spread and started a prairie fire.

I like to think that Matthew Bayswater is the average man who has achieved enormous success and can't really believe it will last. Or put it another way—having climbed to the top of many ladders—he can't understand why he hasn't slid down the back of at least one snake. Nothing succeeds like success, nothing fails like failure. Speaking for myself I have never been a Matthew—pray God I will never become a Luke.

Of course I rather enjoyed developing the characters, trying to imagine how they would react under bizarre circumstances, then pray for another idea. The essential twist in the tail.

I think—I hope—everyone will agree my prayer was answered.

—R. Chetwynd-Hayes

THE MASTER OF THE HOUNDS
Algis Budrys

THE WHITE SAND ROAD LED OFF THE STATE HIGHWAY through the sparse pines. There were no tire tracks in the road, but, as Malcolm turned the car onto it, he noticed the footprints of dogs, or perhaps of only one dog, running along the middle of the road toward the combined general store and gas station at the intersection.

"Well, it's far enough away from everything, all right," Virginia said. She was lean and had dusty black hair. Her face was long, with high cheekbones. They had married ten years ago, when she had been girlish and very slightly plump.

"Yes," Malcolm said. Just days ago, when he'd been turned down for a Guggenheim Fellowship that he'd expected to get, he had quit his job at the agency and made plans to spend the summer, somewhere as cheap as possible, working out with himself whether he was really an artist or just had a certain commercial talent. Now they were here.

He urged the car up the road, following a line of infrequent and weathered utility poles that carried a single strand of power line. The real estate agent already had told them there were no telephones. Malcolm had taken that to be a positive feature, but somehow he did not like the looks of that one thin wire sagging from pole to pole. The wheels of the car sank in deeply on either side of the dog prints, which he followed like a row of bread crumbs through a forest.

Several hundred yards farther along, they came to a sign at the top of a hill:

MARINE VIEW SHORES! NEW JERSEY'S NEWEST, FASTEST GROWING RESIDENTIAL COMMUNITY. WEL- COME HOME! FROM $9,990. NO DN PYT FOR VETS.

Below them was a wedge of land—perhaps ten acres altogether that pushed out into Lower New York Bay. The road became a gullied, yellow gravel street, pointing straight toward the water and ending in three concrete posts, one of which had fallen and left a gap wide enough for a car to blunder through. Beyond that was a low drop-off where the bay ran northward to New York City and, in the other direction, toward the open Atlantic.

On either side of the roughed-out street, the bulldozed land was overgrown with scrub oak and sumac. Along the street were rows of roughly rectangular pits—some with half-finished foundation walls in them—piles of excavated clay, and lesser quantities of sand, sparsely weed-grown and washed into ravaged mounds like Dakota Territory. Here and there were houses with half-completed frames, now silvered and warped.

There were only two exceptions to the general vista. At the end of the street, two identically designed, finished houses faced each other. One looked shabby. The lot around it was free of scrub, but weedy and unsodded. Across the street from it stood a house in excellent repair. Painted a charcoal gray and roofed with dark asphalt shin- gles, it sat in the center of a meticulously green and level lawn, which was in turn surrounded by a wire fence approximately four feet tall and splendid with fresh aluminum paint. False shutters, painted stark white, flanked high, narrow windows along the side Malcolm could see. In front of the house, a line of whitewashed stones the size of men's heads served as curbing. There wasn't a thing about the house and its surroundings that couldn't have been achieved with a straight string, a handsaw, and a three-inch brush. Malcolm saw a chance to cheer things up. "There now, Marthy!" he said to Virginia. "I've led you safe and sound through the howlin' forest to a snug home in the shadder of Fort Defiance."

"It's orderly," Virginia said. "I'll bet it's no joke, keeping up a place like that out here."

As Malcolm was parking the car parallel to where the curb would have been in front of their house, a pair of handsome young Doberman pinschers came out from behind the gray house across the street and stood together on the lawn with their noses just short of the fence, looking out. They did not bark. There was no movement at the front window, and no one came out into the yard. The dogs simply stood there, watching, as Malcolm walked over the clay to his door.

The house was furnished—that is to say, there were chairs in the living room, although there was no couch, and a chromium-and-plastic dinette set in the area off the kitchen. Though one of the bedrooms was completely empty, there was a bureau and a bed in the other. Malcolm walked through the house quickly and went back out to the car to get the luggage and groceries. Nodding toward the dogs, he said to Virginia, "Well! The latest thing in iron deer." He felt he had to say something light, because Virginia was staring across the street.

He knew perfectly well, as most people do and he assumed Virginia did, that Doberman pinschers are nervous, untrustworthy, and vicious. At the same time, he and his wife did have to spend the whole summer here. He could guess how much luck they'd have trying to get their money back from the agent now.

"They look streamlined like that because their ears and tails are trimmed when they're puppies," Virginia said. She picked up a bag of groceries and carried it into the house.

When Malcolm had finished unloading the car, he slammed the trunk lid shut. Although they hadn't moved until then, the Dobermans seemed to regard this as a sign. They turned smoothly, the arc of one inside the arc of the other, and keeping formation, trotted out of sight behind the gray house.

Malcolm helped Virginia put things away in the closets and in the lone bedroom bureau. There was enough to do to keep both of them busy for several hours, and it was dusk when Malcolm happened to look out through the living-room window. After he had glanced that way, he stopped.

Across the street, floodlights had come on at the four corners of the gray house. They poured illumination downward in cones that lighted the entire yard. A crippled man was walking just inside the fence, his legs stiff and his body bent forward from the waist, as he gripped the projecting handles of two crutch-canes that supported his weight at the elbows. As Malcolm watched, the man took a precise square turn at the corner of the fence and began walking along the front of his property. Looking straight ahead, he moved regularly and purposefully, his shadow thrown out through the fence behind the composite shadow of the two dogs walking immediately ahead of him. None of them was looking in Malcolm's direction. He watched as the man made another turn, followed the fence toward the back of his property, and disappeared behind the house.

Later Virginia served cold cuts in the little dining alcove. Putting the house in order seemed to have had a good effect on her morale.

"Listen, I think we're going to be all right here, don't you?" Malcolm said.

"Look," she said reasonably, "any place you can get straightened out is fine with me."

This wasn't quite the answer he wanted. He had been sure in New York that the summer would do it—that in four months a man would come to *some* decision. He had visualized a house for them by the ocean, in a town with a library and a movie and other diversions. It had been a shock to discover how expensive summer rentals were and how far in advance you had to book them. When the last agent they saw described this place to them and told them how low the rent was, Malcolm had jumped at it immediately. But so had Virginia, even though there wasn't anything to do for distraction. In fact, she had made a point of asking the agent again about the location of the house, and the agent, a fat, gray man with ashes on his shirt, had said earnestly, "Mrs. Lawrence, if you're looking for a place where nobody will bother your husband from working, I can't think of anything better." Virginia had nodded decisively.

It had bothered her, his quitting the agency; he could understand that. Still, he wanted her to be happy, because he expected to be surer of what he wanted to do by the end of the summer. She was looking at him steadily now. He cast about for something to offer her that would interest her and change the mood between them. Then he remembered the scene he had witnessed earlier that evening. He told her about the man and his dogs, and this did raise her eyebrows.

"Do you remember the real estate agent telling us anything about him?" she asked. "I don't."

Malcolm, searching through his memory, did recall that the agent had mentioned a custodian they could call on if there were any problems. At the time he had let it pass, because he couldn't imagine either agent or custodian really caring. Now he realized how dependent he and Virginia were out here if it came to things like broken plumbing or bad wiring, and the custodian's importance altered accordingly. "I guess he's the caretaker," he said.

"Oh."

"It makes sense—all this property has got to be worth something. If they didn't have someone here, people would just carry stuff away or come and camp or something."

"I suppose they would. I guess the owners let him live here rent free, and with those dogs he must do a good job."

"He'll get to keep it for a while, too," Malcolm said. "Whoever started to build here was a good ten years ahead of himself. I can't see anybody buying into these places until things have gotten completely jammed up closer to New York."

"So, he's holding the fort," Virginia said, leaning casually over the table to put a dish down before him. She glanced over his shoulder toward the living room window, widened her eyes, and automatically touched the neckline of her housecoat, and then snorted at herself.

"Look, he can't possibly see in here," Malcolm said. "The living room, yes, but to look in here he'd have to be standing in the far corner of his yard. And he's back inside his house." He turned his head to look, and it was indeed true, except that one of the dogs was standing at that corner looking toward their house, eyes glittering. Then its head seemed to melt into a new shape, and it was looking down the road. It pivoted, moved a few steps away from the fence, turned, soared, landed in the street, and set off. Then, a moment later, it came back down the street running side by side with its companion, whose jaws were lightly pressed together around the rolled-over neck of a small paper bag. The dogs trotted together companionably and briskly, their flanks rubbing against one another, and when they were a few steps from the fence they leaped over it in unison and continued across the lawn until they were out of Malcolm's range of vision.

"For heaven's sake! He lives all alone with those dogs!" Virginia said.

Malcolm turned quickly back to her. "How do you come to think that?"

"Well, it's pretty plain. You saw what they were doing out there just now. They're his servants. He can't get around himself, so they run errands for him. If he had a wife, she would do it."

"You learned all that already?"

"Did you notice how happy they were?" Virginia asked. "There was no need for that other dog to go meet its friend. But it wanted to. They can't be anything but happy." Then she looked at Malcolm, and he saw the old, studying reserve coming back into her eyes.

"For Pete's sake! They're only dogs—what do they know about anything?" Malcolm said.

"They know about happiness," Virginia said. "They know what they do in life."

Malcolm lay awake for a long time that night. He started by thinking about how good the summer was going to be, living here and working, and then he thought about the agency and about why he didn't seem to have the kind of shrewd, limited intuition that let a man do advertising work easily. At about four in the morning he wondered if perhaps he wasn't frightened, and had been frightened for a long time. None of this kind of thinking was new to him, and he knew that it would take him until late afternoon the following day to reach the point where he was feeling pretty good about himself.

When Virginia tried to wake him early the next morning he asked her to please leave him alone. At two in the afternoon, she brought him a cup of coffee and shook his shoulder. After a while, he walked out to the kitchen in his pajama pants and found that she had scrambled up some eggs for the two of them.

"What are your plans for the day?" Virginia said when he had finished eating.

He looked up. "Why?"

"Well, while you were sleeping, I put all your art things in the front bedroom. I think it'll make a good studio. With all your gear in there now, you can be pretty well set up by this evening."

At times she was so abrupt that she shocked him. It upset him that she might have been thinking that he wasn't planning to do anything at all today. "Look," he said, "you know I like to get the feel of a new thing."

"I know that. I didn't set anything up in there. I'm no artist. I just moved it all in."

When Malcolm had sat for a while without speaking, Virginia cleared away their plates and cups and went into the bedroom. She came out wearing a dress, and she had combed her hair and put on lipstick. "Well, you do what you want to," she said. "I'm going to go across the street and introduce myself."

A flash of irritability hit him, but then he said, "If you'll wait a minute, I'll get dressed and go with you. We might as well both meet him."

He got up and went back to the bedroom for a T-shirt and blue jeans and a pair of loafers. He could feel himself beginning to react to pressure. Pressure always made him bind up; it looked to him as if Virginia had already shot the day for him.

They were standing at the fence, on the narrow strip of lawn between it and the row of whitewashed stones, and nothing was happening. Malcolm saw that although there was a gate in the fence, there was no break in the little grass border opposite it. And there was no front walk. The lawn was lush and all one piece, as if the house had been lowered onto it by helicopter. He began to look closely at the ground just inside the fence, and when he saw the regular pockmarks of the man's crutches, he was comforted.

"Do you see any kind of bell or anything?" Virginia asked.

"No."

"You'd think the dogs would bark."

"I'd just as soon they didn't."

"Will you look?" she said, fingering the gate latch. "The paint's hardly scuffed. I'll bet he hasn't been out of his yard all summer." Her touch rattled the gate lightly, and at that the two dogs came out from behind the house. One of them stopped, turned, and went back. The other dog came and stood by the fence, close enough for them to hear its breathing, and watched them with its head cocked alertly.

The front door of the house opened. At the doorway there was a wink of metal crutches, and then the man came out and stood on his front steps. When he had satisfied himself as to who they were, he nodded, smiled, and came toward them. The other dog walked beside him. Malcolm noticed that the dog at the fence did not distract himself by looking back at his master.

The man moved swiftly, crossing the ground with nimble swings of his body. His trouble seemed to be not in the spine, but in the legs themselves, for he was trying to help himself along with them. It could not be called walking, but it could not be called total helplessness either.

Although the man seemed to be in his late fifties, he had not gone to seed any more than his property had. He was wiry and clean-boned, and the skin on his face was tough and tanned. Around his small blue eyes and at the corners of his thin lips were many fine, deep-etched wrinkles. His yellowish white hair was brushed straight back from his temples in the classic British military manner. And he even had a slight mustache. He was wearing a tweed jacket with leather patches at the elbows, which seemed a little warm for this kind of day, and a light flannel pale gray shirt with a pale-blue bow tie. He stopped at the fence, rested his elbows on the crutches, and held out a firm hand with short nails the color of old bones.

"How do you do," he said pleasantly, his manner polished and well-bred. "I have been looking forward to meeting my new neighbors. I am Colonel Ritchey." The dogs stood motionless, one to each side of him, their sharp black faces pointing outward.

"How do you do," Virginia said. "We are Malcolm and Virginia Lawrence."

"I'm very happy to meet you," Colonel Ritchey said.

"I was prepared to believe Cortelyou would fail to provide anyone this season."

Virginia was smiling. "What beautiful dogs," she said. "I was watching them last night."

"Yes. Their names are Max and Moritz. I'm very proud of them."

As they prattled on, exchanging pleasantries, Malcolm wondered why the Colonel had referred to Cortelyou, the real estate agent, as a provider. There was something familiar, too, about the colonel.

Virginia said, "You're the famous Colonel Ritchey."

Indeed he was, Malcolm now realized, remembering the big magazine series that had appeared with the release of the movie several years before.

Colonel Ritchey smiled with no trace of embarrassment. "I am the famous Colonel Ritchey, but you'll notice I certainly don't look much like that charming fellow in the motion picture."

"What in hell are you doing *here*?" Malcolm asked.

Ritchey turned his attention to him. "One has to live somewhere, you know."

Virginia said immediately, "I was watching the dogs last night, and they seemed to do very well for you. I imagine it's pleasant having them to rely on."

"Yes, it is, indeed. They're quite good to me, Max and Moritz. But it is much better with people here now. I had begun to be quite disappointed in Cortelyou."

Malcolm began to wonder whether the agent would have had the brass to call Ritchey a custodian if the colonel had been within earshot.

"Come in, please," the colonel was saying. The gate latch resisted him momentarily, but he rapped it sharply with the heel of one palm and then lifted it. "Don't be concerned about Max and Moritz—they never do anything they're not told."

"Oh, I'm not the least bit worried about them," Virginia said.

"Ah, to some extent you should have been," the colonel said. "Dobermans are not to be casually trusted, you know. It takes many months before one can be at all confident in dealing with them."

"But you trained them yourself, didn't you?" Virginia said.

"Yes, I did," Colonel Ritchey said, with a pleased smile. "From imported pups." The voice in which he now spoke to the dogs was forceful, but as calm as his manner had been to Virginia. "Kennel," he said, and Max and Moritz stopped looking at Malcolm and Virginia and smoothly turned away.

The colonel's living room, which was as neat as a sample, contained beautifully cared for, somewhat old-fashioned furniture. The couch, with its needlepoint upholstery and carved framing, was the sort of thing Malcolm would have expected in a lady's living room. Angling out from one wall was a Morris chair, placed so that a man might relax and gaze across the street or, with a turn of his head, rest his eyes on the distant lights of New York. Oil paintings in heavy gilded frames depicted landscapes, great eye-stretching vistas of rolling, open country. The furniture in the room seemed sparse to Malcolm until it occurred to him that the colonel needed extra clearance to get around in and had no particular need to keep additional chairs for visitors.

"Please do sit down," the colonel said. "I shall fetch some tea to refresh us."

When he had left the room, Virginia said, "Of all people! Neighborly, too."

Malcolm nodded. "Charming," he said.

The colonel entered holding a silver tray perfectly steadily, its edges grasped between his thumbs and forefingers, his other fingers curled around each of the projecting black-rubber handgrips of his crutches. He brought tea on the tray and, of all things, homemade cookies. "I must apologize for the tea service," he said, "but it seems to be the only one I have."

When the colonel offered the tray, Malcolm saw that the

utensils were made of the common sort of sheet metal used to manufacture food cans. Looking down now into his cup, he saw it had been enameled over its original tinplate, and he realized that the whole thing had been made literally from a tin can. The teapot—handle, spout, vented lid, and all—was the same. "Be damned—you made this for yourself at the prison camp, didn't you?"

"As a matter of fact, I did, yes. I was really quite proud of my handiwork at the time, and it still serves. Somehow, living as I do, I've never brought myself to replace it. It's amazing, the fuddy-duddy skills one needs in a camp and how important they become to one. I find myself repainting these poor objects periodically and still taking as much smug pleasure in it as I did when that attitude was quite necessary. One is allowed to do these things in my position, you know. But I do hope my *ersatz* Spode isn't uncomfortably hot in your fingers."

Virginia smiled. "Well, of course, it's trying to be." Malcolm was amazed. He hadn't thought Virginia still remembered how to act so coquettish. She hadn't grown apart from the girl who'd always attracted a lot of attention at other people's gallery openings; she had simply put that part of herself away somewhere else.

Colonel Ritchey's blue eyes were twinkling in response. He turned to Malcolm. "I must say, it will be delightful to share this summer with someone as charming as Mrs. Lawrence."

"Yes," Malcolm said, preoccupied now with the cup, which was distressing his fingers with both heat and sharp edges. "At least, I've always been well satisfied with her," he added.

"I've been noticing the inscription here," Virginia said quickly, indicating the meticulous freehand engraving on the tea tray. She read out loud, " 'To Colonel David N. Ritchey, R.M.E., from his fellow officers at *Oflag* XXXI*b*, on the occasion of their liberation, May 14, 1945. Had he not been there to lead them, many would not have been present to share of this heartfelt token.' " Virginia's eyes shone, as she looked up at the colonel. "They must all have been very fond of you."

"Not all," the colonel said, with a slight smile. "I was senior officer over a very mixed bag. Mostly younger officers gathered from every conceivable branch. No followers at all—just budding leaders, all personally responsible for having surrendered once already, some apathetic, others desperate. Some useful, some not. It was my job to weld them into a disciplined, responsive body, to choose whom we must keep safe and who was best suited to keeping the Jerries on the jump. And we were in, of course, from the time of Dunkirk to the last days of the war, with the strategic situation in the camp constantly changing in various ways. All most of them understood was tactics—when they understood at all."

The colonel grimaced briefly, then smiled again. "The tray was presented by the survivors, of course. They'd had a tame Jerry pinch it out of the commandant's sideboard a few days earlier, in plenty of time to get the inscription on. But even the inscription hints that not all survived."

"It wasn't really like the movie, was it?" Virginia said.

"No, and yet—" Ritchey shrugged, as if remembering a time when he had accommodated someone on a matter of small importance. "That was a question of dramatic values, you must realize, and the need to tell an interesting and exciting story in terms recognizable to a civilian audience. Many of the incidents in the motion picture are literally true—they simply didn't happen in the context shown. The Christmas tunnel was quite real, obviously. I did promise the men I'd get at least one of them home for Christmas if they'd pitch in and dig it. But it wasn't a serious promise, and they knew it wasn't. Unlike the motion picture actor, I was not being fervent; I was being ironic.

"It was late in the war. An intelligent man's natural desire would be to avoid risk and wait for liberation. A great many of them felt exactly that way. In fact, many of them had turned civilian in their own minds and were talking about their careers outside, their families—all that sort of thing. So by couching in sarcasm trite words about Christmas tunnels, I was reminding them what and where they still were. The tactic worked quite well. Through devices of that sort, I was able to keep them from going to seed and coming out no use to anyone.'' The colonel's expression grew absent. ''Some of them called me 'The Shrew,' '' he muttered. ''*That* was in the movie, too, but they were all shown smiling when they said it.''

''But it was your duty to hold them all together any way you could,'' Virginia said encouragingly.

Ritchey's face twisted into a spasm of tension so fierce that there might have been strychnine in his tea. But it was gone at once. ''Oh, yes, yes, I held them together. But the expenditure of energy was enormous. And demeaning. It ought not to have made any difference that we were cut off from higher authority. If we had all still been home, there was not a man among the prisoners who would have dared not jump to my simplest command. But in the camp they could shilly-shally and evade; they could settle down into little private ambitions. People will do that. People will not hold true to common purposes unless they are shown discipline.'' The colonel's uncompromising glance went from Virginia to Malcolm. ''It's no good telling people what they ought to do. The only surety is in being in a position to tell people what they *must* do.''

''Get some armed guards to back you up. That the idea, Colonel? Get permission from the Germans to set up your own machine-gun towers inside the camp?'' Malcolm liked working things out to the point of absurdity.

The colonel appraised him imperturbably. ''I was never quite that much my own man in Germany. But there is a little story I must tell you. It's not altogether off the point.'' He settled back, at ease once again.

''You may have been curious about Max and Moritz. The Germans, as you know, have always been fond of training dogs to perform all sorts of entertaining and useful things. During the war the Jerries were very much given to using Dobermans for auxiliary guard duty at the various prisoner-of-war camps. In action, Mr. Lawrence, or simply in view, a trained dog is far more terrifying than any soldier with a machine pistol. It takes an animal to stop a man without hesitation, no matter if the man is cursing or praying.

"Guard dogs at each camp were under the charge of a man called the *Hundführer*—the master of the hounds, if you will—whose function, after establishing himself with the dogs as their master and director, was to follow a few simple rules and to take the dogs to wherever they were needed. The dogs had been taught certain patrol routines. It was necessary only for the *Hundführer* to give simple commands such as 'Search' or 'Arrest,' and the dogs would know what to do. Once we had seen them do it, they were very much on our minds, I assure you.

"A Doberman, you see, has no conscience, being a dog. And a trained Doberman has no discretion. From the time he is a puppy, he is bent to whatever purpose has been preordained for him. And the lessons are painful—and autocratic. Once an order has been given, it must be enforced at all costs, for the dog must learn that all orders are to be obeyed unquestioningly. That being true, the dog must also learn immediately and irrevocably that only the orders from one particular individual are valid. Once a Doberman has been trained, there is no way to retrain it. When the American soldiers were seen coming, the Germans in the machine-gun towers threw down their weapons and tried to flee, but the dogs had to be shot. I watched from the hospital window, and I shall never forget how they continued to leap at the kennel fencing until the last one was dead. Their *Hundführer* had run away. . . . "

Malcolm found that his attention was wandering, but Virginia asked, as if on cue, "How did you get into the hospital—was that the Christmas tunnel accident?"

"Yes," the colonel said to Virginia, gentleman to lady. "The sole purpose of the tunnel was, as I said, to give the men a focus of attention. The war was near enough its

end. It would have been foolhardy to risk actual escape
attempts. But we did the thing up brown, of course. We
had a concealed shaft, a tunnel lined with bed slats, a
trolley for getting to and from the tunnel entrance, fat
lamps made from shoe-blacking tins filled with marga-
rine—all the normal appurtenances. The Germans at that
stage were quite experienced in ferreting out this sort of
operation, and the only reasonable assurance of continued
progress was to work deeply and swiftly. Tunneling is always a calculated risk—the accounts of that sort of operation are biased in favor of the successes, of course.

"At any rate, by the end of November, some of the men
were audibly thinking it was my turn to pitch in a bit, so
one night I went down and began working. The shoring
was as good as it ever was, and the conditions weren't any
worse than normal. The air was breathable, and as long
as one worked—ah—unclothed, and brushed down immediately on leaving the tunnel, the sand was not particularly damaging to one's skin. Clothing creates chafes in
those circumstances. Sand burns coming to light at medical inspections were one of the surest signs that such an
operation was under way.

"However that may be, I had been down there for about
an hour and a half, and was about to start inching my way
back up the tunnel, feetfirst on the trolley like some Freud-
ian symbol, when there was a fall of the tunnel roof that
buried my entire chest. It did not cover my face, which
was fortunate, and I clearly remember my first thought was
that now none of the men would be able to feel the senior
officer hadn't shared their physical tribulations. I discovered, at once, that the business of clearing the sand that
had fallen was going to be extremely awkard. First, I
had to scoop some extra clearance from the roof over my
face. Handfuls of sand began falling directly on me, and
all I could do about that was to thrash my head back and
forth. I was becoming distinctly exasperated at that when
the fat lamp attached to the shoring loosened from its fas-
tenings and spilled across my thighs. The hot fat was quite

painful. What made it rather worse was that the string wick was not extinguished by the fall, and accordingly, the entire lower part of my body between navel and knees, having been saturated with volatile fat . . . ." The colonel grimaced in embarrassment.

"Well, I was immediately in a very bad way, for there was nothing I could do about the fire until I had dug my way past the sand on my chest. In due course, I did indeed free myself and was able to push my way backward up the tunnel after extinguishing the flames. The men at the shaft head had seen no reason to become alarmed—tunnels always smell rather high and sooty, as you can imagine. But they did send a man down when I got near the entrance shaft and made myself heard.

"Of course, there was nothing to do but tell the Jerries, since we had no facilities whatever for concealing my condition or treating it. They put me in the camp hospital, and there I stayed until the end of the war with plenty of time to lie about and think my thoughts. I was even able to continue exercising some control over my men. I shouldn't be a bit surprised if that hadn't been in the commandant's mind all along. I think he had come to depend on my presence to moderate the behavior of the men.

"That is really almost the end of the story. We were liberated by the American Army, and the men were sent home. I stayed in military hospitals until I was well enough to travel home, and there I dwelt in hotels and played the retired, invalided officer. After that journalist's book was published and the dramatic rights were sold, I was called to Hollywood to be the technical adviser for the movie. I was rather grateful to accept the employment, frankly—an officer's pension is not particularly munificent—and what with selectively lending my name and services to various organizations while my name was still before the public, I was able to accumulate a sufficient nest egg.

"Of course, I cannot go back to England, where the Inland Revenue would relieve me of most of it, but, having established a relationship with Mr. Cortelyou and acquired and trained Max and Moritz, I am content. A man must make his way as best he can and do whatever is required for survival.'' The colonel cocked his head brightly and regarded Virginia and Malcolm. ''Wouldn't you say?''

''Y—es,'' Virginia said slowly. Malcolm couldn't decide what the look on her face meant. He had never seen it before. Her eyes were shining, but wary. Her smile showed excitement and sympathy, but tension too. She seemed caught between two feelings.

''Quite!'' the colonel said, smacking his hands together. ''It is most important to me that you fully understand the situation.'' He pushed himself up to his feet and, with the same move, brought the crutches out smoothly and positioned them to balance him before he could fall. He stood leaning slightly forward, beaming. ''Well, now, having given my story, I imagine the objectives of this conversation are fully attained, and there is no need to detain you here further. I'll see you to the front gate.''

''That won't be necessary,'' Malcolm said.

''I insist,'' the colonel said in what would have been a perfectly pleasant manner if he had added the animated twinkle to his eyes. Virginia was staring at him, blinking slowly.

''Please forgive us,'' she said. ''We certainly hadn't meant to stay long enough to be rude. Thank you for the tea and cookies. They were very good.''

''Not at all, my dear,'' the colonel said. ''It's really quite pleasant to think of looking across the way, now and then, and catching glimpses of someone so attractive at her domestic preoccupations. I cleaned up thoroughly after the last tenants, of course, but there are always little personal touches one wants to apply. And you will start some plantings at the front of the house, won't you? Such little activities are quite precious to me—someone as charming as you, in her summer things, going about her little fussings and tendings, resting in the sun after weeding—that sort of thing. Yes, I expect a most pleasant summer. I assume there was never any question you wouldn't

stay all summer. Cortelyou would hardly bother with anyone who could not afford to pay him that much. But little
more, eh?'' The urbane, shrewd look returned to the colonel's face. ''Pinched resources and few ties, eh? Or what
would you be doing here, if there were somewhere else to
turn to?''

''Well, good afternoon, Colonel,'' Virginia said with
noticeable composure. ''Let's go, Malcolm.''

''Interesting conversation, Colonel,'' Malcolm said.

''Interesting and necessary, Mr. Lawrence,'' the colonel said, following them out onto the lawn. Virginia
watched him closely as she moved toward the gate, and
Malcolm noticed a little downward twitch at the corners
of her mouth.

''Feeling a bit of a strain, Mrs. Lawrence?'' the colonel
asked solicitously. ''Please believe that I shall be as con-
siderate of your sensibilities as intelligent care of my own
comfort will permit. It is not at all in my code to offer
offense to a lady, and in any case—'' the colonel smiled
deprecatingly ''—since the mishap of the Christmas tunnel, one might say the spirit is willing but . . .'' The colonel frowned down absently at his canes. ''No, Mrs.
Lawrence,'' he went on, shaking his head paternally, ''is
a flower the less for being breathed of? And is the cultivated flower, tended and nourished, not more fortunate
than the wild rose that blushes unseen? Do not regret your
present social situation too much, Mrs. Lawrence—some
might find it enviable. Few things are more changeable
than points of view. In the coming weeks your viewpoint
might well change.''

''Just what the hell are you saying to my wife?'' Malcolm asked.

Virginia said quickly, ''We can talk about it later.''

The colonel smiled at Virginia. ''Before you do that, I
have something else to show Mr. Lawrence.'' He raised
his voice slightly: ''Max! Moritz! Here!''—and the dogs
were there. ''Ah, Mr. Lawrence, I would like to show you
first how these animals respond, how discriminating they

can be." He turned to one of the dogs. "Moritz," he said sharply, nodding toward Malcolm, "Kill."

Malcolm couldn't believe what he had heard. Then he felt a blow on his chest. The dog was on him, its hind legs making short, fast, digging sounds in the lawn as it pressed its body against him. It was inside the arc of his arms, and the most he could have done was to clasp it closer to him. He made a tentative move to pull his arms back and then push forward against its rib cage, but the minor shift in weight made him stumble, and he realized if he completed the gesture he would fall. All this happened in a very short time, and then the dog touched open lips with him. Having done that, it dropped down and went back to stand beside Colonel Ritchey and Max.

"You see, Mr. Lawrence?" the colonel asked conversationally. "A dog does not respond to literal meaning. It is conditioned. It is trained to perform a certain action when it hears a certain sound. The cues one teaches a dog with pain and patience are not necessarily cues an educated organism can understand. Pavlov rang a bell and a dog salivated. Is a bell food? If he had rung a different bell, or said, 'Food, doggie,' there would have been no response. So, when I speak in a normal tone, rather than at command pitch, 'kill' does not mean 'kiss,' even to Moritz. It means nothing to him—unless I raise my voice. And I could just as easily have conditioned him to perform that sequence in association with some other command— such as, oh, say, 'gingersnaps'—but then you might not have taken the point of my little instructive jest. There is no way anyone but myself can operate these creatures. Only when I command do they respond. And now you respond, eh, Mr. Lawrence? I dare say. . . . Well, good day. As I said, you have things to do."

They left through the gate, which the colonel drew shut behind them. "Max," he said, "watch," and the dog froze in position. "Moritz, come." The colonel turned, and he and the other dog crossed the lawn and went into his house.

Malcolm and Virginia walked at a normal pace back to the rented house, Malcolm matching his step to Virginia's. He wondered if she were being so deliberate because she wasn't sure what the dog would do if she ran. It had been a long time since Virginia hadn't been sure of something.

In the house, Virginia made certain the door was shut tight, and then she went to sit in the chair that faced away from the window. "Would you make me some coffee, please?" she said.

"All right, sure. Take a few minutes. Catch your breath a little."

"A few minutes is what I need," she said. "Yes, a few minutes, and everything will be fine." When Malcolm returned with the coffee, she continued. "He's got some kind of string on Cortelyou, and I bet those people at the store down at the corner have those dogs walking in and out of there all the time. He's got us. We're locked up."

"Now, wait," Malcolm said, "there's the whole state of New Jersey out there, and he can't—"

"Yes, he can. If he thinks he can get away with it, and he's got good reasons for thinking he can. Take it on faith. There's no bluff in *him*."

"Well, look," he said, "just what can he do to us?"

"Any damn thing he pleases."

"That can't be right." Malcolm frowned. "He's got us pretty well scared right now, but we ought to be able to work out some way of—"

Virginia said tightly, "The dog's still there, right?" Malcolm nodded. "Okay," she said. "What did it feel like when he hit you? It looked awful. It looked like he was going to drive you clear onto your back. Did it feel that way? What did you *think?*"

"Well, he's a pretty strong animal," Malcolm said. "But, to tell you the truth, I didn't have time to believe it. You know, a man just saying 'kill' like that is a pretty hard thing to believe. Especially just after tea and cookies."

"He's very shrewd," Virginia said. "I can see why he

had the camp guards running around in circles. He deserved to have a book written about him.''

''All right, and then they should have thrown him into a padded cell.''

''Tried to throw,'' Virginia amended.

''Oh, come on. This is his territory, and he dealt the cards before we even knew we were playing. But all he is is a crazy old cripple. If he wants to buffalo some people in a store and twist a two-bit real estate salesman around his finger, fine—if he can get away with it. But he doesn't own us. We're not in his army.''

''We're inside his prison camp,'' Virginia said.

''Now, look,'' Malcolm said. ''When we walk in Cortelyou's door and tell him we know all about the colonel, there's not going to be any trouble about getting the rent back. We'll find someplace else, or we'll go back to the city. But whatever we do to get out of this, it's going to work out a lot smoother if the two of us think about it. It's not like you to be sitting there and spending a lot of time on how we can't win.''

''Well, Malcolm. Being a prisoner certainly brings out your initiative. Here you are, making noises just like a senior officer. Proposing escape committees and everything.''

Malcolm shook his head. Now of all times, when they needed each other so much, she wouldn't let up. The thing to do was to move too fast for her.

''All right,'' he said, ''let's get in the car.'' There was just the littlest bit of sweat on his upper lip.

''What?'' He had her sitting up straight in the chair, at least. ''Do you imagine that that dog will let us get anywhere near the car?''

''You want to stay here? All right. Just keep the door locked. I'm going to try it, and once I'm out I'm going to come back here with a nice healthy state cop carrying a nice healthy riot gun. And we're either going to do something about the colonel and those two dogs, or we're at least going to move you and our stuff out of here.''

He picked up the car keys, stepped through the front door very quickly, and began to walk straight for the car. The dog barked sharply, once. The front door of Ritchey's house opened immediately, and Ritchey called out, "Max! Hold!" The dog on the lawn was over the fence and had its teeth thrust carefully around Malcolm's wrist before he could take another eight steps, even though he had broken into a run. Both the dog and Malcolm stood very still. The dog was breathing shallowly and quietly, its eyes shining. Ritchey and Moritz walked as far as the front fence. "Now, Mr. Lawrence," Ritchey said, "in a moment I am going to call to Max, and he is to bring you with him. Do not attempt to hold back, or you will lacerate your wrist. Max! Bring here!"

Malcolm walked steadily toward the colonel. By some smooth trick of his neck, Max was able to trot alongside him without shifting his grip. "Very good, Max," Ritchey said soothingly when they had reached the fence. "Loose now," and the dog let go of Malcolm's wrist. Malcolm and Ritchey looked into each other's eyes across the fence, in the darkening evening. "Now, Mr. Lawrence," Ritchey said, "I want you to give me your car keys." Malcolm held out the keys, and Ritchey put them into his pocket. "Thank you." He seemed to reflect on what he was going to say next, as a teacher might reflect on his reply to a child who has asked why the sky is blue. "Mr. Lawrence, I want you to understand the situation. As it happens, I also want a three-pound can of Crisco. If you will please give me all the money in your pocket, this will simplify matters."

"I don't have any money on me," Malcolm said. "Do you want me to go in the house and get some?"

"No, Mr. Lawrence, I'm not a thief. I'm simply restricting your radius of action in one of the several ways I'm going to do so. Please turn out your pockets."

Malcolm turned out his pockets.

"All right, Mr. Lawrence, if you will hand me your wallet and your address book and the thirty-seven cents, they will all be returned to you whenever you have a legitimate use for them.'' Ritchey put the items away in the pockets of his jacket. ''Now, a three-pound can of Crisco is ninety-eight cents. Here is a dollar bill. Max will walk with you to the corner grocery store, and you will buy the Crisco for me and bring it back. It is too much for a dog to carry in a bag, and it is three days until my next monthly delivery of staples. At the store you will please tell them that it will not be necessary for them to come here with monthly deliveries any longer—that you will be in to do my shopping for me from now on. I expect you to take a minimum amount of time to accomplish all this and to come back with my purchase, Mr. Lawrence. Max!'' The colonel nodded toward Malcolm. ''Guard. Store.'' The dog trembled and whined. ''Don't stand still, Mr. Lawrence. Those commands are incompatible until you start toward the store. If you fail to move, he will grow increasingly tense. Please go now. Moritz and I will keep Mrs. Lawrence good company until you return.''

The store consisted of one small room in the front of a drab house. On unpainted pine shelves were brands of goods that Malcolm had never heard of. ''Oh! You're with one of those nice dogs,'' the tired, plump woman behind the counter said, leaning down to pat Max, who had approached her for that purpose. It seemed to Malcolm that the dog was quite mechanical about it and was pretending to itself that nothing caressed it at all. He looked around the place, but he couldn't see anything or anyone that offered any prospect of alliance with him.

''Colonel Ritchey wants a three-pound can of Crisco,'' he said, bringing the name out to check the reaction.

''Oh, you're helping him?''

''You could say that.''

''Isn't he brave?'' the woman said in low and confidential tones, as if concerned that the dog would overhear. ''You know, there are some people who would think you should feel sorry for a man like that, but I say it would be a sin to do so. Why, he gets along just fine, and he's got more pride and spunk than any whole man I've ever seen. Makes a person proud to know him. You know, I think it's just wonderful the way these dogs come and fetch little things for him. But I'm glad he's got somebody to look out for him now. 'Cept for us, I don't think he sees anybody from one year to the next—'cept summers, of course.''

She studied Malcolm closely. "You're summer people too, aren't you? Well, glad to have you, if you're doin' some good for the colonel. Those people last year were a shame. Just moved out one night in September, and neither the colonel nor me or my husband seen hide nor hair of them since. Owed the colonel a month's rent, he said when we was out there.''

"Is he the landloard?" Malcolm asked.

"Oh, sure, yes. He owns a lot of land around here. Bought it from the original company after it went bust.''

"Does he own this store, too?"

"Well, we lease it from him now. Used to own it, but we sold it to the company and leased it from them. Oh, we was all gonna be rich. My husband took the money from the land and bought a lot across the street and was gonna set up a real big gas station there—figured to be real shrewd—but you just can't get people to live out here. I mean, it isn't as if this was *ocean*-front property. But the colonel now, he's got a head on his shoulders. Value's got to go up someday, and he's just gonna hold on until it does.''

The dog was getting restless, and Malcolm was worried about Virginia. He paid for the can of Crisco, and he and Max went back up the sand road in the dark. There really, honestly, didn't seem to be much else to do.

At his front door, he stopped, sensing that he should knock. When Virginia let him in, he saw that she had changed to shorts and a halter. "Hello," she said, and then stood aside quietly for him and Max. The colonel, sitting pertly forward on one of the chairs, looked up.

"Ah, Mr. Lawrence, you're a trifle tardy, but the company has been delightful, and the moments seemed to fly."

Malcolm looked at Virginia. In the past couple of years, a little fat had accumulated above her knees, but she still had long, good legs. Colonel Ritchey smiled at Malcolm. "It's a rather close evening. I simply suggested to Mrs. Lawrence that I certainly wouldn't be offended if she left me for a moment and changed into something more comfortable."

It seemed to Malcolm that she could have handled that. But apparently she hadn't.

"Here's your Crisco," Malcolm said. "The change is in the bag."

"Thank you very much," the colonel said. "Did you tell them about the grocery deliveries?"

Malcolm shook his head. "I don't remember. I don't think so. I was busy getting an earful about how you owned them, lock, stock, and barrel."

"Well, no harm. You can tell them tomorrow."

"Is there going to be some set time for me to run your errands every day, Colonel? Or are you just going to whistle whenever something comes up?"

"Ah, yes. You're concerned about interruptions in your mood. Mrs. Lawrence told me you were some sort of artist. I'd wondered at your not shaving this morning." The colonel paused and then went on crisply. "I'm sure we'll shake down into whatever routine suits best. It always takes a few days for individuals to hit their stride as a group. After that, it's quite easy—regular functions, established duties, that sort of thing. A time to rise and wash, a time to work, a time to sleep. Everything and everyone in his proper niche. Don't worry, Mr. Lawrence, you'll be surprised how comfortable it becomes. Most people find it a revelation." The colonel's gaze grew distant for a moment. "Some do not. Some are as if born on another planet, innocent of human nature. Dealing with that sort, there comes a point when one must cease to try; at the camp, I found that the energy for overall success depended on my admitting the existence of the individual failure. No, some do not respond. But we needn't dwell on what time will tell us.''

Ritchey's eyes twinkled. ''I have dealt previously with creative people. Most of them need to work with their hands; do stupid, dull, boring work that leaves their minds free to soar in spirals and yet forces them to stay away from their craft until the tension is nearly unbearable.'' The colonel waved in the direction of the unbuilt houses. ''There's plenty to do. If you don't know how to use a hammer and saw as yet, I know how to teach that. And when from time to time I see you've reached the proper pitch of creative frustration, then you shall have what time off I judge will best serve you artistically. I think you'll be surprised how pleasingly you'll take to your studio. From what I gather from your wife, this may well be a very good experience for you.''

Malcolm looked at Virginia. ''Yes. Well, that's been bugging her for a long time. I'm glad she's found a sympathetic ear.''

''Don't quarrel with your wife, Mr. Lawrence. That sort of thing wastes energy and creates serious morale problems.'' The colonel got to his feet and went to the door. ''One thing no one could ever learn to tolerate in a fellow *Kriegie* was pettiness. That sort of thing was always weeded out. Come, Max. Come, Moritz. Good night!'' He left.

Malcolm went over to the door and put the chain on. ''Well?'' he said.

''All right, now, look—''

Malcolm held up one finger. ''Hold it. Nobody likes a quarrelsome *Kriegie*. We're not going to fight. We're going to talk, and we're going to think.'' He found himself looking at her halter and took his glance away. Virginia blushed.

''I just want you to know it was exactly the way he described it,'' she said. ''He said he wouldn't think it impolite if I left him alone in the living room while I went to change. And I wasn't telling him our troubles. We were talking about what you did for a living, and it didn't take much for him to figure out—''

''I don't want you explaining,'' Malcolm said. ''I want you to help me tackle this thing and get it solved.''

''How are you going to solve it? This is a man who always uses everything he's got! He never quits! How is somebody like *you* going to solve that?''

All these years, it occurred to Malcolm, at a time like this, now, she finally had to say the thing you couldn't make go away.

When Malcolm did not say anything at all for a while but only walked around frowning and thinking, Virginia said she was going to sleep. In a sense, he was relieved; a whole plan of action was forming in his mind, and he did not want her to badger him.

After she had closed the bedroom door, he went into the studio. In a corner was a carton of his painting stuff, which he now approached, detached but thinking. From this room he could see the floodlights on around the colonel's house. The colonel had made his circuit of the yard, and one of the dogs stood at attention, looking across the way. The setting hadn't altered at all from the night before. Setting, no, Malcolm thought, bouncing a jar of brown tempera in his hand; mood, *si*. His arm felt good all the way from his shoulder, into the forearm, wrist, and fingers.

When Ritchey had been in his house a full five minutes, Malcolm said to himself aloud, ''Do first, analyze later.'' Whipping open the front door, he took two steps forward on the bare earth to gather momentum and pitched the jar of paint in a shallow arc calculated to end against the aluminum fence.

It was going to fall short, Malcolm thought, and it did, smashing with a loud impact against one of the white-washed stones and throwing out a fan of gluey, brown spray over the adjacent stones, the fence, and the dog, which jumped back but, lacking orders to charge, stood its ground, whimpering. Malcolm stepped back into his open doorway and leaned in it. When the front door of Ritchey's house opened he put his thumbs to his ears and waggled his fingers, "*Gute Nacht, Herr Kommandant,*" he called, then stepped back inside and slammed and locked the door, throwing the spring-bolt latch. The dog was already on its way. It loped across the yard and scraped its front paws against the other side of the door. Its breath sounded like giggling.

Malcolm moved over to the window. The dog sprang away from the door with a scratching of toenails and leaped upward, glancing off the glass. It turned, trotted away for a better angle, and tried again. Malcolm watched it; this was the part he'd bet on.

The dog didn't make it. Its jaws flattened against the pane, and the whole sheet quivered, but there was too much going against success. The window was pretty high above the yard, and the dog couldn't get a proper combination of momentum and angle of impact. If he did manage to break it, he'd never have enough momentum left to clear the break; he'd fall on the sharp edges of glass in the frame while other chunks fell and cut his neck, and then the colonel would be down to one dog. One dog wouldn't be enough; the system would break down somewhere.

The dog dropped down, leaving nothing on the glass but a wet brown smear.

It seemed to Malcolm equally impossible for the colonel to break the window himself. He couldn't stride forward to throw a small stone hard enough to shatter the pane, and he couldn't balance well enough to heft a heavy one from nearby. The lock and chain would prevent him from entering through the front door. No, it wasn't efficient for the colonel any way you looked at it. He would rather take a few days to think of something shrewd and economical. In fact, he was calling the dog back now. When the dog reached him, he shifted one crutch and did his best to kneel while rubbing the dog's head. There was something rather like affection in the scene. Then the colonel straightened up and called again. The other dog came out of the house and took up its station at the corner of the yard. The colonel and the dirty dog went back into the colonel's house.

Malcolm smiled, then turned out the lights, double-checked the locks, and went back through the hall to the bedroom. Virginia was sitting up in bed, staring in the direction from which the noise had come.

"What did you do?" she asked.

"Oh, changed the situation a little," Malcolm said, grinning. "Asserted my independence. Shook up the colonel. Smirched his neatness a little bit. Spoiled his night's sleep for him, I hope. Standard *Kriegie* tactics. I hope he likes them."

Virginia was incredulous. "Do you know what he could do to you with those dogs if you step outside this house?"

"I'm not going to step outside. Neither are you. We're just going to wait a few days."

"What do you mean?" Virginia said, looking at him as if he were the maniac.

"Day after tomorrow, maybe the day after that," Malcolm explained, "he's due for a grocery delivery I didn't turn off. Somebody's going to be here with a car then, lugging all kinds of things. I don't care how beholden those storekeepers are to him; when we come out the door, he's not going to have those dogs tear us to pieces right on the front lawn in broad daylight and with a witness. We're going to get into the grocery car, and sooner or later we're going to drive out in it, because *that* car and driver have to turn up in the outside world again."

Virginia sighed. "Look," she said with obvious control, "all he has to do is send a note with the dogs. He can stop the delivery that way."

Malcolm nodded. "Uh-huh. And so the groceries don't come. Then what? He starts trying to freight flour and eggs in here by dog back? By remote control? What's he going to do? All right, so it doesn't work out so neatly in two or three days. But we've got a fresh supply of food, and he's almost out. Unless he's planning to live on Crisco, he's in a bad way. And even so, he's only got three pounds of that.'' Malcolm got out of his clothes and lay down on the bed. "Tomorrow's another day, but I'll be damned if I'm going to worry any more about it tonight. I've got a good head start on frustrating the legless wonder, and tomorrow I'm going to have a nice clear mind, and I'm going to see what other holes I can pick in his defense. I learned a lot of snide little tricks from watching jolly movies about clever prisoners and dumb guards.'' He reached up and turned out the bed light. "Good night, love,'' he said. Virginia rolled away from him in the dark. "Oh, my God,'' she said in a voice with a brittle edge around it.

It was a sad thing for Malcolm to lie there thinking that she had that kind of limitation in her, that she didn't really understand what had to be done. On the other hand, he thought sleepily, feeling more relaxed than he had in years, he had his own limitations. And she had put up with them for years. He fell asleep wondering pleasantly what tomorrow would bring.

He woke to a sound of rumbling and crunching under the earth, as if there were teeth at the foundations of the house. Still sleeping in large portions of his brain, he cried out silently to himself with a madman's lucidity, "Ah, of course, he's been tunneling!" And his mind gave him all the details—the careful transfer of supporting timber from falling houses, the disposal of the excavated clay in the piles beside the other foundations, too, for when the colonel had more people. . . .

Now one corner of the room showed a jagged line of yellow, and Malcolm's hands sprang to the light switch. Virginia jumped from sleep. In the corner was a trapdoor, its uneven joints concealed by boards of different angles. The trapdoor crashed back, releasing a stench of body odor and soot.

A dog popped up through the opening and scrambled into the bedroom. Its face and body were streaked, and it shook itself to get the sand from its coat. Behind it, the colonel dragged himself up, naked, and braced himself on his arms, half out of the tunnel mouth. His hair was matted down with perspiration over his narrow-boned skull. He was mottled yellow-red with dirt, and half in the shadows. Virginia buried her face in her hands, one eye glinting out between spread fingers, and cried to Malcolm, "Oh my God, what have you done to us?"

"Don't worry, my dear," the colonel said crisply to her. Then he screamed at Malcolm, "I will not be abused!" Trembling with strain as he braced on one muscle-corded arm, he pointed at Malcolm. He said to the dog at command pitch: "Kiss!"

AUTHOR'S NOTE

I'M A RATHER QUIET PERSON, CONSIDERING THAT I WRITE about tense, eventually violent individuals with compulsions.

I can't help that; I was born in Nazi Germany and was puzzled and frightened by the time I was five. I didn't fit in all that well when I came to the States in 1936; people tended to speak loudly at me in an only gradually comprehensible language. I still have a great deal of trouble with people who know they're in the right and think they know better than I do. It's been fifty-eight years of that, now, so you can imagine what it was like inside while I gradually attained my present level of benign serenity. (I rarely tremble anymore, and when I do it's only for a little while or, at most, overnight.)

I got off the chicken farm, figuratively and literally, by becoming a science fiction writer who could live on the income from that, if he also cut almost all the corners. My science fiction is marked by a preoccupation with identity, and violent death and mutilation as character-formers. I never knew why this was; I'm not truly a conscious writer; first an idea has to feel right to me, and then I can put some skill into its manuscript. It has dawned on me that a universe of violence, overweening forces, and great difficulty is what feels most right. And perhaps that the reason I wrote so much for science fiction markets was because there weren't any horror markets at the time.

Here and there, I placed a few non-SF stories, some of them pretty good. "The Master of the Hounds" is the best of those, perhaps because even in the "real" world there are times and places where surreal situations can plausibly occur. I am not comfortable writing "straight" fiction; it doesn't feel right or seem to have any sufficient purpose.

"Master of the Hounds" did well; it's even been made into a (very peculiar) movie called To Kill a Clown, *which most video stores will sell you, new, for less than $20. I recommend it to film students as an exercise in guessing what might have gone wrong.*

But never mind all that. In these, the—of course—prime years of my life, I have behind me a record of being a pretty successful teacher of novice writers, a critic with a certain flair for being overweening, a historian of SF with approximate data but some showy interpretations, and a small but elegant production of short stories and novels since 1952. (The production of inelegant short stories and novels took place simultaneously.)

In the world that puzzles me, I've been an advertising and PR man, a senior editor at a few famous places, the author and production designer of a very effective bicycle-repair manual that died in the publishers' warehouse, and an interesting political biography of President Harry S Truman that died on the book racks.

And I'm happy in my work. At present, I have some role in L. Ron Hubbard's Writers of the Future and Illustrators of the Future contests, am working on a sequel to my award-winning book of reviews, on a novel that's been fifteen years in the writing so far, and a couple of other projects.

—Algis Budrys

JUDGMENT DAY
L. Sprague de Camp

IT TOOK ME A LONG TIME TO DECIDE WHETHER TO LET the earth live. Some might think this an easy decision. Well, it was and it wasn't. I wanted one thing, while the mores of my culture said to do the other.

This is a decision that few have to make. Hitler might give orders for the execution of ten million, and Stalin orders that would kill another ten million. But neither could send the world up in a puff of flame by a few marks on a piece of paper.

Only now has physics got to the point where such a decision is possible. Yet, with due modesty, I don't think my discovery was inevitable.

Somebody might have come upon it later—say in a few centuries, when such things might be better organized. My equation was far from obvious. All the last three decades' developments in nuclear physics have pointed away from it.

My chain reaction uses *iron*, the last thing that would normally be employed in such a series. It's at the bottom of the atomic energy curve. Anything else can be made into iron with a release of energy, while it takes energy to make iron into anything else.

Really, the energy doesn't come from the iron, but from the . . . the other elements in the reaction. But the iron is necessary. It is not exactly a catalyst, as it is transmuted and then turned back into iron again, whereas a true catalyst remains unchanged. But the effect is the same. With iron so common in the crust of the earth, it should be possible to blow the entire crust off with one big *poof.*

I recall how I felt when I first saw these equations, here in my office last month. I sat staring at my name on the glass of the door, Dr. Wade Ormont, only it appears backwards from the inside. I was sure I had made a mistake. I checked and rechecked and calculated and recalculated. I went through my nuclear equations at least thirty times. Each time my heart, my poor old heart, pounded harder and the knot in my stomach grew tighter. I had enough sense not to tell anybody else in the department about my discovery.

I did not even then give up trying to find something wrong with my equations. I fed them through the computer, in case there was some glaring, obvious error I had been overlooking. Didn't that sort of thing—a minus for a plus or something—once happen to Einstein? I'm no Einstein, even if I am a pretty good physicist, so it could happen to me.

However, the computer said it hadn't. I was right.

The next question was: What to do with these results? They would not help us toward the laboratory's objectives: more powerful nuclear weapons and more efficient ways of generating nuclear power. The routine procedure would be to write up a report. This would be typed and photostated and stamped Top Secret. A few copies would be taken around by messenger to those who needed to know about such things. It would go to the AEC and the others. People in this business have learned to be pretty closemouthed, but the knowledge of my discovery would still spread, even though it might take years.

I don't think the government of the United States would ever try to blow up the world, but others might. Hitler might have, if he had known how, when he saw he faced inevitable defeat. The present Commies are pretty cold-blooded calculators, but one can't tell who'll be running their show in ten or twenty years. Once this knowledge gets around, anybody with a reasonable store of nuclear facilities could set the thing off. Most would not, even in revenge for defeat. But some might threaten to do so as blackmail, and a few could actually touch it off if thwarted. What's the proportion of paranoids and other crackpots in the world's population? It must be high enough, as a good fraction of the world's rulers and leaders have been of this type. No government yet devised—monarchy, aristocracy, theocracy, timocracy, democracy, dictatorship, soviet, or what have you—will absolutely stop such people from coming to the top. So long as these tribes of hairless apes are organized into sovereign nations, the nuclear Ragnarök is not only possible but probable.

For that matter, am I not a crackpot myself, calmly to contemplate blowing up the world?

No. At least the psychiatrist assured me my troubles were not of that sort. A man is not a nut if he goes about gratifying his desires in a rational manner. As to the kind of desires, that's nonrational anyway. I have adequate reasons for wishing to exterminate my species. It's no high-flown farfetched theory either; no religious mania about the sinfulness of man, but a simple, wholesome lust for revenge. Christians pretend to disapprove of vengeance, but that's only one way of looking at it. Many other cultures have deemed it right and proper, so it can't be a sign of abnormality.

For instance, when I think back over my fifty-three years, what do I remember? Well, take the day I first entered school . . .

I suppose I was a fearful little brute at six: skinny, stubborn, and precociously intellectual. Because my father was a professor, I early picked up a sesquipedalian way of speaking—which has been defined as a tendency to use words like "sesquipedalian." At six I was sprinkling my conversation with words like "theoretically" and "psychoneurotic." Because of illnesses I was as thin as a famine victim, with just enough muscle to get me from here to there.

While I always seemed to myself a frightfully good little boy whom everyone picked on, my older relatives in their last years assured me I was nothing of the sort, but the most intractable creature they ever saw. Not that I was naughty or destructive. On the contrary, I meticulously obeyed all formal rules and regulations with a zeal that would have gladdened the heart of a Prussian drill sergeant. It was that in those situations that depend, not on formal rules, but on accommodating oneself to the wishes of others, I never considered any wishes but my own. These I pursued with fanatical single-mindedness. As far as I was concerned, other people were simply inanimate things put into the world to minister to my wants. What they thought I neither knew nor cared.

Well, that's my relatives' story. Perhaps they were prejudiced, too. Anyway, when I entered the first grade in a public school in New Haven, the fun started the first day. At recess a couple grabbed my cap for a game of "siloochee." That meant that they tossed the cap from one to the other while the owner leaped this way and that like a hooked fish trying to recover his headgear.

After a few minutes I lost my temper and tried to brain one of my tormentors with a rock. Fortunately, six-year-olds are not strong enough to kill each other by such simple means. I raised a lump on the boy's head, and then the others piled on me. Because of my weakness I was no match for any of them. The teacher dug me out from the bottom of the pile.

With the teachers I got on well. I had none of the normal boy's spirit of rebellion against all adults. In my precocious way I reasoned that adults probably knew more than I, and when they told me to do something I assumed they had good reasons and did it. The result was that I became teacher's pet, which made my life that much harder with my peers.

They took to waylaying me on my way home. First, they would snatch my cap for a game of siloochee. The game would develop into a full-fledged baiting session, with boys running from me in front, jeering, while others ran up behind to hit or kick me. I must have chased them all over New Haven. When they got tired of being chased they would turn around, beat me—which they could do with absurd ease—and chase me for a while. I screamed, wept, shouted threats and abuse, made growling and hissing noises, and indulged in pseudofits like tearing my hair and foaming at the mouth in hope of scaring them off. This was just what they wanted. Hence, during most of my first three years in school, I was let out ten minutes early so as to be well on my way to my home on Chapel Street by the time the other boys got out.

This treatment accentuated my bookishness. I was digging through Millikan's *The Electron* at the age of nine.

My father worried vaguely about my troubles but did little about them, being a withdrawn bookish man himself. His line was medieval English literature, which he taught at Yale, but he still sympathized with a fellow intellectual and let me have my head. Sometimes he made fumbling efforts to engage me in ball-throwing and similar outdoor exercises. This had little effect, since he really hated exercise, sport, and the outdoors as much as I did, and was as clumsy and uncoordinated as I to boot. Several times I resolved to force myself through a regular course of exercises to make myself into a young Tarzan, but when it came to executing my resolution I found the calisthenics such a frightful bore that I always let them lapse before they had done me any good.

I'm no psychologist. Like most followers of the exact sciences, I have an urge to describe psychology as a ''science," in quotes, implying that only the exact sciences like physics are entitled to the name. That may be unfair, but it's how many physicists feel.

For instance, how can the psychologists all these years have treated sadism as something abnormal, brought on by some stupid parent's stopping his child from chopping up the furniture with a hatchet, thereby filling him with frustration and insecurity? On the basis of my own experience I will testify that all boys—well, perhaps 99 percent—are natural-born sadists. Most of them have it beaten out of them. Correct that: most of them have it beaten down into their subconscious, or whatever the headshrinkers call that part of our minds nowadays. It's still there, waiting a chance to pop up. Hence crime, war, persecution, and all the other ills of society. Probably this cruelty was evolved as a useful characteristic back in the stone age. An anthropological friend once told me this idea was fifty years out of date, but he could be wrong also.

I suppose I have my share of it. At least I never wanted anything with such passionate intensity as I wanted to kill those little fiends in New Haven by lingering and horrible tortures. Even now, forty-five years after, that wish is still down there at the bottom of my mind, festering away. I still remember them as individuals, and can still work myself into a frenzy of hatred and resentment just thinking about them. I don't suppose I have ever forgotten or forgiven an injury or insult in my life. I'm not proud of that quality, but neither am I ashamed of it. It is just the way I am.

Of course I had reasons for wishing to kill the little tyrants, while they had no legitimate grudge against me. I had done nothing to them except to offer an inviting target, a butt, a punching bag. I never expected, as I pored over Millikan's book, that this would put me on the track of as complete a revenge as anybody could ask.

So much for boys. Girls I don't know about. I was the middle one of three brothers; my mother was a masterful character, lacking the qualities usually thought of as feminine; and I never dated a girl until I was nearly thirty. I married late, for a limited time, and had no children. It would neatly have solved my present problem if I had found how to blow up the male half of the human race while sparing the female. That is not the desire for a super-harem, either. I had enough trouble keeping one woman satisfied when I was married. It is just that the female half has never gone out of its way to make life hell for me, day after day for years, even though one or two women, too, have done me dirt. So, in a mild detached way, I should be sorry to destroy the women along with the men.

By the time I was eleven and in the sixth grade, things had got worse. My mother thought that sending me to a military academy would "make a man of me." I should be forced to exercise and mix with the boys. Drill would teach me to stand up and hold my shoulders back. And I could no longer slouch into my father's study for a quiet session with the encyclopedia.

My father was disturbed by this proposal, thinking that sending me away from home would worsen my lot by de-priving me of my only sanctuary. Also he did not think we could afford a private school on his salary and small private income.

As usual, my mother won. I was glad to go at first. Anything seemed better than the torment I was enduring. Perhaps a new crowd of boys would treat me better. If they didn't, our time would be so fully organized that no-body would have an opportunity to bully me.

So in the fall of 1927, with some fears but more hopes, I entered Rogers Military Academy at Waukeegus, New Jersey. . . .

The first day, things looked pretty good. I admired the gray uniforms with the little brass strip around the edge of the visors of the caps.

But it took me only a week to learn two things. One was that the school, for all its uniforms and drills, was loosely run. The boys had plenty of time to think up mischief. The other was that, by the mysterious sense boys have, they immediately picked me as fair game.

On the third day somebody pinned a sign to my back, reading, "Call Me Sally." I went around all day unconscious of the sign and puzzled by being called "Sally." "Sally" I remained all the time I was at Rogers. The reason for calling me by a girl's name was merely that I was small, skinny, and unsocial, as I have never had any tendencies towards sexual abnormality.

To this day I wince at the name Sally. Some years ago, before I married, matchmaking friends introduced me to an attractive girl and could not understand why I dropped her like a hot brick. Her name was Sally.

There was much hazing of new boys at Rogers; the teachers took a fatalistic attitude and looked the other way. I was the favorite hazee, only with me it did not taper off after the first few weeks. They kept it up all through the first year. One morning in March 1928, I was awakened around five by several boys seizing my arms and legs and holding me down while one of them pinched my nose and another forced a cake of soap into my mouth.

"Look out he don't bite you," said one.

"Castor oil would be better."

"We ain't got none. Hold his nose; that'll make him open up."

"We should have shaved the soap up into little pieces. Then he'd have foamed better."

"Let me tickle him; that'll make him throw a fit."

"There, he's foaming fine, like a old geyser."

"Stop hollering, Sally," one of them addressed me, "or we'll put the suds in your eyes."

"Put the soap in 'em anyway. It'll make a red-eyed monster out of him. You know how he glares and shrieks when he gits mad?"

"Let's cut his hair all off. That'll *reely* make him look funny."

My yells brought one of the masters, who sharply ordered the tormentors to cease. They stood up while I rose to a sitting position on my bunk, spitting out soapsuds. The master said:

"What's going on here? Don't you know this is not allowed? It will mean ten rounds for each of you!"

"Rounds" were Rogers' form of discipline. Each round consisted of marching once around the track in uniform with your piece on your shoulder. (The piece was a Springfield 1903 army rifle with the firing pin removed, lest some student get .30 cartridges to fit and blow somebody's head off.) I hoped my tormentors would be at least expelled and was outraged by the lightness of their sentence. They on the other hand were indignant that they had been so hardly treated and protested with the air of outraged virtue:

"But Mr. Wilson, sir, we was only *playing* with him!"

At that age I did not know that private schools do not throw out paying students for any but the most heinous offenses; they can't afford to. The boys walked their ten rounds and hated me for it. They regarded me as a tattletale because my howls had drawn Mr. Wilson's attention and devoted themselves to thinking up new and ingenious ways to make me suffer. Now they were more subtle. There was nothing so crude as forcing soap down my throat. Instead it was hiding parts of my uniform, putting horse manure and other undesirable substances in my bed, and tripping me when I was drilling so my nine-pound Springfield and I went sprawling in the dirt.

I fought often, always getting licked and usually being caught and given rounds for violating the school's rules. I was proud when I actually bloodied one boy's nose, but it did me no lasting good. He laid for me in the swimming pool and nearly drowned me. By now I was so terrorized that I did not dare to name my attackers, even when the masters revived me by artificial respiration and asked me. Wilson said:

"Ormont, we know what you're going through, but we can't give you a bodyguard to follow you around. Nor can we encourage you to tattle as a regular thing; that'll only make matters worse.''

''But what can I *do*, sir? I try to obey the rules—''

''That's not it.''

''What, then? I don't do anything to these kids; they just pick on me all the time.''

''Well, for one thing, you could deprive them of the pleasure of seeing you yelling and making wild swings that never land—'' He drummed on his desk with his fingers. ''We have this sort of trouble with boys like you, and if there's any way to stop it I don't know about it. You . . . let's face it; you're *queer*.''

''How?''

''Oh, your language is much too adult—''

''But isn't that what you're trying to teach us in English?''

''Sure, but that's not the point. Don't argue about it; I'm trying to help you. Then another thing. You argue about everything, and most of the time you're right. But you don't suppose people like you for putting them in the wrong, do you?''

''But people *ought*—''

''Precisely, they ought, but they don't. You can't change the world by yourself. If you had muscles like Dempsey you could get away with a good deal, but you haven't. So the best thing is to adopt a protective coloration. Pay no attention to their attacks or insults. Never argue; never complain; never criticize. Flash a glassy smile at everybody, even when you feel like murdering them. Keep your language simple and agree with what's said whether you feel that way or not. I hate to give you a counsel of hypocrisy, but I don't see any alternative. If we could only make some sort of athlete out of you—''

This was near the end of the school year. In a couple of weeks I was home. I complained about the school and asked to return to public school in New Haven. My parents objected on the ground that I was getting a better education at Rogers than I should get locally, which was true.

One day some of my old pals from public school caught me in a vacant lot and gave me a real beating, so that my face was swollen and marked. I realized that, terrible though the boys at Rogers were, they did not include the most fearful kind of all: the dimwitted muscular lout who has been left behind several grades in public school and avenges his boredom and envy by tormenting his puny classmates. After that I did not complain about Rogers.

People talk of "School days, school days, dear old golden rule days—" and all that rubbish. Psychologists tell me that, while children suffer somewhat, they remember only the pleasant parts of childhood and hence idealize it later.

Both are wrong as far as I am concerned. I had a hideous childhood, and the memory of it is as sharp and painful forty years later as it was then. If I want to spoil my appetite, I have only to reminisce about my dear, dead childhood.

For one thing, I have always hated all kinds of roughhouse and horseplay, and childhood is full of them unless the child is a cripple or other shut-in. I have always had an acute sense of my own dignity and integrity, and any japery or ridicule fills me with murderous resentment. I have always hated practical jokes. When I'm asked "Can't you take a joke," the truthful answer is no, at least not in that sense. I want to kill the joker, then and for years afterwards. Such humor as I have is expressed in arch, pedantic little witticisms which amuse my academic friends but which mean nothing to most people. I might have got on better in the era of duelling. Not that I should have made much of a duellist, but I believe men were just a bit more careful then how they insulted others who might challenge them.

I set out in my second year at Rogers to try out Wilson's advice. Nobody will ever know what I went through, learning to curb my hot temper and proud, touchy spirit, and literally to turn the other cheek. All that year I sat on my inner self, a mass of boiling fury and hatred. When I was teased, mocked, ridiculed, poked, pinched, punched, hair-pulled, kicked, tripped, and so on, I pretended that nothing had happened, in the hope that the others would get tired of punching a limp bag.

It didn't always work. Once I came close to killing a teaser by hitting him over the head with one of those long window openers with a bronze head on a wooden pole with which every classroom was equipped in the days before air-conditioned schools. Luckily I hit him with the wooden shaft and broke it, instead of with the bronze part.

As the year passed and the next began, I made myself so colorless that sometimes a whole week went by without my being baited. Of course, I heard the hated nickname Sally every day, but the boys often used it without malice from habit. I also endured incidents like this: Everybody, my father, the masters, and the one or two older boys who took pity on me had urged me to go in for athletics. Now, at Rogers one didn't have to join a team. One had compulsory drill and calisthenics, but beyond that things were voluntary. (It was, as I said, a loosely-run school.)

So I determined to try. One afternoon in the spring of 1929 I wandered out to the athletic field, to find a group of my classmates getting up a game of baseball. I quietly joined them.

The two self-appointed captains squared off to choose their teams. One of them looked at me incredulously and asked: "Hey, Sally, are *you* in on this?"

"Yeah."

They began choosing. There were fifteen boys there, counting the captains and me. They chose until there was one boy left: me. The boy whose turn it was to choose said to the other captain:

"You can have him."

"Naw, I don't want him. You take him."

They argued while the subject of their mutual generosity

squirmed and the boys already chosen grinned unsympathetically. Finally one captain said:

"Suppose we let him bat for both sides. That way, the guys the side of he's on won't be any worse off than the other."

"O.K. That suit you, Sally?"

"No, thanks," I said. "I guess I don't feel good anyway." I turned away before visible tears disgraced a thirteen-year-old.

Just after I started my third year, in the fall of 1929, the stock market fell flat. Soon my father found that his small private income had vanished as the companies in which he had invested, such as New York Central, stopped paying dividends. As a result, when I went home for Christmas, I learned that I could not go back to Rogers. Instead I should begin again with the February semester at the local high school.

In New Haven my 'possum-tactics were put to a harder test. Many boys in my class had known me in former days and were delighted to take up where they had left off. For instance—

For decades, boys who found study hall dull have enlivened the proceedings with rubber bands and bits of paper folded into a V-shape for missiles. The trick is to keep your missile-weapon palmed until the teacher is looking elsewhere, and then to bounce your wad off the neck of some fellow-student in front of you. Perhaps this was tame compared to nowadays, when, I understand, the students shoot ball bearings and knock the teacher's teeth and eyes out, and carve him with switch blade knives if he objects. All this happened before the followers of Dewey and Watson, with their lunacies about "permissive" training, had made classrooms into a semblance of the traditional cannibal feast with teacher playing the role of the edible missionary.

Right behind me sat a small boy named Patrick Hanrahan: a wiry, red-haired young hellion with a South Boston accent. He used to hit me with paper wads from time to time. I paid no attention because I knew he could lick me with ease. I was a head taller than he, but though I had begun to shoot up I was as skinny, weak, and clumsy as ever. If anything I was clumsier, so that I could hardly get through a meal without knocking over a glass.

One day I had been peppered with unusual persistence. My self-control slipped, as it would under a determined enough assault. I got out my own rubber band and paper missiles. I knew Hanrahan had shot at me before, but, of course, one never saw the boy who shot a given wad at you.

When a particularly hard-driven one stung me behind the ear, I whipped around and let Hanrahan have one in the face. It struck just below his left eye, hard enough to make a red spot. He looked astonished, then furious, and savagely whispered:

"What you do that for?"

"You shot me," I whispered back.

"I did not! I'll git you for this! You meet me after class."

"You did, too—" I began, when the teacher barked: "Ormont!" I shut up.

Perhaps Hanrahan really had not shot that last missile. One could argue that it was no more than his due for the earlier ones he *had* shot. But that is not how boys' minds work. They reason like the speaker of Voltaire's lines:

> *"Cet animal est trés méchant;*
> *Quand on l'attaque, il se défend!"*

I knew if I met Hanrahan on the way out I should get a fearful beating. When I saw him standing on the marble steps that led up from the floor of the study hall to the main exit, I walked quietly out the rear door.

I was on my way to the gym when I got a kick in the behind. There was Paddy Hanrahan, saying: "Come on, you yellow dog, fight!"

''Hello there,'' I said with a sickly grin.

He slapped my face.

''Having fun?'' I said.

He kicked me in the leg.

''Keep right on,'' I said, ''I don't mind.''

He slapped and kicked me again, crying: ''Yellow dog! Yellow dog!'' I walked on toward the gymnasium as if nothing were happening, saying to myself: pay no attention, never criticize or complain, keep quiet, ignore it, pay no attention— At last Paddy had to stop hitting and kicking me to go to his own next class.

Next day I had a few bruises where Hanrahan had struck me—nothing serious. When he passed me he snarled: ''Yellow dog!'' but did not renew his assault. I have wasted much time in the forty years since then, imagining revenges on Paddy Hanrahan. Hanrahan coming into my office in rags and pleading for a job, and my having him thrown out—All that nonsense. I never saw him again after I finished school in New Haven.

There were a few more such incidents during that year and the following one. For instance at the first class meeting in the autumn of 1930, when the student officers of my class were elected for the semester, after several adolescents had been nominated for president, somebody piped up: ''I nominate Wade Ormont!''

The whole class burst into a roar of laughter. One of the teachers pounced on the nominator and hustled him out for disturbing an orderly session by making frivolous nominations. Not knowing how to decline a nomination, I could do nothing but stare stonily ahead as if I hadn't heard. I need not have worried; the teachers never even wrote my name on the blackboard with those of the other nominees, nor did they ask for seconds. They just ignored the whole thing, as if the nominator had named Julius Caesar.

Then I graduated. As my marks put me in the top one percentile in scientific subjects and pretty high in the others, I got a scholarship at MIT. Without it I don't think my father could have afforded to send me.

When I entered MIT I had developed my protective shell to a good degree of effectiveness, though not so perfectly as later: the automatic, insincere, glassy smile turned on as by a switch; the glad hand; the subdued, modest manner that never takes an initiative or advances an opinion unless it agrees with somebody else's. And I never, *never* showed emotion no matter what. How could I, when the one emotion inside me, overwhelming all others, was a blazing homicidal fury and hatred, stored up from all those years of torment? If I really let myself go I should kill somebody. The incident with the window opener had scared me. Much better never to show what you're thinking. As for feeling, it is better not to feel—to view the world with the detachment of a visitor at the zoo.

MIT was good to me: It gave me a sound scientific education without pulverizing my soul in a mortar every day. For one thing, many other undergraduates were of my own introverted type. For another, we were kept too busy grinding away at heavy schedules to have time or energy for horseplay. For another, athletics did not bulk large in our program, so my own physical inferiority did not show up so glaringly. I reached medium height—about five-eight—but remained thin, weak, and awkward. Except for a slight middle-aged bulge around the middle, I am that way yet.

For thousands of years, priests and philosophers have told us to love mankind without giving any sound reason for loving the creatures. The mass of them are a lot of cruel, treacherous, hairless apes. They hate us intellectuals, longhairs, highbrows, eggheads, or double-domes, despite—or perhaps because—without us they would still be running naked in the wilderness and turning over flat stones for their meals. Love them? Hah!

Oh, I admit I have known a few of my own kind who

were friendly. But by the time I had learned to suppress all emotion to avoid baiting, I was no longer the sort of man to whom many feel friendly. A bright enough physicist, well-mannered and seemingly poised, but impersonal and aloof, hardly seeing my fellow men except as creatures whom I had to manipulate in order to live. I have heard my colleagues describe others of my type as a "dry stick" or "cold fish," so no doubt they say the same of me. But who made me that way? I might not have become a fascinating *bon-vivant* even if I had not been bullied, but I should probably not have become such an extreme aberrant. I might even have been able to like individuals and to show normal emotions.

The rest of my story is routine. I graduated from MIT in 1936, took my PhD from Chicago in 1939, got an instructorship at Chicago, and next year was scooped up by the Manhattan Engineer District. I spent the first part of the war at the Argonne Labs and the last part at Los Alamos. More by good luck than good management, I never came in contact with the Communists during the bright pink era of 1933–45. If I had, I might easily, with my underdog complex and my store of resentment, have been swept into their net. After the war I worked under Lawrence at Berkeley—

I've had a succession of such jobs. They think I'm a sound man, perhaps not a great creative genius like Fermi or Teller, but a bear for spotting errors and judging the likeliest line of research to follow. It's all part of the objective, judicious side of my nature that I have long cultivated. I haven't tried to get into administrative work, which you have to do to rise to the top in bureaucratic setups like this. I hate to deal with people as individuals. I could probably do it—I have forced myself to do many things—but what would be the purpose? I have no desire for power over my fellows. I make enough to live on comfortably, especially since my wife left me—

* * *

Oh, yes, my wife. I had got my PhD before I had my first date. I dated girls occasionally for the next decade, but in my usual reserved, formal manner.

Why did I leave Berkeley to go to Columbia University, for instance? I had a hobby of noting down people's conversation in shorthand when they weren't noticing. I was collecting this conversation for a statistical analysis of speech: the frequency of sounds, of words, combinations of words, parts of speech, topics of conversation, and so on. It was a purely intellectual hobby with no gainful objective, though I might have written up my results for one of the learned periodicals. One day my secretary noticed what I was doing and asked me about it. In an incautious moment I explained. She looked at me blankly, then burst into laughter and said:

"My goodness, Dr. Ormont, you *are* a nut!"

She never knew how close she came to having her skull bashed in with the inkwell. For a few seconds I sat there, gripping my pad and pencil and pressing my lips together. Then I put the paper quietly away and returned to my physics. I never resumed the statistical study, and I hated that secretary. I hated her particularly because I had had my own doubts about my mental health and so could not bear to be called a nut even in fun. I closed my shell more tightly than ever.

But I could not go on working next to that secretary. I could have framed her on some manufactured complaint, or just told the big boss I didn't like her and wanted another. But I refused to do this. I was the objective, impersonal man. I would never let an emotion make me unjust, and even asking to have her transferred would put a little black mark on her record. The only thing was for *me* to go away. So I got in touch with Columbia—

There I found a superior job with a superior secretary: Georgia Ehrenfels, so superior in fact that in 1958 we were married. I was already in my forties. She was twelve years younger and had been married and divorced once.

I think it took her about six months to realize that she

had made an even bigger mistake than the first time. I never realized it at all. My mind was on my physics, and a wife was a nice convenience but nobody to open up one's shell for. Later, when I finally realized that things had begun to go bad, I tried to open my shell and found that the hinges were stuck.

My wife tried to make me over, but that is not easy with a middle-aged man even under the most favorable conditions. She pestered me to get a house in the country until I gave in. I had never owned a house and proved an inefficient householder. I hated the tinkering, gardening, and other minutiae of suburban life. Georgia did most of the work. Then one day later I came home from work to find her gone and a note beginning:

Dear Wade:
It is no use. It is not your fault. You are as you are, as I should have realized at the beginning. Perhaps I am foolish not to appreciate your many virtues and to insist on that human warmth you do not have—

Well, she got her divorce and married another academic man. I don't know how they have got on, but the last I heard they were still married. Psychologists say people tend to repeat their marital mistakes rather than to learn from them. I resolved not to repeat mine by the simple expedient of having nothing more to do with women. So far I have kept to it.

This breakup did disturb me for a time, more than Iron Man Ormont would care to admit. I drank heavily, which I had never done. I began to make mistakes in my work. Finally I went to a psychiatrist. They might be one-third quackery and one-third unprovable speculation, but to whom else could one turn?

The psychiatrist was a nice little man, stout and square-built, with a subdued manner—a rather negative, colorless personality. I was surprised, for I had expected something with a pointed beard, Viennese gestures, and aggressive garrulity. Instead he quietly drew me out. After a few months he told me:

"You're not the least psychotic, Wade. You do have what we call a schizoidal personality. Such people always have a hard time in personal relations. Now, you have found a solution for your problem in your pose of good-natured indifference. The trouble is that the pose has been practiced so long that it's become the real Dr. Ormont, and it has raised up its own difficulties. You practiced so long and so hard suppressing your emotions that now you can't let them go when you want to—"

There was more of the same, much of which I had already figured out for myself. That part was fine; no disagreement. But what to do about it? I learned that the chances of improvement by psychoanalytical or similar treatment go down rapidly after the age of thirty, and over forty it is so small as hardly to be worth bothering with. After a year of spending the psychiatrist's time and my money, we gave up.

I had kept my house all this time. I had in fact adapted myself intelligently to living in a house, and I had accumulated such masses of scientific books, magazines, pamphlets, and other printed matter that I could no longer have got into an ordinary apartment. I had a maid, old and ugly, and I spent my time, away from the office, alone in my house. I learned to plant the lot with groundcover that required no mowing and to hire a gardener a few times a year so as not to outrage the neighbors too much.

Then I got a better job here. I sold my house on Long Island and bought another here, which I have run in the same style as the last one. I let the neighbors strictly alone. If they had done likewise I might have had an easier time deciding what to do with my discovery. As it is, many suburbanites seem to think that if a man lives alone and doesn't wish to be bothered, he must be some sort of ogre.

If I write up the chain reaction, the news will probably get out. No amount of security regulations will stop people from talking about the impending end of the world. Once having done so, the knowledge will probably cause the blowing up of the earth—not right away, but in a decade or two. I shall probably not live to see it, but it wouldn't displease me if it did go off in my lifetime. It would not deprive me of much.

I'm fifty-three and look older. My doctor tells me I'm not in good shape. My heart is not good; my blood pressure is too high; I sleep badly and have headaches. The doctor tells me to cut down on coffee, to stop this and stop that. But even if I do, he can't assure me a full decade more. There is nothing simple wrong with me that an operation would help; just a poor weak body further abused by too intensive mental work over most of my life.

The thought of dying does not much affect me. I have never got much fun out of life, and such pleasures as there are have turned sour in recent years. I find myself getting more and more indifferent to everything but physics, and even that is becoming a bore.

The one genuine emotion I have left is hatred. I hate mankind in general in a mild, moderate way. I hate the male half of mankind more intensely, and the class of boys most bitterly of all. I should love to see the severed heads of all the boys in the world stuck on spikes.

Of course I am objective enough to know why I feel this way. But knowing the reason for the feeling doesn't change the feeling, at least not in a hardened old character like me.

I also know that to wipe out all mankind would not be just. It would kill millions who have never harmed me, or for that matter harmed anybody else.

But why should I be just? When have these glabrous primates been just to me? The headshrinker tried to tell me to let my emotions go, and then perhaps I could learn to be happy. Well, I have just one real emotion. If I let it go, that's the end of the world.

On the other hand, I should destroy not only all the billions of bullies and sadists, but the few victims like myself. I have sympathized with the downtrodden because I knew how they felt. If there were some way to save them while destroying the rest— But my sympathy is probably wasted; most of the downtrodden would persecute others, too, if they had the power.

I had thought about the matter for several days without a decision. Then came Mischief Night. This is the night before Hallowe'en, when the local kids raise hell. The following night they go out again to beg candy and cookies from the people whose windows they have soaped and whose garbage pails they have upset.

All the boys in my neighborhood hate me. I don't know why. It's one of those things like a dog's sensing the dislike of another dog. Though I don't scream or snarl at them and chase them, they somehow know I hate them even when I have nothing to do with them.

I was so buried in my problem that I forgot about Mischief Night, and as usual stopped in town for dinner at a restaurant before taking the train out to my suburb. When I got home, I found that in the hour of darkness before my arrival, the boys had given my place the full treatment. The soaped windows and the scattered garbage and the toilet-paper spread around were bad but endurable. However, they had also burgled my garage and gone over my little British two-seater. The tires were punctured, the upholstery slashed, the paint scratched, and the wiring ripped out of the engine. There were other damages like uprooted shrubbery—

To make sure I knew what they thought, they had lettered a lot of shirt cardboards and left them around, reading: "OLD LADY ORMONT IS A NUT! BEWARE THE MAD SCIENTIST!"

That decided me. There is one way I can be happy during my remaining years, and that is by the knowledge that all these bullies will get theirs some day. I hate them. I hate them. I hate everybody. I want to kill mankind. I'd kill them by slow torture if I could. If I can't, blowing up the earth will do. I shall write my report.

AUTHOR'S NOTE

IF ANY READER WONDERS WHETHER THIS TALE IS AUTO-*biographical, the answer is: yes, in part. Several incidents in Ormont's childhood and youth were taken from things that happened to me. (A consolation of the writer's life is that whatever befalls you, no matter how unpleasant at the time, can eventually be turned into salable copy.) Other persons and events in the story, such as Ormont's parents and wife, are purely made-up.*

The kind of youth that Ormont had seems not unusual among writers. Several colleagues, among them John W. Campbell and Horace Gold, have confided that they, too, had gone through stressful times like those of the story.

Right now I am amid stress of another sort, in the process of moving from Pennsylvania, where Catherine and I lived for nearly fifty years, to Texas. I am scrunched in my new study, wedged into a strait among forty-odd meter-high piles of books and papers awaiting sorting and shelving. Now, if I could only find my thesaurus . . . But these unstable stacks have a strangely threatening aspect. Their polychromatic jackets seem to leer. They are all leaning towards me at once! They are toppling! Help—urk—xxxxxxxxxxxxxxxx.

—*L. Sprague de Camp*

IN THE HILLS, THE CITIES
Clive Barker

IT WASN'T UNTIL THE FIRST WEEK OF THE YUGOSLAVIAN trip that Mick discovered what a political bigot he'd chosen as a lover. Certainly he'd been warned. One of the queens at the baths had told him Judd was to the right of Atilla the Hun, but the man had been one of Judd's ex-affairs, and Mick had presumed there was more spite than perception in the character assassination.

If only he'd listened. Then he wouldn't be driving along an interminable road in a Volkswagen that suddenly seemed the size of a coffin, listening to Judd's views on Soviet expansionism. Jesus, he was so boring. He didn't converse, he lectured—and endlessly. In Italy, the sermon had been on the way the Communists had exploited the peasant vote. Now, in Yugoslavia, Judd had really warmed to his theme, and Mick was just about ready to take a hammer to his opinionated head.

It wasn't that he disagreed with everything Judd said. Some of the arguments (the ones Mick understood) seemed quite sensible. But then, what did he know? He was a dance teacher. Judd was a journalist, a professional pun-

197

dit, who felt, like most journalists Mick had encountered, that he was obliged to have an opinion on everything under the sun. Especially politics; that was the best trough to wallow in. You could get your snout, eyes, head and front hooves in that mess of muck and have a fine old time splashing around. It was an inexhaustible subject to devour, a swill with a little of everything in it, because everything, according to Judd, was political. The arts were political. Sex was political. Religion, commerce, gardening, eating, drinking and farting—all political.

Jesus, it was mind-blowing boring . . . killingly, love-deadeningly boring.

Worse still, Judd didn't seem to notice how bored Mick had become, or if he noticed, he didn't care. He just rambled on, his arguments getting windier and windier, his sentences lengthening with every mile they drove.

Judd, Mick had decided, was a selfish bastard, and as soon as their honeymoon was over he'd part with the guy.

It was not until their trip—that endless, motiveless caravan through the graveyards of mid-European culture—that Judd realized what a political lightweight he had in Mick. The guy showed precious little interest in the economics or the politics of the countries they passed through. He registered indifference to the full facts behind the Italian situation and yawned, yes, yawned when Judd tried (and failed) to debate the Russian threat to world peace. He had to face the bitter truth: Mick was a queen, there was no other word for him. All right, perhaps he didn't mince or wear jewelry to excess, but he was a queen nevertheless, happy to wallow in a dreamworld of early Renaissance frescoes and Yugoslavian icons. The complexities, the contradictions, even the agonies that made those cultures blossom and wither were just tiresome to him. His mind was no deeper than his looks; he was a well-groomed nobody.

Some honeymoon.

* * *

The road south from Belgrade to Novi Pazar was, by Yugoslavian standards, a good one. There were fewer potholes than on many of the roads they'd traveled, and it was relatively straight. The town of Novi Pazar lay in the valley of the River Raska, south of the city named after the river. It wasn't an area particularly popular with the tourists. Despite the good road, it was still inaccessible and lacked sophisticated amenities. However, Mick was determined to see the monastery at Sopocani, to the west of the town, and after some bitter argument he'd won.

The journey had proved uninspiring. On either side of the road the cultivated fields looked parched and dusty. The summer had been unusually hot, and droughts were affecting many of the villages. Crops had failed, and livestock had been prematurely slaughtered to prevent them dying of malnutrition. There was a defeated look about the few faces they glimpsed at the roadside. Even the children had dour expressions, brows as heavy as the stale heat that hung over the valley.

Now, with the cards on the table after a row at Belgrade, they drove in silence most of the time; yet the straight road, like most straight roads, invited dispute. When the driving was easy, the mind rooted for something to keep it engaged. What better than a fight?

"Why the hell do you want to see this damn monastery?" Judd demanded.

It was an unmistakable invitation.

"We've come all this way . . ." Mick tried to keep the tone conversational. He wasn't in the mood for an argument.

"More fucking Virgins, is it?"

Keeping his voice as even as he could, Mick picked up the guide and read aloud from it: " ' . . . there, some of the greatest works of Serbian painting can still be seen and enjoyed, including what many commentators agree to be the enduring masterpiece of the Raska school: *The Dormition of the Virgin*.' "

Silence.

Then Judd: "I'm up to here with churches."

"It's a masterpiece."

"They're all masterpieces according to that bloody book."

Mick felt his control slipping.

"Two and a half hours at most—"

"I told you, I don't want to see another church; the smell of the places makes me sick. Stale incense, old sweat and lies . . ."

"It's a short detour; then we can get back onto the road and you can give me another lecture on farming subsidies in the Sandzak."

"I'm just trying to get some decent conversation going instead of this endless tripe about Serbian fucking masterpieces—"

"Stop the car!"

"What?"

"Stop the car!"

Judd pulled the Volkswagen onto the side of the road. Mick got out.

The road was hot, but there was a slight breeze. He took a deep breath and wandered into the middle of the road. Empty of traffic and of pedestrians in both directions. In every direction, empty. The hills shimmered in the heat off the fields. There were wild poppies growing in the ditches. Mick crossed the road, squatted on his haunches and picked one.

Behind him he heard the VW's door slam.

"What did you stop us for?" Judd said. His voice was edgy, still hoping for that argument, begging for it.

Mick stood up, playing with the poppy. It was close to seeding, late in the season. The petals fell from the receptacle as soon as he touched them, little splashes of red fluttering down on to the gray tarmac.

"I asked you a question," Judd said again.

Mick looked around. Judd was standing at the far side of the car, his brows a knitted line of burgeoning anger. But handsome, oh yes—a face that made women weep with frustration that he was gay. A heavy black moustache (perfectly trimmed) and eyes you could watch forever and never see the same light in them twice. Why, in God's name, thought Mick, does a man as fine as that have to be such an insensitive little shit?

Judd returned the look of contemptuous appraisal, staring at the pouting pretty boy across the road. It made him want to puke, seeing the little act Mick was performing for his benefit. It might just have been plausible in a sixteen-year-old virgin. In a twenty-five-year-old, it lacked credibility.

Mick dropped the flower and untucked his T-shirt from his jeans. A tight stomach, then a slim, smooth chest were revealed as he pulled it off. His hair was ruffled when his head reappeared, and his face wore a broad grin. Judd looked at the torso. Neat, not too muscular. An appendix scar peering over his faded jeans. A gold chain, small but catching the sun, dipped in the hollow of his throat. Without meaning to, he returned Mick's grin, and a kind of peace was made between them.

Mick was unbuckling his belt.

"Want to fuck?" he said, the grin not faltering.

"It's no use," came an answer, though not to that question.

"What isn't?"

"We're not compatible."

"Want a bet?"

Now he was unzipped and turning away towards the wheat field that bordered the road.

Judd watched as Mick cut a swathe through the swaying sea, his back the color of the grain so that he was almost camouflaged by it. It was a dangerous game, screwing in the open air—this wasn't San Francisco or even Hampstead Heath. Nervously, Judd glanced along the road. Still empty in both directions. And Mick was turning, deep in the field, turning and smiling and waving like a swimmer buoyed up in a golden surf. What the hell . . . there was nobody to see, nobody to know. Just the hills, liquid in the heat haze, their forested backs bent to the business of the earth, and a lost dog, sitting at the edge of the road, waiting for some lost master.

Judd followed Mick's path through the wheat, unbuttoning his shirt as he walked. Field mice ran ahead of him, scurrying through the stalks as the giant came their way, his feet like thunder. Judd saw their panic, and smiled. He meant no harm to them, but then how were they to know that? Maybe he'd put out a hundred lives, mice, beetles, worms, before he reached the spot where Mick was lying, stark bollock naked, on a bed of trampled grain, still grinning.

It was good love they made, good, strong love, equal in pleasure for both; there was a precision to their passion, sensing the moment when effortless delight became urgent, when desire became necessity. They locked together, limb around limb, tongue around tongue, in a knot only orgasm could untie, their backs alternately scorched and scratched as they rolled around exchanging blows and kisses. In the thick of it, creaming together, they heard the phut-phut-phut of a tractor passing by; but they were past caring.

They made their way back to the Volkswagen with body-threshed wheat in their hair and their ears, in their socks and between their toes. Their grins had been replaced with easy smiles: the truce, if not permanent, would last a few hours at least.

The car was baking hot, and they had to open all the windows and doors to let the breeze cool it before they started towards Novi Pazar. It was four o'clock, and there was still an hour's driving ahead.

As they got into the car Mick said, "We'll forget the monastery, eh?"

Judd gaped.

"I thought—"

"I couldn't bear another fucking Virgin—"

They laughed lightly together, then kissed, tasting each

other and themselves, a mingling of saliva, and the after-
tastes of salt semen.

The following day was bright but not particularly warm.
No blue skies: just an even layer of white cloud. The
morning air was sharp in the lining of the nostrils, like
ether or peppermint.

Vaslav Jelovsek watched the pigeons in the main square
of Popolac courting death as they skipped and fluttered
ahead of the vehicles that were buzzing around. Some
about military business, some civilian. An air of sober
intention barely suppressed the excitement he felt on this
day, an excitement he knew was shared by every man,
woman, and child in Popolac. Shared by the pigeons, too
for all he knew. Maybe that was why they played under
the wheels with such dexterity, knowing that on this day
of days no harm could come to them.

He scanned the sky again, that same white sky he'd
been peering at since dawn. The cloud layer was low—not
ideal for the celebrations. A phrase passed through his
mind, an English phrase he'd heard from a friend, "to
have your head in the clouds." It meant, he'd gathered, to
be lost in reverie, in a white, sightless dream. That, he
thought wryly, was all the West knew about clouds, that
they stood for dreams. It took a vision they lacked to make
a truth out of that casual turn of phrase. Here, in these
secret hills, wouldn't they create a spectacular reality from
those idle words? A living proverb.

A head in the clouds.

Already the first contingent was assembling in the
square. There were one or two absentees owing to illness,
but the auxiliaries were ready and waiting to take their
places. Such eagerness! Such wide smiles when an auxiliary heard his or her name and number called and was
taken out of line to join the limb that was already taking
shape. On every side, miracles of organization. Everyone
with a job to do and a place to go. There was no shouting
or pushing; indeed, voices were scarcely raised above an

eager whisper. He watched in admiration as the work of positioning and buckling and roping went on.

It was going to be a long and arduous day. Vaslav had been in the square since an hour before dawn, drinking coffee from imported plastic cups, discussing the half-hourly meteorological reports coming in from Pristina and Mitrovica, and watching the starless sky as the gray light of morning crept across it. Now he was drinking his sixth coffee of the day, and it was still barely seven o'clock. Across the square, Metzinger looked as tired and as anxious as Vaslav felt.

They'd watched the dawn seep out of the east together, Metzinger and he. But now they had separated, forgetting previous companionship, and would not speak until the contest was over. After all, Metzinger was from Podujevo. He had his own city to support in the coming battle. Tomorrow they'd exchange tales of their adventures, but for today they must behave as if they didn't know each other, not even to exchange a smile. For today they had to be utterly partisan, caring only for the victory of their own city over the opposition.

Now the first leg of Popolac was erected, to the mutual satisfaction of Metzinger and Vaslav. All the safety checks had been meticulously made, and the leg left the square, its shadow falling hugely across the face of the Town Hall.

Vaslav sipped his sweet, sweet coffee and allowed himself a little grunt of satisfaction. Such days, such days. Days filled with glory, with snapping flags and high, stomach-turning sights, enough to last a man a lifetime. It was a golden foretaste of heaven.

Let America have its simple pleasures, its cartoon mice, its candy-coated castles, its cults and its technologies, he wanted none of it. The greatest wonder of the world was here, hidden in the hills.

Ah, such days.

In the main square of Podujevo, the scene was no less animated and no less inspiring. Perhaps there was a muted sense of sadness underlying this year's celebration, but that was understandable. Nita Obrenovic, Podujevo's loved and respected organizer, was no longer living. The previous winter had claimed her at the age of ninety-four, leaving the city bereft of her fierce opinions and her fiercer proportions. For sixty years Nita had worked with the citizens of Podujevo, always planning for the next contest and improving on the designs, her energies spent on making the next creation more ambitious and more lifelike than the last.

Now she was dead and sorely missed. There was no disorganization in the streets without her, the people were far too disciplined for that, but they were already falling behind schedule, and it was almost seven twenty-five. Nita's daughter had taken over in her mother's stead, but she lacked Nita's power to galvanize the people into action. She was, in a word, too gentle for the job in hand. It required a leader who was part prophet and part ringmaster, to coax and bully and inspire the citizens into their places. Maybe, after two or three decades and with a few more contests under her belt, Nita Obrenovic's daughter would make the grade. But for today Podujevo was behindhand; safety checks were being overlooked; nervous looks replaced the confidence of earlier years.

Nevertheless, at six minutes before eight the first limb of Podujevo made its way out of the city to the assembly point, to wait for its fellow.

By that time the flanks were already lashed together in Popolac, and armed contingents were awaiting orders in the town square.

Mick woke promptly at seven, though there was no alarm clock in their simply furnished room at the Hotel Beograd. He lay in his bed and listened to Judd's regular breathing from the twin bed across the room. A dull morning light whimpered through the thin curtains, not encouraging an early departure. After a few minutes' staring at the cracked paintwork on the ceiling and a while longer at the crudely carved crucifix on the opposite wall, Mick got up and went to the window. It was a dull day, as he had guessed. The sky was overcast, and the roofs of Novi Pazar were gray and featureless in the flat morning light. But beyond the roofs, to the east, he could see the hills. There was sun there. He could see shafts of light catching the blue-green of the forest, inviting a visit to their slopes.

Today maybe they would go to Kosovska Mitrovica. There was a market there, wasn't there, and a museum? And they could drive down the valley of the Ibar, following the road beside the river, where the hills rose wild and shining on either side. The hills, yes; today he decided they would see the hills.

It was eight-fifteen.

By nine the main bodies of Popolac and Podujevo were substantially assembled. In their allotted districts, the limbs of both cities were ready and waiting to join their expectant torsos.

Vaslav Jelovsek capped his gloved hands over his eyes and surveyed the sky. The cloud base had risen in the last hour, no doubt of it, and there were breaks in the clouds to the west—even, on occasion, a few glimpses of the sun. It wouldn't be a perfect day for the contest perhaps, but certainly adequate.

Mick and Judd breakfasted late on *hemendeks*—roughly translated as "ham and eggs"—and several cups of good black coffee. It was brightening up, even in Novi Pazar, and their ambitions were set high. Kosovska Mitrovica by lunchtime, and maybe a visit to the hill-castle of Zvecan in the afternoon.

About nine-thirty they motored out of Novi Pazar and took the Srbovac road south to the Ibar valley. Not a good road, but the bumps and potholes couldn't spoil the new day.

The road was empty except for the occasional pedestrian; and in place of the maize and corn fields they'd passed on the previous day, the road was flanked by undulating hills, whose sides were thickly and darkly forested. Apart from a few birds, they saw no wildlife. Even their infrequent traveling companions petered out altogether after a few miles, and the occasional farmhouse they drove by appeared locked and shuttered up. Black pigs ran unattended in the yard, with no child to feed them. Washing snapped and billowed on a sagging line, with no washerwoman in sight.

At first this solitary journey through the hills was refreshing in its lack of human contact, but as the morning drew on, an uneasiness grew on them.

"Shouldn't we have seen a signpost to Mitrovica, Mick?" He peered at the map.

"Maybe . . ."

". . . we've taken the wrong road."

"If there'd been a sign, I'd have seen it. I think we should try and get off this road, bear south a bit more—meet the valley closer to Mitrovica than we'd planned."

"How do we get off this bloody road?"

"There've been a couple of turnings . . ."

"Dirt tracks."

"Well it's either that or going on the way we are."

Judd pursed his lips.

"Cigarette?" he asked.

"Finished them miles back."

In front of them, the hills formed an impenetrable line. There was no sign of life ahead, no frail wisp of chimney smoke, no sound of voice or vehicle.

"All right," said Judd, "we take the next turning. Anything's better than this."

They drove on. The road was deteriorating rapidly, the potholes becoming craters, the hummocks feeling like bodies beneath the wheels.

Then:

"There!"

A turning: a palpable turning. Not a major road, certainly. In fact, barely the dirt track Judd had described the

other roads as being, but it was an escape from the endless
perspective of the road they were trapped on.

"This is becoming a bloody safari," said Judd as the
VW began to bump and grind its way along the doleful
little track.

"Where's your sense of adventure?"

"I forgot to pack it."

They were beginning to climb now as the track wound
its way up into the hills. The forest closed over them,
blotting out the sky, so a shifting patchwork of light and
shadow scooted over the bonnet as they drove. There was
birdsong suddenly, vacuous and optimistic, and a smell of
new pine and undug earth. A fox crossed the track up
ahead and watched a long moment as the car grumbled up
towards it. Then, with the leisurely stride of a fearless
prince, it sauntered away into the trees.

Wherever they were going, Mick thought, this was better than the road they'd left. Soon maybe they'd stop and
walk a while to find a promontory from which they could
see the valley, even Novi Pazar, nestled behind them.

The two men were still an hour's drive from Popolac
when the head of the contingent at last marched out of the
Town Square and took up its position with the main body.

This last exit left the city completely deserted. Not even
the sick or the old were neglected on this day; no one was
to be denied the spectacle and the triumph of the contest.
Every single citizen, however young or infirm—the blind,
the crippled, babes in arms, pregnant women—all made
their way up from their proud city to the stamping ground.
It was the law that they should attend, but it needed no
enforcing. No citizen of either city would have missed the
chance to see that sight—to experience the thrill of that
contest.

The confrontation had to be total, city against city. This
was the way it had always been.

So the cities went up into the hills. By noon they were
gathered, the citizens of Popolac and Podujevo, in the se-

cret well of the hills, hidden from civilized eyes, to do ancient and ceremonial battle.

Tens of thousands of hearts beat faster. Tens of thousands of bodies stretched and strained and sweated as the twin cities took their positions. The shadows of the bodies darkened tracts of land the size of small towns; the weight of their feet trampled the grass to a green milk; their movement killed animals, crushed bushes, and threw down trees. The earth literally reverberated with their passage, the hills echoing with the booming din of their steps.

In the towering body of Podujevo, a few technical hitches were becoming apparent. A slight flaw in the knitting of the left flank had resulted in a weakness there, and there were consequent problems in the swiveling mechanism of the hips. It was stiffer than it should be, and the movements were not smooth. As a result there was considerable strain being put upon that region of the city. It was being dealt with bravely; after all, the contest was intended to press the contestants to their limbs. But breaking point was closer than anyone would have dared to admit. The citizens were not as resilient as they had been in previous contests. A bad decade for crops had produced bodies less well nourished, spines less supple, wills less resolute. The badly knitted flank might not have caused an accident in itself, but further weakened by the frailty of the competitors, it set a scene for death on an unprecedented scale.

They stopped the car.

"Hear that?"

Mick shook his head. His hearing hadn't been good since he was an adolescent. Too many rock shows had blown his eardrums to hell.

Judd got out of the car.

The birds were quieter now. The noise he'd heard as they drove came again. It wasn't simply a noise: it was almost a motion in the earth, a roar that seemed seated in the substance of the hills.

Thunder, was it?

No, too rhythmical. It came again, through the soles of the feet—

Boom.

Mick heard it this time. He leaned out of the car window.

"It's up ahead somewhere. I hear it now."

Judd nodded.

Boom.

The earth-thunder sounded again.

"What the hell is it?" said Mick.

"Whatever it is, I want to see it—"

Judd got back into the Volkswagen, smiling.

"Sounds almost like guns," he said, starting the car. "Big guns."

Through his Russian-made binoculars, Vaslav Jelovsek watched the starting-official raise his pistol. He saw the feather of white smoke rise from the barrel and a second later heard the sound of the shot across the valley.

The contest had begun.

He looked up at the twin towers of Popolac and Podujevo. Heads in the clouds—well, almost. They practically stretched to touch the sky. It was an awesome sight, a breath-stopping, sleep-stabbing sight. Two cities swaying and writhing and preparing to take their first steps towards each other in this ritual battle.

Of the two, Podujevo seemed the less stable. There was a slight hesitation as the city raised its left leg to begin its march. Nothing serious, just a little difficulty in coordinating hip and thigh muscles. A couple of steps and the city would find its rhythm; a couple more and its inhabitants would be moving as one creature, one perfect giant set to match its grace and power against its mirror image.

The gunshot had sent flurries of birds up from the trees that banked the hidden valley. They rose up in celebration of the great contest, chattering their excitement as they swooped over the stamping ground.

* * *

"Did you hear a shot?" asked Judd.

Mick nodded.

"Military exercises . . . ?" Judd's smile had broadened. He could see the headlines already—exclusive reports of secret maneuvers in the depths of the Yugoslavian countryside. Russian tanks perhaps, tactical exercises being held out of the West's prying sight. With luck, he would be the carrier of this news.

Boom.

Boom.

There were birds in the air. The thunder was louder now.

It did sound like guns.

"It's over the next ridge . . ." said Judd.

"I don't think we should go any further."

"I have to see."

"I don't. We're not supposed to be here."

"I don't see any signs."

"They'll cart us away, deport us—I don't know—I just think—"

Boom.

"I've got to see."

The words were scarcely out of his mouth when the screaming started.

Podujevo was screaming: a death-cry. Someone buried in the weak flank had died of the strain and had begun a chain of decay in the system. One man loosed his neighbor and that neighbor loosed him, spreading a cancer of chaos through the body of the city. The coherence of the towering structure deteriorated with terrifying rapidity as the failure of one part of the anatomy put unendurable pressure on the others.

The masterpiece that the good citizens of Podujevo had constructed of their own flesh and blood tottered and then—a dynamited skyscraper—it began to fall.

The broken flank spewed citizens like a slashed artery

spitting blood. Then, with a graceful sloth that made the agonies of the citizens all the more horrible, it bowed towards the earth, all its limbs dissembling as it fell.

The huge head, that had brushed the clouds so recently, was flung back on its thick neck. Ten thousand mouths spoke a single scream for its vast mouth, a wordless and infinitely pitiable appeal to the sky. A howl of loss, a howl of anticipation, a howl of puzzlement. How, that scream demanded, could the day of days end like this, in a welter of falling bodies?

"Did you hear that?"

It was unmistakably human, though almost deafeningly loud. Judd's stomach convulsed. He looked across at Mick, who was as white as a sheet.

Judd stopped the car.

"No," said Mick.

"Listen—for Christ's sake—"

The din of dying moans, appeals and imprecations flooded the air. It was very close.

"We've got to go now," Mick implored.

Judd shook his head. He was prepared for some military spectacle—all the Russian army massed over the next hill—but that noise in his ears was the noise of human flesh, too human for words. It reminded him of his childhood imaginings of hell; the endless, unspeakable torments his mother had threatened him with if he failed to embrace Christ. It was a terror he'd forgotten for twenty years. But suddenly, here it was again, fresh-faced. Maybe the pit itself gaped just over the next horizon, with his mother standing at its lip, inviting him to taste its punishments.

"If you won't drive, I will."

Mick got out of the car and crossed in front of it, glancing up the track as he did so. There was a moment's hesitation, no more than a moment's, when his eyes flickered with disbelief. Then he turned towards the windscreen, his face even paler than it had been previously and said:

"Jesus Christ . . ." in a voice that was thick with suppressed nausea.

His lover was still sitting behind the wheel, his head in his hands, trying to blot out memories.

"Judd . . ."

Judd looked up slowly. Mick was staring at him like a wildman, his face shining with a sudden, icy sweat. Judd looked past him. A few meters ahead, the track had mysteriously darkened, as a tide edged towards the car, a thick, deep tide of blood. Judd's reason twisted and turned to make any other sense of the sight than that inevitable conclusion. But there was no saner explanation. It was blood, in unendurable abundance, blood without end—

And now, in the breeze, there was the flavor of freshly opened carcasses: the smell of the depths of the human body, part sweet, part savory.

Mick stumbled back to the passenger's side of the VW and fumbled weakly at the handle. The door opened suddenly and he lurched inside, his eyes glazed.

"Back up," he said.

Judd reached for the ignition. The tide of blood was already sloshing against the front wheels. Ahead, the world had been painted red.

"Drive, for fuck's sake, drive!"

Judd was making no attempt to start the car.

"We must look," he said, without conviction. "We have to."

"We don't have to do anything," said Mick, "but get the hell out of here. It's not our business . . ."

"Plane crash—"

"There's no smoke."

"Those are human voices."

Mick's instinct was to leave well enough alone. He could read about the tragedy in a newspaper—he could see the pictures tomorrow when they were gray and grainy. Today it was too fresh, too unpredictable.

Anything could be at the end of that track, bleeding—

"We must—"

Judd started the car, while beside him Mick began to moan quietly. The VW began to edge forward, nosing through the river of blood, its wheels spinning in the queasy, foaming tide.

"No," said Mick, very quietly. "Please, no . . ."

"We must," was Judd's reply. "We must. We must."

Only a few yards away, the surviving city of Popolac was recovering from its first convulsions. It stared with a thousand eyes at the ruins of its ritual enemy, now spread in a tangle of rope and bodies over the impacted ground, shattered forever. Popolac staggered back from the sight, its vast legs flattening the forest that bounded the stamping ground, its arms flailing the air. But it kept its balance, even as a common insanity, awakened by the horror at its feet, surged through its sinews and curdled its brain. The order went out—the body thrashed and twisted and turned from the grisly carpet of Podujevo and fled into the hills.

As it headed into oblivion, its towering form passed between the car and the sun, throwing its cold shadow over the bloody road. Mick saw nothing through his tears, and Judd, his eyes narrowed against the sight he feared seeing around the next bend, only dimly registered that something had blotted the light for a minute. A cloud, perhaps. A flock of birds.

Had he looked up at that moment, just stolen a glance out towards the northeast, he would have seen Popolac's head—the vast, swarming head of a maddened city—disappearing below his line of vision, as it marched into the hills. He would have known that this territory was beyond his comprehension and that there was no healing to be done in this corner of hell. But he didn't see the city, and he and Mick's last turning point had passed. From now on, like Popolac and its dead twin, they were lost to sanity and to all hope of life.

They rounded the bend, and the ruins of Podujevo came into sight.

Their domesticated imaginations had never conceived of a sight so unspeakably brutal.

Perhaps in the battlefields of Europe as many corpses had been heaped together . . . but had so many of them been women and children, locked together with the corpses of men? There had been piles of dead as high, but ever so many so recently abundant with life? There had been cities laid waste as quickly, but ever an entire city lost to the simple dictate of gravity?

It was a sight beyond sickness. In the face of it, the mind slowed to a snail's pace, the forces of reason picked over the evidence with meticulous hands, searching for a flaw in it, a place where it could say:

This is not happening. This is a dream of death, not death itself.

But reason could find no weakness in the wall. This was true. It was death indeed.

Podujevo had fallen.

Thirty-eight thousand, seven hundred and sixty-five citizens were spread on the ground, or rather flung in ungainly, seeping piles. Those who had not died of the fall or of suffocation were dying. There would be no survivors from that city except that bundle of onlookers that had traipsed out of their homes to watch the contest. Those few Podujevians—the crippled, the sick, the ancient few— were now staring, like Mick and Judd at the carnage, trying not to believe.

Judd was the first out of the car. The ground beneath his suedes was sticky with coagulating gore. He surveyed the carnage. There was no wreckage: no sign of a plane crash, no fire, no smell of fuel. Just tens of thousands of fresh bodies, all either naked or dressed in an identical gray serge, men, women, and children alike. Some of them, he could see, wore leather harnesses, tightly buckled around their upper chests, and snaking out from these contraptions were lengths of rope, miles and miles of it. The closer he looked, the more he saw of the extraordinary system of knots and lashings that still held the bodies together. For some reason, these people had been tied together side by side. Some were yoked on their neighbors' shoulders, straddling them like boys playing at horseback riding. Others were locked arm in arm, knitted together with threads of rope in a wall of muscle and bone. Yet others were trussed in a ball, with their heads tucked between their knees. All were in some way connected up with their fellows, tied together as though in some insane collective bondage game.

Another shot.

Mick looked up.

Across the field a solitary man, dressed in a drab overcoat, was walking among the bodies with a revolver, dispatching the dying. It was a pitifully inadequate act of mercy, but he went on nevertheless, choosing the suffering children first. Emptying the revolver, filling it again, emptying it, filling it, emptying it—

Mick let go.

He yelled at the top of his voice over the moans of the injured.

"What is this?"

The man looked up from his appalling duty, his face as dead gray as his coat.

"Uh?" he grunted, frowning at the two interlopers through his thick spectacles.

"What's happened here?" Mick shouted across at him. It felt good to shout, it felt good to sound angry at the man. Maybe he was to blame. It would be a fine thing, just to have someone to blame.

"Tell us, for God's sake. Explain."

Gray-coat shook his head. He didn't understand a word this young idiot was saying. It was English he spoke, but that's all he knew.

Mick began to walk towards him, feeling all the time the eyes of the dead on him. Eyes like black, shining gems set in broken faces. Eyes looking at him upside down, on heads severed from their seating. Eyes in heads that had solid howls for voices. Eyes in heads beyond howls, beyond breath.

Thousands of eyes.

He reached Gray-coat, whose gun was almost empty. He had taken off his spectacles and thrown them aside. He, too, was weeping; little jerks ran through his big, ungainly body.

At Mick's feet, somebody was reaching for him. He didn't want to look, but the hand touched his shoe and he had no choice but to see its owner. A young man, lying like a flesh swastika, every joint smashed. A child lay under him, her bloody legs poking out like two pink sticks.

He wanted the man's revolver, to stop the hand from touching him. Better still he wanted a machine gun, a flamethrower, anything to wipe the agony away.

As he looked up from the broken body, Mick saw Gray-coat raise the revolver.

"Judd—" he said, but as the word left his lips the muzzle of the revolver was slipped into Gray-coat's mouth and the trigger was pulled.

Gray-coat had saved the last bullet for himself. The back of his head opened like a dropped egg, the shell of his skull flying off. His body went limp and sank to the ground, the revolver still between his lips.

"We must—" began Mick, saying the words to nobody. "We must . . ."

What was imperative? In this situation, what *must* they do?

"We must—"

Judd was behind him.

"Help—" he said to Mick.

"Yes. We must get help. We must—"

"Go."

Go! That was what they must do. On any pretext, for any fragile, cowardly reason, they must go. Get out of the battlefield, get out of the reach of a dying hand with a wound in place of a body.

"We have to tell the authorities. Find a town. Get help—"

"Priests," said Mick. "They need priests."

It was absurd, to think of giving the last rites to so many people. It would take an army of priests, a water cannon filled with holy water, a loudspeaker to pronounce the benedictions.

They turned away together, from the horror, and wrapped their arms around each other, then picked their way through the carnage to the car.

It was occupied.

Vaslav Jelovsek was sitting behind the wheel and trying to start the Volkswagen. He turned the ignition key once. Twice. Third time the engine caught and the wheels spun in the crimson mud as he put her into reverse and backed down the track. Vaslav saw the Englishmen running towards the car, cursing him. There was no help for it—he didn't want to steal the vehicle, but he had work to do. He had been a referee; he had been responsible for the contest and the safety of the contestants. One of the heroic cities had already fallen. He must do everything in his power to prevent Popolac from following its twin. He must chase Popolac and reason with it. Talk it down out of its terrors with quiet words and promises. If he failed, there would be another disaster the equal of the one in front of him, and his conscience was already broken enough.

Mick was still chasing the VW, shouting at Jelovsek. The thief took no notice, concentrating on maneuvering the car back down the narrow, slippery track. Mick was losing the chase rapidly. The car had begun to pick up speed. Furious, but without the breath to speak his fury, Mick stood in the road, hands on his knees, heaving and sobbing.

"Bastard!" said Judd.

Mick looked down the track. Their car had already disappeared.

"Fucker couldn't even drive properly."

"We have . . . we have . . . to catch . . . up . . ." said Mick through gulps of breath.

"How?"

"On foot . . ."

"We haven't even got a map . . . it's in the car."

"Jesus . . . Christ . . . Almighty."

They walked down the track together, away from the field.

After a few meters, the tide of blood began to peter out. Just a few congealing rivulets dribbled on towards the main road. Mick and Judd followed the bloody tire marks to the junction.

The Srbovac road was empty in both directions. The tire marks showed a left turn. "He's gone deeper into the hills," said Judd, staring along the lovely road towards the blue green distance. "He's out of his mind!"

"Do we go back the way we came?"

"It'll take us all night on foot."

"We'll hop a lift."

Judd shook his head; his face was slack and his look lost. "Don't you see, Mick, they all knew this was happening. The people in the farms—they got the hell out while those people went crazy up there. There'll be no cars along this road, I'll lay you anything—except maybe a couple of shit-dumb tourists like us—and no tourist would stop for the likes of us."

He was right. They looked like butchers—splattered with blood. Their faces were shining with grease, their eyes maddened.

"We'll have to walk," said Judd, "the way he went."

He pointed along the road. The hills were darker now; the sun had suddenly gone out on their slopes.

Mick shrugged. Either way he could see they had a night on the road ahead of them. But he wanted to walk somewhere—anywhere—as long as he put distance between him and the dead.

* * *

In Popolac a kind of peace reigned. Instead of a frenzy of panic, there was a numbness, a sheeplike acceptance of the world as it was. Locked in their positions, strapped, roped and harnessed to each other in a living system that allowed no single voice to be louder than any other nor any back to labor less than its neighbor's, they let an insane consensus replace the tranquil voice of reason. They were convulsed into one mind, one thought, one ambition. They became, in the space of a few moments, the single-minded giant whose image they had so brilliantly re-created. The illusion of petty individuality was swept away in an irresistible tide of collective feeling—not a mob's passion, but a telepathic surge that dissolved the voices of thousands into one irresistible command.

And the voice said: Go!

The voice said: Take this horrible sight away, where I need never see it again.

Popolac turned away into the hills, its legs taking strides half a mile long. Each man, woman and child in that seething tower was sightless. They saw only through the eyes of the city. They were thoughtless but to think the city's thoughts. And they believed themselves deathless, in their lumbering, relentless strength. Vast and mad and deathless.

Two miles along the road Mick and Judd smelled petrol in the air, and a little farther along they came upon the VW. It had overturned in the reed-clogged drainage ditch at the side of the road. It had not caught fire.

The driver's door was open, and the body of Vaslav Jelovsek had tumbled out. His face was calm in unconsciousness. There seemed to be no sign of injury, except for a small cut or two on his sober face. They gently pulled the thief out of the wreckage and up out of the filth of the ditch onto the road. He moaned a little as they fussed about him, rolling Mick's sweater up to pillow his head and removing the man's jacket and tie.

Quite suddenly, he opened his eyes.

He stared at them both.

"Are you all right?" Mick asked.

The man said nothing for a moment. He seemed not to understand.

Then:

"English?" he said. His accent was thick, but the question was quite clear.

"Yes."

"I heard your voices. English."

He frowned and winced.

"Are you in pain?" said Judd.

The man seemed to find this amusing.

"Am I in pain?" he repeated, his face screwed up in a mixture of agony and delight.

"I shall die," he said, through gritted teeth.

"No," said Mick, "You're all right."

The man shook his head, his authority absolute.

"I shall die," he said again, the voice full of determination. "I want to die."

Judd crouched closer to him. His voice was weaker by the moment.

"Tell us what to do," he said. The man had closed his eyes. Judd shook him awake, roughly.

"Tell us," he said again, his show of compassion rapidly disappearing. "Tell us what this is all about."

"About?" said the man, his eyes still closed. "It was a fall, that's all. Just a fall . . ."

"What fell?"

"The city. Podujevo. My city."

"What did it fall from?"

"Itself, of course."

The man was explaining nothing, just answering one riddle with another.

"Where were you going?" Mick inquired, trying to sound as unaggressive as possible.

"After Popolac," said the man.

"Popolac?" said Judd.

Mick began to see some sense in the story.

"Popolac is another city. Like Podujevo. Twin cities. They're on the map—"

"Where's the city now?" said Judd.

Vaslav Jelovsek seemed to choose to tell the truth. There was a moment when he hovered between dying with a riddle on his lips and living long enough to unburden his story. What did it matter if the tale was told now? There could never be another contest—all that was over.

"They came to fight," he said, his voice now very soft, "Popolac and Podujevo. They come every ten years—"

"Fight?" said Judd. "You mean all those people were slaughtered?"

Vaslav shook his head.

"No, no. They fell. I told you."

"Well, how do they fight?" Mick said.

"Go into the hills" was the only reply.

Vaslav opened his eyes a little. The faces that loomed over him were exhausted and sick. They had suffered, these innocents. They deserved some explanation.

"As giants," he said. "They fought as giants. They made a body out of their bodies, do you understand? The frame, the muscles, the bone, the eyes, nose, teeth all made of men and women."

"He's delirious," said Judd.

"You go into the hills," the man repeated. "See for yourselves how true it is."

"Even supposing—" Mick began.

Vaslav interrupted him, eager to be finished. "They were good at the game of giants. It took many centuries of practice, every ten years making the figure larger and larger. One always ambitious to be larger than the other. Ropes to tie them all together flawlessly. Sinews . . . ligaments . . . There was food in its belly . . . there were pipes from the loins, to take away the waste. The best sighted sat in the eye sockets, the best-voiced in the mouth and throat. You wouldn't believe the engineering of it."

"I don't," said Judd, and stood up.

"It is the body of the state," said Vaslav, so softly his

voice was barely above a whisper. "It is the shape of our lives."

There was a silence. Small clouds passed over the road, soundlessly shedding their mass to the air.

"It was a miracle," he said. It was as if he realized the true enormity of the fact for the first time. "It was a miracle."

It was enough. Yes. It was quite enough.

His mouth closed, the words said, and he died.

Mick felt this death more acutely than the thousands they had fled from; or rather this death was the key to unlock the anguish he felt for them all.

Whether the man had chosen to tell a fantastic lie as he died or whether this story was in some way true, Mick felt useless in the face of it. His imagination was too narrow to encompass the idea. His brain ached with the thought of it, and his compassion cracked under the weight of misery he felt.

They stood on the road, while the clouds scudded by, their vague, gray shadows passing over them towards the enigmatic hills.

It was twilight.

Popolac could stride no further. It felt exhaustion in every muscle. Here and there in its huge anatomy deaths had occurred, but there was no grieving in the city for its deceased cells. If the dead were in the interior, the corpses were allowed to hang from their harnesses. If they formed the skin of the city, they were unbuckled from their positions and released, to plunge into the forest below.

The giant was not capable of pity. It had no ambition but to continue until it ceased.

As the sun slunk out of sight Popolac rested, sitting on a small hillock, nursing its huge head in its huge hands.

The stars were coming out, with their familiar caution. Night was approaching, mercifully bandaging up the wounds of the day, blinding eyes that had seen too much.

Popolac rose to its feet again and began to move, step

by booming step. It would not be long, surely, before fatigue overcame it, before it could lie down in the tomb of some lost valley and die.

But for a space yet, it must walk on, each step more agonizingly slow than the last, while the night bloomed black around its head.

Mick wanted to bury the car thief somewhere on the edge of the forest. Judd, however, pointed out that burying a body might seem, in tomorrow's saner light, a little suspicious. And besides, wasn't it absurd to concern themselves with one corpse when there were literally thousands of them lying a few miles from where they stood?

The body was left to lie, therefore, and the car to sink deeper into the ditch.

They began to walk again.

It was cold, and colder by the moment, and they were hungry.

But the few houses they passed were all deserted, locked and shuttered, every one.

"What did he mean?" said Mick, as they stood looking at another locked door.

"He was talking metaphor—"

"All that stuff about giants?"

"It was some Trotskyist tripe—" Judd insisted.

"I don't think so."

"I know so. It was his deathbed speech, he'd probably been preparing for years."

"I don't think so," Mick said again and began walking back towards the road.

"Oh, how's that?" Judd was at his back.

"He wasn't towing some party line."

"Are you saying you think there's some giant around here someplace? For God's sake!"

Mick turned to Judd. His face was difficult to see in the twilight. But his voice was sober with belief.

"Yes. I think he was telling the truth."

"That's absurd. That's ridiculous. No."

Judd hated Mick that moment. Hated his naiveté, his passion to believe any half-witted story if it had a whiff of romance about it. And this? This was the worst, the most preposterous . . .

"No," he said again. "No. No. No."

The sky was porcelain smooth, and the outline of the hills black as pitch.

"I'm fucking freezing," said Mick out of the ink. "Are you staying here or walking with me?"

Judd shouted: "We're not going to find anything this way."

"Well it's a long way back."

"We're just going deeper into the hills."

"Do what you like—I'm walking."

His footsteps receded, the dark encased him.

After a minute, Judd followed.

The night was cloudless and bitter. They walked on, their collars up against the chill, their feet swollen in their shoes. Above them the whole sky had become a parade of stars. A triumph of spilled light from which the eye could make as many patterns as it had patience for. After a while, they slung their tired arms around each other for comfort and warmth.

About eleven o'clock, they saw the glow of a window in the distance.

The woman at the door of the stone cottage didn't smile, but she understood their condition and let them in. There seemed to be no purpose in trying to explain to either the woman or her crippled husband what they had seen. The cottage had no telephone, and there was no sign of a vehicle, so even had they found some way to express themselves, nothing could be done.

With mimes and face-pullings they explained that the were hungry and exhausted. They tried further to explain they were lost, cursing themselves for leaving their phrase book in the VW. She didn't seem to understand very much

of what they said, but sat them down beside a blazing fire
and put a pan of food on the stove to heat.

They ate thick unsalted pea soup and eggs, and occasionally smiled their thanks to the woman. Her husband
sat beside the fire, making no attempt to talk or even look
at the visitors.

The food was good. It buoyed their spirits.

They would sleep until morning and then begin the long
trek back. By dawn the bodies in the field would be being
quantified, identified, parceled up and dispatched to their
families. The air would be full of reassuring noises, can-
celing out the moans that still rang in their ears. There
would be helicopters, truck loads of men organizing the
clearing-up operations. All the rites and paraphernalia of
a civilized disaster.

And in a while, it would be palatable. It would become
part of their history—a tragedy, of course, but one they
could explain, classify and learn to live with. All would
be well, yes, all would be well. Come morning.

The sleep of sheer fatigue came on them suddenly. They
lay where they had fallen, still sitting at the table, their
heads on their crossed arms. A litter of empty bowls and
bread crusts surrounded them.

They knew nothing. Dreamed nothing. Felt nothing.

Then the thunder began.

In the earth, in the deep earth, a rhythmical tread, as of
a titan, that came by degrees closer and closer.

The woman woke her husband. She blew out the lamp
and went to the door. The night sky was luminous with
stars; the hills black on every side.

The thunder still sounded . . . a full half minute between every boom, but louder now. And louder with every
new step.

They stood at the door together, husband and wife, and
listened to the night-hills echo back and forth with the
sound. There was no lightning to accompany the thunder.

Just the boom—

Boom—

Boom—

It made the ground shake; it threw dust down from the door lintel and rattled the window latches.

Boom—

Boom—

They didn't know what approached, but whatever shape it took and whatever it intended, there seemed no sense in running from it. Where they stood, in the pitiful shelter of their cottage, was as safe as any nook of the forest. How could they choose, out of a hundred thousand trees, that which would be standing when the thunder had passed? Better to wait . . . and watch.

The wife's eyes were not good, and she doubted what she saw when the blackness of the hill changed shape and reared up to block the stars. But her husband had seen it, too: the unimaginably huge head, vaster in the deceiving darkness, looming up and up, dwarfing the hills themselves with its ambition.

He fell to his knees, babbling a prayer, his arthritic legs twisted beneath him.

His wife screamed. No words she knew could keep this monster at bay—no prayer, no plea, had power over it.

In the cottage, Mick woke, and his outstretched arm, twitching with a sudden cramp, wiped the plate and the lamp off the table.

They smashed.

Judd woke.

The screaming outside had stopped. The woman had disappeared from the doorway into the forest. Any tree, any tree at all, was better than this sight. Her husband still let a string of prayers dribble from his slack mouth, as the great leg of the giant rose to take another step—

Boom—

The cottage shook. Plates danced and smashed off the dresser. A clay pipe rolled from the mantelpiece and shattered in the ashes of the hearth.

The lovers knew the noise that sounded in their substance: that earth-thunder.

Mick reached for Judd and took him by the shoulder.

"You see," he said, his teeth blue-gray in the darkness of the cottage. "See? See?"

There was a kind of hysteria bubbling behind his words. He ran to the door, stumbling over a chair in the dark. Cursing and bruised, he staggered out into the night—

Boom—

The thunder was deafening. This time it broke all the windows in the cottage. In the bedroom, one of the roof joists cracked and flung debris downstairs.

Judd joined his lover at the door. The old man was now facedown on the ground, his sick and swollen fingers curled, his begging lips pressed to the damp soil.

Mick was looking up towards the sky. Judd followed his gaze.

There was a place that showed no stars. It was a darkness in the shape of a man, a vast, broad human frame, a colossus that soared up to meet heaven. It was not quite a perfect giant. Its outline was not tidy; it seethed and swarmed.

He seemed broader, too, this giant, than any real man. His legs were abnormally thick and stumpy, and his arms were not long. The hands, as they clenched and unclenched, seemed oddly jointed and overdelicate for its torso.

Then it raised one huge, flat foot and placed it on the earth, taking a stride towards them.

Boom—

The step brought the roof collapsing in on the cottage. Everything that the car thief had said was true. Popolac was a city and a giant; and it had gone into the hills . . .

Now their eyes were becoming accustomed to the night light. They could see in ever more horrible detail the way this monster was constructed. It was a masterpiece of human engineering: a man made entirely of men. Or rather, a sexless giant, made of men and women and children. All the citizens of Popolac writhed and strained in the body of this flesh-knitted giant, their muscles stretched to breaking point, their bones close to snapping.

Mick and Judd could see how the architects of Popolac had subtly altered the proportions of the human body, how the thing had been made squatter to lower its center of gravity, how its legs had been made elephantine to bear the weight of the torso, how the head was sunk low on to the wide shoulders so that the problems of a weak neck had been minimized.

Despite these malformations, it was horribly lifelike. The bodies that were bound together to make its surface were naked but for their harnesses, so that its surface glistened in the starlight like one vast human torso. Even the muscles were well copied, though simplified. They could see the way the roped bodies pushed and pulled against each other in solid cords of flesh and bone. They could see the intertwined people that made up the body: the backs like turtles packed together to offer the sweep of the pectorals; the lashed and knotted acrobats at the joints of the arms and the legs alike, rolling and unwinding to articulate the city.

But surely the most amazing sight of all was the face.

Cheeks of bodies; cavernous eye sockets in which heads stared, five bound together for each eyeball; a broad, flat nose and a mouth that opened and closed as the muscles of the jaw bunched and hollowed rhythmically. And from that mouth, lined with teeth made of bald children, the voice of the giant—now only a weak copy of its former powers—spoke a single note of idiot music.

Popolac walked and Popolac sang.

Was there ever a sight in Europe the equal of it?

They watched, Mick and Judd, as it took another step towards them.

The old man had wet his pants. Blubbering and begging, he dragged himself away from the ruined cottage into the surrounding trees, dragging his dead legs after him.

The Englishmen remained where they stood, watching

the spectacle as it approached. Neither dread nor horror touched them now, just an awe that rooted them to the spot. They knew this was a sight they could never hope to see again; this was the apex—after this, there was only common experience. Better to stay then, though every step brought death nearer, better to stay and see the sight while it was still there to be seen. And if it killed them, this monster, then at least they would have glimpsed a miracle, known this terrible majesty for a brief moment. It seemed a fair exchange.

Popolac was within two steps of the cottage. They could see the complexities of its structure quite clearly. The faces of the citizens were becoming detailed: white, sweat-wet, and content in their weariness. Some hung dead from their harnesses, their legs swinging back and forth like the hanged. Others, children particularly, had ceased to obey their training and had relaxed their positions, so that the form of the body was degenerating, beginning to seethe with the boils of rebellious cells.

Yet it still walked, each step an incalculable effort of coordination and strength.

Boom—

The step that trod the cottage came sooner then they thought.

Mick saw the leg raised and saw the faces of the people in the shin and ankle and foot—they were as big as he was now—all huge men chosen to take the full weight of this great creation. Many were dead. The bottom of the foot, he could see, was a jigsaw of crushed bloody bodies, pressed to death under the weight of their fellow citizens.

The foot descended with a roar.

In a matter of seconds, the cottage was reduced to splinters and dust.

Popolac blotted the sky utterly. It was, for a moment, the whole world, Heaven and Earth; its presence filled the senses to overflowing. At this proximity one look could not encompass it. The eye had to range backwards and forwards over its mass to take it all in, and even then the mind refused to accept the whole truth.

A whirling fragment of stone, slung off from the cottage as it collapsed, struck Judd full in the face. In his head, he heard the killing stroke like a ball hitting a wall—a play-yard death. No pain, no remorse. Out like a light, a tiny, insignificant light; his death-cry lost in the pandemonium, his body hidden in the smoke and darkness. Mick neither saw nor heard Judd die.

He was too busy staring at the foot as it settled for a moment in the ruins of the cottage, while the other leg mustered the will to move.

Mick took his chance. Howling like a banshee, he ran towards the leg, longing to embrace the monster. He stumbled in the wreckage and stood again, bloodied, to reach for the foot before it was lifted and he was left behind. There was a clamor of agonized breath as the message came to the foot that it must move; Mick saw the muscles of the shin bunch and marry as the leg began to lift. He made one last lunge at the limb as it began to leave the ground, snatching a harness or a rope or human hair or flesh itself—anything to catch this passing miracle and be part of it. Better to go with it wherever it was going and serve it in its purpose, whatever that might be; better to die with it than live without it.

He caught the foot and found a safe purchase on its ankle. Screaming his sheer ecstasy at his success he felt the great leg raised and glanced down through the swirling dust to the spot where he had stood, already receding as the limb climbed.

The earth was gone from beneath him. He was a hitchhiker with a god: The mere life he had left was nothing to him now, or ever. He would live with this thing, yes, he would live with it—seeing it and seeing it and eating it with his eyes until he died of sheer gluttony.

He screamed and howled and swung on the ropes, drinking up his triumph. Below, far below, he glimpsed Judd's body, curled up pale on the dark ground, irretrievable. Love and life and sanity were gone, gone like the memory of his name or his sex or his ambition.

It all meant nothing. Nothing at all.

Boom—

Boom—

Popolac walked, the noise of its steps receding to the east. Popolac walked, the hum of its voice lost in the night.

After a day, birds came, foxes came, flies, butterflies, wasps came. Judd moved, Judd shifted, Judd gave birth. In his belly, maggots warmed themselves; in a vixen's den the good flesh of his thighs was fought over. After that, it was quick. The bones yellowing, the bones crumbling . . . soon, an empty space which he had once filled with breath and opinions.

Darkness, light, darkness, light. He interrupted neither with his name.

AUTHOR'S NOTE

BEFORE IT WAS PUBLISHED, "IN THE HILLS, THE CITIES" had the dubious distinction of being the most scorned of those stories contained in The Books of Blood. *Nobody liked it. Not my agent or my agent's assistant; not my editor, nor her assistant. The repeated objection was that the conceit of the story was so far beyond the parameters of the believable that no reader would embrace it. The story would be laughed off the page, I was told.*

They were wrong. The readers of popular horror fiction will devour the most outlandish ideas if publishers will only give them a chance to demonstrate their appetite.

I'm proud of the story, but in a way I'm even more

proud of the readership that proved the cynics wrong; the readership which will take horror fiction kicking and screaming into the 21st Century because it wants to stretch its imagination beyond the limits. . . .

—*Clive Barker*

JAMBOREE
Jack Williamson

THE SCOUTMASTER SLIPPED INTO THE CAMP ON BLACK
plastic tracks. Its slick yellow hood shone in the cold early
light like the shell of a bug. It paused in the door, listening
for boys not asleep. Then its glaring eyes began to swivel,
darting red beams into every corner, looking for boys out
of bed.

"Rise and smile!" Its loud merry voice bounced off the
gray iron walls. "Fox Troop rise and smile! Hop for old
Pop! Mother says today is Jamboree!"

The Nuke Patrol, next to the door, was mostly tenderfeet, still in their autonomic prams. They all began squall-
ing, because they hadn't learned to love old Pop. The
machine's happy voice rose louder than their howling, and
it came fast down the narrow aisle to the cubs in the Anthrax Patrol.

"Hop for Pop! Mother says it's Jamboree!"

The cubs jumped up to attention, squealing with delight.
Jamboree was bright gold stars to paste on their faces.
Jamboree was a whole scoop of pink ice milk and maybe
a natural apple. Jamboree was a visit to Mother's.

The older scouts in the Scavanger Patrol and the Skull Patrol were not so noisy, because they knew Mother wouldn't have many more Jamborees for them. Up at the end of the camp, three boys sat up without a sound and looked at Joey's empty pallet.

"Joey's late," Ratbait whispered. He was a pale, scrawny, wise-eyed scout who looked too old for twelve. "We oughta save his hide. We oughta fix a dummy and fool old Pop."

"Naw!" muttered Butch. "He'll get us all in bad."

"But we oughta—" Blinkie wheezed. "We oughta help—"

Ratbait began wadding up a pillow to be the dummy's head, but he dropped flat when he saw the scoutmaster rushing down with a noise like wind, red lamps stabbing at the empty bed.

"Now, now, scouts!" Its voice fluttered like a hurt bird. "You can't play pranks on poor old Pop. Not today. You'll make us late for Jamboree."

Ratbait felt a steel whip twitch the blanket from over his head and saw red light burning through his tight-shut lids.

"Better wake up, Scout R-8." Its smooth, sad voice dripped over him like warm oil. "Better tell old Pop where J-0 went."

He squirmed under that terrible blaze. He couldn't see and he couldn't breathe and he couldn't think what to say. He gulped at the terror in his throat and tried to shake his head. At last the red glare went on to Blinkie.

"Scout Q-2, you're a twenty-badger." The low, slow voice licked at Blinkie like a friendly pup. "You like to help old Pop keep a tidy camp for Mother. You'll tell us where J-0 went."

Blinkie was a fattish boy. His puffy face was toadstool-pale, and his pallet had a sour smell from being wet. He sat up and ducked back from the steel whip over him.

"Please d-d-d-d-d—" His wheezy stammer stalled his voice, and he couldn't dodge the bright whip that looped

around him and dragged him up to the heat and the hum
and the hot smell of Pop's yellow hood.

"Well, Scout Q-2?"

Blinkie gasped and stuttered and finally sagged against
the plastic tracks like gray jelly. The shining coils rippled
around him like thin snakes, constricting. His breath
wheezed out and his fat arm jerked up, pointing to a black
sign on the wall.

DANGER!
Power Access
ROBOTS ONLY!

The whips tossed him back on his sour pallet. He lay there,
panting and blinking and dodging, even after the whips
were gone. The scoutmaster's eye flashed to the sign and
the square grating under it, and swiveled back to Butch.

Butch was a slow, stocky, bug-eyed boy, young enough
to come back from another Jamboree. He had always been
afraid of Pop, but he wanted to be the new leader of Skull
Patrol in Joey's place, and now he thought he saw his
chance.

"Don't hit me, Pop!" His voice squeaked and his face
turned red, but he scrambled off his pallet without waiting
for the whips. "I'll tell on Joey. I been wantin' all along
to tell, but I was afraid they'd beat me."

"Good boy!" The scoutmaster's loud words swelled out
like big soap-bubbles bursting in the sun. "Mother wants
to know all about Scout J-0."

"He pries that grating—" His voice quavered and caught
when he saw the look on Ratbait's face, but when he turned
to Pop it came back loud. "Does it every night. Since
three Jamborees ago. Sneaks down in the pits where the
robots work. I dunno why, except he sees somebody there.
An' brings things back. Things he shouldn't have. Things
like this!"

He fumbled in his uniform and held up a metal tag.

"This is your good turn today, Scout X-6." The thin

tip of a whip took the tag and dangled it close to the hot red lamps. "Whose tag is this?"

"Lookit the number—"

Butch's voice dried up when he saw Ratbait's pale lips making words without a sound. "What's so much about an ID tag?" Ratbait asked. "Anyhow, what were you doing in Joey's bed?"

"It's odd!" Butch looked away and squeaked at Pop. "A girl's number!"

The silent shock of that bounced off the iron walls, louder than old Pop's boom. Most of the scouts had never seen a girl. After a long time, the cubs near the door began to whisper and titter.

"Shhhhh!" Pop roared like steam. "Now we can all do a good turn for Mother. And play a little joke on Scout J-0! He didn't know today would be Jamboree, but he'll find out." Pop laughed like a heavy chain clanking. "Back to bed! Quiet as robots!"

Pop rolled close to the wall near the power-pit grating, and the boys lay back on their pallets. Once Ratbait caught his breath to yell, but he saw Butch's bug-eyes watching. Pop's hum sank, and even the tenderfeet in their prams were quiet as robots.

Ratbait heard the grating creak. He saw Joey's head, tangled-yellow hair streaked with oil and dust. He frowned and shook his head and saw Joey's sky-blue eyes go wide.

Joey tried to duck, but the quick whips caught his neck. They dragged him out of the square black pit and swung him like a puppet toward old Pop's eyes.

"Well, Scout J-0!" Pop laughed like thick oil bubbling. "Mother wants to know where you've been."

Joey fell on his face when the whip uncoiled, but he scrambled to his feet. He gave Ratbait a pale grin before he looked up at Pop, but he didn't say anything.

"Better tell old Pop the truth." The slick whips drew back like lean snakes about to strike. "Or else we'll have to punish you, Scout J-0."

Joey shook his head, and the whips went to work. Still

he didn't speak. He didn't even scream. But something fell out of his torn uniform. The whip-tips snatched it off the floor.

"What's this thing, Scout J-0?" The whip-fingers turned it delicately under the furious eyes and nearly dropped it again. "Scout J-0, this is a book."

Silence echoed in the iron camp.

"Scout J-0, you've stolen a book." Pop's shocked voice changed into a toneless buzz, reading the title. *"Operator's Handbook, Nuclear Reactor, Series 9-Z."*

Quiet sparks of fear crackled through the camp. Two or three tenderfeet began sobbing in their prams. When they were quiet, old Pop made an ominous, throat-clearing sound.

"Scout J-0, what are you doing with a book?"

Joey gulped and bit his under lip till blood seeped down his chin, but he made no sound. Old Pop rolled closer, while the busy whips were stowing the book in a dark compartment under the yellow hood.

"Mother won't like this." Each word clinked hard, like iron on iron. "Books aren't for boys. Books are for robots only. Don't you know that?"

Joey stood still.

"This hurts me, Scout J-0." Pop's voice turned downy soft, the slow words like tears of sadness now. "It hurts your poor Mother. More than anything can ever hurt you."

The whips cracked and cracked and cracked. At last they picked him up and shook him and dropped him like a red-streaked rag on the floor. Old Pop backed away and wheeled around.

"Fox Troop rise and smile!" Its roaring voice turned jolly again, as if it had forgotten Joey. "Hop for Pop. Today is Jamboree, and we're on our way to visit Mother. Fall out in marching order."

The cubs twittered with excitement until their leaders threatened to keep them home from Jamboree, but at last old Pop led the troop out of camp and down the paved trail toward Mother's. Joey limped from the whips, but he set his teeth and kept his place at the head of his patrol.

Marching through boy territory, they passed the scattered camps of troops whose Jamborees came on other days. A few scouts were out with their masters, but nobody waved or even looked straight at them.

The spring sun was hot and Pop's pace was too fast for the cubs. Some of them began to whimper and fall out of line. Pop rumbled back to warn them that Mother would give no gold stars if they were late for Jamboree. When Pop was gone, Joey glanced at Ratbait and beckoned with his head.

"I gotta get away!" he whispered low and fast. "I gotta get back to the pits—"

Butch ran out of his place, leaning to listen. Ratbait shoved him off the trail.

"You gotta help!" Joey gasped. "There's a thing we gotta do—an' we gotta do it now. 'Cause this will be the last Jamboree for most of us. We'll never get another chance."

Butch came panting along the edge of the trail, trying to hear, but Blinkie got in his way.

"What's all this?" Ratbait breathed. "What you gonna do?"

"It's all in the book," Joey said. "Something called manual override. There's a dusty room, down under Mother's, back of a people-only sign. Two red buttons. Two big levers. With a glass wall between. It takes two people."

"Who? One of us?"

Joey shook his head, waiting for Blinkie to elbow Butch. "I got a friend. We been working together, down in the pits. Watching the robots. Reading the books. Learning what we gotta do—"

He glanced back. Blinkie was scuffling with Butch to keep him busy, but now the scoutmaster came clattering back from the rear, booming merrily, "Hop for Pop! Hop a lot for Pop!"

"How you gonna work it?" Alarm took Ratbait's breath. "Now the robots will be watching—"

"We got a back door," Joey's whisper raced. "A drainage tunnel. Hot water out of the reactor. Comes out under Black Creek bridge. My friend'll be there. If I can dive off this end of the bridge—"

"Hey, Pop!" Butch was screaming. "Ratbait's talking! Blinkie pushed me! Joey's planning something bad!"

"Good boy, Scout X-6!" Pop slowed beside him. "Mother wants to know if they're plotting more mischief."

When Pop rolled on ahead of the troop, Ratbait wanted to ask what would happen when Joey and his friend pushed the two red buttons and pulled the two big levers, but Butch stuck so close they couldn't speak again. He thought it must be something about the reactor. Power was the life of Mother and the robots. If Joey could cut the power off—

Would they die? The idea frightened him. If the prams stopped, who would care for the tenderfeet? Who would make chow? Who would tell anybody what to do? Perhaps the books would help, he thought. Maybe Joey and his friend would know.

With Pop rolling fast in the lead, they climbed a long hill and came in sight of Mother's. Old gray walls that had no windows. Two tall stacks of dun-colored brick. A shimmer of heat in the pale sky.

The trail sloped down. Ratbait saw the crinkled ribbon of green brush along Black Creek, and then the concrete bridge. He watched Butch watching Joey, and listened to Blinkie panting, and tried to think how to help.

The cubs stopped whimpering when they saw Mother's mysterious walls and stacks, and the troop marched fast down the hill. Ratbait slogged along, staring at the yellow sun-dazzle on old Pop's hood. He couldn't think of anything to do.

"I got it!" Blinkie was breathing, close to his ear. "I'll take care of Pop."

"You?" Ratbait scowled. "You were telling on Joey—"

"That's why," Blinkie gasped. "I wanta make it up. I'll handle Pop. You stop Butch—an' give the sign to Joey."

They came to the bridge and Pop started across.

"Wait, Pop!" Blinkie darted out of line, toward the brushy slope above the trail. "I saw a girl! Hiding in the bushes to watch us go by."

Pop roared back off the bridge.

"A girl in boy territory!" Its shocked voice splashed them like cold rain. "What would Mother say?" Black tracks spurting gravel, it lurched past Blinkie and crashed into the brush.

"Listen, Pop!" Butch started after it, waving and squealing. "They ain't no girl—"

Ratbait tripped him and turned to give Joey the sign, but Joey was already gone. Something splashed under the bridge and Ratbait saw a yellow head sliding under the steam that drifted out of a black tunnel mouth.

"Pop! Pop!" Butch rubbed gravel out of his mouth and danced on the pavement. "Come back, Pop. Joey's in the creek! Ratbait and Blinkie—they helped him get away."

The scoutmaster swung back down the slope, empty whips waving. It skidded across the trail and down the bank to the hot creek. Its yellow hood faded into the stream.

"Tattletale!" Blinkie clenched his fat fists. "You told on Joey."

"An' you'll catch it!" Murky eyes bugging, Butch edged away. "You just wait till Pop gets back."

They waited. The tired cubs sat down to rest and the tenderfeet fretted in their hot prams. Breathing hard, Blinkie kept close to Butch. Ratbait watched till Pop swam back out of the drain.

The whips were wrapped around two small bundles that dripped pink water. Unwinding, the whips dropped Joey and his friend on the trail. They crumpled down like rag dolls, but the whips set them up again.

"How's this, scouts?" Old Pop laughed like steel gears clashing. "We've caught ourselves a real live girl!"

In a bird-quick way, she shook the water out of her sand-colored hair. Standing straight, without the whips to hold her, she faced Pop's glaring lamps. She looked tall for twelve.

Joey was sick when the whips let him go. He leaned off the bridge to heave, and limped back to the girl. She wiped his face with her wet hair. They caught hands and smiled at each other as if they were all alone.

"They tripped me, Pop." Braver now, Butch thumbed his nose at Blinkie and ran toward the machine. "They tried to stop me telling you—"

"Leave them to Mother," Pop sang happily. "Let them try their silly tricks on her." It wheeled toward the bridge, and the whips pushed Joey and the girl ahead of the crunching tracks. "Now hop with Pop to Jamboree!"

They climbed that last hill to a tall iron door in Mother's old gray wall. The floors beyond were naked steel, alive with machinery underneath. They filed into a dim round room that echoed to the grating squeal of Pop's hard tracks.

"Fox Troop, here we are for Jamboree!" Pop's jolly voice made a hollow booming on the curved steel wall, and its red lights danced in tall reflections there. "Mother wants you to know why we celebrate this happy time each year."

The machine was rolling to the center of a wide black circle in the middle of the floor. Something drummed far below like a monster heart, and Ratbait saw that the circle was the top of a black steel piston. It slid slowly up, lifting Pop. The drumming died, and Pop's eyes blazed down on the cubs in the Anthrax Patrol to stop their awed murmuring.

"Once there wasn't any Mother." The shock of that crashed and throbbed and faded. "There wasn't any yearly Jamboree. There wasn't even any Pop, to love and care for little boys."

The cubs were afraid to whisper, but a stir of troubled wonder spread among them.

"You won't believe how tenderfeet were made." There was a breathless hush. "In those bad old days, boys and girls were allowed to change like queer insects. They changed into creatures called adults—"

The whips writhed and the red lamps glared and the black cleats creaked on the steel platform.

"Adults!" Pop spewed the word. "They malfunctioned and wore out and ran down. Their defective logic circuits programmed them to damage one another. In a kind of strange group malfunction called war, they systematically destroyed one another. But their worst malfunction was making new tenderfeet."

Pop turned slowly on the high platform, sweeping the silent troop with blood-red beams that stopped on Joey and his girl. All the scouts but Ratbait and Blinkie had edged away from them. Her face white and desperate, she was whispering in Joey's ear. Listening with his arm around her, he scowled at Pop.

"Once adults made tenderfeet, strange as that may seem to you. They used a weird natural process we won't go into. It finally broke down, because they had damaged their genes in war. The last adults couldn't make new boys and girls at all."

The red beams darted to freeze a startled cub.

"Fox Troop, that's why we have Mother. Her job is to collect undamaged genes and build them into whole cells with which she can assemble whole boys and girls. She has been doing that a long time now, and she does it better than those adults ever did.

"And that's why we have Jamboree! To fill the world with well-made boys and girls like you, and to keep you happy in the best time of life—even those old adults always said childhood was the happy time. Scouts, clap for Jamboree!"

The cubs clapped, the echo like a spatter of hail on the high iron ceiling.

"Now, Scouts, those bad old days are gone forever," Pop burbled merrily. "Mother has a cozy place for each of you, and old Pop watched over you, and you'll never be adult—"

"Pop! Pop!" Butch squealed. "Lookit Joey an' his girl!"

Pop spun around on the high platform. Its blinding beams picked up Joey and the girl, sprinting toward a bright sky-slice where the door had opened for the last of the prams.

"Wake up, guys!" Joey's scream shivered against the red steel wall. "That's all wrong. Mother's just a runaway machine. Pop's a crazy robot—"

"Stop for Pop!" The scoutmaster was trapped on top of that huge piston, but its blazing lamps raced after Joey and the girl. "Catch 'em, cubs! Hold 'em tight. Or there'll be no Jamboree!"

"I told you, Pop!" Butch scuttled after them. "Don't forget I'm the one that told—"

Ratbait dived at his heels, and they skidded together on the floor.

"Come on, scouts!" Joey was shouting. "Run away with us. Our own genes are good enough."

The floor shuddered under him and that bright sky-slice grew thinner. Lurching on their little tracks, the prams formed a line to guard it. Joey jumped the shrieking tenderfeet, but the girl stumbled. He stopped to pick her up.

"Help us, scouts!" he gasped. "We gotta get away—"

"Catch 'em for Pop!" that metal bellow belted them. "Or there'll be no gold stars for anybody!"

Screeching cubs swarmed around them. The door clanged shut. Pop plunged off the sinking piston, almost too soon. It crunched down on the yellow hood. Hot oil splashed and smoked, but the whips hauled it upright again.

"Don't mess around with M-M-M-M-Mother!" Its anvil voice came back with a stuttering croak. "She knows best!"

The quivering whips dragged Joey and the girl away from the clutching cubs and pushed them into a shallow black pit, where now that great black piston had dropped below the level of the floor.

"Sing for your Mother!" old Pop chortled. "Sing for the Jamboree!"

The cubs howled out their official song, and the Jamboree went on. There were Pop-shaped balloons for the tenderfeet, and double scoops of pink ice milk for the cubs, and gold stars for nearly everybody.

"But Mother wants a few of you." Old Pop was a fat cat purring.

When a pointing whip picked Blinkie out, he jumped into the pit without waiting to be dragged. But Butch turned white and tried to run when it struck at him.

"Pop! Not m-m-m-m-me!" he squeaked. "Don't forget I told on Joey. I'm only going on eleven, and I'm in line for leader, and I'll tell on everybody—"

"That's why Mother wants you." Old Pop laughed like a pneumatic hammer. "You're getting too adult."

The whip snaked Butch into the pit, dull eyes bulging more than ever. He slumped down on the slick black piston and struggled like a squashed bug and then lay moaning in a puddle of terror.

Ratbait stood sweating, as the whip came back to him. His stomach felt cold and strange, and the tall red wall spun like a crazy wheel around him, and he couldn't move till the whip pulled him to the rim of the pit.

But there Blinkie took his hand. He shook the whip off, and stepped down into the pit. Joey nodded, and the girl gave him a white, tiny smile. They all closed around her, arms linked tight, as the piston dropped.

"Now hop along for Pop! You've had your Jamboree—" That hooting voice died away far above, and the pit's round mouth shrank into a blood-colored moon. The hot dark drummed like thunder all around them, and the slick floor tilted. It spilled them all into Mother's red steel jaws.

AUTHOR'S NOTE

"Jamboree" was written in the aftermath of one of Damon Knight's historic Milford Conferences. These were annual workshops for science fiction writers, founded in 1956 at Milford, Pennsylvania, by Damon and Jim Blish, and moved whenever Damon and Kate Wilhelm moved, to Florida, to Michigan, and finally to Eugene, Oregon. The invited members of each conference included about a dozen seasoned professionals and as many promising newcomers to the field.

Each member brought several copies of an unpublished manuscript. Through the conference week we read them and gathered every afternoon, at first in the living room of Damon's big house in Milford, for a critical session. The rules required the victim to sit silent while he listened to the critics. The comments were often merciless and sometimes wrongheaded, but the conference proved to be a new and remarkable way of teaching writing. After Robin Scott Wilson attended, he went home to Clarion College to establish the first Clarion Conference, which has carried on the tradition with notable success.

I enjoyed attending, not only for insights and information, but for all the writers I came to know there, old pros and emerging stars, Harlan Ellison among them. Harlan always brought his typewriter and his canned music. After the meetings, when others were relaxing or asleep, he played his music and wrote a story that he sold to Damon for Orbit when the conference was over.

At a conference in Florida, he asked me to do a story

for Again, Dangerous Visions. *"Jamboree" is what I wrote when I got back to New Mexico. It's darker than most of my work, but it came out pretty much the way I wanted it, with visible influences from the conference and from Harlan. I think he would have bought it, but my agent sold it to Galaxy instead. I did write another for Harlan, "Prelude to Paradise," which I understand is to be the last story in the last volume of* The Last Dangerous Visions, *if and when that does appear.*

—Jack Williamson

FAMILY
Joyce Carol Oates

THE DAYS WERE BRIEF AND ATTENUATED AND THE SEASON appeared to be fixed—neither summer nor winter, spring nor fall. A thermal haze of inexpressible sweetness (though bearing tiny bits of grit or mica) had eased into the valley from the industrial regions to the north and there were nights when the sun set slowly at the western horizon as if sinking through a porous red mass, and there were days when a hard-glaring moon like bone remained fixed in a single position, prominent in the sky. Above the patchwork of excavated land bordering our property—*all* of which had formerly been our property, in Grandfather's time: thousands of acres of fertile soil and open grazing land—a curious fibrillating rainbow sometimes appeared, its colors shifting even as you stared, shades of blue, turquoise, iridescent-green, russet-red, a lovely translucent gold that dissolved to moisture as the thermal breeze stirred, warm and stale as an exhaled breath. And if I'd run excited to tell others of the rainbow, it was likely to have vanished when they came.

248

"Liar!" my older brothers and sisters said, "—don't promise rainbows when there aren't any!"

Father laid his hand on my head, saying, with a smiling frown, "Don't speak of anything if you aren't certain it will be true for others, not simply for yourself. Do you understand?"

"Yes Father," I said quietly. Though I did not understand.

This story begins in the time of family celebration— after Father made a great profit selling all but fifteen acres of his inheritance from Grandfather; and he and Mother were like a honeymoon couple, giddy with relief at having escaped the fate of most of our neighbors in the Valley, rancher-rivals of Grandfather's, and their descendants, who had sold off their property before the market began to realize its full potential. ("Full potential" was a term Father often uttered, as if its taste pleased him.) Now these old rivals were without land, and their investments yielded low returns; they'd gone away to live in cities of ever-increasing disorder, where no country people, especially once-aristocratic country people, could endure to live for long. They'd virtually prostituted themselves, Father said,—"And for so little!"

It was a proverb of Grandfather's time that a curse would befall anyone in the Valley who gloated over a neighbor's misfortune but, as Father observed, "It's damned difficult *not* to feel superior, sometimes." And Mother said, kissing him, "Darling—you're absolutely right!"

Our house was made of granite, limestone, and beautiful red-orange brick; the new wing, designed by a famous Japanese architect, was mainly tinted glass, overlooking the Valley where on good days we could see for many miles and on humid-hazy days we could barely see beyond the fence at the edge of our property. Father, however, preferred the roof of the house: in his white suit (linen in warm weather, light wool in cold), cream-colored fedora cocked back on his head, high-heeled leather-tooled boots, he spent most of his waking hours on the highest peak of the highest roof, observing through high-powered binoculars the astonishing progress of construction in the Valley—for overnight, it seemed, there had appeared roads, expressways, sewers, drainage pipes, "planned communities" with such melodic names as Whispering Glades, Murmuring Oaks, Pheasant Run, Deer Willow, all of them walled to keep out trespassers, and, even more astonishing, immense towers of buildings made of aluminum, and steel, and glass, and bronze, buildings whose magnificent windows winked and glimmered like mirrors, splendid in sunshine like pillars of flame . . . such beauty, where once there'd been mere earth and sky, it caught at your throat like a bird's talons. "The ways of beauty are as a honeycomb," Father told us mysteriously.

So hypnotized was Father by the transformation of the Valley, he often forgot where he was; failed to come downstairs for meals, or for bed; if Mother, meaning to indulge him, or hurt by his growing indifference to her, did not send a servant to summon him, he was likely to spend an entire night on the roof . . . in the morning, smiling sheepishly, he would explain that he'd fallen asleep; or, conversely, he'd been troubled by having seen things for which he could not account—shadows the size of longhorns moving ceaselessly beyond our twelve-foot barbed wire fence, and inexplicable winking red lights fifty miles away in the foothills. "Optical illusions!" Mother said, "—or the ghosts of old slaughtered livestock, or airplanes. Have you forgotten, darling, you sold thirty acres of land, for an airport at Furnace Creek?" "These lights more resemble fires," Father said stubbornly. "And they're in the foothills, not in the plain."

There came then times of power black-outs, and financial losses, and Father was forced to surrender all but two or three of the servants, but he maintained his rooftop vigil, white-clad, a noble ghostly figure holding binoculars to his eyes, for he perceived himself as a *witness*; and believed, if he lived to a ripe old age like Grandfather (who was in his hundredth year when at last he died—of a riding accident), he would be a chronicler of these troubled times, like Thucydides. For, as Father said, "Is there a new world struggling to be born—or only struggle?"

Around this time—because of numerous dislocations in the Valley: the abrupt abandoning of homes, for instance—it happened that packs of dogs began to roam about looking for food, particularly by night, poor starving creatures that became a nuisance and should be, as authorities urged, shot down on sight,—these dogs being not feral by birth but former household pets, highly bred beagles, setters, cocker spaniels, terriers, even the larger and coarser type of poodle—and it was the cause of some friction between Mother and Father that, despite his rooftop presence by day and by night, Father nonetheless failed to spy a pack of these dogs dig beneath our fence and make their way to the dairy barn where they tore out the throats—surely this could not have been in silence!—of our remaining six Holsteins, and our last two she-goats, before devouring the poor creatures; nor did Father notice anything unusual the night two homeless derelicts, formerly farmhands of ours, impaled themselves on the electric fence and died agonizing deaths, their bodies found in the morning by Kit, our sixteen-year-old.

Kit, who'd liked the men, said, "—I hope I never see anything like that again in my life!"

It's true that our fence was charged with a powerful electric current—but in full compliance with County Farm and Home Bureau regulations.

Following this, Father journeyed to the state capitol with the intention of taking out a sizable loan, and reestablishing, as he called it, old ties with his political friends, or with their younger colleagues; and Mother joined him a few days later for a greatly needed change of scene—"Not that I don't love you all, and the farm, but I need to see other sights for a while!—and I need to be *seen*." Leaving us when they did, under the care of Mrs.

Hoyt (our housekeeper) and Cory (our eldest sister), was possibly not a good idea: Mrs. Hoyt was aging rapidly, and Cory for all the innocence of her marigold eyes and melodic voice, was desperately in love with one of the National Guardsmen who patrolled the Valley in jeeps, authorized to shoot wild dogs, and, when necessary, vandals, arsonists, and squatters who were considered a menace to the public health and well-being. And when Mother returned from the capitol, unaccompanied by Father, after what seemed to the family a long absence (two weeks? two months?), it was with shocking news: she and Father were going to separate.

Mother said, "Children, your father and I have decided, after much soul-searching deliberation, that we must dissolve our wedding bond of nearly twenty years." As she spoke Mother's voice wavered like a girl's but fierce little points of light shone in her eyes.

We children were so taken by surprise we could not speak, at first.

Separate! Dissolve! We stood staring and mute; not even Cory, Kit, and Dale,—not even Lona who was the most impulsive of us—could find words with which to protest; the younger children began whimpering helplessly, soon joined by the rest. Mother clutched at her hair, saying, "Oh please don't! I can hardly bear the pain as it is!" With some ceremony she then played for us a video of Father's farewell to the family, which drew fresh tears . . . for there, framed astonishingly on our one hundred-inch home theater screen, where we'd never seen his image before, was Father, dressed not in white but in somber colors, his hair in steely bands combed wetly across the dome of his skull, and his eyes puffy, an unnatural sheen to his face as if it had been scoured, hard. He was sitting stiffly erect; his fingers gripped the arms of his chair so tightly the blood had drained from his knuckles; his words came slow, halting, and faint, like the faltering progress of a gut-shot deer across a field. *Dear children, your mother and I . . . after years of marriage . . . of very happy*

marriage . . . have decided to . . . have decided . . .
One of the vexatious low-flying helicopters belonging to
the National Guard soared past our house, making the
screen shudder, but the sound was garbled in any case, as
if the tape had been clumsily cut and spliced; Father's
beloved face turned liquid and his eyes began to melt ver-
tically, like oily tears; his mouth was distended like a
drowning man's. As the tape ended we could discern only
sounds, not words, resembling *Help me* or *I am innocent*
or *Do not forget me beloved children I AM YOUR FA-
THER*—and then the screen went dead.

That afternoon Mother introduced us to the man who
was to be Father's successor in the household!—and to his
three children, who were to be our new brothers and sister, and we shook hands shyly, in a state of mutual shock,
and regarded one another with wide staring wary eyes.
Our new father! Our new brothers and sister! So suddenly,
and with no warning! Mother explained patiently, yet forcibly, her new husband was no mere *step*-father but a true
father; which meant that we were to address him "Father"
at all times, with respect, and even in our most private
innermost thoughts we were to think of him as "Father":
for otherwise he would be hurt, and displeased. And
moved to discipline us.

So too with Einar and Erastus, our new *brothers* (not
step-brothers), and Fifi, our new *sister* (not *step*-sister).

New Father stood before us smiling happily, a man of
our old Father's age but heavier and far more robust than
that Father, with an unusually large head, the cranium particularly developed, and small shrewd quick-darting eyes
beneath brows of bone. He wore a tailored suit with wide
shoulders that exaggerated his bulk, and sported a red car-
nation in his lapel; his black shoes, a city man's shoes,
shone splendidly, as if phosphorescent. "Hello Father,"
we murmured shyly, hardly daring to raise our eyes to his,
"—Hello Father." The man's jaws were strangely elongated, the lower jaw at least an inch longer than the upper,
so that a wet malevolent ridge of teeth was revealed; as so

often happened in those days, a single thought passed like lightning among us children, from one to the other to the other, each of us smiling guiltily as it struck us: *Crocodile! Why, here's Crocodile!* Only little Jori burst into frightened tears and New Father surprised us all by stooping to pick her up gently in his arms and comfort her . . . "Hush, hush little girl! Nobody's going to hurt *you*!" and we others could see how the memory of our beloved former Father began to pass from her, like dissolving smoke. Jori was three years old at this time, too young to be held accountable.

New Father's children were tall, big-boned, and solemn, with a faint greenish-peevish cast to their skin, like many city children; the boys had inherited their father's large head and protruding jaws but the girl, Fifi, seventeen years old, was striking in her beauty, with pale blond fluffy hair as lovely as Cory's, and thickly lashed honey-brown eyes in which something mutinous glimmered. That evening certain of the boys—Dale, Kit, and Hewett—gathered around Fifi to tell her wild tales of the Valley, how we all had to protect ourselves with Winchester rifles and shotguns, from trespassers, and how there was a mysterious resurgence of rats on the farm, as a consequence of excavation in the countryside, and these tales, just a little exaggerated, made the girl shudder and shiver and giggle, leaning toward the boys as if to invite their protection. Ah, Fifi was so pretty! But when Dale hurried off to fetch her a goblet of ice water at her request she took the goblet from him, lifted it prissily to the light to examine its contents, and asked rudely, "Is this water *pure*? Is it safe to *drink*?" It was true, our well water had become strangely effervescent, and tasted of rust; after a heavy rainfall there were likely to be tiny red-wiggly things in it, like animated tails; so we had learned not to examine it too closely, just to drink it, and as our attacks of nausesa, diarrhea, dizziness, and amnesia, were only sporadic, we rarely worried but tried instead to be grateful, as Mrs. Hoyt used to urge us, that unlike many of our neighbors we had any drinking water at all. So it was offensive to us to see our new sister Fifi making such a face, handing the goblet back to Dale, and asking haughtily how anyone in his right mind could drink such—*spilth*. Dale said, red-faced,"*How?* This is *how*!" and drank the entire glass in a single thirsty gulp. And he and Fifi stood staring at each other, trembling with passion.

As Cory observed afterward, smiling, yet with a trace of envy or resentment, "It looks as if 'New Sister' has made a conquest!"

"But what will she do," I couldn't help asking, "—if she can't drink our water?"

"She'll drink it," Cory said, with a grim little laugh. "And she'll find it delicious, just like the rest of us."

Which turned out, fairly quickly, to be so.

Poor Cory! Her confinement came in a time of ever-increasing confusion . . . prolonged power failures, a scarcity of all food except canned foods, a scarcity too of ammunition so that the price of shotgun shells doubled, and quadrupled; and the massive sky by both day and night was criss-crossed by the contrails of unmarked jet planes (Army or Air Force bombers?) in designs both troubling and beautiful, like the web of a gigantic spider. By this time construction in most parts of the Valley, once so energetic, had been halted; part-completed high-rise buildings punctuated the landscape; some were no more than concrete foundations upon which iron girders had been erected, like exposed bone. How we children loved to explore! The "Mirror Tower" (as we called it: once, it must have had a real, adult name) was a three-hundred-storey patchwork of interlocking slots of reflecting glass with a subtle turquoise tint, and where its elegant surface had once mirrored scenes of sparkling natural beauty there was now a drab scene, or succession of scenes, as on a video screen no one was watching: clouds like soiled cotton batting, smouldering slag heaps, decomposing garbage, predatory thistles and burdocks grown to the height of trees. Traffic, once so congested on the expressways, had dwindled to four or five diesel trucks per day hauling their heavy cargo (rumored to be diseased livestock bound for northern slaughterhouses) and virtually no passenger cars; sometimes, unmarked but official-looking vehicles, like jeeps, but much larger than jeeps, passed in lengthy convoys, bound for no one knew where. There were strips of pavement, cloverleafs, that coiled endlessly upon themselves, beginning to be cracked and overgrown by weeds, and elevated highways that broke off abruptly in mid-air, thus as state authorities warned travelers they were in grave danger, venturing into the countryside, of being attacked by roaming gangs—but the rumor was, as Father insisted, the most dangerous gangs were rogue Guardsmen who wore their uniforms inside-out and gas-masks strapped over their faces, preying upon the very citizens they were sworn to protect! None of the adults left our family compound without being armed and of course we younger children were forbidden to leave at all—when we did, it was by stealth.

All schools, private and public, had been shut down indefinitely.

"One long holiday!"—as Hewett said.

The most beautiful and luxurious of the model communities, which we called "The Wheel" (its original name was Paradise Hollow), had suffered some kind of financial collapse, so that its well-to-do tenants were forced to emigrate back to the cities from which they'd emigrated to the Valley only about eighteen months before. (We called the complex "The Wheel" because its condominiums, office buildings, shops, schools, hospitals, and crematoria were arranged in spokes radiating outward from a single axis; and were ingeniously protected at their twenty-mile circumference not by a visible wall, which the Japanese architect who'd designed it had declared a vulgar and outmoded concept, but by a force-field of electricity of lethal voltage.) Though the airport at Furnace Creek was officially closed we sometimes saw, late at night, small air-

craft including helicopters taking off and landing there;
were wakened by the insect-like whining of their engines,
and their winking red lights; and one night when the sun
remained motionless at the horizon for several hours and
visibility was poor, as if we were in a dust storm, yet a
dust storm without wind, a ten-seater airplane crashed in
a slag-heap that had once been a grazing pasture for our
cows, and some of the older boys went by stealth to investigate . . . returning with sober, stricken faces, refusing to tell us, their sisters, what they had seen except to
say, "Never mind! Don't ask!" Fifteen miles away in the
western foothills were mysterious encampments, said to
be unauthorized settlements of city dwellers who had fled
their cities at the time of the "urban collapse" (as it was
called), as well as former ranch-families, and various wan-
derers and evicted persons, criminals, the mentally ill,
and victims and suspected carriers of contagious diseases
. . . all of these considered "outlaw parties" subject to
severe treatment by the National Guardsmen, for the region was now under martial law, and only within family
compounds maintained by state-registered property owners and heads of families were civil rights, to a degree,
still operative. Eagerly, we scanned the Valley for signs of
life, passing among us a pair of heavy binoculars, unknown to Father and Mother,—like forbidden treasure
these binoculars were, though their original owner was
forgotten. (Cory believed that this person, a man, had lived
with us before Father's time, and had been good to us,
and kind. But no one, not even Cory, could remember his
name, nor even what he'd looked like.)

Cory's baby was born the very week of the funerals of
two of the younger children, who had died, poor things,
of a violent dysentery, and of Uncle Darrah, who'd died
of shotgun wounds while driving his pick-up truck along
a familiar road in the Valley; but this coincidence, Mother
and Father assured us, was only that—a coincidence, and
not an omen. Mother led us one by one into the drafty
attic room set aside for Cory and her baby and we stared

in amazement at the puppy-sized, florid-faced, screaming, yet so wonderfully alive creature . . . with its large soft-looking head, its wizened angry features, its smooth, pore-less skin. How had Cory, one of us, accomplished *this*! Sisters and brothers alike, we were in awe of her, and a little fearful.

Mother's reaction was most surprising. She seemed furious with Cory, saying that the attic room was good enough for Cory's "outlaw child," sometimes she spoke of Cory's "bastard child"—though quick to acknowledge, in all fairness, the poor infant's parentage was no fault of its own. But it was "fit punishment," Mother said, that Cory's breasts ached when she nursed her baby, and that her milk was threaded with pus and blood . . . "fit punishment for shameful sluttish behavior." Yet, the family's luck held for only two days after the birth Kit and Erastus came back from a nocturnal hunting expedition with a dairy cow: a healthy, fat-bellied, placid creature with black-and-white-marbled markings similar to those of our favorite cow, who had died long ago. This sweet-natured cow, named Daisy, provided the family with fresh, delicious, seemingly pure milk, thus saving Cory's bastard-infant's life, as Mother said spitefully—"Well, the way of Providence *is* a honeycomb!"

Those weeks, Mother was obsessed with learning the identity of Cory's baby's father; Cory's "secret lover," as Mother referred to him. Cory, of course, refused to say— even to her sisters. She may have been wounded that the baby's father had failed to come forward to claim his child, or her; poor Cory, once the prettiest of the girls, now disfigured with skin rashes like fish scales over most of her body, and a puffy, bloated appearance, and eyes red from perpetual weeping. Mother herself was frequently ill with a similar flaming rash, a protracted respiratory infection, intestinal upsets, bone-aches, and amnesia; like everyone in the family except, oddly, Father, she was plagued with ticks—the smallest species of deer tick that could burrow secretly into the skin, releasing an analgesiac spittle to numb the skin, thus able to do its damage, sucking blood contentedly for weeks until, after weeks, it might drop off with a *ping*! to the floor, black, shiny, now the size of a watermelon seed, swollen with blood. What loathsome things!—Mother developed a true horror of them, for they seemed drawn to her, especially to her white, wild-matted hair.

By imperceptible degrees Mother had shrunk to a height of less than five feet, very unlike the statuesque beauty of old photographs; with that head of white hair, and pebble-colored eyes as keen and suspicious as ever, and a voice so brassy and penetrating it had the power to paralyze any of us where we stood . . . even the eldest of her sons, Kit, Hewett, Dale, tall bearded men who carried firearms even inside the compound were intimidated by Mother, and, like Cory, were inclined to submit to her authority. When Mother interrogated Cory, "*Who* is your lover? Why are you so ashamed of him? Did you find him in the drainage pipe, or in the slag-heap?—in the compost?" Cory bit her lip, and said quietly, "Even if I see his face sometimes, Mother, in my sleep, I can't recall his name. Or who he was, or is. Or claimed to be."

Yet Mother continued, risking Father's displeasure—for she began to question *all males* with whom she came into contact, not excluding Cory's own blood-relations—cousins, uncles, even brothers!—even those ravaged men and boys who made their homes, so to speak, beyond the compound, as she'd said jeeringly, in the drainage pipe, in the slag-heap, in the compost. (These men and boys were not official residents on our property but were enlisted by the family in times of crisis and emergency.) But no one confessed—no one acknowledged Cory's baby as his. And one day when Cory lay upstairs in the attic with a fever and I was caring for the baby, excitedly feeding it from a bottle, in the kitchen, Mother entered with a look of such determination I felt a sudden fear for the baby, hugging it to my chest, and Mother said, "Give me the bastard, girl," and I said weakly, "No Mother, don't make me," and

Mother said, "Are you disobeying me, girl? *Give me the bastard,*" and I said, backing away, daringly, yet determined too, "No Mother, Cory's baby belongs to Cory, and to all of us, and it isn't a bastard." Mother advanced upon me, furious; her pebble-colored eyes now rimmed with white; her fingers—what talons they'd become, long, skinny, clawed!—outstretched. Yet I saw that in the very midst of her passion she was forgetting what she intended to do, and that this might save Cory's baby from harm.

(For often in those days when the family had little to eat except worm-riddled apples from the old orchard, and stunted blackened potatoes, and such game, or wildlife, that the men and boys could shoot, and such canned goods as they could acquire, we often, all of us, young as well as old, forgot what we were doing in the very act of doing it; plucking bloody feathers from a quail, for instance, and stopping vague and dreamy wondering what on earth am I doing? here? at the sink? *is* this a sink? what is this limp little body? this instrument—a knife?—in my hands? and naturally in the midst of speaking we might forget the words we meant to speak, for instance *water*, *rainbow*, *grief*, *love*, *filth*, *Father*, *deer-tick*, *God*, *milk*, *sky* . . . and Father who'd become brooding with the onset of age worried constantly that we, his family, might one day soon lose all sense of ourselves as a family should we forget, in the same instant, all of us together, the sacred word *family*.)

And indeed, there in the kitchen, reaching for Cory's baby with her talon-like fingers, Mother was forgetting. And indeed within the space of a half-minute she had forgotten. Staring at the defenseless living thing, the quivering, still-hungry creature in my arms, with its soft flat shallow face of utter innocence, its tiny recessed eyes, its mere holes for nostrils, its small pursed mouth set like a manta ray's in its shallow face, Mother could not, simply could not, summon back the word *baby*, or *infant*, nor even the cruel *Cory's bastard*, always on her lips. And at that moment there was a commotion outside by the compound gate, an outburst of gunfire, familiar enough yet always jarring when unexpected, and Mother hurried out to investigate. And Cory's baby returned to sucking hungrily and contentedly at the bottle's frayed rubber nipple, and all was safe for now.

But Cory, my dear sister, died a few days later.

Lona discovered her in her place of exile in the attic, in her bed, eyes opened wide and pale mouth contorted, the bedclothes soaked in blood . . . and when in horror Lona drew the sheet away she saw that Cory's breasts had been partly hacked away, or maybe devoured?—and her chest cavity exposed; she must have been attacked in the night by rats, and was too weak or too terrified to scream for help. Yet her baby was sleeping placidly in its crib beside the bed, miraculously untouched . . . sunk in its characteristic sleep to that profound level at which organic matter seems about to revert to the inorganic, to perfect peace. For some reason the household rats with their glittering amaranthine eyes and stiff hairless tails and unpredictable appetites had spared it!—or had missed it altogether!

Lona snatched the baby up out of its crib and ran downstairs screaming for help; and so fierce was she in possession she would not give up the baby to anyone, saying, dazed, sobbing, yet in a way gloating, "This is my baby. This is Lona's baby now." Until Father, with his penchant for logic, rebuked her: "Girl, it is the family's baby now."

And Fifi too had a baby; beautiful blond Fifi; or, rather, the poor girl writhed and screamed in agony for a day and a night, before giving birth to a perfectly formed but tiny baby weighing only two pounds, that lived only a half-hour. How we wept, how we pitied our sister!—in the weeks that followed nothing would give her solace, even the smallest measure of solace, except our musical evenings, at which she excelled. For if Dale tried to touch her, to comfort her, she shrank from him in repugnance; nor would she allow Father, or any male, to come near.

One night she crawled into my bed and hugged me in her icy bone-thin arms. "What I love best," she whispered, "—is the black waves that splash over us, endlessly, at night,—do you know those waves, sister? and do you love them as I do?" And my heart was so swollen with feeling I could not reply, as I wished to, "Oh *yes*."

Indeed, suddenly the family had taken up music. In the evenings by kerosene lamp. In the pre-dawn hours, roused from our bed by aircraft overhead, or the barking of wild dogs, or the thermal winds. We played such musical instruments as fell into our hands discovered here and there in the house, or by way of strangers at our gate eager to barter anything they owned for food. Kit took up the violin shyly at first and then with growing confidence and joy for, it seemed, he had musical talent—practicing for hours on the beautiful though scarified antique violin that had once belonged to Grandfather, or Great-grandfather (so we surmised: an old portrait depicted a child of about ten posed with the identical violin tucked under his chin); Jori and Vega took up the piccolo, which they shared; Hewett the drums, Dale the cymbals, Einar the oboe, Fifi the piano . . . and the rest of us sang, sang our hearts out.

We sang after Mother's funeral and we sang that week a hot feculent wind blew across the Valley bearing the odor of decomposing flesh and we sang (though often coughing and choking, from the smoke) when fires raged out of control in the dry woodland areas to the east, an insidious wind then too blowing upon our barricaded compound and handsome house atop a high hill, a wind intent upon seeking us out, it seemed, carrying sparks to our sanctuary, our place of privilege, destroying us in fire as others both human and beast were being destroyed . . . and how else for us to endure such odors, such sights, such sounds, than to take up our instruments and play them as loudly as possible, and sing as loudly as possible, and sing and sing and sing until our throats were raw, how else.

Yet, the following week became a time of joy and feast-
ing, since Daisy the cow was dying in any case and might
as well be quickly slaughtered, when Father, surprising us
all, brought his new wife home to meet us: New Mother
we called her, or Young Mother, or Pretty Mother, and
Old Mother that fierce stooped wild-eyed old woman was
soon forgotten, even the mystery of her death soon forgotten (for had she like Cory died of household rats? or
had she, like poor Erastus, died of a burst appendix? had
she drowned somehow in the cistern, had she died of thirst
and malnutrition locked away in the attic, had she died of
a respiratory infection, of toothache, of heartbreak, of her
own rage, or of age, or of Father's strong fingers closing
around her neck . . . or had she not "died" at all but
passed quietly into oblivion, as the black waves splashed
over her, and Young Mother stepped forward smiling happily to take her place).

Young Mother was so pretty!—plump, and round-faced,
her complexion rich and ruddy, her breasts like large balloons filled to bursting with warm liquid, and she gave off
a hot intoxicating smell of nutmeg, and tiny flames leapt
from her when in a luxury of sighing, yawning, and
stretching, she lifted the heavy mass of red-russet hair that
hung between her shoulder blades, and fixed upon us her
smiling-dark gaze. "Mother!" we cried, even the eldest
of us, "—oh Mother!" hoping would she hug us, would
she kiss and hug us, fold us in those plump strong arms,
cuddle our faces against those breasts, each of us, all of
us, weeping, in her arms, those arms, oh Mother, *there*.

Lona's baby was not maturing as it was believed babies
should normally mature, nor had it been named since we
could not determine whether it was male or female, or
somehow both, or neither; and this household problem
Young Mother addressed herself to at once. No matter
Lona's desperate love of the baby, Young Mother was
"practical-minded" as she said: for why else had Father
brought her to this family but to take charge, to reform it,

to give *hope*? She could not comprehend, she said, laughing incredulously, how and why an extra mouth, a useless mouth, perhaps even a dangerous mouth, could be tolerated at such a time of near-famine, in violation of certain government edicts as she understood them. "Drastic remedies in drastic times," Young Mother was fond of saying. Lona said, pleading, "I'll give it my food, Mother—I'll protect it with my life!" And Young Mother simply repeated, smiling, so broadly her eyes were narrowed almost to slits, "Drastic remedies in drastic times!"

There were those of us who loved Lona's baby, for it *was* flesh of our flesh, it *was* part of our family; yet there were others, mainly the men and boys, who seemed nervous in its presence, keeping a wary distance when it crawled into a room to nudge its large bald head or pursed mouth against a foot, an ankle, a leg. Though it had not matured in the normal fashion Lona's baby weighed now about thirty pounds; but it was soft as a slug is soft, or an oyster; with an oyster's general shape; apparently boneless; the hue of unbaked bread dough, and hairless. As its small eyes lacked an iris, being entirely white, it must have been blind; its nose was but a rudimentary pair of nostrils, holes in the center of its face; its fish-like mouth was deceptive in that it seemed to possess its own intelligence, being ideally formed, not for human speech, but for seizing, sucking, and chewing. Though it had at best only a cartilaginous skeleton it did boast two fully formed rows of tiny needle-sharp teeth, which it was not shy of using, particularly when ravenous for food, and it was often ravenous. At such times it groped its way around the house, silent, by instinct, sniffing and quivering, and if by chance it was drawn by the heat of your blood to your bed it would burrow beneath the covers, and nudge, and nuzzle, and begin like a nursing infant to suck virtually any part of the body though preferring of course a female's breasts . . . and if not stopped in time it would start to bite, chew, *eat* . . . in all the brute innocence of appetite. So some of us surmised, though Lona angrily denied it, that the baby's first mother (a sister of ours whose name we had forgotten) had not died of rat bites after all but of having been attacked in the night and partly devoured by her own baby.

(In this, Lona was duplicitous. She took care never to undress in Mother's presence for fear Mother's sharp eye would discover the numerous wounds on her breasts, belly, and thighs.)

As the family had a time-honored custom of debating issues, in a democratic manner, for instance should we pay the exorbitant price a cow or a she-goat now commanded on the open market, or should the boys be given permission to acquire one of these beasts however they could, for instance should we try to feed the starving men, women, and children who gathered outside our fence, even if it was food too contaminated for the family's consumption,—so naturally the issue of Lona's baby was taken up too, and soon threatened to split the family into two warring sides. Mother argued persuasively, almost tearfully, that the baby was "worthless, repulsive, and might one day be dangerous,"—not guessing that it had already proved dangerous; and Lona argued persuasively, and tearfully, that "Lona's baby," as she called it, was a living human being, a member of the family, one of *us*. Mother said hotly, "It is not one of *us*, girl, if by *us* you mean a family that includes *me*," and Lona said, daringly, "It is one of *us* because it predates any family that includes *you*— 'Mother.' "

So they argued; and others joined in; and emotions ran high. It was strange how some of us changed our minds several times, now swayed by Mother's reasoning, and now by Lona's; now by Father who spoke on behalf of Mother, or by Hewett who spoke on behalf of Lona. Was it weeks, or was it months, that the debate raged?—and subsided, and raged again?—and Mother dared not put her power to the vote for fear that Lona's brothers and sisters would side with Lona out of loyalty if not love for the baby. And Father acknowledged reluctantly that however any of us felt about the baby it *was* our flesh and blood, and embodied the Mystery of Life: ". . . Its soul bounded by its skull and its destiny no more problematic than the sinewy tubes that connect its mouth and its anus. Who are we to judge!"

Yet Mother had her way, as slyboots Mother was always to have her way . . . one March morning soliciting the help of several of us, who were sworn to secrecy, and delighted to be her handmaidens, in a simple scheme: Lona being asleep in the attic, Mother led the baby out of the house by holding a piece of bread soaked in chicken blood in front of its nostrils, led it crawling across the hard-packed wintry earth, to the old hay barn, and, inside, led it to a dark corner where we helped her lift it and lower it carefully into an aged rain barrel empty except for a wriggling mass of half-grown rats, that squealed in great excitement at being disturbed, and at the smell of the blood-soaked bread which Mother dropped with the baby. We than nailed a cover in place; and, as Mother said, her skin warmly flushed and her breath coming fast, "There girls—it is entirely out of our hands."

And then one day it was spring. And Kit, grinning, led a she-goat proudly into the kitchen, her bags primed with milk, swollen pink dugs leaking milk! How grateful we all were, those of us who were with child especially, after the privations of so long a winter, or winters, during which time certain words have all but faded from our memories, for instance *she-goat* and *milk*, and as we realized *rainbow*, for the rainbow too re-appeared, one morning, shimmering and translucent across the Valley, a phenomenon as of the quivering of millions of butterflies' iridescent wings. In the fire-scorched plain there grew a virtual sea of fresh green shoots and in the sky enormous dimpled clouds and that night we gathered around Fifi at the piano to play our instruments and to sing. Father had passed away but Mother had remarried: a husky bronze-skinned horseman whose white teeth flashed in his beard, and whose rowdy pinches meant love and good cheer, not meanness. We were so happy we debated turning the calendar ahead to the New Year. We were so happy we debated abolishing the calendar entirely and declaring this the First Day of Year One, and beginning Time anew.

AUTHOR'S NOTE

"FAMILY" WAS WRITTEN AFTER A FEVER-DREAM IN WHICH it seemed absolutely self-evident to me that our civilization was shortly to begin its inevitable decline; had, perhaps, already begun. The images in my dream and its setting were totally different from those of "Family," but the one definitely led to the other. I was thinking too of a recent visit to Dallas, Texas and its environs. But I was thinking also that humankind has a stubborn propensity for survival, in however altered a form; and that there will always be the phenomenon we call "family."

—Joyce Carol Oates

TWILIGHT OF THE DAWN
Dean R. Koontz

"SOMETIMES YOU CAN BE THE BIGGEST JACKASS WHO EVER lived," my wife said the night I took Santa Claus away from my son.

We were in bed, but she was clearly not in the mood for either sleep or romance.

Her voice was sharp, scornful. "What a terrible thing to do to a little boy."

"He's seven years old—"

"He's a little boy," Ellen said harshly, though we rarely spoke to each other in anger. For the most part ours was a happy, peaceful marriage.

We lay in silence. The drapes were drawn back from the French doors that opened onto the second-floor balcony, so the bedroom was limned by ash-pale moonlight. Even in that dim glow, even though Ellen was cloaked in blankets, her anger was apparent in the tense, angular position in which she was pretending to seek sleep.

Finally she said, "Pete, you used a sledgehammer to shatter a little boy's fragile fantasy, a *harmless* fantasy, all because of your obsession—"

"It wasn't harmless," I said patiently. "And I don't have an obsession—"

"Yes, you do," she said.

"I simply believe in rational—"

"Oh, shut up," she said.

"Won't you even talk to me about it?"

"No. It's pointless."

I sighed. "I love you, Ellen."

She was silent a long while.

Wind soughed in the eaves, an ancient voice.

In the boughs of one of the backyard cherry trees, an owl hooted.

At last Ellen said, "I love you, too, but sometimes I want to kick your ass."

I was angry with her because I felt that she was not being fair, that she was allowing her least admirable emotions to overrule her reason. Now, many years later, I would give anything to hear her say that she wanted to kick my ass, and I'd bend over with a smile.

From the cradle, my son Benny was taught that god did not exist under any name or in any form, and that religion was the refuge of weak-minded people who did not have the courage to face the universe on its own terms. I would not permit Benny to be baptised, for in my view that ceremony was a primitive initiation rite by which the child would be inducted into a cult of ignorance and irrationalism.

Ellen—my wife and Benny's mother—had been raised as a Methodist and still was stained (as I saw it) by lingering traces of faith. She called herself an agnostic, unable to go further and join me in the camp of the atheists. I loved her so much that I was able to tolerate her equivocation on the subject. However I had nothing but scorn for others who could not face the fact that the universe was godless and that human existence was nothing more than a biological accident.

I despised all those who bent their knees to humble

themselves before an imaginary lord of creation, all the Methodists and Lutherans and Catholics and Baptists and Mormons and Jews and others. They claimed many labels but in essence shared the same sick delusion.

My greatest loathing was reserved, however, for those who had once been clean of the disease of religion, rational men and women like me who had slipped off the path of reason and fallen into the chasm of superstition. They were surrendering their most precious possessions— their independent spirit, self-reliance, intellectual integrity—in return for half-baked, dreamy promises of an afterlife with togas and harp music. I was more disgusted by the rejection of their previously treasured secular enlightenment than I would have been to hear some old friend confess that he had suddenly developed an all-consuming obsession for canine sex and had divorced his wife in favor of a German shepherd bitch.

Hal Sheen, my partner with whom I had founded Fallon and Sheen Design, had been as proud of his atheism too. In college we were best friends, and together we were a formidable team of debaters whenever the subject of religion arose; inevitably, anyone harboring a belief in a supreme being, anyone daring to disagree with our view of the universe as a place of uncaring forces, any of *that* ilk was sorry to have met us, for we stripped away his pretensions to adulthood and revealed him for the idiot child he was. Indeed we often didn't even wait for the subject of religion to arise but skillfully baited fellow students who, to our certain knowledge, were believers.

Later, with degrees in architecture, neither of us wished to work for anyone but ourselves, so we formed a company. We dreamed of creating brawny yet elegant, functional yet beautiful buildings that would astonish—and win the undiluted admiration of—not only the world but our fellow professionals. And with brains, talent, and dogged determination, we began to attain some of our goals while we were still very young men. Fallon and Sheen Design, a wunderkind company, was the focus of a revolution in design that excited university students as well as long-time professionals.

The most important aspect of our tremendous success was that our atheism lay at the core of it, for we consciously set out to create a new architecture that owed nothing to religious inspiration. Most laymen are not aware that virtually all the structures around them, including those resulting from modern schools of design, incorporate architectural details originally developed to subtly reinforce the rule of God and the place of religion in life. For instance vaulted ceilings, first used in churches and cathedrals, were originally meant to draw the gaze upward and to induce, by indirection, contemplation of heaven and its rewards. Underpitch vaults, barrel vaults, grain vaults, fan vaults, quadripartite and sexpartite and tierceron vaults are more than mere arches; they were conceived as agents of religion, quiet advertisements for Him and His authority. From the start Hal and I were determined that no vaulted ceilings, no spires, no arched windows or doors, no slightest design element born of religion would be incorporated into a Fallon and Sheen building. In reaction we strove to direct the eye earthward and, by a thousand devices, to remind those who passed through our structures that they were born of the earth, not children of any god but merely more intellectually advanced cousins of apes.

Hal's reconversion to the Roman Catholicism of his childhood was, therefore, a shock to me. At the age of thirty-seven, when he was at the top of his profession, when by his singular success he had proven the supremacy of unoppressed, rational man over imagined divinities, he returned with apparent joy to the confessional, humbled himself at the communion rail, dampened his forehead and breast with so-called holy water, and thereby rejected the intellectual foundation on which his entire adult life, to that point, had been based.

The horror of it chilled my heart, my marrow.

For taking Hal Sheen from me, I despised religion more

than ever. I redoubled my efforts to eliminate any wisp of religious thought or superstition from my son's life, and I was fiercely determined that Benny would never be stolen from me by incense-burning, bell-ringing, hymn-singing, self-deluded, mush-brained fools. When he proved to be a voracious reader from an early age, I carefully chose books for him, directing him away from works that even indirectly portrayed religion as an acceptable part of life, firmly steering him to strictly secular material that would not encourage unhealthy fantasies. When I saw that he was fascinated by vampires, ghosts, and the entire panoply of traditional monsters that seem to intrigue all children, I strenuously discouraged that interest, mocked it, and taught him the virtue and pleasure of rising above such childish things. Oh, I did not deny him the enjoyment of a good scare, for there's nothing religious in that. Benny was permitted to savor the fear induced by books about killer robots, movies about the Frankenstein monster, and other threats that were the work of man. It was only monsters of satanic origin that I censored from his books and films, for belief in things satanic is merely another facet of religion, the flip side of God worship.

I allowed him Santa Claus until he was seven, though I had a lot of misgivings about that indulgence. The Santa Claus legend includes a Christian element, of course. Good *Saint* Nick and all that. But Ellen was insistent that Benny would not be denied that fantasy. I reluctantly agreed that it was probably harmless, but only as long as we scrupulously observed the holiday as a secular event having nothing to do with the birth of Jesus. To us Christmas was a celebration of the family and a healthy indulgence in materialism.

In the backyard of our big house in Buck's County, Pennsylvania, grew a pair of enormous, long-lived cherry trees, under the branches of which Benny and I often sat in the milder season, playing checkers or card games. Beneath those boughs, which already had lost most of their leaves to the tugging hands of autumn, on an unusually

warm day in early October of his seventh year, as we were
playing Uncle Wiggly, Benny asked if I thought Santa was
going to bring him lots of stuff that year. I said it was too
early to be thinking about Santa, and he said that *all* the
kids were thinking about Santa and were starting to com-
pose want lists already. Then he said, "Daddy, how's Santa
know we've been good or bad? He can't watch all us kids
all the time, can he? Do our guardian angels talk to him
and tattle on us, or what?"

"Guardian angels?" I said, startled and displeased.
"What do you know about guardian angels?"

"Well, they're supposed to watch over us, help us when
we're in trouble, right? So I thought maybe they also talk
to Santa Claus."

Only months after Benny was born, I had joined with
like-minded parents in our community to establish a private school guided by the principles of secular humanism,
where even the slightest religious thought would be kept
out of the curriculum; in fact our intention was to insure
that, as our children matured, they would be taught history, literature, sociology, and ethics from an anti-clerical
viewpoint. Benny had attended our preschool and, by that
October of which I write, was in second-grade of the el-
ementary division, where his classmates came from families guided by the same rational principles as our own. I
was surprised to hear that in such an environment he was
still subjected to religious propagandizing.

"Who told you about guardian angels?"

"Some kids."

"They believe in these angels?"

"Sure. I guess."

"Why?"

"They saw it on TV."

"They did, huh?"

"It was a show you won't let me watch. *Highway to
Heaven*."

"And just because they saw it on TV they think it's
true?"

Benny shrugged and moved his game piece five spaces along the Uncle Wiggly board.

I believed then that popular culture—especially television—was the bane of all men and women of reason and goodwill, not least of all because it promoted a wide variety of religious superstitions and, by its saturation of every aspect of our lives, was inescapable and powerfully influential. Books and movies like *The Exorcist* and television programs like *Highway to Heaven* could frustrate even the most diligent parent's attempts to raise his child in an atmosphere of untainted rationality.

The unseasonably warm October breeze was not strong enough to disturb the game cards, but it gently ruffled Benny's fine brown hair. Wind-mussed, sitting on a pillow on his redwood chair in order to be at table level, he was so small and vulnerable. Loving him, wanting the best possible life for him, I grew angrier by the second; my anger was directed not at Benny but at those who, intellectually and emotionally stunted by their twisted philosophy, would propagandize an innocent child.

"Benny," I said, "listen, there are no guardian angels. They don't exist. It's all an ugly lie told by people who want to make you believe that you aren't responsible for your own successes in life. They want you to believe that the bad things in life are the result of your sins and *are* your fault, but that all the good things come from the grace of God. It's a way to control you. That's what all religion is—a tool to control and oppress you."

He blinked at me. "Grace who?"

It was my turn to blink. "What?

"Who's Grace? You mean Mrs. Grace Keever at the toy shop? What tool will she use to press me with?" He giggled. "Will I be all mashed flat and on a hanger when they're done? Daddy, you're silly."

He was only a seven-year-old boy, after all, and I was solemnly discussing the oppressive nature of religious belief as if we were two intellectuals drinking espresso in a coffee house. Blushing at the realization of my own capacity for foolishness, I pushed aside the Uncle Wiggly board and struggled harder to make him understand why believing in such nonsense as guardian angels was not merely innocent fun but was a step toward intellectual and emotional enslavement of a particularly pernicious sort. When he seemed alternately bored, confused, embarrassed, and utterly baffled—but never for a moment even slightly enlightened—I grew frustrated, and at last (I am now ashamed to admit this) I made my point by taking Santa Claus away from him.

Suddenly it seemed clear to me that by allowing him to indulge in the Santa myth, I'd laid the groundwork for the very irrationality that I was determined to prevent him from adopting. How could I have been so misguided as to believe that Christmas could be celebrated entirely in a secular spirit, without giving credence to the religious tradition that was, after all, the genesis of the holiday. Now I saw that erecting a Christmas tree in our home and exchanging gifts, by association with such other Christmas paraphernalia as manger scenes on church lawns and trumpet-tooting plastic angels in department-store decorations, had generated in Benny an assumption that the spiritual aspect of the celebration had as much validity as the materialistic aspect, which made him fertile ground for tales of guardian angels and all the other rot about sin and salvation.

Under the boughs of the cherry trees, in an October breeze that was blowing us slowly toward another Christmas, I told Benny the truth about Santa Claus, explained that the gifts came from his mother and me. He protested that he had evidence of Santa's reality: the cookies and milk that he always left out for the jolly fat man and that were unfailingly consumed. I convinced him that Santa's sweet tooth was in fact my own and that the milk—which I don't like—was always poured down the drain. Methodically, relentlessly—but with what I thought was kindness and love—I stripped from him all of the so-called magic of Christmas and left him in no doubt that the Santa stuff had been a well-meant but mistaken deception.

He listened with no further protest, and when I was finished he claimed to be sleepy and in need of a nap. He rubbed his eyes and yawned elaborately. He had no more interest in Uncle Wiggly and went straight into the house and up to his room.

The last thing I said to him there beneath the cherry trees was that strong, well-balanced people have no need of imaginary friends like Santa Claus and guardian angels. "All we can count on is ourselves, our friends, and our families, Benny. If we want something in life, we can't get it by asking Santa Claus and certainly not by praying for it. We get it only by earning it—or by benefiting from the generosity of friends or relatives. There's no reason ever to *wish* for or pray for anything."

Three years later, when Benny was in the hospital and dying of bone cancer, I understood for the first time why other people felt a need to believe in God and to seek comfort in prayer. Our lives are touched by some tragedies so enormous and so difficult to bear that the temptation to seek mystical answers to the cruelty of the world is powerful indeed.

Even if we can accept that our own deaths are final and that no souls survive the decomposition of our flesh, we often can't endure the idea that our *children*, when stricken in youth, are also doomed to pass from this world into no other. Children are special, so how can it be that they too will be wiped out as completely as if they had never existed? I have seen atheists, despising religion and incapable of praying for themselves, suddenly invoke the name of God in behalf of their own seriously ill children—then realize, sometimes with embarrassment but often with regret, that their philosophy denies them the foolishness of petitioning for divine intercession.

When Benny was afflicted with bone cancer, I was not shaken from my convictions; not once during the ordeal did I put principles aside and turn blubberingly to God. I was stalwart, steadfast, stoical, and determined to bear the burden by myself, though there were times when the weight bowed my head and when the very bones of my shoulders felt as if they would splinter and collapse under a mountain of grief.

That day in October of Benny's seventh year, as I sat beneath the cherry trees and watched him return to the house to nap, I did not know how severely my principles and self-reliance would be tested in the days to come. I was proud of having freed my son of his Christ-related fantasies about Santa Claus, and I was pompously certain that the day would come when Benny, grown to adulthood, would eventually thank me for the rigorously rational upbringing that he had received.

When Hal Sheen told me that he had returned to the fold of the Catholic church, I thought he was setting me up for a joke. We were having an after-work cocktail at a hotel bar near our offices, and I was under the impression that the purpose of our meeting was to celebrate some grand commission that Hal had won for us. "I've got news for you," he had said cryptically that morning. "Let's meet at the Regency for a drink at six o'clock." But instead of telling me that we had been chosen to design a building that would add another chapter to the legend of Fallon and Sheen, he told me that after more than a year of quiet debate with himself, he had shed his atheism as if it were a moldy cocoon and had flown forth into the realm of faith once more. I laughed, waiting for the punch line, and he smiled, and in his smile there was something—perhaps pity for me—that instantly convinced me that he was serious.

I argued quietly, then not so quietly. I scorned his claim to have rediscovered God, and I tried to shame him for his surrender of intellectual dignity.

"I've decided a man can be both an intellectual and a practicing Christian or Jew or Buddhist," Hal said with annoying self-possession.

"Impossible!" I said, striking our table with one fist to emphasize my rejection of that muddle-headed contention. Our cocktail glasses rattled, and an unused ashtray nearly fell on the floor, which caused other patrons to look our way.

"Look at Malcolm Muggeridge," Hal said. "Or C.S. Lewis. Isaac Singer. Christians and a Jew—*and* undisputed intellectuals."

"Listen to you!" I said, appalled. "On how many occasions have other people raised those names—and others—when we were arguing the intellectual supremacy of atheism, and you joined me in proving what fools the Muggeridges, Lewises, and Singers of this world really are."

He shrugged. "I was wrong."

"Just like that?"

"No, not just like that. Give me some credit, Pete. I've spent a year reading, thinking . . . I've actively resisted the urge to return to the faith, and yet I've been won over."

"By whom? What propagandizing priest or—"

"No one won me over. It's been entirely an inner debate, Pete. No one but me has known that I've been wavering on this tightrope."

"Then what started you wavering?"

"Well, for a couple of years now, my life has been empty. . . ."

"Empty? You're young and healthy. You're married to a smart and beautiful woman. You're at the top of your profession, admired by one and all for the freshness and vigor of your architectural vision, and you're wealthy! You call that an empty life?"

He nodded. "Empty. But I couldn't figure out why. Just like you, I added up all that I've got, and it seemed like I should be the most fulfilled man on the face of the earth. But I felt hollow, and each new project we approached had less interest for me. Gradually I realized that all I'd built and that all I might build in the days to come was not going to satisfy me because the achievements were not lasting. Oh, sure, one of our buildings might stand for two hundred years, but a couple of centuries are but a grain of sand falling in the hourglass of Time. Structures of stone and steel and glass are not enduring monuments; they're not, as we once thought, testimonies to the singular genius of mankind. Rather the opposite: they're reminders that even our mightiest structures are fragile, that our greatest achievements can be quickly erased by earthquakes, wars, tidal waves, or simply by the slow gnawing of a thousand years of sun and wind and rain. So what's the point?''

"The point," I reminded him angrily, "is that by erecting those structures, by creating better and more beautiful buildings, we are improving the lives of our fellow men and encouraging others to reach toward higher goals of their own, and then together all of us are making a better future for the whole human species."

"Yes, but to what end?" he pressed. "If there's no afterlife, if each individual's existence ends entirely in the grave, then the *collective* fate of the species is precisely that of the individual: death, emptiness, blackness, nothingness. Nothing can come from nothing. You can't claim a noble, higher purpose for the species as a whole when you allow no higher purpose for the individual spirit." He raised one hand to halt my response. "I know, I know. You've arguments against that statement. I've supported you in them through countless debates on the subject. But I can't support you anymore, Pete. I think there *is* some purpose to life besides just living, and if I didn't think so then I would leave the business and spend the rest of my life having fun, enjoying the precious finite number of days left to me. However, now that I believe there is something called a soul and that it survives the body, I can go on working at Fallon and Sheen because it's my destiny to do so, which means the achievements there are meaningful. I hope you'll be able to accept this. I'm not going to proselytize. This is the first and last time you'll hear me mention religion because I'll respect your right *not* to believe. I'm sure we can go on as before."

But we could not.

I felt that religion was a hateful degenerative sickness of the mind, and I was thereafter uncomfortable in Hal's presence. I still pretended that we were close, that nothing had changed between us, but I felt that he was not the same man he had been.

Besides, Hal's new faith inevitably began to infect his fine architectural vision. Vaulted ceilings and arched windows began to appear in his designs, and everywhere his new buildings encouraged the eye and mind to look up and regard the heavens. This change of direction was welcomed by certain clients and even praised by critics in prestigious journals, but I could not abide it because I knew he was regressing from the man-centered architecture that had been our claim to originality. Fourteen months after his embrace of the Roman Catholic Church, I sold out my share of the company to him and set up my own organization free of his influence.

"Hal," I told him the last time I saw him, "even when you claimed to be atheist, you evidently never understood that the nothingness at the end of life isn't to be feared or raged against. Either accept it regretfully as a fact of life . . . or welcome it."

Personally, I welcomed it, because not having to concern myself about my fate in the afterlife was liberating. Being a nonbeliever, I could concentrate entirely on winning the rewards of *this* world, the one and only world.

The night of the day that I took Santa Claus away from Benny, the night Ellen told me that she wanted to kick me in the ass, as we lay in our moonlit bedroom on opposite sides of the large four-poster bed, she also said, "Pete, you've told me all about your childhood, and of course I've met your folks, so I have a good idea what it must've been like to be raised in that crackpot atmosphere. I can understand why you'd react against their religious fanaticism by embracing atheism. But sometimes . . . you get carried away. You aren't happy to just *be* an atheist; you're so eager to impose your philosophy on everyone else, no matter the cost, that sometimes you behave very much like your own parents . . . except instead of selling God, you're selling godlessness.''

I raised up on the bed and looked at her blanket-shrouded form. I couldn't see her face; she was turned away from me. "That's just plain nasty, Ellen."

"It's true."

"I'm nothing like my parents. Nothing like them. I don't *beat* atheism into Benny the way they tried to beat God into me."

"What you did to him today was as bad as beating him."

"Ellen, all kids learn the truth about Santa Claus eventually, some of them even sooner than Benny did."

She turned toward me, and suddenly I could see her face just well enough to discern the anger in it but, unfortunately, not well enough to glimpse the love that I knew was also there. She said, "Sure, they all learn the truth about Santa Claus, but they don't have the fantasy ripped away from them by their own fathers, damn it!"

"I didn't *rip* it away. I reasoned him out of it."

"He's not a college boy on a debating team," she said. "You can't reason with a seven-year-old. They're all emotion at that age, all heart. Pete, he came into the house today after you were done with him, and he went up to his room, and an hour later when I went up there he was still crying."

"Okay, okay," I said. "I feel like a shit."

"Good. You should."

"And I'll admit that I could have handled it better, been more tactful about it."

She turned away from me again and said nothing.

"But I didn't do anything wrong," I said. "I mean, it was a real mistake to think we could celebrate Christmas in a strictly secular way. Innocent fantasies can lead to some that aren't so innocent."

"Oh, shut up," she said again. "Shut up and go to sleep before I forget I love you."

The trucker who killed Ellen was trying to make more money to buy a boat. He was a fisherman whose passion was trolling; to afford the boat he had to take on more work. He was using amphetamines to stay awake. The truck was a Peterbilt, the biggest one they make. Ellen was driving her blue BMW. They hit head-on, and though she apparently tried to take evasive action, she never had a chance.

Benny was devastated. I put all work aside and stayed home with him the entire month of July. He needed a lot of hugging, reassuring, and some gentle guidance toward acceptance of the tragedy. I was in bad shape too, for Ellen had been more than my wife and lover: she had been my toughest critic, my greatest champion, my best friend, and my only confidant. At night, alone in the bedroom we had shared, I put my face against the pillow upon which she had slept, breathed in the faintly lingering scent of her, and wept; I couldn't bear to wash the pillowcase for weeks. But in front of Benny, I managed for the most part to maintain control of myself and provide him with the example of strength that he so terribly needed.

There was no funeral. Ellen was cremated, and her ashes were dispersed at sea.

A month later, on the first Sunday in August, when we had begun to move grudgingly and sadly toward acceptance, forty or fifty friends and relatives came to the house, and we held a quiet memorial service for Ellen, a purely secular service with not even the slightest thread of religious content. We gathered on the patio near the pool, and half a dozen friends stepped forward to tell amusing stories about Ellen and to explain what an impact she'd had on their lives.

I kept Benny at my side throughout that service, for I wanted him to see that his mother had been loved by others, too, and that her existence had made a difference in more lives than his and mine. He was only eight years old, but he seemed to take from the service the very comfort that I had hoped it would give him. Hearing his mother praised, he was unable to hold back his tears, but now there was something more than grief in his face and eyes: now he was also proud of her, amused by some of the practical jokes that she had played on friends and that they now recounted, and intrigued to hear about aspects of her that had theretofore been invisible to him. In time these new emotions were certain to dilute his grief and help him adjust to his loss.

The day following the memorial service, I rose late. When I went looking for Benny, I found him beneath one of the cherry trees in the backyard. He sat with his knees drawn up against his chest and his arms around his legs, staring at the far side of the broad valley on one slope of which we lived, but he seemed to be looking at something still more distant.

I sat beside him. "How you doin'?"

"Okay," he said.

For a while neither of us spoke. Overhead the leaves of the tree rustled softly. The dazzling white-pink blossoms of spring were long gone, of course, and the branches were bedecked with fruit not yet quite ripe. The day was hot, but the tree threw plentiful, cool shade.

At last he said, "Daddy?"

"Hmmmm?"

"If it's all right with you . . ."

"What?"

"I know what you say . . ."

"What I say about what?"

"About there being no heaven or angels or anything like that."

"It's not just what I say, Benny. It's true."

"Well . . . just the same, if it's all right with you, I'm going to picture Mommy in heaven, wings and everything."

I knew he was still in a fragile emotional condition even

a month after her death and that he would need many more months if not years to regain his full equilibrium, so I did not rush to respond with one of my usual arguments about the foolishness of religious faith. I was silent for a moment, then said, "Well, let me think about that for a couple minutes, okay?"

We sat side by side, staring across the valley, and I know that neither of us was seeing the landscape before us. I was seeing Ellen as she had been on the Fourth of July the previous summer, wearing white shorts and a yellow blouse, tossing a Frisbee with me and Benny, radiant, laughing, laughing. I don't know what poor Benny was seeing, though I suspect his mind was brimming with gaudy images of heaven complete with haloed angels and golden steps spiraling up to a golden throne.

"She can't just end," he said after a while. "She was too nice to j-j-just end. She's got to be . . . somewhere."

"But that's just it, Benny. She *is* somewhere. Your mother goes on in you. You've got her genes, for one thing. You don't know what genes are, but you've got them: her hair, her eyes . . . And because she was a good person who taught you the right values, you'll grow up to be a good person, as well, and you'll have kids of your own some day, and your mother will go on in them and in *their* children. Your mother still lives in our memories, too, and in the memories of her friends. Because she was kind to so many people, those people were shaped to some small degree by her kindness; they'll now and then remember her, and because of her they might be kinder to people, and that kindness goes on and on."

He listened solemnly, although I suspected that the concepts of immortality through bloodline and impersonal immortality through one's moral relationships with other people were beyond his grasp. I tried to think of a way to restate it so a child could understand.

But he said, "Nope. Not good enough. It's nice that lots of people are gonna remember her. But it's not good enough. *She* has to be somewhere. Not just her memory.

She has to go on . . . so if it's all right with you, I'm gonna figure she's in heaven.''

"No, it's not all right, Benny." I put an arm around him. "The healthy thing to do, son, is to face up to unpleasant truths—"

He shook his head. "She's all right, Daddy. She didn't just end. She's somewhere now. I know she is. And she's happy."

"Benny—"

He stood, looked up into the trees, and said, "We have cherries to eat soon?"

"Benny, let's not change the subject. We—"

"Can we drive into town for lunch at Mrs. Foster's restaurant—burgers and fries and Cokes and then a cherry sundae?"

"Benny—"

"Can we, can we?"

"All right. But—"

"I get to drive!" he shouted and ran off toward the garage, giggling at his joke.

During the next year Benny's stubborn refusal to let his mother go was at first frustrating, then annoying, and finally intensely aggravating. He talked to her nearly every night as he lay in bed, waiting for sleep to come, and he seemed confident that she could hear him. Often, after I tucked him in and kissed him goodnight and left the room, he slipped out from under the covers, knelt beside the bed, and prayed that his mother was happy and safe where she had gone.

Twice I accidentally heard him. On other occasions I stood quietly in the hall after leaving his room, and when he thought I had gone downstairs, he humbled himself before God, though he could know nothing more of God than what he had illicitly learned from television shows or other pop culture that I had been unable to monitor.

I was determined to wait him out, certain that his childish faith would expire naturally when he realized that God would never answer him. As the days passed without a miraculous sign assuring him that his mother's soul had survived death, Benny would begin to understand that all he had been taught about religion was true, and he eventually would return quietly to the realm of reason where I had made—and was patiently saving—a place for him. I did not want to tell him I knew of his praying, did not want to force the issue because I knew that in reaction to a too heavy-handed exercise of parental authority, he might cling even longer to his irrational dream of life everlasting.

But after four months, when his nightly conversations with his dead mother and with God did not cease, I could no longer tolerate even whispered prayers in my house, for though I seldom heard them, I *knew* they were being said, and knowing was somehow as maddening as hearing every word of them. I confronted him. I reasoned with him at great length on many occasions. I argued, pleaded. I tried the classic carrot-and-stick approach: I punished him for the expression of any religious sentiment; and I rewarded him for the slightest antireligious statement, even if he made it unthinkingly or even if it was only my *interpretation* of what he'd said that was antireligious. He received few rewards and much punishment. I did not spank him or in any way physically abuse him; that much, at least, is to my credit; I did not attempt to beat God out of him the way my parents had tried to beat Him *into* me.

I took Benny to Dr. Gerton, a psychiatrist, when everything else had failed. "He's having difficulty accepting his mother's death," I told Gerton. "He's just not . . . coping. I'm worried about him."

After three sessions with Benny over a period of two weeks, Dr. Gerton called to say he no longer needed to see Benny. "He's going to be all right, Mr. Fallon. You've no need to worry about him."

"But you're wrong," I insisted. "He needs analysis. He's still not . . . coping."

"Mr. Fallon, you've said that before, but I've never been able to get a clear explanation of what behavior strikes you as evidence of his inability to cope. What's he *doing* that worries you so?''

"He's praying," I said. "He prays to God to keep his mother safe and happy. And he talks to his mother as if he's sure she hears him, talks to her *every* night.''

"Oh, Mr. Fallon, if that's all that's been bothering you, I can assure you there's no need to worry. Talking to his mother, praying for her, all that's perfectly ordinary and—''

"Every night!" I repeated.

"Ten times a day would be all right. Really, there's nothing unhealthy about it. Talking to God about his mother and talking to his mother in heaven . . . it's just a psychological mechanism by which he can slowly adjust to the fact that she's no longer actually here on earth with him. It's perfectly ordinary.''

I'm afraid I shouted: "It's not perfectly ordinary in *this* house, Dr. Gerton. We're atheists!''

He was silent for a moment, then sighed. "Mr. Fallon, you've got to remember that your son is more than your son—he's a person in his own right. A *little* person but a person nonetheless. You can't think of him as property or as an unformed mind to be molded—''

"I have the utmost respect for the individual, Dr. Gerton. Much more respect than do the hymn-singers who value their fellow men less than they do their imaginary master in the sky.''

His silence lasted longer than before. Finally he said, "All right. Then surely you realize there's no guarantee the son will be the same person in every respect as the father. He'll have ideas and desires of his own. And ideas about religion might be one area in which the disagreement between you will widen over the years rather than narrow. This might not be *only* a psychological mechanism that he's using to adapt to his mother's death; it might also turn out to be the start of lifelong faith. At least you have to be prepared for the possibility.''

"I won't have it," I said firmly.

His third silence was the longest of all. Then: "Mr.
Fallon, I have no need to see Benny again. There's nothing
I can do for him because there's nothing he really needs
from me. But perhaps you should consider some counseling for yourself."

I hung up on him.

For the next six months Benny infuriated and frustrated
me by clinging to his fantasy of heaven. Perhaps he no
longer spoke to his mother every evening, and perhaps
sometimes he even forgot to say his prayers, but his stubborn faith could not be shaken. When I spoke of atheism,
when I made a scornful joke about God, when I tried to
reason with him, he would only say, "No, Daddy, you're
wrong," or "No, Daddy, that's not the way it is," and he
would either walk away from me or try to change the subject. Or he would do something even more infuriating: he
would say, "No, Daddy, you're wrong," and then he
would throw his small arms around me, hug me very tight,
and tell me that he loved me, and at these moments there
was a too-apparent sadness about him that included an
element of pity, as if he was afraid for me and felt that *I*
needed guidance and reassurance. Nothing made me angrier than that. He was nine years old, not an ancient
guru! As punishment for his willful disregard of my
wishes, I took away his television privileges for days—and
sometimes weeks—at a time, forbid him to have dessert
after dinner, and once refused to allow him to play with
his friends for an entire month. Nothing worked.

Religion, the disease that had turned my parents into
stern and solemn strangers, the disease that had made my
childhood a nightmare, the very sickness that had stolen
my best friend, Hal Sheen, from me when I least expected
to lose him, *religion* had now wormed its way into my
house again. It had contaminated my son, the only important person left in my life. No, it wasn't any particular
religion that had a grip on Benny. He didn't have any formal theological education, so his concepts of God and

heaven were thoroughly nondenominational, vaguely Christian, yes, but only vaguely. It was religion without structure, without dogma or doctrine, religion based entirely on childish sentiment; therefore some might say that it was not really religion at all, and that I should not have worried about it. But I knew Dr. Gerton's observation was true: this childish faith might be the seed from which a true religious conviction would grow in later years. The virus of religion was loose in my house, and I was dismayed, distraught, and perhaps even somewhat deranged by my failure to find a cure for it.

To me, this was the essence of horror. It wasn't the acute horror of a bomb blast or plane crash, mercifully brief, but a chronic horror that went on day after day, week after week.

I was sure that the worst of all possible troubles had befallen me and that I was in the darkest time of my life.

Then Benny got bone cancer.

Nearly two years after his mother died, on a blustery day in late February, we were in the park by the river, flying a kite. When Benny ran with the control stick, paying out string, he fell down. Not just one. Not twice. Repeatedly. When I asked what was wrong, he said he had a sore muscle in his right leg: "Must've twisted it when the guys and I were climbing trees yesterday."

He favored the leg for a couple of days, and when I suggested he ought to see a doctor, he said he was feeling better.

A week later he was in the hospital, undergoing tests, and in another two days, the diagnosis was confirmed: bone cancer. It was too widespread for surgery. His physicians instituted an immediate program of radium treatments and chemotherapy.

Benny lost his hair, lost weight. He grew so pale that each morning I was afraid to look at him because I had the crazy idea that if he got any paler he would begin to turn transparent and, when he was finally as clear as glass, would shatter in front of my eyes.

After five weeks he took a sudden turn for the better and was, though not in remission, at least well enough to come home. The radium and chemotherapy were continued on an outpatient basis.

I think now that he improved not due to the radium or cytotoxic agents or drugs but simply because he wanted to see the cherry trees in bloom one last time. His temporary turn for the better was an act of sheer will, a triumph of mind over body.

Except for one day when a sprinkle of rain fell, he sat in a chair under the blossom-laden boughs, enjoying the spring greening of the valley and delighting in the antics of the squirrels that came out of the nearby woods to frolic on our lawn. He sat not in one of the redwood lawn chairs but in a big, comfortably padded easy chair that I brought out from the house, his legs propped on a hassock, for he was thin and fragile; a harder chair would have bruised him horribly.

We played card games and Chinese checkers, but usually he was too tired to concentrate on a game for long, so mostly we just sat there, relaxing. We talked of days past, of the many good times he'd had in his ten short years, and of his mother. But we sat in silence a lot, too. It was never an awkward silence; sometimes melancholy, yes, but never awkward.

Neither of us spoke of God or guardian angels or heaven. I know he had not lost his belief that his mother had survived the death of her body in some form and that she had gone on to a better place. But he said nothing more of that and did not discuss his own hopes for the afterlife. I believe he avoided the subject out of respect for me and because he wanted no friction between us during those last days.

I will always be grateful to him for not putting me to the test. I am afraid that I'd have tried to force him to embrace rationalism even in his last days, thereby making a bigger jackass of myself than usual.

After only nine days at home, he suffered a relapse and returned to the hospital. I booked him into a semi-private room with two beds: he took one, and I took the other.

Cancer cells had migrated to his liver, and a tumor was found there. After surgery he improved for a few days, was almost buoyant, but then sank again.

Cancer was found in his lymphatic system, in his spleen, tumors everywhere.

His condition improved, declined, improved, and declined again. However each improvement was less encouraging than the one before it, while each decline was steeper.

I was rich, intelligent, and talented. I was famous in my field. But I could do nothing to save my son. I had never felt so small, so powerless.

At least I could be strong for Benny. In his presence I tried to be cheerful. I did not let him see me cry, but I wept quietly at night, curled in the fetal position, reduced to the helplessness of a child, while he lay in troubled, drug-induced slumber on the other side of the room. During the day, when he was away for therapy or tests or surgery, I sat at the window, staring out, seeing nothing.

As if some alchemical spell had been cast, the world became gray, entirely gray. I was aware of no color in anything; I might have been living in an old black-and-white movie. Shadows became more stark and sharp-edged. The air itself seemed gray, as though contaminated by a toxic mist so fine that it could not be seen, only sensed. Voices were fuzzy, the audial equivalent of gray. The few times that I switched on the TV or the radio, the music seemed to have no melody that I could discern. My interior world was as gray as the physical world around me, and the unseen but acutely sensed mist that fouled the outer world had penetrated to my core.

Even in the depths of that despair, I did not step off the path of reason, did not turn to God for help or condemn

God for torturing an innocent child. I did not consider seeking the counsel of clergymen or the help of faith healers.

I endured.

If I had slipped and sought solace in superstition, no one could have blamed me. In little more than two years, I'd had a falling out with my only close friend, had lost my wife in a traffic accident, and had seen my son succumb to cancer. Occasionally you hear about people with bad runs of luck like that, or you read about them in the papers, and strangely enough they usually talk about how they were brought to God by their suffering and how they found peace in faith. Reading about them always makes you sad and stirs your compassion, and you can even forgive them their witless religious sentimentality. Of course, you always quickly put them out of your mind because you know that a similar chain of tragedies could befall you, and such a realization does not bear contemplation. Now I not only had to contemplate it but *live* it, and in the living I did not bend my principles.

I faced the void and accepted it.

After putting up a surprisingly long, valiant, painful struggle against the virulent cancer that was eating him alive, Benny finally died on a night in August. They had rushed him into the intensive care unit two days before, and I had been permitted to sit with him only fifteen minutes every second hour. On that last night, however, they allowed me to come in from the ICU lounge and stay beside his bed for several hours because they knew he did not have long.

An intravenous drip pierced his left arm. An aspirator was inserted in his nose. He was hooked up to an EKG machine that traced his heart activity in green light on a bedside monitor, and each beat was marked by a soft beep. The lines and the beeps frequently became erratic for as much as three or four minutes at a time.

I held his hand. I smoothed the sweat-damp hair away from his brow. I pulled the covers up to his neck when he was seized by chills and lowered them when the chills gave way to fevers.

Benny slipped in and out of consciousness. Even when awake he was not always alert or coherent.

"Daddy?"

"Yes, Benny?"

"Is that you?"

"It's me."

"Where am I?"

"In bed. Safe. I'm here, Benny."

"Is supper ready?"

"Not yet."

"I'd like burgers and fries."

"That's what we're having."

"Where're my shoes?"

"You don't need shoes tonight, Benny."

"Thought we were going for a walk."

"Not tonight."

"Oh."

Then he sighed and slipped away again.

Rain was falling outside. Drops pattered against the ICU windows and streamed down the panes. The storm contributed to the gray mood that had claimed the world.

Once, near midnight, Benny woke and was lucid. He knew exactly where he was, who I was, and what was happening. He turned his head toward me and smiled. He tried to rise up on one arm, but he was too weak even to lift his head.

I got out of my chair, stood at the side of his bed, held his hand, and said, "All these wires . . . I think they're going to replace a few of your parts with robot stuff."

"I'll be okay," he said in a faint, tremulous voice that was strangely, movingly confident.

"You want a chip of ice to suck on?"

"No. What I want . . ."

"What? Anything you want, Benny."

"I'm scared, Daddy . . ."

My throat grew tight, and I was afraid that I was going

to lose the composure that I had strived so hard to hold onto during the long weeks of his illness. I swallowed and said, "Don't be scared, Benny. I'm with you. Don't—"

"No," he said, interrupting me. "I'm not scared . . . for me. I'm afraid . . . for you."

I thought he was delirious again, and I didn't know what to say.

But he was not delirious, and with his next few words he made himself painfully clear: "I want us all . . . to be together again . . . like we were before Mommy died . . . together again someday. But I'm afraid that you . . . won't . . . find us."

The rest is agonizing to recall. I was indeed so obsessed with holding fast to my atheism that I could not bring myself to tell my son a harmless lie that would make his last minutes easier. If only I had promised to believe, had told him that I would seek him in the next world, he would have gone to his rest more happily. Ellen was right when she called it an obsession. I merely held Benny's hand tighter, blinked back tears, and smiled at him.

He said, "If you don't believe you can find us . . . then maybe you won't find us."

"It's all right, Benny," I said soothingly. I kissed him on the forehead, on his left cheek, and for a moment I put my face against his and held him as best I could, trying to compensate with affection for the promise of faith that I refused to give.

"Daddy . . . if only . . . you'd look for us?"

"You'll be okay, Benny."

". . . just *look* for us . . ."

"I love you, Benny. I love you with all my heart."

". . . if you look for us . . . you'll find us . . ."

"I love you, I love you, Benny."

". . . don't look . . . won't find . . ."

"Benny, Benny. . . ."

The gray ICU light fell on the gray sheets and on the gray face of my son.

The gray rain streamed down the gray window.

He died while I held him.

Abruptly color came back into the world. Far too much color, too intense, overwhelming. The light brown of Benny's staring, sightless eyes was the purest, most penetrating, most beautiful brown that I had ever seen. The ICU walls were a pale blue that made me feel as if they were not made of plaster but of water, and as if I was about to be drowned in a turbulent sea. The sour-apple green of the EKG monitor screen blazed bright, searing my eyes. The watery blue walls flowed toward me. I heard running footsteps as nurses and interns responded to the lack of telemetry data from their small patient, but before they arrived I was swept away by a blue tide, carried into deep blue currents.

I shut down my company. I withdrew from negotiations for new commissions. I arranged for those commissions already undertaken to be transferred as quickly as possible to other design firms of which I approved and with which my clients felt comfortable. I pink-slipped my employees, though with generous severance pay, and helped them to find new jobs where possible.

I converted my wealth into treasury certificates and conservative savings instruments, investments that required no monitoring. The temptation to sell the house was great, but after considerable thought I merely closed it up and hired a part-time caretaker to look after it in my absence.

Years later than Hal Sheen, I had reached his conclusion that no monuments of man were worth the effort it took to erect them. Even the greatest edifices of stone and steel were pathetic vanities, of no consequence in the long run. When viewed in the context of the vast, cold universe in which trillions of stars blazed down on tens of trillions of planets, even the pyramids were as fragile as origami sculptures. In the dark light of death and entropy, even heroic effort and acts of genius appeared foolish.

Yet relationships with family and friends were no more enduring than humanity's fragile monuments of stone. I had once told Benny that we lived on in memory, in the genetic trace, in the kindness that our own kindnesses encouraged in others. But those things now seemed as insubstantial as shapes of smoke in a brisk wind.

Unlike Hal Sheen, however, I did not seek comfort in religion. No blows were hard enough to crack my obsession.

I had thought that religious mania was the worst horror of all, but now I had found one that was worse: the horror of an atheist who, unable to believe in God, is suddenly also unable to believe in the value of human struggle and courage, and is therefore unable to find meaning in anything whatsoever, neither in beauty nor in pleasure nor in the smallest act of kindness.

I spent that autumn in Bermuda. I bought a Cheoy Lee sixty-six-foot sport yacht, a sleek and powerful boat, and learned how to handle it. Alone, I ran the Caribbean, sampling island after island. Sometimes I dawdled along at quarter-throttle for days at a time, in sync with the lazy rhythms of Caribbean life. But then suddenly I would be overcome with the frantic need to move, to stop wasting time, and I would press forward, engines screaming, slamming across the waves with reckless abandon, as if it mattered whether I got anywhere by any particular time.

When I tired of the Caribbean, I went to Brazil, but Rio held interest for only a few days. I became a rich drifter, moving from one first-class hotel to another in one far-flung city after another: Hong Kong, Singapore, Istanbul, Paris, Athens, Cairo, New York, Las Vegas, Acapulco, Tokyo, San Francisco. I was looking for something that would give meaning to life, though the search was conducted with the certain knowledge that I would not find what I sought.

For a few days I thought I could devote my life to gambling. In the random fall of cards, in the spin of roulette wheels, I glimpsed the strange, wild shape of fate. By committing myself to swimming in that deep river of randomness, I thought I might be in harmony with the pointlessness and disorder of the universe and therefore at peace. In less than a week I won and lost fortunes, and at last I walked away from the gaming tables with a hundred-thousand-dollar loss. That was only a tiny fraction of the millions on which I could draw, but in those few days I learned that even immersion in the chaos of random chance provided no escape from an awareness of the finite nature of life and of all things human.

In the spring I went home to die. I'm not sure if I meant to kill myself. Or, having lost the will to live, perhaps I believed that I could just lie down in a familiar place and succumb to death without needing to lift my hand against myself. But although I did not know how death would be attained, I was certain death was my goal.

The house in Buck's County was filled with painful memories of Ellen and Benny, and when I went into the kitchen and looked out the window at the cherry trees in the backyard, my heart ached as if pinched in a vise. The trees were ablaze with thousands of pink and white blossoms.

Benny had loved the cherry trees when they were at their radiant best, and the sight of their blossoms sharpened my memories of Benny so well that I felt I had been stabbed. For a while I leaned against the kitchen counter, unable to breathe, then gasped painfully for breath, then wept.

In time I went out and stood beneath the trees, looking up at the beautifully decorated branches. Benny had been dead almost nine months, but the trees he had loved were still thriving, and in some way I could not quite grasp, their continued existence meant that at least a part of Benny was still alive. I struggled to understand that crazy idea—

—and suddenly the cherry blossoms fell. Not just a few. Not just hundreds. Within one minute every blossom on both trees dropped to the ground. I turned around, around, startled and confused, and the whirling white flowers were as thick as snowflakes in a blizzard. I had never seen anything like it. Cherry blossoms just don't fall by the thousands, simultaneously, on a windless day.

When the phenomenon ended I plucked blossoms off my shoulders and out of my hair. I examined them closely. They were not withered or seared or marked by any sign of tree disease.

I looked up at the branches.

Not one blossom remained on either tree.

My heart was hammering.

Around my feet, drifts of cherry blossoms began to stir in a mild breeze that sprang up from the west.

"No," I said, so frightened that I could not even admit to myself what I was saying no *to*.

I turned from the trees and ran to the house. As I went, the last of the cherry blossoms blew off my hair and clothes.

In the library, however, as I took a bottle of Jack Daniels from the bar cabinet, I realized that I was still clutching blossoms in my hand. I threw them down on the floor and scrubbed my palm on my pants as if I had been handling something foul.

I went to the bedroom with the Jack Daniels and drank myself unconscious, refusing to face up to the reason why I needed to drink at all. I told myself that it had nothing to do with the cherry tree, that I was drinking only because I needed to escape the misery of the past few years.

Mine was a diamond-hard obsession.

I slept for eleven hours and woke with a hangover. I took two aspirins, stood in the shower under very hot water for fifteen minutes, under a cold spray for one minute, toweled vigorously, took two more aspirin, and went into the kitchen to make coffee.

Through the window above the sink, I saw the cherry trees ablaze with pink and white blossoms.

Hallucination, I thought with relief. Yesterday's blizzard of blossoms was just hallucination.

I ran outside for a closer look at the trees. I saw that

only a few pink-white petals were scattered on the lush grass beneath the boughs, no more than would have blown off in the mild spring breeze.

Relieved but also curiously disappointed, I returned to the kitchen. The coffee had brewed. As I poured a cupful, I remembered the blossoms that I had cast aside in the library.

I drank two cups of fine Colombian before I had the nerve to go to the library. The blossoms were there: a wad of crushed petals that had yellowed and acquired brown edges during the night. I picked them up, closed my hand around them.

All right, I told myself shakily, you don't have to believe in Christ or in God the Father or in some bodiless Holy Spirit.

Religion is a disease.

No, no, you don't have to believe in any of the silly rituals, in the dogma and doctrine. In fact you don't have to believe in *God* to believe in an afterlife.

Irrational, unreasonable.

No, wait, think about it: Isn't it possible that life after death is perfectly natural, not a divine gift but a simple fact of nature? The caterpillar lives one life, then transforms itself to live again as a butterfly. So, damn it, isn't it conceivable that our bodies are the caterpillar stage and that our spirits take flight into another existence when the bodies are no longer of use to us? The human metamorphosis may just be a transformation of a higher order than that of the caterpillar.

Slowly, with dread and yet hope, I walked through the house, out the back door, up the sloped yard to the cherry trees. I stood beneath their flowery boughs and opened my hand to reveal the blossoms I had saved from yesterday.

"Benny?" I said wonderingly.

The blossomfall began again. From both trees, the pink and white petals dropped in profusion, spinning lazily to the grass, catching in my hair and on my clothes.

I turned, breathless, gasping. "Benny? Benny?"

In a minute the ground was covered with a white mantle, and again not one small bloom remained on the trees.

I laughed. It was a nervous laugh that might degenerate into a mad cackle. I was not in control of myself.

Not quite sure why I was speaking aloud, I said, "I'm scared. Oh, shit, am I scared."

The blossoms began to drift up from the ground. Not just a few of them. All of them. They rose back toward the branches that had shed them only moments ago. It was a blizzard in reverse. The soft petals brushed against my face.

I was laughing again, laughing uncontrollably, but my fear was fading rapidly, and this was good laughter.

Within another minute, the trees were cloaked in pink and white as before, and all was still.

I sensed that Benny was not within the tree, that this phenomenon did not conform to pagan belief any more than it did to traditional Christianity. But he was *somewhere*. He was not gone forever. He was out there somewhere, and when my time came to go where he and Ellen had gone, I only needed to believe that they could be found, and then I would surely find them.

The sound of an obsession cracking could probably be heard all the way to China.

A scrap of writing by H.G. Wells came into my mind. I had always admired Wells's work, but nothing he had written had ever seemed so true as that which I recalled while standing under the cherry trees: "The past is but the beginning of a beginning, and all that is and has been is but the twilight of the dawn." He was writing about history, of course, and about the long future that awaited mankind, but those words seemed to apply, as well, to death and to the mysterious rebirth that followed it. A man might live a hundred years, yet his long life is but the twilight of the dawn.

"Benny," I said. "Oh, Benny."

But no blossoms fell, and through the years that followed I received no more signs. Nor did I need them.

From that day forward, I knew that death was not the end and that I would be rejoined with Ellen and Benny on the other side.

And what of God? Does He exist? I don't know. Although I have believed in an afterlife of some kind for ten years now, I have not become a churchgoer. But if, upon my death, I cross into that other plane and find Him waiting for me, I will not be entirely surprised, and I will return to His arms as gratefully and happily as I will return to Ellen's and to Benny's.

AUTHOR'S NOTE

FICTION IS A FORM OF MAGIC. THE AUTHOR IS A PRESTI-digitator who must create a false world exotic enough to engage our imagination, yet sufficiently a reflection of the real world to be relevant to our lives. This legerdemain of language cannot succeed if the author accompanies his story with analysis, any more than a stage magician can induce an abiding sense of wonder in his audience if he follows his illusions with detailed explanations of how the effects were achieved. Good magic requires secrecy, so I am not going to explain here the mechanics that allowed these rabbits to be pulled from hats and these doves from silk handkerchiefs.

All I have to say about "Twilight of the Dawn" is that it was written for Night Visions IV, *an anthology of horror stories, and that it was meant to stretch the definition of the genre. Real-life horrors have nothing to do with vampires and werewolves, or any of the genre's other shopworn de-*

vices. And in real life, unlike the worlds in most horror stories, horror and hope are inextricably intertwined, which makes the former more frightening and the latter more poignant.

—Dean R. Koontz

THE WOMAN IN THE ROOM
Stephen King

THE QUESTION IS: CAN HE DO IT?

He doesn't know. He knows that she chews them sometimes, her face wrinkling at the awful orange taste, and a sound comes from her mouth like splintering popsicle sticks. But these are different pills . . . gelatin capsules. The box says DARVON COMPLEX on the outside. He found them in her medicine cabinet and turned them over in his hands, thinking. Something the doctor gave her before she had to go back to the hospital. Something for the ticking nights. The medicine cabinet is full of remedies, neatly lined up like a voodoo doctor's cures. Gris-gris of the Western world. FLEET SUPPOSITORIES. He has never used a suppository in his life and the thought of putting a waxy something in his rectum to soften by body heat makes him feel ill. There is no dignity in putting things up your ass. PHILLIPS MILK OF MAGNESIA. ANACIN ARTHRITIS PAIN FORMULA. PEPTO-BISMOL. More. He can trace the course of her illness through the medicines.

But these pills are different. They are like regular Darvon only in that they are gray gelatin capsules. But they are bigger, what his dead father used to call hosscock pills. The box says Asp. 350 gr, Darvon 100 gr, and could she chew them even if he was to give them to her? *Would* she? The house is still running; the refrigerator runs and shuts off, the furnace kicks in and out, every now and then the cuckoo bird pokes grumpily out of the clock to announce an hour or a half. He supposes that after she dies it will fall to Kevin and him to break up housekeeping. She's gone, all right. The whole house says so. She

is in the Central Maine Hospital, in Lewiston. Room 312. She went when the pain got so bad she could no longer go out to the kitchen and make her own coffee. At times, when he visited, she cried without knowing it.

The elevator creaks going up, and he finds himself examining the blue elevator certificate. The certificate makes it clear that the elevator is safe, creaks or no creaks. She has been here for nearly three weeks now and today they gave her an operation called a "cortotomy." He is not sure if that is how it's spelled, but that is how it sounds. The doctor has told her that the "cortotomy" involves sticking a needle into her neck and then into her brain. The doctor has told her that this is like sticking a pin into an orange and spearing a seed. When the needle has poked into her pain center, a radio signal will be sent down to the tip of the needle and the pain center will be blown out. Like unplugging a TV. Then the cancer in her belly will stop being such a nuisance.

The thought of this operation makes him even more uneasy than the thought of suppositories melting warmly in his anus. It makes him think of a book by Michael Crichton called *The Terminal Man*, which deals with putting wires in people's heads. According to Crichton, this can be a very bad scene. You better believe it.

The elevator door opens on the third floor and he steps out. This is the old wing of the hospital, and it smells like the sweet-smelling sawdust they sprinkle over puke at a county fair. He has left the pills in the glove compartment of his car. He has not had anything to drink before this visit.

The walls up here are two-tone: brown on the bottom and white on top. He thinks that the only two-tone combination in the whole world that might be more depressing than brown and white would be pink and black. Hospital corridors like giant Good 'n' Plentys. The thought makes him smile and feel nauseated at the same time.

Two corridors meet in a T in front of the elevator, and there is a drinking fountain where he always stops to put things off a little. There are pieces of hospital equipment here and there, like strange playground toys. A litter with chrome sides and rubber wheels, the sort of thing they use to wheel you up to the "OR" when they are ready to give you your "cortotomy." There is a large circular object whose function is unknown to him. It looks like the wheels you sometimes see in squirrel cages. There is a rolling IV tray with two bottles hung from it, like a Salvador Dali dream of tits. Down one of the two corridors is the nurses' station, and laughter fueled by coffee drifts out to him.

He gets his drink and then saunters down toward her room. He is scared of what he may find and hopes she will be sleeping. If she is, he will not wake her up.

Above the door of every room there is a small square light. When a patient pushes his call button his light goes on, glowing red. Up and down the hall patients are walking slowly, wearing cheap hospital robes over their hospital underwear. The robes have blue and white pinstripes and round collars. The hospital underwear is called a "johnny." The "johnnies" look all right on the women but decidedly strange on the men because they are like knee-length dresses or slips. The men always seem to wear brown imitation-leather slippers on their feet. The women favor knitted slippers with balls of yarn on them. His mother has a pair of these and calls them "mules."

The patients remind him of a horror movie called *The Night of the Living Dead*. They all walk slowly, as if someone had unscrewed the tops of their organs like mayonnaise jars and liquids were sloshing around inside. Some of them use canes. Their slow gait as they promenade up and down the halls is frightening but also dignified. It is the walk of people who are going nowhere slowly, the walk of college students in caps and gowns filing into a convocation hall.

Ectoplasmic music drifts everywhere from transistor radios. Voices babble. He can hear Black Oak Arkansas singing "Jim Dandy" ("Go Jim Dandy, go Jim Dandy!" a falsetto voice screams merrily at the slow hall walkers). He can hear a talk-show host discussing Nixon in tones that have been dipped in acid like smoking quills. He can hear a polka with French lyrics—Lewiston is still a French-speaking town and they love their jigs and reels almost as much as they love to cut each other in the bars on lower Lisbon Street.

He pauses outside his mother's room and

for a while there he was freaked enough to come drunk. It made him ashamed to be drunk in front of his mother even though she was too doped and full of Elavil to know. Elavil is a tranquilizer they give to cancer patients so it won't bother them so much that they're dying.

The way he worked it was to buy two six-packs of Black Label beer at Sonny's Market in the afternoon. He would sit with the kids and watch their afternoon programs on TV. Three beers with *Sesame Street*, two beers during *Mister Rogers*, one beer during *Electric Company*. Then one with supper.

He took the other five beers in the car. It was a twenty-two-mile drive from Raymond to Lewiston, via Routes 302 and 202, and it was possible to be pretty well in the bag by the time he got to the hospital, with one or two beers left over. He would bring things for his mother and leave them in the car so there would be an excuse to go back and get them and also drink another half beer and keep the high going.

It also gave him an excuse to piss outdoors, and somehow that was the best of the whole miserable business. He always parked in the side lot, which was rutted, frozen November dirt, and the cold night air assured full bladder contraction. Pissing in one of the hospital bathrooms was too much like an apotheosis of the whole hospital experience: the nurse's call button beside the hopper, the chrome handle bolted at a 45-degree angle, the bottle of pink disinfectant over the sink. Bad news. You better believe it.

The urge to drink going home was nil. So leftover beers collected in the icebox at home and when there were six of them, he would

never have come if he had known it was going to be this bad. The first thought that crosses his mind is *She's no orange* and the second thought is *She's really dying quick now*, as if she had a train to catch out there in nullity. She is straining in the bed, not moving except for her eyes, but straining inside her body, something is moving in there. Her neck has been smeared orange with stuff that looks like Mercurochrome, and there is a bandage below her left ear where some humming doctor put the radio needle in and blew out 60 per cent of her motor controls along with the pain center. Her eyes follow him like the eyes of a paint-by-the-numbers Jesus.

—I don't think you better see me tonight, Johnny. I'm not so good. Maybe I'll be better tomorrow.

—What is it?

—It itches. I itch all over. Are my legs together?

He can't see if her legs are together. They are just a raised V under the ribbed hospital sheet. It's very hot in the room. No one is in the other bed right now. He thinks: Roommates come and roommates go, but my mom stays on forever. Christ!

—They're together, Mom.

—Move them down, can you, Johnny? Then you better go. I've never been in a fix like this before. I can't move anything. My nose itches. Isn't that a pitiful way to be, with your nose itching and not able to scratch it?

He scratches her nose and then takes hold of her calves through the sheet and pulls them down. He can put one hand around both calves with no trouble at all, although his hands are not particularly large. She groans. Tears are running down her cheeks to her ears.

—Momma?

—Can you move my legs down?

—I just did.

—Oh. That's all right, then. I think I'm crying. I don't mean to in front of you. I wish I was out of this. I'd do anything to be out of this.

—Would you like a smoke?

—Could you get me a drink of water first, Johnny? I'm as dry as an old chip.

—Sure.

He takes her glass with a flexible straw in it out and around the corner to the drinking fountain. A fat man with an elastic bandage on one leg is sailing slowly down the corridor. He isn't wearing one of the pin-striped robes and is holding his "johnny" closed behind him.

He fills the glass from the fountain and goes back to Room 312 with it. She has stopped crying. Her lips grip the straw in a way that reminds him of camels he has seen in travelogues. Her face is scrawny. His most vivid memory of her in the life he lived as her son is of a time when he was twelve. He and his brother Kevin and this woman had moved to Maine so that she could take care of her parents. Her mother was old and bed-ridden. High blood pressure had made his grandmother senile, and, to add insult to injury, had struck her blind. Happy eighty-sixth birthday. Here's one to grow on. And she lay in a bed all day long, blind and senile, wearing large diapers and rubber pants, unable to re-member what breakfast had been but able to recite all the Presidents right up to Ike. And so the three generations of them had lived together in that house where he had so recently found the pills (although both grandparents are now long since dead) and at twelve he had been lipping off about something at the breakfast table, he doesn't remember what, but something, and his mother had been washing out her mother's pissy diapers and then running them through the wringer of her ancient washing machine, and she had turned around and laid into him with one of them, and the first snap of the wet, heavy diaper had upset his bowl of Special K and sent it spinning wildly across the table like a large blue tiddlywink, and the second blow had stropped his back, not hurting but stunning the smart talk out of his mouth and the woman now lying shrunken in this bed in this room had whopped him again and again, saying: You keep your big mouth *shut*, there's nothing big about you right now but your *mouth* and so you keep it shut until the rest of you grows the same *size*, and each italicized word was accompanied by a strop of his grandmother's wet diaper—*WHACKO!*—and any other smart things he might have had to say just evaporated. There was not a chance in the world for smart talk. He had discovered on that day and for all time that there is nothing in the world so perfect to set a twelve-year-old's impression of his place in the scheme of things into proper perspective as being beaten across the back with a wet grandmother-diaper. It had taken four years after that day to relearn the art of smarting off.

She chokes on the water a little and it frightens him even though he has been thinking about giving her pills. He asks her again if she would like a cigarette and she says:

—If it's not any trouble. Then you better go. Maybe I'll be better tomorrow.

He shakes a Kool out of one of the packages scattered on the table by her bed and lights it. He holds it between the first and second fingers of his right hand, and she puffs it, her lips stretching to grasp the filter. Her inhale is weak. The smoke drifts from her lips.

—I had to live sixty years so my son could hold my cigarettes for me.

—I don't mind.

She puffs again and holds the filter against her lips so long that he glances away from it to her eyes and sees they are closed.

—Mom?

The eyes open a little, vaguely.

—Johnny?

—Right.

—How long have you been here?

—Not long. I think I better go. Let you sleep.

—Hnnnnn.

He snuffs the cigarette in her ashtray and slinks from the room, thinking: I want to talk to that doctor. Goddamn it, I want to talk to the doctor who did that.

Getting into the elevator he thinks that the word "doctor" becomes a synonym for "man" after a certain degree of proficiency in the trade has been reached, as if it was an expected, provisioned thing that doctors must be cruel and thus attain a special degree of humanity. But

"I don't think she can really go on much longer," he tells his brother later that night. His brother lives in Andover, seventy miles west. He only gets to the hospital once or twice a week.

"But is her pain better?" Kev asks.

"She says she itches." He has the pills in his sweater pocket. His wife is safely asleep. He takes them out, stolen loot from his mother's empty house, where they all once lived with the grandparents. He turns the box over and over in his hand as he talks, like a rabbit's foot.

"Well then, she's better." For Kev everything is always better, as if life moved toward some sublime vertex. It is a view the younger brother does not share.

"She's paralyzed."

"Does it matter at this point?"

"Of course it *matters*!" he bursts out, thinking of her legs under the white ribbed sheet.

"John, she's dying."

"She's not dead yet." This in fact is what horrifies him. The conversation will go around in circles from here, the profits accruing to the telephone company, but this is the nub. Not dead yet. Just lying in that room with a hospital tag on her wrist, listening to phantom radios up and down the hall. And

she's going to have to come to grips with time, the doctor says. He is a big man with a red, sandy beard. He stands maybe six foot four, and his shoulders are heroic. The doctor led him tactfully out into the hall when she began to nod off.

The doctor continues:

—You see, some motor impairment is almost unavoidable in an operation like the "cortotomy." Your mother has some movement in the left hand now. She may reasonably expect to recover her right hand in two to four weeks.

—Will she walk?

The doctor looks at the drilled-cork ceiling of the corridor judiciously. His beard crawls all the way down to the collar of his plaid shirt, and for some ridiculous reason Johnny thinks of Algernon Swinburne; why, he could not say. This man is the opposite of poor Swinburne in every way.

—I should say not. She's lost too much ground.

—She's going to be bedridden for the rest of her life?

—I think that's a fair assumption, yes.

He begins to feel some admiration for this man who he hoped would be safely hateful. Disgust follows the feeling; must he accord admiration for the simple truth?

—How long can she live like that?

—It's hard to say. (That's more like it.) The tumor is

blocking one of her kidneys now. The other one is operating fine. When the tumor blocks it, she'll go to sleep.

—A uremic coma?

—Yes, the doctor says, but a little more cautiously. "Uremia" is a techno-pathological term, usually the property of doctors and medical examiners alone. But Johnny knows it because his grandmother died of the same thing, although there was no cancer involved. Her kidneys simply packed it in and she died floating in internal piss up to her ribcage. She died in bed, at home, at dinnertime. Johnny was the one who first suspected she was truly dead this time, and not just sleeping in the comatose, open-mouthed way that old people have. Two small tears had squeezed out of her eyes. Her old toothless mouth was drawn in, reminding him of a tomato that has been hollowed out, perhaps to hold egg salad, and then left forgotten on the kitchen shelf for a stretch of days. He held a round cosmetic mirror to her mouth for a minute and when the glass did not fog and hide the image of her tomato mouth, he called for his mother. All of that had seemed as right as this did wrong.

—She says she still has pain. And that she itches.

The doctor taps his head solemnly, like Victor DeGroot in the old psychiatrist cartoons.

—She *imagines* the pain. But it is nonetheless real. Real to her. That is why time is so important. Your mother can no longer count time in terms of seconds and minutes and hours. She must restructure those units into days and weeks and months.

He realizes what this burly man with the beard is saying, and it boggles him. A bell dings softly. He cannot talk more to this man. He is a technical man. He talks smoothly of time, as though he has gripped the concept as easily as a fishing rod. Perhaps he has.

—Can you do anything more for her?

—Very little.

But his manner is serene, as if this were right. He is, after all, "not offering false hope."

—Can it be worse than a coma?

—Of course it *can*. We can't chart these things with any real degree of accuracy. It's like having a shark loose in your body. She may bloat.

—Bloat?

—Her abdomen may swell and then go down and then swell again. But why dwell on such things now? I believe we can safely say

that they would do the job, but suppose they don't? Or suppose they catch me? I don't want to go to court on a mercy-killing charge. Not even if I can beat it. I have no causes to grind. He thinks of newspaper headlines screaming MATRICIDE and grimaces.

Sitting in the parking lot, he turns the box over and over in his hands. DARVON COMPLEX. The question still is: *Can he do it?* Should he? She has said: *I wish I were out of this. I'd do anything to be out of this*. Kevin is talking of fixing her a room at his house so she won't die in the hospital. The hospital wants her out. They gave her some new pills and she went on a raving bummer. That was four days after the "cortotomy." They'd like her someplace else because no one has perfected a really foolproof "cancerectomy" yet. And at this point if they got it all out of her she'd be left with nothing but her legs and her head.

He has been thinking of how time must be for her, like something that has gotten out of control, like a sewing basket full of threaded spools spilled all over the floor for a big mean tomcat to play with. The days in Room 312. The nights in Room 312. They have run a string from the call button and tied it to her left index finger because she can no longer move her hand far enough to press the button if she thinks she needs the bedpan.

It doesn't matter too much anyway because she can't feel the pressure down there; her midsection might as well be a sawdust pile. She moves her bowels in the bed and pees in the bed and only knows when she smells it. She is down to ninety-five pounds from one-fifty and her body's muscles are so unstrung that it's only a loose bag tied to her brain like a child's sack puppet. Would it be any different at Kev's? Can he do murder? He knows it is murder. The worst kind, matricide, as if he were a sentient fetus in an early Ray Bradbury horror story, determined to turn the tables and abort the animal that has given it life. Perhaps it is his fault anyway. He is the only child to have been nurtured inside her, a change-of-life baby. His brother was adopted when another smiling doctor told her she would never have any children of her own. And of course, the cancer now in her began in the womb like a second child, his own darker twin. His life and her death began in the same place. Should he not do what the other is doing already, so slowly and clumsily?

He has been giving her aspirin on the sly for the pain she *imagines* she has. She has them in a Sucrets box in her hospital table drawer, along with her get-well cards and her reading glasses that no longer work. They have taken away her dentures because they are afraid she might pull them down her throat and choke on them, so now she simply sucks the aspirin until her tongue is slightly white.

Surely he could give her the pills; three or four would be enough. Fourteen hundred grains of aspirin and four hundred grains of Darvon administered to a woman whose body weight has dropped 33 per cent over five months.

No one knows he has the pills, not Kevin, not his wife. He thinks that maybe they've put someone else in Room 312's other bed and he won't have to worry about it. He can cop out safely. He wonders if that wouldn't be best, really. If there is another woman in the room, his options will be gone and he can regard the fact as a nod from Providence. He thinks

* * *

—You're looking better tonight.

—Am I?

—Sure. How do you feel?

—Oh, not so good. Not so good tonight.

—Let's see you move your right hand.

She raises it off the counterpane. It floats splay-fingered in front of her eyes for a moment, then drops. Thump. He smiles and she smiles back. He asks her,

—Did you see the doctor today?

—Yes, he came in. He's good to come every day. Will you give me a little water, John?

He gives her some water from the flexible straw.

—You're good to come as often as you do, John. You're a good son.

She's crying again. The other bed is empty, accusingly so. Every now and then one of the blue and white pin-striped bathrobes sails by them up the hall. The door stands open halfway. He takes the water gently away from her, thinking idiotically: Is this glass half empty or half full?

—How's your left hand?

—Oh, pretty good.

—Let's see.

She raises it. It has always been her smart hand, and perhaps that is why it has recovered as well as it has from the devastating effects of the "cortotomy." She clenches it. Flexes it. Snaps the fingers weakly. Then it falls back to the counterpane. Thump. She complains.

—But there's no feeling in it.

—Let me see something.

He goes to her wardrobe, opens it, and reaches behind the coat she came to the hospital in to get at her purse. She keeps it in here because she is paranoid about robbers; she has heard that some of the orderlies are rip-off artists who will lift anything they can get their hands on. She has heard from one of her room-mates who has since gone home that a woman in a new wing lost five hundred dollars which she kept in her shoe. His mother is paranoid about a great many things lately, and has once told him a man sometimes hides under her bed in the late-at-night. Part of it is the combination of drugs they are trying on her. They make the bennies he occasionally dropped in college look like Excedrin. You can have your pick from the locked drug cabinet at the end of the corridor just past the nurses' station: ups and downs, highs and bummers. Death, maybe, merciful death like a sweet black blanket. The wonders of modern science.

He takes the purse back to her bed and opens it.

—Can you take something out of here?

—Oh, Johnny, I don't know . . .

He says persuasively:

—Try it. For me.

The left hand rises from the counterpane like a crippled helicopter. It cruises. Dives. Comes out of the purse with a single wrinkled Kleenex. He applauds:

—Good! Good!

But she turns her face away.

—Last year I was able to pull two full dish trucks with these hands.

If there's to be a time, it's now. It is very hot in the room but the sweat on his forehead is cold. He thinks: If she doesn't ask for aspirin, I won't. Not tonight. And he knows if it isn't tonight it's never. Okay.

Her eyes flick to the half-open door slyly.

—Can you sneak me a couple of my pills, Johnny?

It is how she always asks. She is not supposed to have any pills outside of her regular medication because she has lost so much body weight and she has built up what his druggie friends of his college days would have called "a heavy thing." The body's immunity stretches to within a fingernail's breadth of lethal dosage. One more pill and you're over the edge. They say it is what happened to Marilyn Monroe.

—I brought some pills from home.

—Did you?

—They're good for pain.

He holds the box out to her. She can only read very close. She frowns over the large print and then says,

—I had some of that Darvon stuff before. It didn't help me.

—This is stronger.

Her eyes rise from the box to his own. Idly she says,

—Is it?

He can only smile foolishly. He cannot speak. It is like the first time he got laid, it happened in the back of some friend's car and when he came home his mother asked him if he had a good time and he could only smile this same foolish smile.

—Can I chew them?

—I don't know. You could try one.

—All right. Don't let them see.

He opens the box and pries the plastic lid off the bottle. He pulls the cotton out of the neck. Could she do all that with the crippled helicopter of her left hand? Would they believe it? He doesn't know. Maybe they don't either. Maybe they wouldn't even care.

He shakes six of the pills into his hand. He watches her watching him. It is many too many, even she must know that. If she says anything about it, he will put them all back and offer her a single Arthritis Pain Formula.

A nurse glides by outside and his hand twitches, clicking the gray capsules together, but the nurse doesn't look in to see how the ''cortotomy kid'' is doing.

His mother doesn't say anything, only looks at the pills like they were perfectly ordinary pills (if there is such a thing). But on the other hand, she has never liked ceremony; she would not crack a bottle of champagne on her own boat.

—Here you go,

he says in a perfectly natural voice, and pops the first one into her mouth.

She gums it reflectively until the gelatin dissolves, and then she winces.

—Taste bad? I won't . . .

—No, not too bad.

He gives her another. And another. She chews them
with that same reflective look. He gives her a fourth.
She smiles at him and he sees with horror that her
tongue is yellow. Maybe if he hits her in the belly she
will bring them up. But he can't. He could never hit his
mother.

—Will you see if my legs are together?

—Just take these first.

He gives her a fifth. And a sixth. Then he sees if her
legs are together. They are. She says,

—I think I'll sleep a little now.

—All right. I'm going to get a drink.

—You've always been a good son, Johnny.

He puts the bottle in the box and tucks the box into
her purse, leaving the plastic top on the sheet beside
her. He leaves the open purse beside her and thinks:
*She asked for her purse. I brought it to her and opened
it just before I left. She said she could get what she
wanted out of it. She said she'd get the nurse to put it
back in the wardrobe.*

He goes out and gets his drink. There is a mirror
over the fountain, and he runs out his tongue and looks
at it.

When he goes back into the room, she is sleeping with
her hands pressed together. The veins in them are big,
rambling. He gives her a kiss and her eyes roll behind
their lids, but do not open.

Yes.

He feels no different, either good or bad.

He starts out of the room and thinks of something else.
He goes back to her side, takes the bottle out of the box,
and rubs it all over his shirt. Then he presses the limp
fingertips of her sleeping left hand on the bottle. Then he
puts it back and goes out of the room quickly, without
looking back.

He goes home and waits for the phone to ring and wishes

puts it back and goes out of the room quickly, without looking back.

He goes home and waits for the phone to ring and wishes he had given her another kiss. While he waits, he watches TV and drinks a lot of water.

AUTHOR'S NOTE

CHILDREN WHO HAVE SUFFERED PHYSICAL OR SEXUAL *abuse are often unable to talk in a straightforward way about the suffering they have undergone. Knowing this, wise child psychologists often get at the truth by employing a technique called "play therapy." They give the children dolls and ask them to re-enact certain events—events they may find too traumatic to simply relate. Writers of fiction are more like these sad, abused children than they sometimes like to admit, I think, and some of our best stories serve a purpose which is strikingly similar to this sort of therapy.*

Writing is play for many of us; I have certainly never thought of writing stories as work (copyediting, now . . . that's work). But sometimes the play serves a sadder, more serious purpose than it does at others. For me, "The Woman in the Room" was one of those more difficult stories. My mother's cancer was diagnosed in the summer of 1972, far too late to do anything constructive about it. She was a woman who had worked all her adult life, and during the second half of 1972 and the first two months of 1973, she did her hardest job, which was waiting to die with dignity and patience.

She did a good job of it—as she did with most things—but it was a dark and difficult time for her loved ones (as anyone who has been through a similar experience will testify). This story is about a young man who collaborates with his mother in an act which might be murder, or suicide, or simple mercy. The actions are fictitious; the feel-

ings are not. As my mother's end drew nearer, there were many times when I wished I'd had the guts to do what the character in the story does.

When my mother's dying was done, I wrote this story. The characters were my dolls. The story, while fictional, was my therapy. I have never enjoyed re-reading it, but at times I do . . . because my mother's death was also a part of my life. And, you know, writing it made me feel better. If there is a stronger moral justification for the reading and writing of stories, I have never found it.

—Stephen King

NOTES ON THE CONTRIBUTORS

CLIVE BARKER is our newest master, though his first stories did not appear until 1984, when three volumes of his *Books of Blood* were published simultaneously. Three more volumes followed a year later, as did the British Fantasy and World Fantasy Awards, the novel *The Damnation Game*, and a feature film, *Underworld*, based upon his original script. He has since published *Cabal* and *Weaveworld*; his novella "The Hellbound Heart" was adapted for the screen and directed by Barker as *Hellraiser*, and spawned an immediate sequel, *Hellraiser II: Hellbound*. Another film, *Rawhead Rex*, was released in 1986: the more recent *Nightbreed* (1989) was again directed by Barker himself. One wonders where this Liverpool prodigy really came from, though he had a reputation as a playwright (*Frankenstein in Love*, *The History of the Devil*, *The Secret Life of Cartoons*) before taking the publishing world by storm. His oft-stated motto is "There Are No Limits," and he certainly lives up to his principles. "We who write and read and celebrate horror fiction," he has said, "have our fingers on a pulse which beats where most people won't even look, never mind explore. . . . At its best [it is] a visionary literature, with its feet in blood and its eyes on transformation.'' Other books include *Shadows in Eden* and *The Great and Secret Show*.

ALGIS BUDRYS served as an editor at Gnome Press, *Galaxy*, and Royal Publications, Editor-in-Chief of Regency Books and Editorial Director of Playboy Press, all the while quietly establishing himself as one of science fiction's finest critics and a superb novelist and short story writer in his own right. ''Most fiction,'' he has said, ''is devoted to perpetuating easy, comforting ideas that make life softer for us.'' His work is proof of science fiction's particular affinity for probing deeper issues: what is real, the nature of the universe and our place in it. The novels *Rogue Moon*, *The Falling Torch*, *Some Will Not Die*, *Who?* and *Michaelmas* are examinations of the search for identity and human values under political pressure—not surprising for this immigrant who as a child saw Adolf Hitler pass in a black Mercedes and then the accompanying hysteria that swept through Europe. Some of his best short fiction has been collected in *Budrys' Inferno*, *The Unexpected Dimension* and *Blood and Burning*; others are included in many of the most distinguished anthologies of recent years. ''Any given story springs from my general background as a human being who is unreservedly bound to express reactions to what he notes around him . . . that is, who is an artist.'' His selection for this book, ''The Master of the Hounds,'' was originally published in *The Saturday Evening Post*, and won an Edgar Award from the Mystery Writers of America.

HUGH B. CAVE was born in England, moved to the United States at age five and grew up in New England, attending Boston University. He then departed for Haiti, where he lived for five years, exploring that land of mystery and voodoo; soon after, he bought an old ruinate coffee plantation in Jamaica's Blue Mountains and spent the next fifteen years turning it into a producer of the world's highest priced coffee. Fortunately for those of us who prefer tea, he also became a freelance writer: first some 800 stories for *Weird Tales* and virtually every other pulp-paper magazine of the 30's and 40's, then another 300 or so for *The Saturday Evening Post*, *Good Housekeeping*, *Redbook*, *Collier's*, *Esquire* and others printed on coated stock, as well as travel books, war reports, mainstream and horror novels—some 30 volumes in all. Many of his stories have been reprinted around the world and adapted for radio and television. A collection of 26 of these, *Murgunstrumm and Others*, appeared in 1977 under Karl Edward Wagner's Carcosa imprint, and deservedly won the World Fantasy Award for that year. In 1988 Cave received the Life Achievement Award from the World Fantasy Convention, the field's highest honor. More recent books by one of our most restless and prolific authors include *Disciples of Dread*, *The Lower Deep*, *The Voyage*, and *Conquering Kilmarnie*. For a fuller report, see *The Hugh B. Cave Story*, published by Starmont House.

R. CHETWYND-HAYES was evacuated from Dunkirk in World War II, only to be returned to France on D-Day plus six. In the years following he worked as a salesman at Harrod's, among other places, and for some reason put off becoming a full-time writer until the early 70's. But since then he has earned the title "Britain's Prince of Chill" by publishing (at last count) 18 collections of stories, including *The Unbidden*, *Cold Terror*, *The Elemental*, *Terror By Night*, *Tales of Darkness*, *The Night Ghouls*, *Tales of Fear and Fantasy* and *Ghosts from the Mist of Time*, from which "Doppelgänger" is taken—all of them since 1971. Like the early career of America's Ray Bradbury, this example is heartening for writers who prefer to work in short-form fiction. Chetwynd-Hayes has also inspired versatility with several novels, and is the editor of nearly three dozen anthologies, among them many volumes in the *Fontana Book of Great Ghost Stories* (taking over for the late Robert Aickman) and *Armada Monster Book* series. Two feature films, *From Beyond the Grave* and *The Monster Club*, were based on his tales, as are a number of episodes in the *Haunted House of Hammer* TV series. It seemed only fitting that in 1989 the Horror Writers of America should vote not one but two Bram Stoker Awards for Life Achievement to those stalwart practitioners of the short story, Ray Bradbury and Ronald Chetwynd-Hayes. Recent books: *The Grange*, *The Other Side*, *The Curse of the Snake God* and *Shudders and Shivers*.

AVRAM DAVIDSON was Executive Editor of *The Magazine of Fantasy and Science Fiction* from April 1962 through November 1964, an important transitional period in the history of that seminal publication; under his editorship the magazine won a 1963 Hugo Award. Those who submitted promising though less than perfect manuscripts then were likely to receive not rejection slips but lengthy and provocative notes written in Davidson's unique hand, filled with kind and thoughtful advice that did much to encourage new writers at exactly the point in their lives when it mattered most. For others, Davidson's own superbly crafted and defiantly eclectic works were enough to inspire careers that would further test the boundaries of genre fiction, revitalizing and enriching the field, so that the weight of his influence will continue to be felt for many years to come. From "My Boy Friend's Name Is Jello" in 1954, through his Hugo, Edgar, Ellery Queen and World Fantasy Award winning stories ("Or All the Seas With Oysters," "The Affair of Lahore Cantonement," "The Necessity of His Condition," "Naples"), his reputation remains impeccable, his position assured. *The Enquiries of Doctor Eszterhazy* earned the Howard Award for Best Anthology or Collection at the World Fantasy Convention in 1976. Others among his 23 books are *What Strange Stars and Skies*, *The Phoenix and the Mirror*, *Vergil in Averno*, *The Adventures of Doctor Eszterhazy*, and *Marco*

Polo and the Sleeping Beauty (co-authored with Grania Davis).

L. SPRAGUE DE CAMP has published a greater number of books, stories and articles than the total most people will read in a lifetime (according to a 1982 bibliography, well over 800 already). To accomplish this he had to begin more than a half-century ago. De Camp achieved great popularity in John W. Campbell's *Unknown* and *Astounding*, in the "Gavagan's Bar" series with Fletcher Pratt, and as a champion of heroic adventure with his many *Conan* volumes, some written in (posthumous) collaboration with the Cimmerian's creator, Robert E. Howard. His most frequent collaborator, however, has been his wife, Catherine Crook de Camp, herself a poet, anthologist, critic and prolific author of fiction and nonfiction. Among his many books are *Divide and Rule*, *Lest Darkness Fall*, *The Incomplete Enchanter* (with Pratt), *Genus Homo* (with P. Schuyler Miller), the collection *A Gun For Dinosaur*, classic biographies of Lovecraft and Howard, and the popular *Science-Fiction Handbook*. Nonetheless de Camp may be best remembered as a humorist; his penchant for broad satire has left an indelible mark on science fiction's often dry literal-mindedness. It is with surprise, then, that some readers will encounter "Judgment Day" for the first time, a chilling moral history that may be more disturbing today than the author had intended it to be at the height of the Cold War.

JAMES HERBERT, born in East London in 1943, worked as an art director at an advertising agency while writing his first novel. Published in 1974, *The Rats* immediately sold out its print run and went back to press—22 times so far, for a total of more than one million copies. He now designs his own book covers and publicity. Subsequent novels have also been phenomenally successful, installing Herbert as Europe's most popular living horror writer: *The Fog* (another million copies), *The Survivor*, *Fluke*, *The*

Spear, *Lair*, *The Dark*, *The Jonah*, *Domain*, *Moon*, *The Magic Cottage* and *Sepulchre*. It is worth noting that these books operate against the grain, daring readers to confront images of modern-day catastrophe and the darkness just outside the window rather than the more familiar subjects of traditional British horror fiction. Their extraordinary popularity may attest to the field's growing maturity as the comfort of escapism continues to lose currency in an uncertain time. Herbert is represented in this book by one of three published examples of his short fiction, and the only one that is not excerpted from a longer work. He is married, with three daughters, and now lives in Sussex, where for relaxation he plays guitar and indulges in stock car racing. In 1988 he was quite understandably chosen to be Guest of Honor at the World Fantasy Convention in England. Latest: *Haunted*, a new and disturbing treatment of psychic phenomena, and *Creed*.

STEPHEN KING published his first short story, "I Was a Teenage Graverobber," in 1965. Since then he has become the most popular horror writer of all time, with perhaps 100 million copies of his books in print, surpassing not only Blatty and Levin but Lovecraft and Poe. That he has done so without pandering to his audience makes the accomplishment all the more impressive. In his books—*Carrie*, *'Salem's Lot*, *The Shining*, *Night Shift*, *The Stand*, *The Dead Zone*, *Firestarter*, the nonfiction *Danse Macabre*, *Cujo*, *Different Seasons*, *The Dark Tower*, *Christine*, *Cycle of the Werewolf*, *Pet Sematary*, *The Talisman* (with Peter Straub), *The Eyes of the Dragon*, *Skeleton Crew*, *It*, *The Tommyknockers*, *Misery*, *The Dark Half*, the pseudonomymous novels as "Richard Bachman," et al.—he reveals himself to be a natural-born storyteller with an abiding concern for his characters, who live for him and for his audience. He has kept faith with readers, who know they can trust him not to lie when that would be easier than telling the truth, not to take the facile way out when an opportunity exists to say something honest about the real world, and not to reassure with pious sentiment in the face of evil. All this is both more and less than comforting. "I think of writing as an act of communication," he has said. "What comes out of your fiction is what you live." This commitment is nowhere more evident than in "The Woman in the Room," the searingly honest story chosen to represent him here.

NIGEL KNEALE is promptly recognized in science fiction circles as the creator of Professor Quatermass, the headstrong protagonist of a famous series of BBC TV plays: *The Quatermass Experiment*, *Quatermass II* and *Quatermass and the Pit*, all later filmed to great cult success (US: *The Creeping Unknown*, *Enemy From Space* and *Five Million Years to Earth*—"terrible titles," observes Kneale). He also scripted the BBC production of Orwell's *1984* and the screen versions of John Osborne's *Look Back in Anger* and *The Entertainer*, as well as *The Stone Tape* and *The Beasts* for television. More significantly for readers, he is the author of *Tomato Cain*, the memorable collection of 29 stories that won the Somerset Maugham Award in 1950. It is a legendary book and a landmark not only in this field but in the history of the art of the short story. The contents have been frequently anthologized but the collection itself remains long out of print, an appalling oversight requiring immediate correction. In the 80's Kneale worked in Hollywood, though the "Martin Quatermass" who penned John Carpenter's *Prince of Darkness* was *not* Kneale but perhaps proof of the Professor's indomitable spirit ("Don't tell me what I can and can't do!"). Three of his television scripts have been published in book form under the title *The Year of the Sex Olympics*. His daughter Tacy is an actress, his son Matthew a novelist and winner of the 1988 Somerset Maugham Award.

DEAN R. KOONTZ is one of today's most read novelists; it is hard to believe that this was not always so. Beginning in 1968, he produced dozens of books in the science fiction and suspense fields under a variety of pen names, but not until he ventured into horror did he become a major star with such titles as *Night Chills*, *The Vision* and *Whispers*. How many of his fans know that he was also David Axton, Brian Coffey, K.R. Dwyer, Leigh Nichols, Anthony North and Owen West? More will learn soon enough, as the earlier novels are reissued under his own name, alongside the millions of copies of *Darkfall*, *Twilight Eyes*, *Strangers* and *Watchers* already in print. "I strongly believe that, in addition to entertaining, it is the function of fiction to explore the way we live, reinforce our noble traits, and suggest ways to improve the world where we can," he has said, and his recent writing reveals that the label "horror fiction" is no longer adequate to describe his work. Koontz's worldview is apparent in his selection for our series, "Twilight of the Dawn," an antidote to the splattery misanthropy that informs so much recent dark fantasy. He is presently busy adapting some of his novels, including *The Bad Place*, for movies and television; three others, including *Demon Seed*, *Shattered*, and *Watchers*, have been previously filmed. Koontz is a past President of the Horror Writers of America, and helped create that organization's famed Bram Stoker Awards.

BRIAN LUMLEY was for many years a long-term soldier in the service of Her Majesty; during that same period he somehow found time to build a reputation as one of Britain's leading horror writers. First published by Arkham House (*The Caller of the Black*, 1971), he persisted in turning out a large number of notable books and short stories, all of them dealing with the macabre. Those set against Lovecraft's Mythos backdrop were much loved by the public in general, less so by a hardcore clique of purists who may have seen him as a meddler. Significantly, HPL's former publisher continued to champion Lumley's writing, following that first volume with *The Burrowers*

Beneath, *The Transition of Titus Crow*, *Beneath the Moors* and *The Horror at Oakdeene and Others*. A frequent contributor to a wide range of magazines and anthologies, he has now more or less left the Mythos behind, though he still professes a penchant for Lovecraftian themes. He is retired from the army and married to his literary agent: "One, because she's terrific, and two, because it saves postage." More recent books are part of an ongoing vampire saga (*Necroscope*, *Vamphyri*, *The Source*, etc.), which he wrote because he was "sick of vampires who just suck!" Other books include *The Clock of Dreams*, *Spawn of the Winds*, *In the Moons of Borea*, *Khai of Ancient Khem*, *Psychomech* and *Psychosphere*.

DAVID MORRELL is the best-selling author who created a hero named Rambo in his novel *First Blood*. The character has since attained the status of pop culture icon in a series of films starring Sylvester Stallone. As if in answer to this, Morrell went on to write *Testament*, followed by a Western, *Last Reveille*, and *The Totem*, a reinterpretation of the werewolf myth that is one of the best horror novels of the 70's; then *Blood Oath*, *The Brotherhood of the Rose*, filmed as an NBC mini-series, and *The Fraternity of the Stone*. Horror chronically occupies his imagination, and virtually all of his short stories deal with uncommon terror; they are featured in the *Shadows* and *Whispers* series, *Prime Evil* and other prestigious anthologies. Two were nominated for World Fantasy Awards, and another, "Orange Is for Anguish, Blue for Insanity," won the Horror Writers of America Bram Stoker Award in 1989. Morrell teaches at the University of Iowa Writers Workshop, as have Kurt Vonnegut, John Irving, Vance Bourjaily, Raymond Carver, John Cheever, Flannery O'Conner, Philip Roth, Walter Tevis and Tennessee Williams. One hopes that the students in Iowa City are learning as much from his visceral treatment of fear as from his accomplished style, for as he said to one interviewer, "I find it impossible to eliminate the grotesque from my work.'' Readers of the present volume will thank him for that.

JOYCE CAROL OATES is one of today's most gifted and honored writers, with more than 20 novels, 16 short story collections, nine volumes of poetry, four of literary criticism, three essay collections, several plays, and numerous book reviews and articles to her credit. Though this winner of a Guggenheim Fellowship, the O. Henry Award and the National Book Award may be found more often in the pages of *Paris Review*, *Atlantic*, *Esquire* and *Best American Short Stories* than in the pages of science fiction, fantasy or mystery publications, readers will surely recall her remarkable story ''The Bingo Master'' from Kirby McCauley's *Dark Forces* anthology. ''It would have been impossible for me to translate this parable into conventional naturalistic terms,'' she wrote of that piece, ''which is a reason why many of us choose to write, at times, in the surreal mode: the psychological truths to impart are simply too subtle, too complex, for any other technique.'' Which points up the reason why *Masters of Darkness* is not limited to writers making their careers in the horror field; were it otherwise, readers of this series might have missed some of the most brilliant short stories of our time. Particularly recommended: the collection *Night Side*, the Gothic *Bellefleur* and *A Bloodsmoor Romance*, and *Night Walks: A Bedside Companion*. Recent novels include *American Appetites* and *The Crosswicks Horror*. Oates is a Professor of Humanities at Princeton University and editor of *Ontario Review*.

JACK VANCE, a master of science fiction and fantasy, is the author of dozens of memorable books—such classics as *The Dying Earth*, *The Dragon Masters*, *The Eyes of the Overworld*, *The Last Castle*, *Big Planet* and *To Live Forever*—and scores of short stories, and has won several justly deserved Hugo and Nebula Awards. He is also the Edgar Award-winning author of mystery and suspense novels under his full name, John Holbrook Vance, and under pseudonyms that include Alan Wade, Peter Held, and Ellery Queen. His prose is always colorful, vivid and full of wit, his imagination unlimited, often reaching millions of years into the future to describe the xenology of alien races and cultures. In these pulp-born fields, where language tends toward either the facelessly utilitarian or the embarrassingly purple, Vance stands out as a mature stylist as well as a marvelous storyteller of astonishing breadth and power. Many of his early titles are available again in handsome editions from Underwood-Miller, along with an apparently endless supply of new works. "The Secret," from his collection *Green Magic*, is of course exotic, witty, anthropologically fascinating and vividly imagined, but not till its unforgettable last lines does the true nature of Vance's story become clear. What more appropriate note of moral awakening could there be to begin the present volume?

JACK WILLIAMSON was born in Arizona Territory in 1908. His first story ("The Metal Man") was published in *Amazing* in 1928, when he was an amazing 20 years old. With time out to work as a weather forecaster for the United States Army Air Force during World War II and as a professor of English at Eastern New Mexico University in Portales, where he still teaches occasional courses, he has been writing science fiction and fantasy more or less steadily ever since. Readers might consider how many—or how few—persons alive today have been actively employed in the same profession for more than six decades; then how many of those are doing the job better now than ever; then be humbled and inspired by Williamson's example. In 1988 the University observed his 80th birthday and the 60th anniversary of his first professional publication by proclaiming "Williamson Year." At the rate he is going, "Williamson Century" would have been more like it. He is the author of the fondly remembered *Legion of Space* and *Seetee* series in *Astounding*, and such books as

After World's End, *Bright New Universe*, the famous were-wolf novel *Darker Than You Think*, *Dragon's Island*, *Golden Blood*, *The Humanoids*, *The Reefs of Space*, *Trapped in Space* and *The Trial of Terra*, and the collaborations *Star Bridge* (with James E. Gunn) and *Starchild* (with Frederik Pohl). Latest: a novel, *Mazeway*, and (with Pohl) *The Turtles of Time*, inspired by Stephen Hawking's nonfiction bestseller *A Brief History of Time*.

BESTSELLING HORROR FICTION FROM TOR

MORE OF THE FINEST IN
SHORT HORROR STORIES